The Year Package

Ajrea Huar

MONTAG

A Montag Press Book
www.montagpress.com
Montag Press
777 Morton Street, Unit B
San Francisco CA 94129 USA

Montag Press, the burning book with the hatchet cover, the skewed word mark and the portrayal of the long-suffering fireman mascot are trademarks of Montag Press.

Printed & Digitally Originated in the United States of America
10 9 8 7 6 5 4 3 2 1

TRIGGER WARNING

This book contains references to bloodletting, explicit sex scenes, prostitution, transphobia, violence, death and murder. Please read at your own discretion.

Dedication

Sometimes, all it takes is a wild dream
in the summer of 2019.

The Hotel Room

I push a stray strand of hair behind my ear, watching the dial tick forward as we pass each floor, the numbers from 1 to 25 lighting up.

"Where are we going?" His low voice pulls me away from the soft hum of the elevator. I look in the mirror at the man stood in the corner

His dirty blond hair is up in a bun, no longer hanging beside his face in flat waves as it was at the club on Eighth Street. The new style makes his five-o-clock shadow more prominent, highlighting the reflective black lenses of his sunglasses.

"To my room, of course," I say. *Confident, but not cocky.* That's the type of person I am meant to be this evening, down to the style of pubic hair, if any.

The doors slide open with a whoosh, revealing barren hallways. I've rented out the floor; goodness knows how loud it's about to get.

I take his hand, pulling him out of the elevator. "This must've set you back?"

I spin around on my heels, walking backwards.

"This place?" I turn back, admiring the hidden lighting fixtures across the ceiling that give the hallway a calm ambience. My hand strokes the cushioned wall, caressing the number on each mahogany door. The Hampshire Hotel is pricey, something that only a select few can afford, and I happen to be one of them.

"Not in the slightest," comes my remark.

He smirks at me, his head low so I don't see his smile. We stop at the end of the hallway, where a large pane of glass separates us from the outside world.

I press my hands against the window and look across the city, where shades of pale yellow decorate the darkness of the night sky.

He wraps one hand around my waist while the other runs down the length of my exposed back. I shiver at his cold touch, my insides warming as he pushes himself against me, the tension in his pants evident against my back.

"Come, Diana."

"It's Delilah," I correct. *What a dick! He's testing me to see if I remember who I'm playing today. I'm a seasoned employee, not some amateur.*

He pulls the keycard out from my back pocket and inserts it into the slot above the handle. The light flashes green, and he pulls me in behind him as the door opens. I take one last look outside behind me before going in with him.

Dropping my bag on the floor, I kick off my heels while he stands and observes me briefly. He turns to the window, opens the mini fridge, and takes out a small bottle of whiskey with a frosted glass.

I remove my clothes, stripping the fabric off and letting it fall gracefully.

He pours the brown liquor just halfway into the glass, brings it to his lips, but stops; seeing my reflection in the window causes him to put the glass down. Smirking his way, I think about how hard I've had to work to get this body, and even more so when it comes to maintaining it, especially against those meokbang people: the creeps that sometimes pay hundreds to watch me binge eat a dozen burgers.

"Come join me, Dominic. I need a shower."

He removes his shades and places them in the pocket of his leather jacket, before taking off the jacket and laying it on the chair. With that, I turn towards the bathroom, swaying my hips seductively.

As I enter, the lights in the bathroom brighten, and I place my hands on the sink. Catching my peripheral in the mirror, I dismiss the view refusing to overthink my appearance. *You look sexy,.*

I flip on the shower and watch the water cascade onto the floor.

The words of Magenta echo in my head, debriefing me around tonight's agenda.

"In no way should your makeup smudge. He wants a natural, refined version of you."

I did as she said, and kept things natural, with gloss on my lips accompanied by a light foundation; chocolate brown with an equally chocolaty fragrance. My hazel eyes fit the description, so I wasn't required to wear contacts, but he had requested that I wore beach waved hair.

Definitely not surprised.

Most clients preferred a more European hairstyle, so I kept an abundance of wigs, ranging from straight and blonde, to dark brown and wavy.

I stand under the shower head, the water caressing my skin, rolling off my breasts before falling onto the grey tiled floor.

"The water looks good running off you."

I grab the soap, lather it between my hands, ignoring Dominic.

"Don't ignore me, Delilah."

The sound of my name rolling off his tongue has my toes curling in desire, the sound of the "i" flicking off the edge of his tongue.

His tongue rolling across my lips, down my chest to my – my body spins around, soapy hands crashing into Dominic's chest.

"I said." He stares me down, his silver eyes narrowing into slits. "Don't. Ignore. Me."

Had we not been under the jet stream of water, a bead of sweat would've slid down my face as my heart beats recklessly in my chest.

Get it together!

"You brought whiskey into the shower," I say, with a scoff to mask my fear. Dominic smiles widely at me, causing dimples to appear on either side of his cheeks.

A smile that seemed to balance insanity and lust. *If he wanted to, he could kill me.*

He brings the glass to his lips, taking a loud gulp. I watch his Adam's apple bob.

"Nothing has given me a reason to put it down." His silver eyes roam over me, taking in each delicate curve of my body, dissecting every inch of my skin, watching the droplets roll off me before bringing his eyes back to mine.

"Well, except when you walked into the bathroom," he finishes.

I smile and roll my eyes, my hands running across his bare chest. He's as naked as I.

My long red nails dig slightly into his skin, making a red circle through the soap suds. Dominic growls, and I watch his penis stand to attention. I trace my nails across the circle, making him growl louder.

I jump as he throws the glass and the mirror cracks behind us. I watch our distorted reflection in the fragmented pieces.

"That's going to cost me," I retort.

He spins me around, sandwiching me between himself and the glass wall of the shower. The sound of his palm making skin contact with my ass resonates around the room.

I shriek, rising on the tips of my toes.

"This little mark is going to cost you," he growls, his hold on my waist tightening fiercely as he aligns my ass with his growing erection. I look out the window at the city, admiring it as the reds and blues dart around like buzzing bees while Dominic pushes himself into me.

There's no electricity or rhythm between us, just pure, unadulterated, animalistic pounding.His hand snakes around my neck and squeezes, my disobedience to his rhythm only fueling his lust-induced state. I hold onto his hand as my vision begins to blur, my other hand making a path down my body, heading for my sweet spot.

He grabs my hand before it reaches its destination, squeezing until I whimper before he slams the open palm against the glass.

"This isn't about you," he groans in my ear between each breathy thrust. My watery eyes stay glued to the city outside. False sensations of the cold autumn breeze touch my body, a stark contrast to the hot water washing over us. A feeling that seems to lull me to sleep.

Stay awake!

His hold around my neck tightens, and my eyes start to droop as Dominic's thrusts become sloppy and erratic.

A sharp pain whizzes around my body, forcing my eyes open.

Blonde hair brushes my face as Dominic sinks his teeth in deeper, his thrusts not letting up. My hand slides off the glass, and the only thing holding me up is Dominic's hand around my throat. My eyes drift shut as Dominic explodes inside of me, blood dripping as he drinks from my neck.

This is not the evening I had planned.

The Wire Transfer

Stretching my arms and legs, I moan as my back cracks from a blissful slumber, one which I hadn't had in years.

"Is this what Mr. Dominic spent his money on?"

One eye immediately flies open at the sound of the voice, and I try to make out the blurry image, but my eye closes of its own accord before I can.

What the fuck am I doing here? Did I sleep over? No... I don't think so. Does that mean he owns the hotel? Nonsense, he can't own the hotel...can he? No, I paid for this hotel, I organized this. Did he leave me after...after he...FUCKING BIT ME!? Fucking new clients.

"The creases between your brows mean that you're mulling over your current situation."

I open my eyes. The curtains are drawn morning sun concentrates its rays on the bed as it filters through the room. I sit, sliding on the silk bed sheet that's most definitely not the hotel's. It creases around my legs, exposing the striped lavender pajama set I am wearing.

"Where is Dominic?" Maintaining my composure, I stare at the woman dressed in black. She has her back to me, tying the curtains to one side.

"He's having breakfast." She tuts loudly as she turns to face me, pulls a bobby pin from her pocket, and slides her greying blonde hair back into place.

"My clothes?"

We are in a large room with pale, salmon-colored walls, a cedar door to my right, and another to my left, with an archway behind me. *There's no way to escape if I wanted to.*

"Back at the hotel, I suppose," she replies nonchalantly.

Back at the hotel, I suppose! He brought me here naked! I smile sweetly.

"And my phone?"

She moves to the side, revealing a swivel chair with my navy leather bag on top of it. She picks it up and flings it in front of me.

"When you're ready, I'll be outside. I suggest you dress warm, it's a bit nippy outside. Clothes are through the archway." She takes her leave walking out the door to my right.

As the door closes, I pull out my phone to check the invoice, and find out exactly how long I was asleep. I unlock it and slide across to the company app, hidden amongst my online shopping and games. When I tap on the seemingly harmless green icon, the phone goes black momentarily. I trace a star across the screen, and it brightens once more.

One the display is a timer that reads 13:38:29. I sigh. *So, I've been asleep for eight hours. Another 10 hours of work until I'm done for the day.* It comes as no surprise, but that isn't my main concern as I slide the screen across to the invoice.

Full Day: 2400
-Employee Lead: 3000 (Hotel)
Dangerous Situation (V): 1000
Total: 8400.

It was looking like a good day, and an expensive one at that. As I tap on the last entry, i begin to amend the invoice, biting the inside of my cheek. **FD: 2400**

-E. L: 3000 (H)
DS (V): 13000
-BL (1)(M): 12000
30400.

I exit the app and put the phone back in my bag as I slide off the bed. *She said clothes are through the archway.*

I head in, staring at the walk-in closet, which is practically empty, shy of a red, longline jumper, and a pair of brown suede boots. I put on the clothes and head out the door.

The lady from before stands on the side of the hallway, her hands behind her back as she awaits my appearance.

"Come along, no time like the present."

I follow behind her as she walks down the hallway, my shoes padding across the beige carpet. *The place isn't that bad, I suppose.*

For the next 10 hours, this is my home. We walk down the spiral staircase. Dominic sure does have a lot of staff – down the stairs are two similarly dressed members dusting the flowerpots and hanging art on the wall. We walk past them, but their heads hang low, and I can't make eye contact.

"You said Dominic was having breakfast." I say, but instead of replying, she waves her hand, dismissing the statement. I silently follow as she takes a sharp right through another archway.

He is sitting at the head of an obnoxiously long table, one hand around a coffee cup while the other effortlessly scrolls through his phone. "Mr. Dominic, I've brought her."

He sets his coffee down, giving me a brief look, and strokes his light stubble before he goes back to his phone. Pulling out a chair from his left, the lady grips me by the shoulder, forcefully shoving me into the seat despite her size.

"Thank you, Sybil," Dominic says, and she saunters off. He puts his phone face down.

"Good morning," I say. I twiddle my thumbs under the table.

"Good morning, Delilah, sleep well?" His lips twitch as though he wishes to smirk.

"Very well. Had I known we'd be having a sleepover, I would've brought extra clothes."

"Are the clothes I provided not enough?" His silver eyes pierce mine intensely. But I do not shy away. Instead, I smile at him.

"They aren't mine."

He raises his brows, hesitating, but then he just clears his throat and leans back in his chair.

"I noticed you made some changes to the invoice." His brows settle back to their original place.

Finally, business. I rest my hands on the table.

"I did. Are you not satisfied with the prices?"

A plate is placed in front of me with a close to perfect English breakfast. *Hmm, almost* .

"Would you prefer black pudding as well?" Dominic asks, and I breathe in through my nose as he tries to pick my thoughts apart.

"No, I never liked black pudding."

"I know. In response to your statement, the prices aren't what concern me; it's what they are under: RS and BL. I would like to know exactly what I'm paying for."

I pull out a sheet of paper, hidden in the lining of my bag so no one could steal it. Sybil had brought it along with my food.

There's something about seeing the "menu" of what we offer that reassures the client, as though seeing it in black and white distracts from the fact that they are soliciting a prostitute. *Each to their own, I guess.*

I scoot closer to the table and unfold the paper, pushing my plate aside.

"FD is a full day. You requested that I make the arrangements, which is the EM. L employer lead and the H is the hotel, which I booked with your money."

"And what about DS with the V in the parentheses?" he asks

Does no one read the menu anymore?

"I'm a busy man, Delilah."

"Could...could you not read my thoughts? It's very invasive."

Dominic raises a brow at me, his lips tilting upwards before he says, "I'm down by $30,400. I can be as invasive as I want."

Resisting the urge to roll my eyes, as I cannot argue with him on that note.

I clear my throat before rolling up my sleeve, revealing the silver bracelet decorated with crystals imbued with Magenta's magic. I pluck the yellow one from its holder, crush the tiny gem between my fingers, and then sprinkle the gold dust on the paper.

"Citrine the money stone, how convenient," he remarks.

I grab his hand, making him go stiff and rigid. As I gently put it on the paper, his eyes narrow at me. The yellow dust turns a deep red, swirling around the paper, and Dominic yanks his hand away as the dust settles before burning into the paper, leaving more acronyms and numbers in its wake.

"This means dangerous situation. The standard price is $1,000," I explain as I point to the DS acronym first.

"And why is that?" he asks mockingly.

I glare at him.

"Because I'm being put in harm's way," I scold.

"You're an escort for the supernatural; your job entails that you will get harmed," he says cockily.

I can't help but mutter *asshole* in my head.

"Now, now Delilah, you're still on the clock."

"BL is bloodletting. I believe you're the only person that has drunk from me."

"I don't play well with others, Delilah," he adds warningly.

"Great." I run my hand over the puncture wound on my neck, feeling it crusted over.

"It doesn't feel deep, and I'm not lethargic or anything this morning to suggest you caused real damage, so 'M' is for minor."

"With bloodletting, wouldn't the starting damage be minor anyway?"

At his question, I smirk, my thoughts tumbling over the various stories I've heard from other colleagues and their escapades.

"There are other ways to draw blood without making an incision, Dominic." *Does that cover everything?*

"It does, Delilah."

I place the paper back into its hiding place and bring the plate back to its rightful place. *It's probably cold now.* I pout as I put the now soggy bread in my mouth.

"Delilah."

I look at Dominic, who is gazing at me intently, and I swallow my food.

"Yes?"

"I've decided to employee you."

"For how long?" I ask.

"For a year."

My eyes go wide as I try to solve the math in my head, a full day minimum not even including extras daily that would be like-

"$876,000." Dominic shows me his phone with his online banking, the deposit he is ready to make to my employer.

I gulp loudly.

The Price for a Year

I watch Delilah eat slowly, her mind a complete mess as she discusses with herself what she'll do with the money. Questions like how she's going to survive the year here, and where exactly *here* is.

I run my hands through my hair as I admire just how innocent she looks. Despite her trying to eat calmly, I hear her heart hammering away in her chest, pumping delicious blood through her curvaceous body.

My trousers tighten as images of last night come to mind, the defiance she showed by trying to pleasure herself without my consent. I was a bit shocked, and even more entranced by her.

A whole year, imagine the things I can do to her body. I slide further down into my chair. I clear my throat, sitting up.

"Delilah, do we have a deal?"

She looks up at me and puts her knife and fork down. She smiles politely. I am still paying for her time.

"That's not for me to decide."

My teeth clench as she speaks, but I quickly compose myself. "Then who decides?" I ask.

"My employers. Call them. They'll tell you what arrangements to make for such situations."

Sybil comes in with a jug of water in hand, completely ignoring Delilah's presence, and takes away her plate. Sybil's grey eyes bore into mine.

I know she isn't happy with Delilah being here because she has a low opinion of the service. When I walked in with a sleeping Delilah in my arms, she shut off her thoughts, preventing me from hearing her array of curses.

"Sybil."

The wrinkles around Sybil's eyes seem to hiss at me.

"Take Delilah and give her something to wear. Preferably black."

Sybil pulls out her chair and takes her bag.

"Come along dear," Sybil says, as she walks away.

Delilah smiles at me before following after.

When Delilah disappears from my line of view, I pull out my phone, along with the business card from inside my jacket pocket. I flip the card over and realize that the last three digits have changed from 208 to 481, no doubt as a result of the witch's magic. Nonetheless, I type the number and hold the phone to my ear.

"Mr. Aldrek, is everything OK? I see here that you still have another nine and a half hours before your time with Delilah comes to an end."

"Everything is fine. I wish to extend my time with her." The person taps away on the keyboard before speaking again.

"That's fine. How long are you looking to extend her time with you, sir?"

15

"A year."

There's a sharp intake of breath, and her chair screeches against the floor. I smirk at her reaction. Clearly, they hardly come by such offers, as not many can afford it. Finally, her voice drifts back through the line.

"Hi, Mr. Aldrek, are you still there?"

"Of course."

"Extensions over a week, or costs over $50,000, must be overseen by Magenta. Both you and Delilah should please report to our Seattle branch this afternoon to draft a contract. Thank you." With that, she hangs up, and I sigh.

I straighten my jacket, and grab both my coffee and phone before heading to Delilah's room. I don't bother knocking. Sybil has left a black dress on the bed as requested. Steam flows from underneath the bathroom door.

Delilah's hair is tied up in a bun, and she rubs soap over her body. She stops humming when she notices my presence but doesn't otherwise acknowledge me.

"What have I said about ignoring me?" I ask.

She turns around, soap running off her body. Her hands cover her breasts, and I watch as the soap seeps through her fingers.

"Don't do it," she replies in a small voice, and I walk over to her, backing her into a corner, water drenching me.

"That is correct."

"Are we going to have a repeat of last night?" Her thoughts drift through my head as she looks up at me.

"No. They've asked that we head to their main branch this afternoon to draft a contract," I reply.

"OK, I'll just finish showering and then-"

"Did I say I was finished?" I hear her heart skip a beat. My clothes cling to me, and I step closer, forcing her onto the tips of her toes.

"No, Dominic. Do you plan on showering with me?" She steadies her breathing, refusing to tear her gaze away from mine, and I smirk. *She remembers, confident, but not cocky.*

I trace my hand over her neck, feeling her pulsing heartbeat dance across my skin. The desire to squeeze runs through me. *If you do that, she'll be asleep for another eight hours or more.* I drop my hand, and a small sigh escapes her lips, making my cock twitch as I step out of the shower.

"Meet me downstairs when you're ready." With that, I turn and head out of the room.

I'm now unnecessarily wet and extremely horny. If this contract had been done over the phone, I would've bent Delilah over the table and had my way with her. I can see it clearly: her smooth back hunches over as her breasts smack against her wet body. or maybe her legs wrap around me as I fuck her on the bathroom sink, biting down on her neck and tasting her blood as it coats my tongue. *Stop it, Dominic. Focus.*

I roll my shoulders and remove the clinging fabric from my body. That was incredibly foolish of me. I was all dressed and ready, and now I have to get dressed again. The thought of having her here to do with as I please excites me, and I can't help myself. No more hovering around shitty bars and social events for a quick release.

Lincoln is going to have a field day when I tell him. I grind my teeth at the thought of his smug face seeing her. Seeing the branded 'H' underneath her left breast and not just him any-one who has ever signed a contract, both client and employee, saw the branding. A beacon for all horny supernatural beings – another one of that witch's tricks, free advertisement for her business.

I head to the closet in my boxers and search for a new outfit. I unhook the light grey sweater, a white collared shirt, and jeans, then opt for camel-colored Chelsea boots. I fix a watch onto my wrist. A knock sounds from the door.

"Enter, Sybil."

She walks in, her face sunken as she hides her thoughts from me.

"Mr. Dominic, you can't be serious."

I sigh and head for the door, Sybil following close behind.

"Sybil, we've had this conversation already."

"I know, Mr. Dominic, but it's dangerous."

"For whom?" I reply curtly. We head past the first staircase to the second at the end of the hallway.

"For everyone involved. The girls have been talking," she explains.

"The girls shouldn't be talking."

We move down the stairs, the light thinning to a hazy blue.

"She can't stay here for a year."

"Do you not have self-control, Sybil?" I ask, then feel a sharp pain at the back of my head. I spin around to face her. My eyes narrow into slits, but Sybil stands her ground. I smile, shaking my head.

"You best remember who you're talking to, Mr. Dominic. I taught you self-control," she argues, with a wagging finger.

I continue into the garage, heading for the noticeboard on the wall. I pick out a random key and press the button, and a white Audi beeps across the room.

"As long as you have self-control, the girls will follow suit."

"What if they don't?" she asks, as I climb into the Audi.

"Then their employment will be terminated immediately, and they'll have to find somewhere else to live. Now open the garage door so I can go pick her up."

Sybil nods begrudgingly and heads back to the noticeboard. She flicks one of the switches and the door rumbles open.

I rev the engine and smoothly drive out from underneath the house, parking in front.

Sybil and I stand at the bottom of the stairs as I wait for Delilah. *How long does it take to put on a fucking dress and a pair of heels?*

My shoulders relax as I hear the clipping of Delilah's footsteps. She bounds down the steps, the bottom half of her dress barely visible under the red sweater she wore this morning.

"Why are you wearing that sweater?" I ask, and she looks down.

"Sybil mentioned it was cold. Do you want me to take it off?"

«*It's 44 degrees out, I'll get ill.* »

I frown at her thought. "No, we don't want you getting ill." I turn to Sybil.

"We will be back tonight. Have dinner ready for us."

Sybil nods, glances at Delilah, then heads to the kitchen.

"Let's get this contract drafted." I move to get back into the car, "I need to drive."

I turn around, smirking.

"Company policy," she adds.

"What company policy?" I ask. She closes her eyes as she recites her next words.

"No client should know the whereabouts of the branches. Should a client require access to the branches, a car will be provided, or an employee will have to drive them." She opens her eyes and stretches out her hand.

"Please? It's a lot easier than sending for a car."

I grumble under my breath and slap the keys into her hand. "Let's go then."

She opens the car door and slides into the driver's seat while I begrudgingly settle into the passenger. She starts the engine and heads towards the highway that will lead us back to the city.

I train my eyes on the road even though I'm not the one driving, as we go further into the city, my mind trying to come up with different locations for the branch. *I know Seattle, where could Magenta have possibly put her business without me knowing?*

Delilah turns into a car park and settles into a space on the ground floor.

"We walk from here," she says, switching off the engine and handing me the keys.

"How far do we have to walk?"

"Just around the corner." She hides her hands in her sleeves and hugs her body, walking quickly. Mae pushes the door to a costume store open and lets out a heavy breath as the warmth engulfs her.

I glance up at the sign that reads: *FolkWore*.

Welcome to FolkWore

What an obscene sign is the first thing that crosses my mind, but I follow Delilah through the aisles of costumes to the assistant at the back.

"Hello, stranger, didn't see you last night," the man behind the counter says.

"Hi Klaus, Magenta is expecting us. He's the year package."

Klaus's eyes widen. He looks me over before putting a manicured hand over his mouth, and then turning to Delilah. She screeches as he smacks her ass. I stiffen as my teeth clench.

"Well go on in, and don't forget me when you become rich."

Delilah laughs, causing tingles to run through me as she walks past him through a green curtain. I eye Klaus suspiciously, noticing iridescent wings attached to his back fluttering against the light. *Fucking faery.*

Liberal polyamorous little creatures with an equally liberal mother: Seraphine, Queen of the Fae. I descend the stairs behind Delilah, and the lights stop abruptly, now replaced by the warm glow of candles.

There is another curtain which we push through, revealing an ambient office space filled with rows of hallways and closed doors. In front of us sits another faery with burnt-orange hair.

"Gretchin," Delilah calls, catching her attention as the female types furiously.

"Magenta wants you and Mr. Aldrek in her room."

Delilah nods and glances over her shoulder at me, signaling for me to follow. She heads down the frosted hallway, glass and wooden doors on either side of us along with a black metal staircase at the end.

I follow closely behind Delilah, watching her thighs move as she ascends the stairs. Delilah opens the door to the office, moving aside for me to step through ahead of her.

The room is drowning in light, downtown Seattle's skyscrapers standing proud out of the window.

Magenta sits in a light grey chair behind a white marble desk held up by four thin, golden legs. Her hands run over a stack of papers, no doubt the contract I'm here to sign.

She lifts her head, and her fiery orange hair tumbles over her shoulder, the strands splaying on the desk. She is truly breathtaking – porcelain skin with a bit of flush around the cheeks, accompanied by deep amethyst eyes that are currently boring holes into me.

"Please, Mr. Aldrek, take a seat," she says, her silky voice wraps around me like a vine. I sit, my eyes still lingering on hers as Delilah stands beside me. Her jasmine scent pulls my eyes away from Magenta's and onto the papers on the desk.

"I have come to sign the contract," I say, and she slides it towards me.

"This may take a while, Delilah. I see you've already eaten and had a shower. Go see a medic for that wound of yours, and when we are done, I'll send someone for you," Magenta says to a patiently waiting Delilah.

"Yes, Magenta." Delilah turns on her heels and leaves the room, silently closing the door behind her. Magenta returns her gaze to me.

"If you have any questions, please don't hesitate to ask." She pulls her laptop close, opens it, and begins her work while I am left to read.

I flip the last page of the contract then let them drop on the table with a loud thud. Magenta raises her head from the computer and closes the screen.

"Do you have any questions, Mr. Aldrek?" Magenta asks, getting comfortable in her office chair.

I lean back in mine.

"I do. As I will be paying for a year, how will the payment schedule work?"

"You will pay the standard 24-hour fee of $2,400 across the year, making your total."

"$876,000," I finish for her, and she licks her lips at the thought of all that money.

"Yes, Mr. Aldrek, both you and Delilah will be using our FW app to pay for any extras that may come up along the way."

I scoff loudly.

"So, the extras don't come free? Considering a transaction so large, are there not some sort of discounts that are applied?"

"Oh no, Mr. Aldrek, things such as bloodletting are extra. My employee would be at risk," Magenta says her words with an air of concern.

This is starting to look like a significant spend.

"What insurance do I have to guarantee an excellent service for the whole year? After all, it is a lot of money."

"Each of my girls go to their jobs with 110% dedication. Should anything happen to the agreement, whether Delilah should come to severe harm or even death, that would be on you, Mr. Aldrek. While this is a large transaction for you, this is my employee's year spoken for. Should you wish it, she may spend her year locked in a small room with minimal food. We don't tend to lend our employees for long durations to just anyone. If anything, the fact that we are even discussing this agreement is already a privilege."

I am a businessman, and negotiations aren't alien to me, but somehow, while Magenta talks, the meeting turns in her favor. Me the client about to hand over thousands of dollars didn't provide any sort of VIP treatment. She can see as well as I do that Delilah has left a lasting impression: one that will cost me thousands. Should I back out, Delilah will be booked for another who can afford it.

"Fine, where do I sign?"

Magenta puts her hand on the contract before speaking again. "There are some things you must know first."

I sit back in my chair, shoulders aching from hunching over and reading.

"Delilah is human, meaning she will require you to look after her. Depending on the arrangement you have with her, she may rely on you to feed her and take care of any human problems she may encounter."

"Besides food and transport, I don't expect she'd need much," I say.

"Whatever you do with Delilah is your business, Mr. Aldrek. As Delilah will be in your care for a long duration, we will require her to have bi-monthly visits with our medic team."

"I have my own doctors."

"With all due respect, Mr. Aldrek, we've known clients to keep underlying problems hidden from us during these types of arrangements, so I am afraid this is non-negotiable."

"Fine, but it has to be done on neutral ground, and my doctors will work alongside yours."

"That is fine, Mr. Aldrek. Delilah has a safe place which she submitted when she joined us; it will be done there."

"Anything else?"

"Delilah has been booked for this December also in April and August of next year. She will be gone for a couple of weeks." I frown, feeling the dip in my brow.

"So, I'm not even guaranteed her for the whole year?"

"Please understand, Mr. Aldrek, that this booking was made in advance by a subscribing and very loyal client who only requests Delilah. From August, Delilah will be solely yours, meaning we will have to decline this subscribing client or suggest another employee," Magenta explains.

"What has this got to do with me?" I ask.

"Everything. After this agreement, Delilah will still be required to work, and her connection with returning customers must be kept intact."

"Then I would like a deduction of her time spent away," I say.

"Rightly so. As you are paying for the year, during the monthly overview for any extras, the deduction will be added. Should you move into credit, it will roll over to the next month."

"May I sign now?" My words come out impatient and strained.

"I have a few questions, just to make sure we're on the same page."

I sigh, running my hands through my hair.

"You are a vampire, correct?"

"Yes."

"Will you be bloodletting regularly?"

"I may."

"You have Delilah's blood type should the worst happen. In the time that Delilah is with you, will anyone else be involved in your activities?"

"They better not be."

Magenta gives me a look, unimpressed by my answer.

"No," I say clearly.

"Excellent. You are free to create your own contract with Delilah, providing it does not conflict with ours. Delilah will have her character pack on her, which you can review when you get home." Magenta flips to the last page and points to the signature column. She hands me a silver pen. I sign with my name and date, and she does the same underneath mine. *November 1st, my year package begins.*

"Right, I will go and send for Delilah, and then we can focus on the payment." She presses a button on the phone at the edge of the table.

"What is her name?" I ask. I had chosen the name Delilah on accident, but since she'll be staying with me for a year, I'd like to know.

"Her name is Mae, Mr. Aldrek." She turns to the phone, speaking into it. "Could you go retrieve Mae for me, please?"

The Escort Named Mae

I sit cross-legged as Lara puts crushed yellow flower paste onto my neck over the puncture wound.

"A whole year, Mae," she exclaims. Sadness coats her voice as she breaks the silence. My hand strokes hers, brushing a thumb over the Elvish markings across her skin.

"Magenta will definitely come up with some sort of check-up to make sure he isn't hurting me," I reassure her as she crosses over to sit in front of me. She twirls her single, long purple braid around her finger while rubbing her chest, a motion she does whenever she's stressed.

"And if he is?"

At her question, I frown. I know Magenta is very money-oriented, but with a deal like this, my welfare should also be one of her priorities, even if only a little.

"He won't. He hasn't," I say, convincing myself and Lara.

She motions to the dry healing flower on my neck, and I rub it, embarrassed.

"Well, what did you expect, Lara? After all, he is a vampire. Not getting bitten would have been strange, and Magenta would think that I didn't do my job."

Lara sighs. She pulls out a drawer and grabs a pack of cigarettes.

"Lara, you can't smoke. You've been requested next week."

It is never just one cigarette with Lara, and it is never just cigarettes. They say marijuana is a gateway drug, but for Lara, everything is a gateway.

She puts a cigarette between her lips, rummaging through the drawer for her special lighter. "The thought of you being on a job for a year stresses me out. You're so little, Mae." She finds the lighter, sighing as she flicks it open. A purple flame shoots out and she lights the cigarette.

"I'm not little. I'm human," I counter as she takes a long drag of the cigarette.

Lara loves the human world but not the effect it has on her body. She is addicted to smoking, drugs and sex. This job is the perfect fix for her.

When she first arrived, she was predictably confused. After all, she was forced to marry a woman she did not love, and the man that held her heart was forced into his own troublesome relationship. Things such as homosexuality, transgender and all the aspects in between are alien for elves.

Recreational drugs and sex filled the void in her soul when she first arrived in America, at least until Magenta found her and filled her with hope of becoming the woman she's always wanted to be. What Magenta hadn't banked on was Lara's dependency on drugs, which forced her to put the girl on a strict regime. She could have all the drugs in the world on the condition that she'd do a deep cleanse once a month.

Magenta oversees the brutal purge. Consequently, Lara hasn't become less of an addict, but has gained resilience to the extreme lengths Magenta takes to ensure Lara doesn't succumb to worldly temptations, outside of work that is.

Lara puts away the lighter as she blows out the orange smoke, clearing it with a swat of her hand. The sweet, smoky smell of cocaine-laced cigarettes consistently irritates my nose and makes my chest ache.

Lara's life is difficult at the best of times, her life is like calorie counting, if the calories were substituted for recreational drugs.

"Exactly, pet, you're human. There isn't a lot of sustenance to your kind." She takes another drag, finishing the cigarettes in two draws, making my skin crawl. She blows out the smoke.

"Talk to Magenta. I want you to be there during my check-ups," I say.

"I will do my best, but if I'm working...." She shakes her head, exhausted as the words hang in the air. I nod in understanding.

There is a knock on the door and Gretchin steps in, her hair a pale pink this time, shifting with her mood. Burnt orange means that she's frustrated, and pink means that she's feeling flirtatious. A paling color means that her mood is due for another change.

"Magenta called. The contract is done."

I stand up, my hands trembling as I suddenly feel nervous. I have never been away for longer than a month at a time, and never so abruptly. Usually, a client would get a feel for their match before committing to a long relationship. *What if I am wrong about Dominic, and last night is all it will be?*

I look at Lara, who is more nervous than me. Her eyes have darkened around the rims, full of concern as she pulls me into a tight squeeze.

"You look after yourself, Mae, do you understand?"

I nod against her chest, afraid that if I speak, she'll hear the worry in my voice.

She stretches out her arms, holding me by the shoulder.

"I'll see you in December, Lara," I whisper, smiling slightly as I put on my jumper and grab my bag.

"Also, let the Yarrow do its job before you let Mister Bitey go at your neck again."

I sniff and let out a laugh before following Gretchin out of the room. She motions to Magenta's office, and as I turn to head in that direction, she grabs my wrist.

"Watch yourself, Mae," Gretchin warns. Though she tries to maintain her steely look, I know that she is just as concerned as Lara. I raise a brow at the faery, and see blue grow on the tips of her hair.

"Always, Gretchin." I open the door to Magenta's office and see Dominic sitting idly in the chair, scrolling through his phone while Magenta rests her head in her hands.

"Mae, we have finished signing the contract. All that's left now is your signature." I give an open palm to Magenta, who pulls out a small ceremonial knife.

"No," Dominic says, pushing my hand down.

"A blood signature is required," Magenta insists.

"I said no," he says firmly, and Magenta tuts, motioning to me.

I remove my jumper and pull up the halter dress he had picked out for me. Magenta comes around the desk, whispering a small enchantment. I wince slightly as the 'H' mark under my breast begins to sizzle. I will happily take a blood signature any day of the week over a sealing spell.

A small prick can easily be healed and fixed, but a contractual sealing enchantment boils the blood: a quick reminder of what will happen should I attempt to break the rules or underperform.

t's not like being in a sauna or under warm water. I can only imagine this is what it feels like to be cooked in a microwave.

"Mr. Aldrek, if you would please place your hand on the marking."

Dominic rests his hand on my sizzling skin. His cool hand eases the pain that envelops my body, and, for a second, I am able to breathe.

"Thank you. With that settled, I will take the payment."

Dominic takes his hand away and instantly the pain disappears, as though it was never there to begin with.

"I want it to go directly to Mae," Dominic states, and Magenta and I both eye him.

"That is against pro-"

"To Mae or no payment at all. The year payment will go to Mae, and the monthly additions can go through whatever system you've created."

I eye Magenta, who mulls over his proposal before she speaks, "Fine, there will be an additional rush fee of $5,000, bringing your payment to $881,000 paid via..."

"Bank transfer," Dominic completes. Magenta writes a few words down before sliding the post-it notes to Dominic, and I recognize the sequence of numbers as my bank account.

Dominic pulls out his phone and begins tapping away. A few minutes later my phone dings and I pull it out. A notification from the Bank of America stating that my account has exceeded my $300,000 alert. *So much money.*

A part of me wants to be sick, while another imagines how much this money is going to change my life. However, I may not even spend it until the end of the contract.

Dominic stands up, straightening his jacket before grabbing my hand and leading me out the door.

"See you in a year, my dear," Magenta says casually.

I smile meekly at her as I am pulled away.

My heels click quickly, Dominic's massive strides causing me to run alongside him. I give a quick wave to Klaus, no time for a proper goodbye.

As we stand in the street, the sun takes its leave in shades of blue and purple. I hold my arms to my chest. The early November breeze is whipping through the holes of my dress and chilling my skin. Dominic has let go of my arm, but his strides remain as quick as ever. I hold my heels in my hand, chasing after him as he rounds the corner to the car. He stands in front of the vehicle holding his keys.

"Take off your underwear," he says, so low I can just about make out his words.

I drop my bag by the car door, pull my underwear down off my ankles, and place it in my bag.

"Come here." He points directly in front of him, making sure I am between him and the car, and I do as I am told. He lifts me onto the car, spreads my legs, runs his hands up my thigh, and grips me, his throat rumbling as he pulls me close.

When Dominic unbuckles his trousers and pulls out his long throbbing penis, my mouth reflexively salivates.

I have seen it all in my time of working – ranging from uncircumcised to circumcised, thin and long, short and thick with an array of balls to match, but I could never help the tingling feeling of coming out of his jeans, enough to cause tension between my thighs

He pulls me close, pressing me against his chest as his hands grab my ass. He lines himself up and I brace myself. *I bet you've been waiting for this all day.*

"Shut up, Mae." He pushes into me, earning a deep sigh from me, and a loud, deep animalistic moan from Dominic. Enough to distract me from him using my actual name.

He hangs his head back as his hips rock, his knees hitting the brake lights of the car as he holds me close.

But his slow, gentle movements are short-lived, and I find myself being choked as he rams into me, and I sprawl on the back of the car, looking at the car park ceiling lights.

Is this what my year is going to be like?

Who Am I?

Two plates of grilled chicken and vegetables sit on the table, a bottle of chardonnay by Dominic.

I take a small sip of the alcohol, paired perfectly with the meat Sybil has made. The sound of steps approach, Sybil carrying a silver tray.

She places it on Dominic's furthest side and takes his plate. She rounds the table and removes mine, even though I still have over half to eat and wasn't given lunch.

Dominic pulls the tray in front of him, revealing sheets of paper and a red fountain pen.

"Your contract, Mae," he says, as he picks up the stack of sheets.

"During your stay here, you'll only leave this house when instructed to by either your employer or me. You will have breakfast and lunch either in your room or in the dining room – dinner we will always have together.

"You will only see me in the evening. Before that time, you will help Sybil with the daily duties around the house. You'll have a two-hour window before I return home to do what you please.

There is a pool in the garden, a gym on the third floor, and a library across the hall. Sybil will show you around tomorrow.

"You'll be expected to wear black at all times, except during your two-hour window. Sybil has filled your closet with the appropriate clothing and shoes. Your legs must never be covered. Your bathroom has been stocked with the correct toiletries, soaps and oils that Magenta gave me.

"Every night at 10:00, you will meet me in my room, which is the door opposite the staircase, completely naked aside from the red heels provided." Dominic lays the papers on the tray before sliding it across to me. I scan it over, making sure everything he said is indeed everything.

When I am satisfied, I sign. I slide the contract back to Dominic.

"Magenta said you had a character pack for me."

My eyes light up at the mere mention This is my favorite bit: deciding who I am going to be. I pull out several sheets of paper held together by a yellow paperclip. On the first sheet is a plain diagram of the female body with six blank boxes distributed on either side of the picture. Arrows point to parts of the body.

"This is for physical attributes: how you want me to look on a day-to-day basis besides the black dress code and the red heels," I say. "How do you want my hair?"

Dominic glances at my current hair. I have clipped the sides back on this occasion, bringing it off my face, but the brown waves still fall across my chest.

"I'd prefer whatever hair you were born with."

I let out a sigh of relief. I can't imagine a whole year having to live under this wig; it would surely be the death of me. I write down the word "natural" in the box before pointing to the one arrowed at the diagram's face.

"Makeup-wise? And any particular changes to my eyes?"

Again, Dominic surveys my face. He bites the inside of his lip as he considers his choices. "Only wear makeup if the situation calls for it, and no, your eyes are fine."

I smile. This year is looking a lot easier than I envisioned. I write down his answer.

"How do you want my hands? Any particular nail polish?"

"I like the nails you have now."

"Pubic hair?"

"What are my options?" A slightly humorous tone laces his words, complemented with curiosity.

"Well, there's bald, stubble, thick stubble, a small to large-size bush. Then there's the landing strip, the triangle, the martini glass, the square, the arrow, or hell I can get your initials down there." I peek the beginning of a smile.

"Between bald and thick stubble."

"My legs. The hair there is sparce at the moment, but if you want hair, I'm sure we can work something out." *Please say no, please say no.*

Dominic eyes me, and I grimace. He has heard my thoughts. *That was very unprofessional.*

"It was."

Shit.

"But luckily for you, I don't want you to have hairy legs."

I make a note quickly, worried he will change his mind.

"Would you like nail polish on my toes as well?"

"Yes, same as your hands."

I make the final note, discard the diagram sheet to the side, and pull out another.

"This is who you want me to be, from my name down to my dreams and aspirations. What should I call you?"

"Dominic will be enough."

"What would you like to call me?"

"What is your name?"

"Whatever you want it to be," I reply.

"We will stick with Mae. That is your name, right?"

"It is now." I write down the name on the top of the sheet. "Right, my personality." I turn the sheet to Dominic, who surveys the rows of tick box options: sweet, funny, dim-witted, rude, materialistic, sadistic, empathetic, caring, kind, smart. This goes on for a while.

Dominic looks, and the more he looks, the more frustrated he becomes. He runs a hand through his hair, sighing.

"This is ridiculous. I'm not going to fill out this build-a-whore sheet of paper. This is eating into my time. You look over it, Mae. You choose whatever characteristics you want, providing you don't annoy me." Dominic picks up the sheets of paper, ripping them in half. "I don't want to know. Besides the physical attributes, I don't give a shit what your dreams and aspirations are, as long as you do your chores, and fuck me properly. Is that understood?"

I hang my head low at his sudden outburst.

"Yes, Dominic," I murmur.

Dominic stands up from his chair.

"Be at my door in half an hour as discussed." He leaves the room.

I give it a few seconds before I pick up the ripped pieces of paper, trying my best to order them and pair the halves together. I place what I can under the yellow paperclip and put it in my bag before heading to my room.

I stand outside Dominic's room. I have managed to remove the wig and undo my hair before our scheduled time. It isn't as dirty as I expected, and my tight curls just about rest on my shoulders. My feet tap on the padded carpet as I wait for the instruction to enter.

The door opens, and Dominic stands as naked as I am. He grabs my hand, pulling me inside. He shuts the door as I stumble in.

"Did you get that shit off your neck?"

The yarrow flower has done its job, though not as well as Magenta's magic would have. The scar of his bite remains on my neck.

"I did."

Dominic sits on the edge of the bed, watching me. His eyes linger on my jet-black hair.

"Come here."

I do as instructed, standing between his legs. His face is level with my nipples.

His hands cup the cheeks of my ass, pulling me close, so a nipple brushes against his nose. I watch as Dominic opens his mouth, taking it in.

My head falls back as he sucks hungrily. His grip on my ass tightens, and his erection brushes against my thigh.

I run my hands through his blonde locks before resting them around his neck, tracing lines across his nape as his mouth switches to the other breast.

His strong arms lift me, placing me on his lap, situating himself right at my opening. Dominic's hands trail down my thighs, hooking themselves around the backs of my knees and sliding me slowly down his shaft.

My breathing hitches as he stretches and paves his way inside me. A string of curses leaves his lips as he settles inside, adjusting his hips to reach his full depth.

My head lolls on his shoulder. Nothing can beat the first penetration: a perfect balance between pain and pleasure.

One hand returns to my thigh while the other goes for my hair, tugging with a bit of force. I pull myself away, meeting Dominic's piercing silver gaze. His jaw clenches as our eyes meet. He jerks his hips, causing me to bite my lip.

I rock my hips against his, and his eyelids flutter. *He doesn't want me to see him enjoy himself.* Dominic growls in response, taking it up a notch. His hand on my thigh moves to my lower back, pushing me closer.

Dominic's fangs brush over my neck, and I feel my pulse pounding underneath the healed wound. It is hard to focus on anything but his warm breath against my skin, waiting for the moment his teeth will clamp down on my neck.

"Stay still," he murmurs against my skin.

The fangs are sharp enough to cut straight through my skin; there is no pushing feeling, just a burn shooting through my body. I hold onto his shoulder, my grip tight, which does more harm than good.

The animalistic nature of a vampire, and the fear and anxiety that radiate off my body drive Dominic's teeth further into my neck. Blood slithers down between our bodies, imprinting on our skin.

His hold around my waist tightens, leaving me breathless as he erratically thrusts inside me. I feel the swelling of his penis close to exploding, and my light-headedness as he drinks. Dominic keeps me in place as he thrusts a few more times, his moans vibrating against my skin as he comes.

He removes his mouth from my neck, licking his lips to pick up the last of my blood. Dominic lifts me, placing me on the bed beside him.

Dominic picks me up, no doubt the same way he did last night, and opens the door to his bedroom, padding across the floor to mine. He lays me down, swiping a trail of blood that is dripping from my neck and sucks it off his finger.

"Sybil will come and patch you up."

I hum a response, my body suddenly extremely fatigued and aching. Through the strands of my hair, I watch Dominic leave, my claw marks etched on his shoulders.

The Housewife Named Mae

The curtains to my new room fly open. I roll over, curling into a ball before I stretch my legs.

"What time is it, Sybil?" I ask. I sit up, my hair falling over my face as I rub my tired eyes.

"It's time to get ready for a day's work," Sybil replies.

I groggily lift my head to look at her. Dressed in all black like she is in mourning, her hands are placed behind her back.

"I had forgotten Dominic wanted me to do stuff around the house." I groan, pulling myself off the bed and landing on my knees with a soft thud. I lean forward, stretching my back, my hands open wide in the child's pose.

"I'll be down shortly." I sit up and smile at Sybil, who only tuts and walks away. She shuts the door quietly behind her, but I am sure she wants to slam it shut.

I head into the bathroom, practically dragging my feet. Dominic must've given my file to Sybil, as all my products are lined up. I peer out of the window just behind the railing to the garden.

Standing on the tips of my toes, I make out the edge of the covered pool. *I will have to explore this place, see what it's got to offer.*

Knowing that Sybil is on the edge of her patience, I grab a flannel, run it under the golden tap, and wipe my face. By my neck, the rag traces over a bandage. I shut the cabinet, revealing my morning state.

Oh, Lord.

Hair defying gravity, and my eyes look tired. *You just need your morning coffee.* On my neck is a nude brown plaster, almost invisible against my skin. My insides turn when I run my hand over it. *I'll have to make sure Magenta gets rid of this before I see him.*

I pick out a thin, black jumper and tuck it into a black denim skirt. I stare reluctantly at the hoard of various heeled black shoes: boots, pumps, stilettos, open toe, peep toe. *This must've been what Dominic felt last night when he read through the character pack.* I frown, selecting a chunky heeled, laced boot.

Why did he have to rip the paper? The whole act surprisingly makes me feel quite deflated. *Who am I supposed to be? I can't be me. That's not enough.* I open the door to Sybil, who is moments away from banging it down.

"Finally," she says, then turns on her heel, and heads away. "Come along. I'll show you around before breakfast."

As we walk, Sybil points.

"That is the main staircase, takes you to the front door." Then to the door opposite. "I'm sure you know, Mr. Dominic's room." There is a hint of annoyance in her voice as she speaks, like the mere thought of me here is poisonous.

I do not doubt that she's read the contract we signed.

Sybil continues walking to the end of the hallway. "Up there is the entrance to the gym, down here is the garage." Sybil takes a right, descending the stairs, and I follow behind.

We step into the hallway, and three rows of cars– from a practical Volkswagen, to Jaguars, Bugatti, and other obnoxiously expensive vehicles.

"Hmmm... pretty," I say with a hint of disdain, enough to have Sybil look at me. *No doubt she'll go scurrying off to Dominic to report.* Sybil moves past the rows of cars and opens the door to her left, revealing the concrete ground and the chilly fall air.

Instinctively, my hands cradle my chest as I follow her out. I shiver, the wind whipping around my calves, almost scratching my skin.

"The garden," Sybil says.

There are strips of grass between slabs of white stone snaking around before reaching a perimeter decorated with small flowers and towering trees.

"And where do you stay, Sybil?" I ask.

"I live next door while the girls live a further down. Master Dominic owns this gated community so we can live without hassle."

"Is that why he wants me to stay here? Only leave when instructed to, am I hassle?"

Sybil sighs, age showing through her staggered breathing.

"Yes, Miss Mae, you are a hassle, indeed," she replies. "Head in through the garage, breakfast will be ready soon."

I watch her leave through another door and take her instructions back to the dining room.

"Good morning, Mae," Dominic says, his eyes to his phone: a replica of yesterday morning.

I sit down and cross my legs.

"Good morning, Dominic. How is your back?"

Dominic smiles at his phone. I can't tell whether it's because of what I said or something he has seen because, as he looks up, his smile fades.

"Nothing I can't handle. How is your neck?"

My stomach churns and the plaster seems to throb. "I've had worse." I smile at him, challenging his nonchalant attitude with my own.

"As fun as these mornings are, I won't be having breakfast with you but will see you in the evening for dinner when..." He rubs his bottom lip.

"You'll fuck me and bite into my neck," I finish for him.

Dominic looks into my eyes, his silvery gaze stern and mean.

It is what it is, isn't it, Dominic.?

His gaze narrows, but only slightly, as though he is caught off guard by my brashness. As though stating that I'm nothing more than a breathing sex doll and blood vending machine is taboo.

Dominic pushes out of his chair. He grabs his notebook and slots it under his arm, taking his coffee cup and phone between his hands. He gives me one lasting look, expecting to pick up any thoughts I have tumbling through my head.

"See you tonight, Dominic."

He dismisses me by walking off, passing Sybil as she enters with a plate in hand.

She places it in front of me, leaving me to the emptiness of the room alone and very much isolated. I lean my head on my hand, pushing the food back and forth on the plate.

I'm already bored.

The walk to the kitchen gave me too much time to think, and seeing Sybil sat beside a kitchen island, her legs crossed, accompanied by two others.

"Mae, finished already?" None of them look up from their distractions as Sybil speaks.

"Yes, it was lovely, thank you."

Sybil points to the sink installed on the island. One of the girls looks at me, her dark brown eyes studious.

"We clean our plates here." Her New Zealand accent is thick as she speaks.

I bite the inside of my cheek as I grab the sponge on the side and turn on the black tap that extends upwards, creating an elegant arch. I keep my eyes down as I wash the plate. The other woman chucks a cloth to me.

"Here."

"Come sit, Mae."

I do as I am told, the grooves on the bottom of my shoes slotting into the foothold of the stool. Her crystal blue eyes hold my gaze momentarily, as though she is trying to pick through my thoughts. She turns her head to the left, towards the other two beside her.

"This is Amelia."

Amelia raises her hand, revealing herself to be the ginger one.

She attempts a smile, but it looks more like a grimace, her jade eyes narrowing slightly as she takes me in.

"This is Constantia."

"But you can call me Constance." *Italian, definitely Italian.* I had my suspicions with the sun-kissed skin, the dark brunette hair and strong jawline.

The girls appear to be young. Sybil has already confirmed that they are all vampires.

As immortal as they are, Mother Nature always prevails.

I remember distinctively that after the sixth century, the ageing takes hold.

"Right girls, head along to do your chores. One of you will need to go and get some ingredients for tonight. Understood?" Sybil instructs.

"Yes, Sybil," the girls say in unison. With that, they stand up and head out of the kitchen.

"Right, Mae." She pulls out a folded piece of paper from her dress pocket and slides it over to me. "Your chores for the day: mainly dusting I'm afraid.

"Lunch is at 1:00, and it will be waiting in your room. Green bags can be found in the garage by the keys. The laundry room is down there." Sybil points to the archway behind me. "*Should you* finish your list, come find me, and I will give you more to do."

I don't dare look at Sybil, my eyes trained on the paper.

I open it, expecting more sheets to tumble to the floor, but instead just the one decorated with delicate handwriting.

Sweep the leaves in the garden

Vacuum the hallway on the first floor

Wash clothes and hang

Iron Mr. Dominic's shirts

**Change bathroom hand towels in
Mr. Dominic's room**

Restock mini fridge in the gym

Dust the bookshelves in the library

I check the clock on the wall opposite to me – the large black frame decorated with golden roman numerals, *hmmm just gone nine. I* head out of the kitchen to Dominic's room. I can't hear anything – no rustling, no padding footsteps. *Am I the only one here? Nonsense. Dominic would never leave me here unattended.*

I head up the stairs, my strides slowing down as I approach his door. It feels almost unnatural standing outside his room fully clothed and with an agenda that doesn't involve sex and bloodletting. I turn the handle, pushing it open.

The last time I was in here, my heart was beating so fast I couldn't see anything besides Dominic sitting on the bed. The puncture wound seems to throb in anticipation, and I rub it gently.

I try not to linger too much; how much darker it all feels with the grey and black bedding on top of an equally dark headboard. I keep my head down, almost ashamed to be in this room without him. I head into the bathroom, grab the hand towels, and scurry out the door. I step out of Dominic's room and descend the stairs, catching Sybil, Constance and Amelia by the door.

Sybil hands Amelia a card and Constance a sheet of paper. The girls link arms before heading out the door. I'm sure Sybil notices my presence, as she stands there momentarily before heading to the library just behind the staircase.

I have started not to take offense to the blatant disregard of my presence. *If I get too hung up on it, I won't survive the month.*

With the hand towels over my arm, I go to the laundry room. *Does that mean I'm doing my washing as well? Would he request our clothes to be separated? Come on, Mae, I'm sure a few bits of underwear and some tops won't hurt the guy. Besides, he doesn't wash his own clothes.*

I am no stranger to washing clothes. I can't be when I've lived on my own. I empty the container onto the floor, sorting them out before starting the wash.

It whirs to life as it begins vibrating, threatening to shake out of its cramped confinement on the shelf. On the wooden table are two piles of folded clothes. I pull the iron from the top shelf and plug it in.

When I was younger, I found ironing very therapeutic. Most jobs that people find tedious; I find relaxing. It means that I can go on autopilot and don't have to use my brain for a while. More times than not, I don't have to think about what I am going to do next.

I have only been here for less than a day and, not to say that I expected to be held in a cage with a collar around my neck saying *bitch*, but I did expect something a bit more exciting. I feel more like a housewife than anything else.

Is this going to be my year?

A younger me would be crying at the thought of not being able to spend her hard-earned wages, but then again, a younger me is the reason I'm even here.

With all ten shirts ironed and hanging on the rail, I still have another hour on the machine before it is due for a spin, so I go to the kitchen.

Now searching is an understatement. *Where could water bottles be aside from in a cupboard or the fridge?* I close the sixth cupboard for the second time, as though relooking will magically mean the water bottles will be there.

"We don't keep the gym bottles in the kitchen."

I stand up to see Constance, bags in hand as she saunters into the kitchen. She places them on the marble table, the bags collapsing with the weight of their contents.

"Where do you keep them?" I ask, watching as she begins unpacking her bounty from her travels.

"In the gym, you'll notice that there's a cabinet. Take a few bottles from there and place at the back of the fridge."

I sigh in relief. I was down to my last cupboard before giving up and going on to the next task.

"Thanks, Constance," I reply gratefully.

"You're his whore, right?" Constance comments.

The quick change of conversation stops me briefly from leaving the kitchen. Constance, however, does not seem fazed and continues unpacking.

"Well, currently it would seem I am his maid," I correct.

Constance lets out a small chuckle, taking me aback. She looks up at me, her deep brown eyes almost trying to drown me.

"You're always his whore. Should Mr. Dominic want it, he could request you now, and as to be expected, you'd go running."

This is not my first heckling, and it will surely not be my last. Women of clients tend to have an issue with my presence, as though I went out of my way to be on the arm of their boyfriend, their husband, or their ex. *It is not my fault. This is a job no different than that of any dull nine to five. It pays the bills and does so well.*

It is as if they negate entirely the man who's hired me. The man who requests I be his plus one to the dinner function he knows his ex-wife will be at. The man who knows that his ex-wife will ultimately ruin the night by throwing a drink over both him and me.

The man who knows that will only make her come across as jealous and banshee-like as security escorts her out of the function, the talk of the evening. The man who knows, for the rest of the night, he will be patted on the back repeatedly by other like-minded men while I continue to pretend that I can't see the lingering gazes and perverted smiles.

This is not my first heckling.

"Luckily Dominic has not requested me. Thank you for your help." I walk out of the kitchen, heading up the staircase towards the gym.

It is difficult not to allow these things to bother me. I have been doing this for six years now, and every encounter with someone like Constance is wearing.

Constance hasn't lied.

There isn't much hoovering needed. Dominic isn't a dirty man, so I can't imagine him tracking filth into the house. To be honest, I can't imagine him being anywhere near dirt.

With the hoover away, I go into my room. Somehow, between my chores, one of the ladies has brought me my lunch, placed on a silver tray with a lid on my bed. I sit down with a huff, suddenly my feet aching and my back sore.

I have not taken in the time, so as I place the first bite of grilled chicken and quinoa in my mouth, I glance at the small analogue clock on the bedside table. *1:00 exactly.* My stomach flutters, as my plan has gone exactly as I've expected.

With the food down, I'm sure no one will collect, so I go back to the kitchen. I leave the dish on the counter before heading into the laundry room to turn the machine on to spin.

I was right to leave the garden it until the afternoon, with the fall breeze grabbing at my knees. The sunshine above me makes the chilly weather a bit more bearable.

With a large maple tree that drops everything but its trunk, I spend the hour raking and plucking leaves in the most inconvenient places.

My hands are dirty, and so are my knees. *No wonder he has us wear black.*

Thankfully, in less than an hour, I'm dragging my feet to my room. Walking around doing mundane chores in four-inch heels makes even the most straightforward task that much harder.

"Sybil..." I call. I have an hour before my allocated two-hour free time. A part of me doesn't want more work – my fingers feel raw, my back aches, I know I need a shower, my hair sags, and there is a heartbeat on my puncture wound.

With no answer, I don't bother to repeat myself, and almost jog to my room.

I dive headfirst into the bed, trying to kick the heels off, I raise my leg, too tired to lift my upper body, and untie them before repeating. I lie there briefly, trying to will the bath to fill itself up.

Realizing I'm not Magenta, I roll off the bed, instantly regretting it as I crawl into the bathroom. I turn on the golden tap and water starts streaming into the bath. I plug up the hole, grab the small bottle of bubble bath, and empty a worrying amount, knowing that if I sit back down, I will forget.

I lean my head on the black tub. Legs stretch as I lazily remove my clothes, almost slithering into the tub like slime. It is not seductive and certainly not sensual, but as the water and soap suds cradle my body, I couldn't care less.

I curl into the fetal position as my eyes close. I am so exhausted that I don't even care if I fall asleep and potentially drown. But as my consciousness begins to leave, my perfectionist brain leave one little sticky note as a last thought.

You forgot to dust!

Prying Eyes

Rebekah is an overachiever; she hands her assignments in on time if not before. She's never been sick on a weekday, always making a miraculous recovery over the weekend. When one wants to get on her good side, handing her a cup of coffee ensures her magnanimity until it runs out.

As she signs off her last refundable credit sheet, her computer beeps. She refuses to look at it before she double-checks her work. Rebekah finally places the paper on a large stack of documents before acknowledging her screen.

It is an email from Bank of America. She clicks on it as she reads through the extensive email, her eyes widen, and a smile grows on her face.

Rebekah isn't an erratic person. Still, this email has Rebekah charging down the hallway, laptop in hand, as she weaves past colleagues who stare dumbfounded.

She slows down as she reaches the transparent door to her manager's office. Without waiting to be let in, Rebekah opens the door, closes it behind her, and places her laptop in front of her boss.

"Look what Bank of America just sent me," Rebekah huffs, sitting down in the brown leather chair as she catches her breath, waiting for Michael to hang up the phone and pay attention.

Michael, still shocked by Rebekah – of all people – rushing into his office and placing her computer down on his desk, goes mute momentarily. He clears his throat, angling his body away as he ends the phone call.

The second the phone is on the hook; Rebekah jumps up and rounds his small desk to show him what she found.

"Look at this, Michael." She points at the screen. Her finger smushes against the LED display.

"Alright, Rebekah calm down, sit... please, you're making me nervous." Michael sneezes, causing Rebekah to jump back, a reaction he has when he becomes nervous and unsettled.

Rebekah sits back in the chair. Her hands drum nervously on her knees. She wants Michael to catch up, to be on the same exciting page as she is. But Michael is painstakingly slow in nearly all his actions that don't involve leaving the office, the only time the man is chipper.

Michael eyes Rebekah, causing her to stop drumming. He pulls down the bifocals from on top of his head and fixes them on his nose.

"Right, what do we have here..."

Rebekah watches, edging almost off her seat as Michael's lips move, reading the email to himself quietly.

Her grin returns as Michael looks at her, astonishment evident on his face.

"Right, right," Rebekah says as she stands to her feet, moving to stand beside Michael as they both read the email together, experiencing the moment simultaneously.

Michael removes his glasses, leaning back into his chair as he rubs his eyes tiredly. He hands Rebekah her laptop, miming her to sit back down. Again.

For a few minutes, Michael is silent, changing from rubbing his eyes to stroking the bridge of his nose as he thinks, the creases of his red skin contorting and relaxing. He clears his throat, coming out of his mind library, and places the glasses back on.

"Forward that email to me," Michael says. Rebekah forwards the email to Michael. There is a *ding*, and he glances at his computer, expecting it to be from anyone but her.

"Have you told anyone about this?" His hand returns to the phone and lifts the receiver off the hook. He dials some numbers.

"No, I came straight to you."

"Right, good, good. That's good. Right." He sighs. Having to string a sentence together is not Michael's favorite task. "I need to call a few people. This goes beyond us."

"Bullshit." Rebekah holds her mouth, shocked at the words that left her lips. "I mean who else could this possibly go to if not us. We are the IRS, Michael. We deal with these sorts of things."

"Yes, I understand, Rebekah, however, the parties involved hold interests to other agencies," he counters.

"Like..."

"Well, the FBI for one. They'd want to know."

Rebekah slams her laptop shut before saying, "Come on, Michael. Give it to them and they'll do a half-assed job and send us all the paperwork. You know how they are in the Seattle branch. If it doesn't involve gangs and guns, they don't want to know."

Michael thinks for a moment, and Rebekah takes that chance to cater to his sentimental side.

"I've been working for you what... six...coming up to seven years? And have I ever had a sick day?" Rebekah implores.

"No," Michael replies.

"Have I ever been late with assignments or to work?"

"No."

"And aren't I the last person to leave the office?"

"Where are you taking this, Calamba?" Michael says, tired.

"I deser- need this big break, Michael. As my manager to oversee it all, imagine what that would do for both our careers." Rebekah raises her brows at Michael. She knows he wants to move to another branch but is always overlooked. With this breakthrough, he could move on, and she could take his spot.

"Fine, you can lend a helping hand, but the FBI has to be involved. Got it?" Michael orders.

Rebekah stands up, giddier than ever. "Yeah, got it."

"And they take the lead, Calamba. I don't want you strong-arming the investigation." He points the phone at her threateningly.

"Yes, yes, of course," Rebekah replies, waving her hand.

"Right, now get out of my office. You just dumped a whole load of shit on my lap."

Rebekah smiles, taking her leave.

"And don't come storming in here again."

She closes the door, her smile never leaving her face.

Conrad sits, arms folded before he runs his hand through his hair. He pushes back onto the chair, lifting the front legs a few inches off the floor.

"Investigations are becoming stagnant, Conrad," Naomi announces.

He leans forward, resting his arms on the table, covering his face briefly. He lifts his gaze to Naomi, who is standing watching him, her arms folded over her buttoned white shirt.

"I know, but just because investigations are stagnant doesn't mean I'm not right," he counters.

Naomi sighs, rubbing her face. She turns to look out of the window the sun reflecting off of her brown skin.

"Right now, all you've got to show a waste of resources and taxpayers' money." Naomi turns to face him. "Right now, people are expecting results. We can't go against the Aldrek family. They'll drown us in lawsuits," Naomi explains.

Conrad strides over to the evidence board, littered with notes and pictures. "Aldrek Enterprise" in big bold letters across the top.

Conrad stares down the center picture; his fist clenches as the silver eyes stare back at him mockingly.

"They've got a hand in every sector, Naomi." Conrad slams his hand against the board. "Nightlife, travel, medicine, property. They are this close to having the whole of Seattle in their hands."

"And the state loves them for it," Naomi adds. "Aldreks have funded many schools and businesses, raised the employment rate exponentially. They even sponsored this year's state governor and, let's be honest, Governor Francis is the closest thing to Jesus, making Dominic Aldrek God."

Naomi is right and Conrad hates himself because of it, he drops his hands in defeat.

The pair turn as the glass door opens. A small, timid woman walks in, no doubt several floors above her pay grade.

"Um... Mister Grier sir, there's a call from the IRS," she whispers.

Conrad narrows his eyes. The last thing he needs is the toddlers down in IRS calling about a missing tax report and expecting them to send all guns blazing into a middle-aged woman's house.

"What is it? What could be so important you trekked floors to relay to me?" Conrad responds angrily.

"He says that over $800,000 was transferred into a Bank of America account," she replies, her voice barely audible.

"So..." Conrad stares at the woman, waiting for a suitable response.

"The receipt was from Aldrek Pharmaceuticals to a Mae Geoffries," she answers. Her hands grip the glass door, waiting anxiously.

Until that moment, Conrad had never smiled so much in his life.

"Are you sure?" Naomi asks.

"Yes, ma'am, I'm sure. He's on the line if you wish to speak to him."

"Transfer the call to conference room three," Naomi orders.

Conrad slams his hand on the table, making everyone in the room jump.

"Fuck! Yes," he screams and heads to the wall, scribbling *Mae Geoffries* next to the picture of Dominic.

"I fucking got you now," Conrad whispers through a lopsided grin.

Medicine

I stand on the raised podium with obnoxiously large scissors in my hand, a red ribbon hovering between the shears.

"A few more pictures and we will be done," Delilah whispers. She stands back as I smile, showcasing my pearly whites as the reporters take a few more shots.

I cut the ribbon and hand the scissors to Delilah before shaking hands with the chief of the hospital, Dr. Hail.

As my PA, she has done well getting word out for today's unveiling. Reporters take a few more photos, the flashes just as blinding as the sun, almost making me feel disoriented and nauseous. I find my way on the podium, running my cold, red hands over the equally freezing microphone.

"Today is a good day, aside from the chilly fall weather." The crowd laughs. "I'm honored to have been a part of the renovations for the children's ward for Tacoma General." I take the mic from the stand and move in front of it.

"There's nothing sadder than seeing a child unwell. Now I'm not a doctor. I leave all the hard work to Dr. Hail and his very talented doctors and nurses." Dr. Hail nods in recognition. "But what I can do is make their stay comfortable, make their life comfortable, because no child should have to suffer. Keep their innocence. Keep them smiling is the motto I live by."

There is a round of applause as I fit the mic to the stand. This is my favorite bit: standing on top of the world as people shower me with praise and adoration. *I am the King of Seattle.*

"Mr. Aldrek, Mr. Aldrek."

I cast my eyes down on the reporter who so eagerly pushes to the front before security stops him. The mere eye contact means that he assumes I let him speak.

"David Hanesley from the Puget Sound Business Journal. Can we assume there won't be a repeat of four years ago?"

I look to Delilah, who waves her hands to security to usher David away. I watch as David scrambles forward.

"When Aldrek Pharmaceuticals came under fire when their self-administered Citalopram caused problems to their users." Security attempts to pick him up, but David resists, continuing his shouts. "And it came to light that FDA trials and protocol had been back benched to get the medicine on the market."

At this point, David has been hoisted up by security. Everyone begins to whisper, and a melancholy air begins to envelop us all.

"Leaving victims tired, fatigued, and in one case, a complete nervous system shutdown."

I look at Delilah. *«These hecklings will only continue.»*

"It's alright, let him speak," I say, raising my hand to the guards. Security drops him, and David hurries to the front. His phone stretches towards me.

"And when victims and parents of victims came forward, Aldrek swamped them in court bills and legal fees. A child died,

Mr. Aldrek." David ruffles through his worn brown satchel, pulls out a sheet of paper, and waves it frantically in my face.

The paper was a photo, a boy no older than 17, he is gazing out of a window, his ashen blond hair swept by his ears.

I sigh, fixing my collar as David continues speaking. "He was 15, Mr. Aldrek, suffering from mild depression and anxiety. He took Citalopram in the hopes it'd make going to school easier, yet three months later, Sean Piers died. Heart failure, Mr. Aldrek. A 15-year-old died of heart failure, and all his parents received were funeral debt and legal fees." David flings the paper at me. It floats and lands just in front of my feet.

"Sean Piers was an honor roll student. Despite his depression, he still maintained his grades. His mom said Sean was into music, but his dad was convinced Sean would go on to play football. I, when I met Sean, was convinced he'd be a musician: the next Jimi Hendrix or Slash. Sean just wanted to be like Mendes, saying the name alone would help him get there." I smile, looking down at the floor before raising my head to the silent crowd.

"When Sean passed, I was in Vienna. His mom called merely hours after, and I hopped on the first plane. I covered those funeral costs, paying for every requirement that would make Sean's resting place as beautiful as his kind soul. Sean was the worst case. By that time, I had made sure that Citalopram had been discontinued until it was thoroughly checked, products stripped from the shelves, and recalls sent out, but that did not stop the other victims.

"Ten other teens faced problems caused by Citalopram, thankfully not as serious as Sean's. There was nothing I could do for Sean's parents. I could not bring their child back, but what

I could do was ensure it didn't happen again." I raise my hand, and the crowd parts as a couple walks forward. I smile as Sean's mom wipes her eyes. His father is cradling her as they step onto the podium.

"Aside from the new state-of-the-art equipment in the children's ward, I have added a new sector for children who suffer from mental illnesses. A recreational hall where children can do their homework, make friends with others around the state. It is the first of many which I hope to include in all hospitals within Seattle. I named it The Pier, and hopefully, these children can envision a brighter future."

Cheers and shouts explode from the crowd. Mr.s. Piers engulfs me in a hug, Mr. Piers patting me firmly on the back. I take her hands into mine as I stare at her.

"You are doing an amazing job, Diane. I hope this does Sean justice."

All Diane can do is nod, tears streaming down her face.

With both parents on either side of me, the press laps it up. I give them a dazzling smile as David slinks away, disheartened at the result.

Delilah takes control of the matter, finally.

"That is all we have time for. Thank you for coming to the unveiling."

With one last hug from the parents, Delilah ushers me away, heading to the double doors of the children's ward.

My shoes squeak across the polished floor, matching with the clicking of Delilah's heels.

"How the FUCK did a reporter from the business journal get in?"

Delilah jumps and turns to face me, her hands tightly clasped around her notebook.

"I'm not sure, Mr. Aldrek. I checked the list, only those approved reporters were allowed. But we were outside. It's a lot harder to keep an area secure when it's on public property. If we had the unveiling insi-"

"No!" I shout, my voice bouncing off the empty halls' walls. "If we did it inside, the press would just deem me some pretentious entrepreneur who's too good to stand in the cold."

Delilah nods, her blond hair falling in front of her face.

"You should count yourself lucky that I was able to handle Mr. Hanesley so well." I continue walking, Delilah trotting behind me.

"Is that why you started the Pier project?" she asks.

"Exactly. I knew that the press wouldn't let me forget the failure that was Citalopram, so I needed to make good again," I reply. We walk to the end of the hallway, to the elevator that will take us down to the car park. I press the button.

"Mr. Aldrek... Mr. Aldrek."

I turn around to see Dr. Hail running down the hall, a bag in hand. The elevator opens, and I usher Delilah inside. "I will see you at the office."

The doors close before she can speak.

"Yes, Dr. Hail?"

Dr. Hail raises his arms, holding out a black leather duffle bag to me.

"For you," he says.

I take the bag from him and place it over my shoulder.

"Thank you, Dr. Hail," I say gratefully. I put my hand on his shoulder, capturing his brown eyes with mine. "Don't forget, this is between you and me." Dr. Hail's body slumps forward suddenly as I compel him. "If anybody asks, you know nothing."

I slap his shoulder, waking him from the trance.

"Thanks again, Dr. Hail." I lift the duffle bag. "Black leather, my favorite. The team didn't need to get me a gift."

Dr. Hail rubs the back of his neck, confused briefly before nodding and smiling.

"Well, it's the least we could do, thanks to all your hard work."

The elevator doors open, and I step in.

"The hard work is done by you, doctor."

With that, the doors close, and I sigh.

I walk out onto the empty car park and unlock the door to my car. I chuck the duffle bag into the passenger side, my inner jacket buzzes, and I pull out my phone. *Ada Aldrek* appears on the screen. I roll my eyes, answering the phone.

"What is it?"

"Is that how you greet your mother?" she barks on the other line.

"No." I rub my eyes. "I'm just stressed. Another reporter tried to dig at me for the Citalopram incident." I can hear the clink of a martini glass being set down.

"Did you mention the Pier project?" she asks.

"I did, Mother, that wasn't a bad idea."

"Dominic honey, your mother is full of them. Where do you think you get it from?"

I laugh, sliding in the driver's seat.

"When are we seeing you?" my mother asks. I groan as she mentions meeting up.

"Not anytime soon, Mother," I reply.

"Not even for Christmas?"

"I'm busy Christmas, and besides, I'm too tired to accompany you to another gala so you can show me off and bid large amounts of money on useless items," I explain.

"Now Dominic, if I want to show off my favorite child, I should be able to."

"Don't let Lincoln and Freya hear you say that." I sit up. "Here's an idea: take Freya. Have her and Christopher make an entrance. Nothing screams wealth like having someone to pass it to, perhaps Elsie could accompany them. Show off your one and only granddaughter. Maybe that'll spark them to have more."

"Freya said she was busy."

Oh, so I wasn't even your first choice.

"And your brother... well, he doesn't own several multimillion companies, and he doesn't have a wife and child, so he's a no. What have you got him doing again?"

"He manages nightlife. Mom, is Dad not enough?"

I hear a laborious sigh. "He's somehow wormed his way out of it, winter golf apparently. We live in Bali. How could he possibly be doing winter golf?"

"I suspect he will be flying out for that, Mom." I rub my chin as I think. "Why don't you skip this year, Mom, spend Christmas with Freya."

"Nonsense," my mother cries. "This is my event: focusing on the charities, making us look humble and charitable."

I rub my head. It isn't about looking more charitable, it is an excuse for her to flaunt our wealth, rub it in every woman's nose.

"Fine, don't skip, we can meet in the New Year, OK?"

There is a loud sip as she drinks from her glass before setting it back down.

"That's all I ask, to see my babies at least once."

I grumble before letting out a sigh.

"I need to get back to work. Bye, Mother," I say quickly.

"Bye, dear."

I hang up the phone and throw it on the passenger's side. I turn to the duffle bag and unzip it, revealing the IV packs filled with blood. I graze my hand over them: *O negative, B positive, AB positive.* I lick my lips as I close the bag.

I push the start button, the engine roars to life, and I pull out of the car park.

The Agents Named Conrad and Rebekah

Rebekah sits, holding a rather large coffee in her hands. Yesterday she spoke with dozens of branch managers, who eagerly turned down her request for a meeting the next day. Their responses ranged from "too short notice" to "we don't cover that in this branch." Finally, after many fruitless efforts, Rebekah managed to meet with a manager of a branch overlooking Lake Washington.

As Michael directed, she forwarded her intentions to her new FBI friend. However, due to her strong-arming nature, she sent him the wrong time: an hour after the actual scheduled meeting.

That'll force him to communicate with me. Rebekah smiles slyly to herself. She uncrosses her legs and then re-crosses them, draping her right leg over the left.

"Miss Calamba?" A small, thin man pokes his head out from behind the oak door, his eyes sunken and his cheeks deflated. Rebekah stands up, clasping her notebook in one hand and her coffee in another.

"Yes, Mr. Islington."

He ushers her forward to walk into his office.

Closing the door slowly and shuffles to his desk. Rebekah lets out a held breath. Her eyes dart to the clock. At this rate, her assigned partner will turn up and take over the investigation, leaving her on the sidelines like a substitute.

"Should we wait for the other one?" he asks, clearly not pressed for time.

"No, that'll be quite alright," Rebekah replies quickly, almost stumbling over her words.

"This transaction – could you tell me the parties involved," she starts. The man makes a series of clicks on the computer, his hand shaking ever so slightly.

"I believe it was a transaction of $881,000 made from Aldrek pharmaceuticals to Mae Geoffries." Rebekah writes down the answer. "I must mention to you, Miss Calamba, th-"

"Rebekah is fine, Mr. Islington," she says, interrupting him. He looks at her momentarily before continuing.

"I had a look over Mae Geoffries' account, and it is not uncommon for large sums of money to be delivered to this account."

"Are you saying that an amount of just under nine hundred thousand dollars is normal for such an account?" Rebekah asks. Mr. Islington shakes his head, causing the man to sway from side to side.

"No, Miss Calamba, such an amount, however common, would still be brought up with suspicion. All I mean to say is that figures ranging from five to nine thousand dollars are dropped periodically – almost weekly in fact – however, not from Aldrek pharmaceuticals."

"Then where, Mr. Islington, does this money come from?" she asks.

"It would seem from-"

The door bursts open and Conrad saunters in. A small line of sweat graces his upper lip as he eyes Rebekah.

"FBI agent Grier, I'm here for the Aldrek Pharmaceuticals transaction."

"Please." Mr. Islington stands up, an action that Rebekah knows will take a long time to undo. "Sit down, Agent Grier."

Conrad plops into the seat next to Rebekah, his eyes skim the shorthand notes she has taken before turning back to Mr. Islington, who has only just begun to lower himself into the chair.

"As I said to Miss Calamba, large sums of money often enter Miss Geoffries account, however, from a different source."

"And what source might that be, Mr..."

"Islington," he finishes.

"Right, Islington," Conrad repeats.

"It would seem from a company named Folk-" He stops as he eyes the name, his throat becoming so unbearably dry that the man has to reach for a glass of water and down it all. He clears his throat.

"I apologize."

"Well, if you can manage, Mr. Islington, I would greatly appreciate it," Conrad replies.

Mr. Islington turns the computer towards the pair so they can see for themselves.

"FolkWore." Rebekah concludes, "What is that?"

Mr. Islington clears his throat, eying the now empty glass.

"It would seem from our records that they are a costume store but have branches internationally. I would also like to mention that while Miss Geoffries receives money from Folk-wore, she also sends money to an account in the UK with a similar surname, a relative perhaps."

It seems grammatically incorrect. At best, it should be referred to as Folk Wear, if not anything else.

"Thank you, Mr. Islington, for your help," Rebekah says. She is the first to stand, but only by a second.

The pair simultaneously stretch their hands to Mr. Islington, who looks almost frightened by the whole ordeal. He looks between the hands that threateningly approach him.

"That is no worries, Miss Calamba. If there's anything you need from the bank or me, please don't hesitate to call." His hands remain firmly on the desk, and Conrad takes that as his cue to leave.

"We will be in touch, Mr. Islington," Conrad says before heading out the door, Rebekah nipping at his heels.

As the pair exit the building, the brisk wind whips around them like a storm. Rebekah instinctively brings her coat in a bunch at her waist, launching her coffee cup in a nearby bin.

"Misinforming me of the meeting time was sneaky of you," Conrad remarks, breaking the silence. "Lucky thing I am a punctual man. Otherwise, I would have missed it." He turns to face Rebekah, his forest green eyes boring into her brown ones.

He easily towers over her at six-foot-five, Rebekah a measly five-five. She cranes her neck to look at him, her short raven hair flying in the wind.

However, what Rebekah lacks in size, she makes up with confidence. She shoves her notebook in her bag.

"If I hadn't done so, you would have put me on the sidelines, Detective Grier."

Conrad steps closer to her, causing Rebekah to stumble only slightly backwards.

"This is no game, Miss Calamba, this is very, VERY dangerous territory you are waltzing into, way beyond your pay grade," Conrad spits.

"Well, this is MY field. You need me as much as I need you," Rebekah counters. Conrad steps back, fishing out his phone.

"Speak for yourself, Calamba." He looks at Rebekah, who is looking for her car keys. "Whatever the case is, both our seniors want us working together. We should focus our efforts on Aldrek pharmaceuticals."

Rebekah shakes her head.

"No, I think this Mae Geoffries is the answer," she replies.

Conrad sighs and flags down a taxi.

"Fine, you take the Mae Geoffries lead. I will take Aldrek. We will meet once every two weeks to get each other up to speed. Deal?" As the car pulls up, he gives his hand to Rebekah, who shakes it.

"Deal."

"I'll see you in a fortnight, Agent Calamba. The name's Conrad, by the way." He shuts the door and winds down the window.

"The name's Rebekah."

The Vampire and the Escort

As I open the front door, Sybil approaches me, taking the duffle and coat from my hands.

"How's she been, Sybil?" I ask.

"She did most of her chores, aside from the dusting, but the chores she did do, she did well. When I went to scold her, I found her asleep in the bathtub. Luckily, the plug had come loose, otherwise she would've drowned." Sybil tuts loudly as though Mae's death would've been an inconvenience. "I forget how simple humans are. I may have worked her too hard, Mr. Dominic."

I wave my hand.

"Nonsense, I'm sure you did fine. Take the bag and distribute it among the community. Don't forget to save some for you and the girls."

Sybil nods before heading to the kitchen. I head to my room, ready to discard the smart, casual outfit I had put together this morning; however, I find myself gravitating to Mae's room. I open it, peering in, and there she is in all her naked glory.

The curtains are drawn, and Mae has lit several candles to illuminate the room, creating a soft glow that causes her shadow to dance across the walls.

"...low lunge. Exhale...pivot towards the front of your mat..." The New Zealand accent floats throughout the room, instantly reminding me of Constance.

Mae does as the voice instructs, moving into a lunge.

"...push through your hands, round your spine. Try to lift your knee towards your chest and feel your core engage. Take a breath in..." I hear her take a large breath in, her back rising. "And exhale."

"You do yoga naked?"

Mae glances at me before standing and switching off the Bluetooth speaker. "It's very freeing," she replies, grabbing a silk robe from her bed and covering her body.

I groan in response, catching her off guard, making her smirk.

"There's no need to cover up on my accord."

"No offense, Dominic, but you kind of disturbed my vinyasa. Besides, dinner will be ready soon, and I should get dressed."

If I could have it my way, you wouldn't wear any clothing. I envision Mae parading around the house with nothing on but heels. My jaw clenches and my pants tighten.

I lean my back on the door as Mae walks past me, heading to the closet.

"Sybil said you didn't complete your chores."

"I forgot to dust. I hardly think the world should end because of it." She drops her robe, exposing her back to me before glancing over her shoulder. "Don't you think?" *She's teasing me... and it's working.*

Mae pulls the dress on, the spaghetti straps hanging delicately on her shoulders as she takes out a pair of black wedge peep-toe heels.

She is dressed for summer, and luckily for her, she isn't leaving for the rest of the night, so her body can afford to be so exposed. She doesn't bother to wear a bra, leaving little points near the top of the dress. Instinctively, I lick my lips.

Mae approaches, her jasmine scent encasing me, making me undeniably horny. She eyes me, and my lower half jumps at the thought of what she'll do next.

"Should we go have some dinner, Dominic?" Her eyes shift to the door I'm blocking. I open it, allowing her to pass, giving me time to adjust my throbbing erection.

I sip my wine as I watch Mae put another forkful into her mouth.

"I researched you."

I raise my brow at Mae as she speaks, patting her lips before laying the napkin on the empty plate.

"I'm not really supposed to 'til... well, I could, I just typically choose not to."

"What did you find?" I ask.

One of the downsides of being a very wealthy man is that I am also rich in scandals, fake news, and every tabloid speculating whether I'm gay. Dissecting the clothes, I wear whether they make me a Democrat or a Republican and whether I funded Trump in his win...I did not.

"Besides the females on your arm, I noticed that your businesses have come under a lot of scrutiny. Like the medical scandal with the young boy."

My eyes flutter shut as I am reminded again of Sean.

"I'm sorry to hear about what happened."

I feel her hand rest on my forearm and open my eyes to look at her.

"You seem like a good person...well, you haven't shown yourself to be a bad person."

"You think so?" I ask her.

"You take some warming up. You are not nearly as big of a dick as you were the first night we met and then consequently the day after."

I watch her smile grow, and my own face frowns. Sex brings out a meaner side, a more vampiric side that at times works wonders at stimulating me, keeping me sharp and focused. However, I don't tend to make a habit of having sex with the same woman more than once, so I can afford to be that fleeting jerk who knows how to fuck. But here Mae is having to see both sides of me daily. I have forgotten my manners.

I look down at her hand on my arm before going back to her. Mae pushes back in her chair and so do I, instinctively, almost parroting her, under her spell.

"Thank you for dinner. I'll be outside your door in an hour." She takes my plate and hers before walking out of the room.

On my feet already, I follow her. Mae is in the dark. Without my hunter-like eyes adjusting to the poor lighting, I would've never made out her silhouette scraping the last of the food in the bin.

"Why a-"

She screams, dropping the plate, and it hits the floor, shattering into far too many pieces. "Don't do that!" She spins around, facing no one, and I switch on the light.

"Why are you in the dark?"

Hearing my voice, Mae is able to direct her next words at me instead of the stairs. "Because I'm only washing the dishes. There's no need to turn the light on. It's a waste of electricity."

My lips curve into a smile, and I just about stifle a laugh. She catches my cover-up, glaring at me.

"Don't be silly, Mae. A few minutes in the light to wash dishes won't through me into bankruptcy. Besides, I have a dishwasher."

"A what!" she shouts, perhaps a little too loudly. "Sorry, Sybil gave me the impression that everything was done by hand."

"Most times, but there are times when it's just me home, so..." I shrug.

Mae goes to the corner and takes out the dustpan and broom before squatting. She begins sweeping up the pieces of china that have scattered across the kitchen.

I watch her shuffling around, her knees to her chest, as she sweeps the pieces, but soon she begins to pick up the pieces.

"Shit!" she shouts, and I'm across the kitchen to her side in three strides, lifting her by her elbows.

"What?"

Mae has her index finger in her mouth, and I pull it out. A line of saliva mixed with blood trails. I narrow my eyes as the red blood oozes out of her finger. Instinctively, I put it in my mouth.

Mae stares at me for a second before casting her eyes to the ceiling, almost embarrassed by the whole thing.

"Done?" She places her finger back in her mouth, despite it not bleeding anymore, and my blood rushes to my growing erection.

"Not in the slightest." I pull her finger out of her mouth and replace it with my lips. Mae is just as shocked as I am when I kiss her, the action entirely alien for me.

The FolkWore Designer

Rebekah stands outside the golden storefront – the name is lined with fake greenery like weeds on an abandoned building snaking around to make the letters.

FolkWore, she smiles. It's starting to grow on her, the name that is, similar to the weeds that cover the shop title, slithering around until the host becomes one with it.

Rebekah pushes the door open as the bell chimes. Before she can even reach the front desk, Rebekah has to weave her way through rows of clothes on a rotating metal frame like something at a dry cleaner.

"Hello... hello," Rebekah calls.

"Back here, babe." A small hand waves from a distance and Rebekah walks over. Finally, in a clearing, she comes face-to-face with Klaus.

He rolls a stick of gum between his fingers before putting it in his mouth and bites his soft pink lips as he surveys Rebekah's whole existence.

Kawaii is the best way to describe her face: pale skin like whipped cream with sprinkles of cinnamon, almond-shaped eyes behind golden, thin-rimmed glasses that magnify the brown.

Small, plump, pink lips that always pout when she's in deep thought. But Rebekah is from the Philippines, and when she speaks, she is anything but cute.

Rebekah stands awkwardly, brushing her short raven hair behind one of her ears. Klaus' eyes trail down her white blouse wrapped under her khaki trench coat, stopping just at the knees of her black cigarette trousers, ending finally on some black brogues.

"A nymph." His eyes find their way to hers as he speaks.

"Excuse me," Rebekah replies as Klaus runs a pink-nailed hand through his golden hair.

"I'm usually good at guessing what a customer is looking for, and if not, I usually already have an answer for them."

"I'm not a customer." She places her coffee cup on the counter and takes her notebook and wallet out of her beige bag before setting it on the ground.

Klaus looks horrified at the caffeine that has made an entrance on his glass countertop.

Rebekah flips open her wallet, showcasing the IRS badge and her picture on the other side. Klaus takes it, surveying the badge as though he assumes it is fake, before handing it back to her, as disgusted as he was when she set down the coffee cup.

"Well, Agent Calamba, what brings you down to FolkWore?"

Rebekah opens her notebook, sliding the pen off the page, and clicks it.

"Does a Mae Geoffries work here?"

Klaus sighs, rubbing his chin.

"Why?"

"I'm hoping to speak to her. I tried her home phone and mobile, but I couldn't reach her through either."

Klaus slips off the desk, naturally towering over Rebekah. For a brief second, she thinks he is about to attack. Instead, he reaches under the desk and pulls out a large black leather book, dust covering the top.

"It's been a while since I had to bring out the diary. We do most of our stuff on the internet, but as I don't have access to it, we keep an overview of jobs the guys are on in here." He opens it up to November and runs his finger over the dates.

"Here we go."

Klaus turns the book around for Rebekah to see. He points at the handwritten note *Mae x Aldrek 10* inside the box dated the 1st.

"Is that it?" Rebekah says, disheartened. She looks to Klaus, who shrugs.

"That's what it is, I couldn't tell you more; you'd have to speak to my boss, and she's not in today. However..."

Rebekah's ears perk up on the off chance of more information.

"It's not uncommon for designers to go off the grid, no doubt Mae is working on outfits for this Aldrek person. The number 10 suggests the time."

"Ten weeks? That'll bring us to mid-February."

"Oh, no, baby girl. Ten months," Klaus corrects.

"She'll be off the grid for ten months!" Rebekah clarifies.

"Looks like it. It must be a massive project."

Rebekah's lips move to the side as she tucks away her notebook and pen. She grabs her coffee cup, to Klaus' relief. The investigation has hit a dead end almost immediately. If Grier doesn't sideline her, this investigative path will.

"Thanks..."

"Klaus," he finishes. Rebekah takes out her business card and hands it to him.

"When your boss gets in, have her give me a call. I really need to speak to Miss Geoffries."

"Will do, Agent."

Rebekah leaves the store, the cold air seeming more brutal than it did when she went in, almost mocking her for the failed attempt of being an IRS agent.

Hopefully, Grier is doing better than I am, she thinks, taking a long, unhappy gulp of her now ice-cold coffee.

A Woman for Every Man

I walk up the stairs to the gym, a hand towel over my shoulder. It is the weekend, meaning that I don't have any chores to complete. I'm finally able to wear something other than heels, so naturally, I put on some trainers that had been hidden behind the wedged shoes.

I push open the door to the well-lit room, the morning sun casting its rays through the floor-to-ceiling windows, covering it in a hazy yellow.

"What are you wearing?" Dominic's breathy voice tickles the back of my neck as his hand runs down the lavender sports bra, tugging slightly on the matching leggings.

"Gym wear." I walk in and kneel to grab a bottle from the mini-fridge I'd stocked two days ago.

"I can see that, but why are your legs covered?" Dominic stands to my left as I survey my options.

I take the water out and stand up, facing Dominic, whose eyes continue to take me in.

"I can't exactly wear a skirt. What is your thing with the no covering of legs policy?" I unscrew the water bottle and place it to my lips.

"Easy access," Dominic smirks, a brow raised, as I try my best not to choke.

I put the bottle down on the bench.

"I see."

Deciding that he's gotten the reaction he desired, Dominic gives me one last, lingering look before going to a rowing machine.

I take my spot on a treadmill. It is very similar to my own at home, so programming it for a short and fast journey is easy enough.

I catch sight of Dominic as he powers away on the machine, his Bluetooth flashing. *A podcast perhaps.* I can't imagine Dominic listening to music for pleasure. In fact, listening to anything for pleasure seems below him.

I turn my gaze to the garden, focusing my attention to the sway of the barren maple tree as the treadmill begins to move.

"You're pretty good at this."

I blink a few times before tearing my gaze away from the maple tree to Dominic, who speaks from the bench, wiping his face on the towel I have brought.

"What do you mean?"

He stands up, pulling his damp shirt off and dropping it onto the bench. His sweat makes his body shine, droplets falling under the creases of his muscles and sliding down to rest on the band of his shorts. My eyes linger on his body for a while longer, watching muscles stretch and contract as he walks over to me and leans an arm on the side of the treadmill.

"Keeping your stamina up, I need a woman who can keep up with me."

"I don't think there's much to keep up with," I argue.

Dominic rubs his chin. I slow down the machine to a slow jog as he speaks, "Mae, you're knocked out after one session. I don't think you'd survive two."

"It could be that, or it could be that I'm also a part-time maid. Besides, I don't keep in shape for you. I keep in shape for me."

Dominic raises a brow at me, something close to curiosity coating his eyes.

"Is that so?"

"Do you know what meokbang is?"

"No, can't say that I do."

"Well, it's a Korean-originated trend where people watch others eat ridiculous amounts of food. Almost like the rise of ASMR., it just blew up one day. People find a way to sexualize anything. There was an introduction to meokbang in the escort business. Men will pay generous amounts of money to watch a slim girl or guy eat."

"That's all?" Dominic says, almost disappointed.

"*That's all?*" I roll my eyes at him. "I have a friend who was hired by such a person – for a month, he didn't touch her, didn't have sex with her, not even a hand job. All he required was for her to eat, and all he wanted to do was watch. At the end of the month, she was over 300 pounds. 300 pounds, Dominic! She had to have a tummy tuck and surgery to remove all the excess skin. Thankfully, Magenta polished her up, but the girl can't look at food the same anymore. Not that I didn't keep in shape before, but seeing Quinny returned to us on a gurney was horrifying."

Dominic's brows furrow as he processes it.

"As weird and unfortunate as that story seems, some men love the power to force people to change, sometimes specifically women. The thought of bringing down a strong woman or at least an independent one is a notch in their masculinity." He shrugs, no longer bothered by the topic, and steps on the treadmill next to me, programming it to match my speed.

"How did you get into this line of work, Mae?" he asks me suddenly.

I look at him as I reply simply, "Like any person, I needed the money."

I sat with my head against the window as the train rushed past the vast fields and tumbling hills that seemed to stretch on for eternity. My mum's hand stroked the back of my head, bringing me back from the landscape. I turned to face her, pulling out my earphones.

"Yup?"

"Are you still mad at me?" she asked quietly. I saw the creases between her brows form as I thought about my answer.

I had done my screaming at her months ago when she told me we were relocating to Scotland. Rent had become so unbearably high that every month was a case of rent or utilities. Not to say that we were poor but living in London had become almost elitist. With support from the government, we could manage on a month-by-month basis, providing that the house didn't need repairing, which it always did.

Soon my mum said, "fuck it" and her job allowed her to relocate. Thankfully, she could work in Inverness as the dance lecturer.

Luckily for her, I had just finished my last year of secondary school and could start sixth form up there with her.

But in no way did that mean I was happy. In fact, throughout the whole process, I went out of my way to avoid her. I refused to speak more than ten words weekly to my mother and would spend all my time away from her. Being an only child meant that if she wasn't at home, there was no one there to talk to, so it wasn't hard to keep myself isolated.

Then as the "to let" sign went up in the front garden, I lost it. I trashed the house. I was angry at my mother for making life-changing decisions without any consideration to me or my own life that I had been living. This wasn't the first time she had done so. She shipped us from the states to live in the UK when I was three.

After the death of my father, she didn't want to be away from her family anymore. So, we moved here, and now we were moving away from those people to the middle of nowhere with no one.

But now I was just tired.

I just about scraped through my exams, spending as much time as I could with friends knowing that, by the time they could visit me in Scotland, our friendships would be reduced to nothing but pleasantries, and had applied to start sixth form in September.

I bit the inside of my cheek as my mother waited for an answer.

"No, I'm just tired, Mum."

I saw relief wash over her as her shoulders relaxed from holding in tension for the last three months. She pulled me close as we sat in the aisle of the train, stroking my hair, caressing my face, and whispering apologies as the train approached our new life.

Night Life

I walk out of the bathroom, a towel around my waist and another in my hand. I glance at the time on the clock hovering over the door frame. *She will be here soon.*

I realize that every night, I look forward to this and this only: to open the door to a naked Mae standing there, hands behind her back, waiting to be ravished.

By me.

The phone on the bed vibrates. I frown. This is the fifth vibration in the space of ten minutes. *If I check it, I'll have to deal with it. Whatever it is, someone else can sort it out.*

I chuck my small towel over it, hoping the cover will stop the constant vibrations, but still they persist. From a periodical buzz to a long drone, whoever texted me has taken to calling.

Knowing I'll regret my decision, I pick up the towel, and pull the phone from underneath. *Lincoln*, I slide across the bar on the phone and press the phone to my ear.

"The club better be on fire for you to be calling me," I hiss.

"Worse. The police are here."

"What!" I head to the closet, already deciding that my evening has been ruined. "Why are the police there?"

"I don't know. They say they want to talk to the owner. I am the owner, but they're not buying it, saying they know you own the building."

I put Lincoln on loudspeaker as I get dressed.

"And what do they want?" I ask as I pull on my jogging bottoms. There is a pause from the other line.

"Words, Lincoln, I can't hear fucking gestures."

"I don't know. They want to talk to you, and if you don't get here, they'll have to close the club. Do you know how many we've got in here tonight, man?" I throw on a shirt before adding another layer. "Fucking 800. 200 have bought a table. Our bar tab is fucking hilarious."

"I don't fucking care about the occupancy tonight. It's 10 pm. If the nightclub gets shut down now, those people will go somewhere else to spend their fucking hilarious bar tab."

"Well, I told them you were at home, and would be here by one."

"Great." I hang up as I throw open the door, revealing a naked Mae waiting to be ravished. She looks down at my casual clothing before looking down at her nude body, slightly confused.

"Are we not on today?"

"Get a coat on. We are going out." I practically usher her towards her room.

"Clothes?" she asks.

"Don't even think about it," I remark, heading to the far staircase. I hear a loud groan as her bedroom door opens.

You and me both.

I pull the car around the back, passing the waiting line as it snakes its way down three blocks.

The alleyway is lit up, deterring horny club-goers and criminals, illuminating the large dumpsters and the silver doors on either side of me. I walk quickly around to the passenger side and open it for Mae. She steps out and wraps the brown lapel coat tighter around herself, tying the matching color belt, covering her erect nipples.

I frown, reminded of what I could've been doing instead of walking outside a nightclub dressed in sweats and palladium boots. I type on the keypad for the back door, and it buzzes. I open it, pulling Mae along with me. The door slams shut behind us as we walk quickly down the empty hallway past the security room and up the stairs to the office.

I open the door to the sleek black office, the tinted window looking onto the dancing, happy clubbers below as the lights strobe and the DJ plays.

"Stay here."

Mae steps into the room and sits down on the leather chair to the right.

"I'm not a dog, Dominic," she replies.

I let out a heavy sigh, running my hand through my hair.

"Mae...just..." Just seeing her sitting there has me pacing. *How quick can I be? Five minutes. Ten tops if I let off some steam and then go to see the police. Fuck the police, God they're not going to fucking wait, but neither can I. Argh. Fuck!*

"Stay here!" I repeat louder than before and leave the room quickly before my erection gets this club closed.

I never understand why people queue outside a nightclub in any weather under the sun. If Crimson is open, they come flocking, and that's what tonight is like.

Streams of people wait patiently under the painful wind. Women grip their small coats and clench their exposed thighs as their hair flies freely in the sky.

The police are waiting off the side by the front entrance as I make my way around, making those who have begun to enter nervous and worried – *they are ruining the mood, fucking idiots.*

"Dominic Aldrek. I hear you want me,"

The police turn around as I introduce myself, making sure their backs are to the entrance so my guests can feel at ease.

"I am Officer Hounders, and this is Officer Staines."

Between the two, I don't give a shit what their names are. I want to know why they are down here, standing and causing unrest.

"Nice to meet you, Officers, what brings you to the Crimson?"

"We believe you may be serving two underage children," one of them says.

My eyebrows dip as I take in their words.

"I can assure you everyone is checked at the door." I motion to the scanner placed by the door. The police turn as partygoers step forward, handing their IDs to the bouncer before they slide under the machine and a green flash goes off.

"Fake IDs, Mr. Aldrek, they aren't hard to come by," one of the officers says.

"Right, names of these so-called underage clubbers?"

One officer pulls out his notepad from his breast pocket and flips it open.

"Kara Baits and Lesley Fisher."

"Thank you. We have a list of all our guests. I will go and collect these two and bring them out."

"Please hurry, Mr. Aldrek, we've wasted enough time waiting for you," one of them remarks.

I head back in the club before they can see my face.

I storm through the corridor – gold, reflecting walls on either side as my shoes stamp along the red carpet. I've forgotten how much I hate the interior. The winding of the path, making the guests feel disoriented, forcing them back inside where everything is straight, and alcohol is flowing freely. It makes me nauseous, and I'm thankful when the path leads me to the open floor space.

The red continues into the lighting: shades of it everywhere, you can always find it paired with black. I push past the crowds to the closest bar of six and slam my hands down to catch the bartender's attention.

Recognizing me, she hurries over, dropping whatever drink she was just making to attend to me.

"Where is the guest list?" I shout, trying to be heard over the rumble of the bass and the chats of others. She looks around, her hand going for a shot glass. I slam my hand down again, making her jump, nearly knocking the stack of glasses onto the floor.

She looks at me, her pale grey eyes frightened, and I beckon her forward with my finger so that I can speak directly into her ear.

"Where is the guest list?" I ask.

The bartender pulls a tablet from under the till and hands it to me. I scroll through the list. *Where there's one, the other should be nearby.* 'Kara Baits' I tap on her name.

She is under a plus one at a table on the second floor behind the DJ. I hand the tablet back to the bartender and head for the stairs.

Lincoln isn't a bad designer. I just hate nightclubs. Too many people and never enough space, to top it off, you can't have a decent conversation with someone without paying ridiculous amounts of money for your own booth. Despite all this, I had requested Mae to meet me at one. Maybe because I had no intention of having a meaningful conversation with her.

I see the girls on top of the black rounded table, dancing as a fat man sits and enjoys it.

Their gold eyes sparkle as they giggle to themselves, like two school children being caught by a teacher outside of school premises during second period. Not a care in the world.

I look to the man, whose face is sweltering under the lights, finding it difficult to contain his human features – his nose already beginning to round into a shape more like a pig's.

"So, pixies and a Zhu Bajie." I look over the trio, the girls holding in uncontrollable laughter. "The police are here. I need you to put on some years."

The girls look to each other. If you didn't know, you'd think they are 18, but the moment I ask them to add some years, it is in their nature to retract them.

Tricksters and immature ones at that. I should consider having their kind banned. It's no surprise, though; their parents are elves and fae. Two opposites, so it's typical to have such troublesome children.

It's a good thing interracial breeding between them is now forbidden.

I roll my eyes as the girls giggle, their features softening out and losing the maturity they had previously. I drop one of them, my hand going from her clothes to her neck.

"I said add some years. Otherwise, I rip your throat out." I bare my teeth, the retractable fangs etching further down my mouth.

The pixie looks at me, her golden eyes dimming as she does as she is told. I wait patiently as she goes from 16 to a lovely legal age of 25. I drop her to the floor, and her equally age-appropriate friend holds her close.

"Thank you, ladies," I smile as I speak, "now let's go see the police."

The police look between me, the girls, and the photo IDs that they have received.

"As you can see, officers, there's been a mistake. These girls are the legal age to enjoy my club," I reassure them, hoping that the girls can contain themselves and hold on a bit longer.

I hear it's very taxing being old for Pixies, despite them ageing mentally and through experience, being physically old is too tiresome, especially on their magic. Keeping a youthful appearance requires less work than ageing gracefully.

I was told once by my mother that when a Pixie dies, it reverts back to its first day of life, and that their cemetery is filled with dead newborns, completely preserved.

I did not sleep that week.

The officers look between them, making sure these are the girls on their list.

"It would appear so, Mr. Aldrek, have a good night." They turn their backs to us, heading to their patrol car on the other side of the road. I face the girls, who have already started to return to their preferred 16-year-old faces.

"The rules, girls: keep the shifting indoors. I don't need this hassle again."

They nod quickly and run back into the club.

I open the back door and come face-to-face with Lincoln.

"There you are. I've been looking all over for you. Did you sort out the issue?"

I push past him, the door slamming shut from the wind.

"Why are the police coming to the club, Lincoln?" I glance behind me as he shrugs.

"It's been like this on and off over the last two months. False reports, from out-of-date club license, to whoring out some of the staff. This, however, is the first time they've asked for you personally," Lincoln explains.

"I can't keep coming to the rescue every time you have a problem," I reply.

"I didn't ask for you to come, Dominic, they did. If you just put my name on the owner-"

"We've talked about this, Lincoln. You're not going on the paperwork," I interject.

"Fuck sake, Dominic, you really want to do everything yourself, don't you?"

There is a reason why I haven't put Crimson under his name. He simply isn't ready for such responsibility. Not only does Lincoln dress like a teenager, but he also acts like one.

You can't tell that he is a manager from the way he dresses black and white vans with a v-neck grey shirt. He could easily be one of the clubbers, even the bartenders have more formality than he does, not to mention Lincoln's inability to separate work and his personal life, continually making moves on the female and male bartenders whenever a small opportunity presents itself.

I open the door to the office to see Mae. She has discarded her lapel coat and is peering at the things at the back of the office. As the door creaks, Mae has her back to us. She stands up straight facing the windows out onto the dance floor. I hear Lincoln's mouth drop open.

"Well, Dominic," he begins, throwing his hands down on my shoulders with considerable force. "Who is this?"

She continues to stare out the window.

"Adding him will cost extra."

"He's not joining." I turn around to Lincoln, who is smiling, his devilish grey eyes never leaving Mae's figure. I push him out the office and shut the door so his focus can return to me.

"A FolkWhore, Dominic, I gave you that calling card on a whim. I didn't think you'd go ahead with it." Lincoln laughs. I roll my eyes as my brother continues to smile at me.

"How long have you got her for?"

"Why do you ask?" I reply.

"Why won't you say?" he counters. Lincoln studies my face.

"Are you using protection?" he asks suddenly.

I make a face, taken aback by Lincoln's concern. I'm sure the guy can't tell the difference between a condom wrapper and a seasoning packet.

"What?"

"Come on, Dominic, are you keeping it wrapped up?" Lincoln persists.

"She's clean, Lincoln. I'm clean," I answer, equally curious and annoyed he's asking me such personal questions.

"Catching something is not what I am concerned about. I'm talking about getting her pregnant."

I scoff loudly as I turn Lincoln around, facing the stairs.

"Just remain vigilant. Magenta is an opportunist if I've ever seen one," Lincoln advises as he walks down the stairs.

"You know as well as I do, I'm not getting her pregnant. She wouldn't go through the process, and I'm not getting a prostitute pregnant. Imagine the PR on that," I laugh.

He glances over his shoulder before he speaks again. "Good, just making sure. It must be lonely in that big house of yours on top of the hill."

"Why do you think I bought her? I'm fucking bored."

Lincoln waves goodbye, heading down the corridor to do his job. I head back into the room. My hands are by her waist in four strides.

"Oh, are you free now?"

I hear the wit in her words as she leans back onto her hands.

"I see you've developed an attitude since last night," I mention.

"You raised my pedestal when *you* kissed *me*." Mae smirks. Her brow rises as she purses her lips.

"Is kissing the whore that monumental?" I question.

Mae trails her hands down my top and pulls the strings to my sweats, letting them fall dramatically as she releases their tie.

"You're not supposed to," she whispers. Her eyes hold mine: a light brown swirl sucking me in. Her warm hands pull me out of my sweats and hold me attentively. I want to see what she is doing, want to see as she strokes it, running her finger over the head.

"And why is that?" I ask.

Mae knows as well as I do as precum smears her finger. Holding my gaze, I see her place her finger in her mouth. Her other hand takes hold of me and slides me between her open legs in one long, glorious motion.

"It's dangerous," she moans.

If I weren't experienced, I would climax right there and then. The feel of Mae wrapping tight around me, clenching. The urge I feel in my stomach rumbles, and my hold on her waist tightens.

I bite into her neck with no warning. I want to taste her as I thrust with hard strokes. The sweet, metallic taste coats my tongue and slithers down my throat.

I feel her heartbeat quicken as it works faster to pump the blood around her body as I suck it out through her neck. Her breath is fanning my ear as I move back and forth inside her, driving myself deeper, and bringing her closer.

The desk screeches as I draw nearer, rocking and pushing it towards the wall. My vision is becoming hazy as I feel myself expand inside of her, feel the clenching of Mae around me that only spurs me on until I come.

I groan into her neck, aware that Mae has become silent. *Two rounds my fucking ass.* I lick the side of her neck to stop the bleeding.

Somehow, I manage to hold her close as I pull up my trousers. I look at the coat on the floor and then an unconscious Mae.

I pick her up, carrying her bridal style, and hook my foot under her coat, chucking it upwards to fall on top of her. Her head hangs back as we head out of the club. I place her on the passenger side, tilting the chair back so she won't flop forward.

I shut the door, heading to the trunk. *This is why I do this at home.* I pop it open and unzip a cube-like freezer bag, revealing stacks of blood. I pull out one of the B positive bags and take it with me to the driver's side. I hang the packet on the hook on the top of the door frame. I wrap the elasticated thick black band around her arm and place the needle into her.

I lean back in my chair, sitting in the darkness of the car staring at the sleeping Mae – her heartbeat the only indication that I haven't gone overboard tonight.

I tuck the coat around her body and start up the engine to head home.

Take your Whore to Work Day

I roll onto my back as I hear some scuttering behind me. I sit up, my eyes still closed.

"Sybil, I can dress myself."

A haul of clothes falls on top of me, and I groan, pulling it off. Dominic strolls out of the walk-in closet, more clothes draped over his shoulder and a pair of heels in his hand.

"I'm sure you can. You're coming to work with me," Dominic says.

I look at Dominic as he takes a seat on the swivel chair in front of me, clothes surrounding me in a mound.

"Why?" I ask, tired.

"Because our meeting at night doesn't work. As a contingency, you will be by my side."

"Easy access," I say simply.

"Easy access," Dominic repeats. I look down at the clothes: nothing black for as far as I can see. I lift the camel-colored skirt.

"Where did these come from?"

Dominic is too busy staring at his phone to pay attention. I roll my eyes, sliding out of bed en route to the bathroom. I step into the shower. I lean into the corner, letting the water hit the sore puncture wound.

I hold my neck, the water droplets starting to sting as though they weigh far more than they should. I hold my hand out, expecting to see it coated in deep red, but nothing. There is a weird churning in my stomach.

With my body soaking wet, I tiptoe to the sink, pull out a plaster, and stick it across my neck. From afar, you wouldn't have noticed the slight shade change, or the fact that there is a red border around the wound – a pulsating warning from my body to me.

I step out of the room, drying my body before letting the towel drop to the floor. Sensing that I am naked, Dominic looks up, rubbing his chin as he takes in my form.

"Mae." Dominic stands up. "I've got to get to work." His eyes narrow as he scrutinizes my body. "Is there something you can do about that?" He points to nowhere in particular.

"What?"

"The branding. I don't need others seeing it."

I look down before running my hand over the raised H under my breast. Magenta told me just before she stamped it on my skin that it's only visible to supernatural beings and continuously on show. It not only serves as advertisement but also security: anyone who tries anything without an arrangement is at risk of Magenta's wrath.

I turn my gaze to Dominic as I speak. "You have to lick it."

Dominic walks towards me and crouches down. He cups my breast and lifts it, exposing the branding, and trails his tongue over it. My body shudders, goosebumps coating every inch of my skin.

"Wear something that complements what I am wearing." He drops me far too quickly, and I stumble slightly.

I give Dominic a glance over – a beige jumper, a white tailored shirt poking from underneath, and slim black trousers with some black suede derby shoes. It won't be too difficult, as it seems I am in an abundance of fall colors.

I stand in the elevator, twirling a loose strand just beside my ear. I hear Dominic grumbling behind me.

"Get over it, Dominic, the boots complement what you're wearing." I flatten out the woolen beige longline jumper touching the midsection of my thighs, followed by black suede boots that go over the knee with a thick heel.

"Doesn't mean that I like it. I'm sure I mentioned specifically that nothing that covers your legs should be in the closet," he mumbles. I roll my eyes, fluffing the low-hanging ponytail before standing by his side, hooking my arm through his.

"Take it up with Sybil," I retort.

"If anyone asks, you're my girlfriend," he says.

I nod, and the elevator doors swing open to the small bustle of people going between offices. Parting like the red sea, I hear whispers as people gape, seeing a woman on Dominic's arm, a woman that none of the newspapers have mentioned.

We stroll across the salt-and-pepper carpet to the end of the hallway, *Dominic Aldrek* displayed in gold lettering on the brown cedar wood door. Unlike all the other offices, Dominic's has blinds across the floor-to-ceiling window, hiding anything that goes on inside.

I walk in, drop my nearly empty bag, and sit down on one of the suede chairs. Dominic removes his long, brown coat, and drapes it over the white desk chair before taking a seat.

"I have some meetings to attend. Do what you please, just don't leave the building." He rifles through his drawer before picking out something and chucking it at me. I just about catch it, fumbling before it falls onto my lap.

"A phone?" I ask.

"A phone," Dominic repeats. "I need to be able to reach you if I'm going to leave you to your own devices."

There is a knock on the door, and we both stand up while the door opens slowly. A young, blonde peeks around the door and looks between Dominic and me. She seems almost embarrassed by our presence, casting her green eyes to the floor.

"Delilah, what is it?"

I try to keep my face straight as I look at the slim woman Dominic named me after.

Her hands are wrapped around a silver notebook matching her blazer that has been rolled at the sleeve, exposing her freshly tanned skin. Delilah drops her arms, revealing the white tailored shirt, the buttons starting just above her cleavage.

"Your scheduled meeting for ten, the board members are here."

Dominic rises and rounds the desk to stand beside me, his arms looping around my waist.

"Delilah, this is Mae. Mae, this is Delilah, my PA."

I stretch out my hand and shake Delilah's.

"Such a pretty name." *Did you name me after your PA?* Dominic pinches my hip lightly as a response to my thought.

For what feels like too long, we all stand there basking in the awkwardness that only Dominic and I know about. I edge out of Dominic's grasp.

"You said Dominic had a meeting." I smile between the two.

Delilah opens the door.

"It was lovely meeting you, Mae." Delilah walks out the door, leaving it open.

He grasps the handle before taking a long look at me.

"I'll be back soon, Mae."

I dismiss his sentiment, waving my hand.

"Go do what you have to do."

I think I prefer being at home, at least I had things to do. Somehow, I make it past 12, and after directions to the café on the ground floor, I sit in a corner on a worn-out armchair, watching the torrential rain outside.

I run my nail over the coffee cup, watching pedestrians run this way and that, trying to avoid the fat droplets of rain hitting the pavement. I take a sip. The chai latte fills my mouth before flowing down my throat and settling in my stomach.

The phone on the table vibrates, moving slightly across the wooden table.

Where are you? - Dominic

I stare at the message as though doing so will make him materialize in front of me.

Having lunch.

Have you finished? - Dominic

Something tells me this is less of an "I'm just curious as to what you're up to" and more of a "get here now" type question.

Deciding that going to his office is more effective than replying to his text, I get up from my comfort, picking up the coffee cup. I head to the elevator, tossing it into a nearby bin.

No one dares get into the elevator with me, as though even being near me means some disrespect towards their boss.

The floor is quiet. I open the door to Dominic's office to find him staring out of the window overlooking midtown Seattle.

As the door closes, Dominic makes his way from the window to me. His body presses me up against the door. He pulls up my jumper, bundles the ends underneath my neck.

With some jangling from his buckle, Dominic pushes down his trousers. His hand curls around the back of my knee, holding it up and forcing me to stand on my toes.

Something is wrong. Dominic doesn't even look at me as he pushes himself inside, doesn't even groan in satisfaction as he starts pumping away.

His head leans against my shoulder with my arms around his neck and legs around his hips. Dominic has both his hands on either side of me, palms open as he works away.

I can only imagine what people outside can hear: no grunts or pleasurable sounds, just a *THUMP, THUMP, THUMP* — *coming from* the other side of the door.

It doesn't work well with the whole "this is my girlfriend" façade. If anything, it does the complete opposite and makes our relationship come across as something cheap and quick. I trail my finger down his neck as he fucks away.

THUMP, THUMP, THUMP.

Property

"I'll be back, Mae."

She waves me off, plopping back into the chair. One covered leg crosses over the other.

"Go do what you have to do."

I shut the door behind me.

Delilah has already reached the conference room six doors down. All the rooms have the same floor-to-ceiling windows and one large, oval, polished wooden table that seats 12.

I open the door, and all the similarly dressed board members stand up, their chatter silent. I place my folders on the table and sit down, the board members following shortly after.

"I didn't expect to be having a meeting so soon. Is the development of the community near Fauntleroy Park exceeding my expectations?"

Immediately the board erupts – one speaking over the other. Some stand up, flapping their sheets of papers at me, others sit quietly.

I raise my hand.

"Gentlemen, gentlemen, please. My assistant can't take minutes if you are all shouting."

The noise quiets down, and the board members take their seats.

One man leans forward, his bald head catching the rays of the morning sun off the top as he grabs my attention. He straightens his red tie, clearing his throat before he speaks.

"We are nowhere near completion, Mr. Aldrek. In fact, construction hasn't even begun."

"And why is that?" I ask.

The man leans back, another taking his place. He runs his hand through his oily, thinning grey hair, sweat beads resting on his forehead.

"There seem to be problems on every avenue, Mr. Aldrek. If it isn't the contracts with the suppliers, it's with the land. If it isn't the land, then it's inspections. All of a sudden, Mr. Aldrek, it would seem everyone is making business with you complicated. Even worse, Mr. Aldrek, up-"

A knock interrupts the nervous man as he speaks.

He slinks back into his chair, and I turn my head to the door. Chrissy steps in. She has an uncommon scowl on her face and rolls her eyes at me. Chrissy walks up to and leans in so she can whisper in my ear.

"A detective Grier is here to speak to you."

She leans back to gauge my reaction, and my frown matches hers. She nods as if to say *I know*.

I stand up quickly.

"Excuse me, gentlemen, I will be back shortly." I follow Chrissy out of the room, shutting the door behind me.

Detective Grier is standing by the reception desk, one hand inside his light grey trousers, another spinning his badge between his index finger and his thumb.

"Detective Grier, is it?" I ask. He lifts his head, and his lip gives a slight upturn, close to a smile. I stretch my hand to him, which he shakes.

We both stand there shaking each other's hand for perhaps too long. I'm the first one to drop the handshake.

"Please, come into my office; we can talk better there." I lead the way, hoping that Mae won't be in there. I open the door to find it vacant and sigh, stepping back to let the detective inside.

"So detective, how can I help you today?" I watch the detective pull out a small notebook and a pen from his inside jacket pocket and flip it open.

"It has come to the IRS' attention that a transaction of just under $900,000 went from your account to a Mae Geoffries, on the 1st of November."

"Yes, it did. Is that a problem?"

"It is. That is a substantial amount. Care to tell me, what exactly did you pay for?"

"Mae Geoffries is a designer. I have a function in the new year, a ball of sorts. I employed Miss Geoffries to make the outfits for all my guests, we will be having an auction. Her outfits will be up for sale."

"How many guests are expected to attend?"

"A good amount, we are expecting business partners, employees, there'd be potential networking opportunities I think shy of about 1,000."

"You're expecting Miss Geoffries to make 1,000 different costumes?" I watch the detective stifle a laugh, making my jaw clench.

"I've paid Miss Geoffries just under nine hundred thousand dollars. She could easily hire out help. However, I have no intention of her making that many at most around 50. These are one-of-a-kind pieces, so I don't expect there to be many of them" I stand up. "If that's all, Detective Grier, I have a meeting to finish."

Grier stands up, but his notebook is still in his hand.

"One more question: is there any way I can reach Miss Geoffries?"

"Unfortunately, no, detective, I don't speak to her directly. Her company liaisons for her."

Grier makes a disappointed face. He folds his notebook and fixes his aviator jacket collar before sliding the items inside.

"Thank you, Mr. Aldrek, for your time. If you do happen to see Miss Geoffries, or speak to her, please." He pulls out a card and places it on the table. "Give me a call. I'll see myself out."

I watch Grier leave the room, shutting the door quietly behind himself. I pick up the card and stare at the small rectangle, hoping it will shoot up in flames.

As if my day couldn't get even more complicated, now I have the IRS and the FBI snooping around.

The urge to return home and utilize the waning time I have with Mae is almost unbearable. However, the door creaks inwards and Delilah peers her head round.

"Everything OK?"

I relax the lines that have gathered between my brows.

"Perfect, Delilah, thank you. Shall we continue with the meeting?" I round the table, heading out of the office.

It is hard to concentrate on the meeting and all the others that follow. After the impromptu disruption from Detective

Grier. I have always been on the FBI's radar. This is not the first time they have come into my building, requesting a meeting.

But this time is different. The legalities surrounding my business are ironclad. FolkWore, however, is not my business and therefore a liability. It doesn't matter if I withdraw my arrangement with Magenta. The money has caught their attention. If anything, a refund would only prove that the FBI has rattled me.

What's worse is that I have put myself in this position. I was so concerned with getting the contract signed and Mae home that I hadn't even considered a deposit of that amount would surely bring attention. Prostitution is illegal in most states in America, and other countries. If Grier finds out who Mae really is, my business troubles will be the least of my problems.

I stand up from my desk and head to the window looking out onto midtown Seattle. I pull out my phone and scroll to find the number I have given Mae.

'Where are you?'

Coffee and Collusion

Conrad sits down on one of the fabric armchairs in the small, independent coffee shop. He slides a cup across to Rebekah

The pair have organized a meeting after their fruitless efforts trying to solve the mystery of the transaction. They are in a small, independent coffee shop near the subway, hidden behind a small alleyway that most people walk past daily. Unlike franchises, this one is homely with dimly lit exposed bulbs hanging across the seating area filled with recycled and millennial furniture: a ladder turned into a shelf and tires used as tables.

"They are both lying," Conrad says, breaking the silence. Rebekah looks up from her laptop.

"Well," Rebekah begins, "it's either this Mae woman doesn't exist, and something is going on between Aldrek and FolkWore, or this costume designing is a façade for something else. Drugs, perhaps?"

Conrad shakes his head before speaking. "It wouldn't be drugs. Aldrek has pharmaceutical companies, they wouldn't need to outsource drugs. They both had the same story. Mae is a designer, and Aldrek has employed her."

Rebekah takes a sip of her coffee while Grier plays with his, running his finger over the ceramic rim.

"It would seem that, despite us taking our own leads, the results are the same," Conrad says. He runs his hand through his hair, shaking the ends as he leans back, staring out the window.

"We have no choice but to work together," she says, placing the coffee down. "Two heads are better than one, right?"

Conrad mumbles what could have been a "yes" or an "I guess so."

Rebekah leans back in her chair.

"This Aldrek guy has really got under your skin."

Conrad stiffens.

"The Aldreks have a lot of influence in Seattle and other places. You can't even shit without them playing a hand in it."

Welcome to FolkWore...again

What a terrible sign, Conrad thinks to himself. For him, the name is far too on the nose and bordering on unoriginal; it frustrates him for reasons not yet known to him. He turns to Rebekah, who is blowing the steam off another cup of coffee.

"You know you can die from too much coffee," Conrad says.

She takes a long sip, almost tempting fate before shrugging.

"That is if you don't die from hypothermia," he adds.

Rebekah glances down at her choice of clothes today: thin, black turtleneck and khaki cigarette trousers that have been rolled up to the ankles. Like always, her trench coat has not been tied up and allows the winter breeze to wrap itself around her body.

"Let's just go in, Conrad. It's cold."

Conrad laughs, opening the door for his temporary partner, who steps in. As he follows, she grabs his arm, pulling him down slightly to speak to him.

"You should talk to the guy; he's already seen me. I'll have a look around."

Conrad nods, watching as Rebekah slinks away, weaving through the aisle of hanging costumes.

Klaus is leaning over the desk, bored, as usual, one hand over his mouth as he covers his tenth yawn in the last five minutes. Conrad takes out his badge and flips it open for Klaus to see. At the sight of it, the male faery perks up, hands pressed flat on the glass countertop.

"What can I do for you..."

"Agent Grier," Conrad finishes. "I am hoping to speak to your boss."

Klaus's eyes trail over Conrad's slim physique, then jabs his thumb toward the green curtains behind him.

"She's in there."

"Calamba, let's go," Conrad shouts.

Klaus' eyes narrow at the mention of the woman that came a week ago. Rebekah's tiny face emerges from a rack of clothes, seemingly pleased with herself as she skips to Conrad's side.

"Thanks so much," Rebekah says, taking the lead through the green curtains.

The room has the same magic used in Magenta's office space. It makes it feel as though it is basking in natural light. Somehow, the pair do not walk through a long corridor as Mae and Dominic had; instead, they walk straight into everything you'd expect from a store that sells luxury costumes.

There are four workbenches decorated with ripped and shredded fabrics. On the wall, farthest from them, is a thin shelf filled with large rolls of fabrics surrounded by desks with sewing machines.

The room is nearly empty, aside from the ginger sitting on a workbench, her head leaning on her hand as she traces something using chalk.

"Miss..." Rebekah starts off.

She raises her head, fixing the fedora hat.

"Just Magenta is fine," she says.

Conrad frowns. She stands up from her chair.

"I hear you've been asking for me?" Magenta approaches the pair, stopping them from walking too far into the room.

Rebekah takes a step towards her with an outstretched hand. Magenta stares at the hand, either unsure of what to do or flat out refusing to shake it. She diverts her attention to Conrad, who has an intense gaze on her.

"Yes. Why did Mr. Aldrek pay $881,000 to Mae Geoffries?" Conrad asks.

Magenta laughs lightly, tucking some hair behind her ear. Her hands are decorated with rings that catch the light at the perfect angle, almost blinding Conrad.

"I doubt you'd be here if you didn't already speak to Mr. Aldrek, and from what Klaus says, this one." She points to Rebekah. "Has already been here."

"I just want to get the story straight," Conrad replies simply.

"Alright then, Miss Geoffries is one of my designers. She has been hired by Mr. Aldrek to design and create outfits for guests to purchase for his event in the new year."

Conrad doesn't bother to write anything down. Rebekah, however, is scribbling away.

"How can we get in touch with Miss Geoffries?"

"Unfortunately, Miss Geoffries requires complete isolation during a project, and this one will last ten months. I'm just a bit confused, Agent Grier."

"What are you confused about?"

"Why come back here when your partner was already informed about everything?"

Conrad looks to Rebekah, who frowns at the attention thrown her way.

Rebekah looks between the pair, who seem to tower over her, and adjusts her glasses.

"That is true, Magenta, but as her boss, you should be able to contact your employee, especially if the IRS and FBI are requesting you to do so," Rebekah argues.

Magenta narrows her eyes, the edge of the brown iris starting to transition to purple.

"Is Mae in trouble?" she asks the agents unexpectedly.

"No," Conrad replies.

"Has she done something illegal?"

"That's what we are trying to ascertain, Magenta."

"Right, so my employee has done nothing wrong but taken a job. Unless you have a warrant, you'll just have to believe what I tell you. I have told you what she is doing, and I have told you for how long. Now please, if you'll excuse me, I have a lot of work to do." Magenta motions her hand to the door, silently asking them to leave.

Conrad and Rebekah stand outside, the dying sun casting a dark glow over the city. The wind whips around their bodies, adding to their annoyance. Conrad runs a hand through his hair while Rebekah sips her coffee.

"I noticed something," Rebekah says.

"What, Calamba?"

"I took a design major before settling with the IRS, and stitching was something that we had to learn from basic to intermediate, both by hand and machine."

"Ok, where are you taking this?"

"Well, while I was wandering through the clothes, I noticed that all the costumes had the same stitching: a very basic straight stitch."

"So?" Conrad lets the word hang in the air for Rebekah to continue.

"Well, anyone who's done designing knows straight stitch isn't the best choice for all fabrics, especially if they are made-to-order and supposedly luxury."

"Yeah..."

"What I'm saying is you use a straight stitch for efficiency and mass production."

Conrad looks blankly at Rebekah, who rolls her eyes.

"I'm saying their clothes aren't luxury, they are mass-produced. I'm saying that being a designer for a company that mass produces their costumes is pointless, especially as it seems Magenta is a designer herself."

"What you're saying is that Mae can't be a designer?"

"I don't know about that, but $881,000 is a lot of money for bad stitching."

Tell Me a Story

I walk out of the bathroom with a wet flannel in my hand, fixing the band of my boxers as I sit down. Mae rolls over. A thin trail of blood escapes from her neck and rolls down, settling in the groove of her shoulder blade.

I hand her the flannel, which she takes, leaning back, looking up at the ceiling as she dabs her neck gently.

Her body is sprawled slightly on the silk sheets, creases outlining her shape, folding and bulging in all the right places.

The curtains have been drawn, shielding the room from the moonlight that would otherwise stream in. Mae has lit her candles. *A definite fire hazard.* But I do enjoy the soft orange glow that lights the room.

"Tell me, Mae." She looks at me, her eyes are half-lidded. "Why did you need the money so desperately?"

It is hard in the poor lighting, but I see her grimace as if the mere mention of her past causes her physical pain.

I was sitting in the empty design & technology room. Everyone had gone for lunch with friends, but I found it better to just eat on my own and finish work.

College was just a pit stop for me – two years that I had to endure before I could go on. Go somewhere else, be someone else. It didn't help that I was not from the area, and my accent was clearly not Scottish.

"Hey, Mae."

I looked up to see Miss Crew by the door. She had her hands in her burnt-orange trousers pockets, her laptop stuck under her arm.

"Hi, Miss."

Miss Crew came up to me and settled down on one of the wooden stools opposite me. She placed the laptop on the table before clasping her light brown hands together.

"Have you checked your phone recently, Mae?"

I frowned at her before pulling my bag up off the floor and placing it on the table.

"No," I replied. I took out my phone. As the screen brightened, I was bombarded with messages, calls from unknown numbers, over a dozen from Mum. I looked up at Miss Crew.

"What's happened?"

"Your mother had an accident at work. It seems she fell down some stairs. She's at the hospital, and she's been trying to reach you."

Before Miss Crew had finished, I was already on my feet, my pencils shoved in my bag alongside my sketchbook, and my jacket flung over my shoulder.

"Thank you." I didn't give her time to reply as I headed out the door.

Raigmore Hospital was like any hospital: large and confusing. Even more so if you needed to get somewhere in a hurry.

When I asked for my mother, they couldn't find her on their records. It was only after an hour that they informed me that she had just come out of surgery and was waiting for me in the post-surgery room.

As I rushed along the corridor, my palms sweaty, I eyed the numbers on the rooms. She was in room 16. 12, 13, 14, 15. Suddenly, my head hurt, and a cold breeze ran through me, striking my chest and causing my vision to blur.

What state could she be in? What if she was on life support? I was not yet 18 and couldn't live on my own. I'd have to move back to London to live with a family member until I was officially an adult.

The door opened, and a tall man walked out dressed in purple scrubs, his hands wrapped around a metal clipboard. I was sure he could hear my hammering heart as he lifted his head from his board and looked right at me.

"You must be Mae."

I swallowed a large lump, almost choking in the process, and nodded.

"Your mother has had a nasty fall and injured her spine in the process. She's only just come out of surgery, so the true extent of the accident is uncertain."

I wanted to collapse, throw up and scream all at the same time. But all I could do was stand there like a gaping fish; eyes wide as my brain processed the information.

My mother was a dancer, an injury was bad enough but a spinal injury. I slumped to the floor, the weight of everything suddenly crushing me. I brought my legs to my chest, resting my head on my knees.

"Mae...." A gentle hand rested on my shoulder, and I looked up at the doctor.

"We have many counselors and groups who can support you and your mother during this difficult time."

I nodded, somehow managing to get to my feet. I wiped my face, feeling the ears that coated it. I hardened my heart, refusing to let another vibration course through me.

"Thank you, doctor, I'll see my mother now."

He nodded as a reply and left me to continue with his job.

I opened the door slightly and stepped in. My mother was on her side, her back turned to me. I heard sniffles from my position. Immediately, I rushed over and wrapped my arms around her.

"I'm so sorry, Mum, I'm so sorry this has happened to you."

Her arms wrapped around mine, cradling me as we both cried into the night.

"The swelling went down and that's when we found out the damage. Paraplegia injury to the lower spinal cord, my mother lost all feeling from her waist down. The university paid my mother after the accident, but she couldn't continue working in the same job."

I watch Mae sigh. This story seems to spur on repressed emotions in her, almost forcing her to shrink into herself.

"What did you do?" I ask quietly, fearing that I might shatter her fragile state if I speak any louder.

"She stopped working altogether. The settlement lasted us another year, and by the time it had run out, I had finished college somehow, and found a job in Glasgow as a bartender."

"Did you enjoy it?"

"It had its ups and downs, but if I hadn't, I wouldn't have gotten involved with FW and Magenta."

Mae covers her mouth as she yawns, stretching out her naked figure on the bed. I stand up and cover her in the sheet.

"Goodnight, Mae."

"Goodnight, Dominic."

I shut the door behind me, heading to my bedroom. I sit at the desk, bringing my laptop towards me. I flip it open and type *Mae Geoffries* into the search bar.

As I've expected, she has no social footprint. FolkWore makes sure their employees can't be traced by clients; only their assigned character would have a background, and I hadn't asked one of Mae. Despite this, that doesn't mean others don't keep track of her. There are only two news reports: one from the Inverness Courier, another from the Scottish Daily news.

The first is about her mother's injury and, like Mae had told me, her mother was a dance teacher. The picture depicts a young Ms. Geoffries, and it is clear that the long hair runs in the family. She is on a billboard for Swan Lake, perhaps in her prime. Beside the large photo is a smaller one, one of Miss Geoffries in a wheelchair smiling as she sits outside the university.

The other report is of a crime. It is a lot less detailed than the first newspaper. I'm only able to get blurry pictures. I can't make out the date, and thus my search ends. I sit back, staring at the black screen and sighing heavily.

Purging of One's Sins

It is the weekend again, and with the problems that are going on with the development of a new community, I have been called out to escort an inspector around the site again – to reconfirm that there are no leaky gas pipes and no creatures that need protecting.

I shut the car door and drop the keys on one of the pins on the noticeboard before walking up the stairs. As I round the corner, I see Mae, and she catches my eyes before heading in my direction.

She doesn't have her heels on, so when she is an arm's length away, I fully appreciate how short she is compared to me: barely shoulder height. I look down slightly at her.

"I have to go see Magenta."

Instantly, I scowl. This is not something I want to hear right about now.

"Why?"

"My other event is coming up soon, and I need to...well... rid myself of you."

I narrow my eyes at her.

"What do you mean rid yourself of me?" I say through a tightly clamped jaw.

"Don't take it personally. Usually, this is something I would do at the end of our arrangement, but because both events overlap, I have to do it now."

"Explain."

"It's a deep cleanse that resets my body to before you came, figuratively and literally. It gets rid of any scars and blemishes."

"Can you not do it here? "

"I can b-"

"Great, you can do it here. I had forgotten you had that other event."

"Fine. If I do it now, I will have to leave straight away, " Mae explains. *Which is the lesser evil, Mae going to Magenta, or doing what she wants here and then leaving immediately?* Either way, I'm annoyed.

A grumble vibrates in the back of my throat, and I sigh.

"Ok, let's go and do it."

Mae looks taken aback by my decision to join but doesn't press on the matter as she turns around and heads to her room, me close on her heels.

I shut the door behind us, watching Mae remove her clothes, and for some reason, it annoys me. I am peeved that her clothes are hitting the floor in piles, but what makes it worse is that she's doing it for someone else, not me.

She almost glides to the bathroom, and her presence seems more ethereal than usual. Could it be that when she's leaving, she's more enticing to me? Could it be jealousy?

Mae sits on the edge of the bath, twiddling her thumbs as the water fills.

"Busy day at work? " she asks, trying to fill the silence.

"Please don't, Mae. I'm. not happy, but at the end of the day, this is your job."

She turns off the tap, throwing her legs into the water. I edge forward, leaning on the sink overlooking the bath, and watch her slip in.

Mae gives me a lasting look before she plucks a smoky-colored crystal from her bracelet. She crushes the gem, the dust dropping into the water. Before it can settle to the bottom, she plucks out another, this one a cloudy-looking color speckled with blue as though a summer sky. Mae crushes the gem and sprinkles it over her face.

She turns to me.

"Please don't worry about me," She yawns. "I'll be fine." She lays her head on her hands.

I don't think much of her last comment until she begins to sink into the water. It isn't until it reaches her eyebrows that I hurry over. As the last of Mae becomes submerged, the ripples created by her breathing stop.

Everything around her seems to be frozen – I see the oxygen bubbles frozen mid-float – *another glimpse into Magenta's magic.* I have been regularly told that I have control issues, but Magenta is a whole different ball game.

As I watch Mae frozen inside the water, the black liquid begins to dance through the stillness, snaking around her body, then settling on the surface. I am not sure what exactly is happening. *Why is Mae leaking out this black liquid, and why is it the only thing moving in her frozen state?*

It is then that I notice her bite mark sizzling, the bite itself falling off her skin and transforming into the same black liquid that is surrounding her body, settling just under the surface creating a thick, black layer. *This is what she meant about ridding herself of me.*

What I'm staring at is a month's worth of me touching her, fucking her with no protection, and overall, being in her presence. Magenta is taking it all, and the worst part is this is just the beginning; every few months, Mae will rid herself of me. Magenta will expect her to go to her next client without even my scent on her skin.

My phone vibrates, and I pull it out, turning my back on the sleeping Mae. The screen flashes with the name *Freya*, and I answer.

"Please tell me the police aren't at your door."

"What? No, but you need to come to Spain now."

I look to Mae. The black liquid has completely covered her sleeping figure. Not even an outline can be seen.

"Sure, that works fine." I reach out to her, but immediately retract my hand, and head out the bathroom straight to my own room.

Girlfriend Material

I pull my suitcase along, moving with the sea of people as we head out of the arrival gate. I am nervous. *How long has it been since I've seen him?*

My thighs ache from sitting on the plane in tight jeans, and my ears are still ringing from the descent. Above everything else, my heart keeps leaping with every step I take towards the double doors.

I emerge into the open, searching the hall for those eyes and that big smile. A hand is stretched above the rest, and my steps hurry towards it. The hand soon turns into a body as he steps out from the crowd.

I drop my suitcase, run to him, and leap into his arms. I press my lips onto his as he wraps his hands underneath me. Just kissing him alone sends waves of pleasure to my underwear, and I have to resist the urge to rub against his toned body.

I pull away, smiling wildly, wrapping my arms around his neck.

"I guess you've missed me, Luna."

"Of course, I've missed you, Stephan. Not seeing you for several months is painful, you know."

"It is you who requires complete isolation between projects, how many have they got you on this year?"

"I've got three more, I timed it well so I can still see you. But you know what I'm like, hidden away in my loft apartment till they are done."

"You mean your hyper fixation." Stephan laughs, placing me down on the ground, and picks up my fallen luggage, which is causing congestion. He slings my duffle over his shoulder, grabs the handle of the suitcase in one hand, and takes my hand in the other.

"I booked a hotel across from the airport just so I could make it on time."

"But you were still late."

Stephan looks at me, his smile wide.

"No, I wasn't."

I pull at his arm, forcing him to spin around.

"Stephan, I know your gym wear when I see it. You went to the gym and got carried away, didn't you?" I tug on his ribbed grey shirt before wrapping a finger around his hoodie strings.

Stephan puts his hands around my waist, bringing me close. I gaze into his emerald-colored eyes, knowing that he can't lie to me when I do. He matches my gaze, his finger running circles across my back.

"What does it matter if I was late? "

I slap his chest playfully, moving out of his grasp.

"So, you *were* late."

He rolls his eyes, taking my hand and leading me out of the airport.

"I was on time for you, Luna, I made sure of it. Booked an apartment in the hotel next door to make things easier."

"For whom?" I enquire.

"For you, I know how much you hate planes, and it means I can get you behind a door even quicker." He glances down at me, winking, causing ripples in my stomach.

"Let's get you back to the hotel."

Stephan isn't kidding; directly next door is the hotel.

Despite it only being a short walk, I find myself squashed against Stephan as we walk the few feet to the hotel doors.

He pushes the golden-rimmed doors open for me, sighing in relief as the warm air cradles our bodies. I take his hand, allowing him to lead me to the elevator of the hotel.

He gives the receptionist a small nod, who looks at me dismissively. I smile at her just to irritate her further. Stephan is handsome, and I'm sure I'd be pissed too if I saw him return with a woman. *A gorgeous one at that,* I try to reassure myself.

"What floor are we on?"

"The twelfth, " is his reply. We are alone in the elevator, and as the doors shut, I grab at him, tugging on his sweats.

Stephan looks at me, his eyes dark with temptation as I slide my hands down his trousers, running a nail over his once flaccid penis.

"Luna." His warning tone contradicts the flutter of his eyes, his head leaning on the back mirror of the elevator.

I stand in front of him, using my free hand to cup his cheek, forcing him to look at me.

I feel him twitch in my hand as our eyes connect.

"Don't. You know I'll stop the elevator."

I grin at him, wrapping all five fingers along his length.

"But we had so much fun when you did." I bite my lip at memories of Stephan and me rushing to fix our clothes as the fire brigade pried the doors open.

"Can I at least have a kiss?" I flutter my lashes at Stephan, who leans down, pressing his lips softly against mine. I open my mouth for him, but as the doors open, he pulls away.

"We are here." Stephan gently removes my hand from his pants, holding it in his own, and leads me out the elevator and down the hallway.

He opens the door, letting me in first, and no doubt getting an eyeful of my form in the process. He shuts the door behind him and leans my things against the wall. I kick off my shoes, tucking them away into the small closet.

Stephan always does an excellent job when it involves booking a hotel. He always seems to know whether I'm in the mood for self-catering or full board.

The small studio apartment is like two hotel rooms in one. Stephan wraps his hands around my waist, kissing the side of the neck. My heart leaps instinctively, forgetting who is breathing on me.

Stephan would never bite me.

"You hungry, babe?"

I nod, holding onto his strong arms as I breathe out in comfort.

"Are you going to cook? Or room service?" I ask.

"You know we have the most fun when we cook together. Besides, after we can shower and head to my parents."

I smile, snuggling up to him. I pull off my jumper and drape it over the sofa, followed by my jeans.

Stephan opens the fridge and brings out the eggs and sausage, laying them on the marble top. I head to the cupboards, looking for a frying pan.

"Mom has been asking after you."

"I haven't been ignoring her calls, I promise you. You know how I am with work. This project has really taken up my time," I explain.

Stephan laughs, catching my eyes from the corner of his.

"I know, you're lucky she isn't your mother. On a day-to-day basis, mom calls ten times. You would hate the family group chat. It's basically my parents having their own conversation for everyone to see."

I let out a small chuckle, pulling out my phone from my jacket.

"That is annoyingly cute. Maybe we can be like that when we have our kids."

"I think we'd be a lot more technologically savvy by that time." Stephan bumps his hip against mine as he cracks an egg into the frying pan.

We sit opposite each other, enjoying the silence and relishing each other's presence as the playlist shuffles through our favorite songs.

Sitting opposite Stephan in our small apartment feels right. I always feel right with him. *You have been dating for almost three years.* I lean my head on my hands as I look at him.

His dark brown hair lifts slightly at the front, and from the side, it looks like he has recently cut it. *Probably because he was seeing me.* I can't help but smile. His tanned skin always looks as if he's just returned from the tropics, and it complements his green eyes that remind me of the fields in Scotland: the blades of grass soaking up the sun. I love the way his face always curves into a smile regardless of what he's doing. It is one of the many things that I love about him.

Sensing I'm staring at him, he looks up and smiles.

"What is it?"

I shake my head, embarrassed that he's caught me staring at him, and look down. Stephan leans over the table, lifting my head to look at him. He brushes the ice-blond chunk of hair behind my ear.

"I...I just missed you," I whisper. I hate how warm he makes me feel, how even a simple touch makes my stomach swirl and my heart burst.

Stephan leans in and kisses me softly, opening his mouth this time, allowing our tongues to stroke alongside one another, rolling around both our mouths. I could happily stay in this moment, with our lips welded together as our bodies warm from the inside.

I'm the first to pull away.

"I love you, Luna."

"I love you, too." I get out from under the table, heading to the suitcase. Being so near to Stephan causes flutters in my stomach.

"How long are we staying at your parents'?" I ask.

"The apartment is ours 'til we're ready to leave. If my mom sees you with a suitcase, she'll think you're here to stay for a while."

"Duffle it is then, " I say.

"Duffle it is," he repeats.

I grab my stuff, heading into the bedroom. Stephan has already made it his own with his suitcase in the corner and the covers clearly slept in.

I don't have much in my duffle, just the things that I could bring on the plane. It is a four-hour journey from Seattle to Colorado.

I pull out the few things in the large, black leather duffle bag before lifting my suitcase onto the bed. My suitcase, on the other hand, is not for two weeks.

It is so cold in Colorado, and Stephan's parents live in a cottage-like house surrounded by forest. *They'll hike at one point; I just know they will.* So, I had no choice but to pack everything.

I take out a few pairs of matching underwear, socks, shirts, knitted jumpers, trousers and two pairs of shoes, including the trainers I had worn on the plane. I zip up the duffle and place the now two-stone-heavier bag next to Stephan's.

"Is it safe to enter? " Stephan says behind the door.

"You wondering whether I'm decent?" I ask, and he pokes his head around, his hands wet and soapy from the dishes.

"No, making sure this place hasn't become a bomb site."

I pick up the closest thing I can get my hands on and chuck it at him.

He catches it and unballs the item, revealing the purple hipster style knickers. He wiggles his eyebrows.

"Sexually frustrated already?"

I roll my eyes, march towards him, and snatch the underwear out of his grasp.

"Extremely, but I'm a patient girl, so I can wait."

He kisses my forehead, stepping into the room.

"Have you decided what you'll take to the house?" he asks, running his hands down his trousers.

I nod, showcasing my excellent work with the duffle in the corner.

"I'm nearly as efficient as you. I'm going to have a bath; my neck aches."

"I did offer to bump you up to first."

"For four hours?" I shake my head furiously. "What a waste of money."

"Well, who else would I spend it on, Luna? "

I point at him as I speak.

"That is a good response." I slide past him, heading to the bathroom.

I'm surprised they managed to get both a bath and a shower cubicle in the clearly not-so-spacious bathroom.

I pull out my hair; with it straightened, you can see its full length. I've been used to curls laying on my shoulders, but when it falls, it sways delicately to the middle of my shoulder blades.

I twirl the ice-blond section at the front. Magenta agrees with me that it plays well with Luna, and undoubtedly makes me stand out. It doesn't matter how often I put magic into my hair; I always marvel at how natural it looks. Even if I were to spend a whole year with Stephan, that small section at the front of my hair would continue to grow an ice-blond color.

I fill the tub, unwrapping the hotel's supplied soap before dropping my clothes and getting into the bath.

The door opens, and Stephan walks in. He has also discarded his clothes, and my stomach swirls at his naked body.

He strides to the shower cubicle and opens the glass door, taking a stance so we can watch each other.

"So, it's decided then?" I ask, watching him as he wipes the water off his face.

"Is what decided? "

"No sex until tonight."

Stephan steps out of the shower, his body dripping wet, and I sit up.

The swirls in my stomach have intensified, and I can't control myself as I bite my lip.

"Do you want me to fuck you, Luna?" His low voice makes me speechless, and I open my mouth senselessly. Stephan holds my chin and tilts it.

I stand up, my eyes never leaving his.

He pulls me close, so our bodies are a few centimeters apart.

"Do you want me to turn you over and fuck you in this tub?" He smirks. "Would you like that?" He lets go of my chin and flicks my right nipple.

My thighs clench, and my body grows goosebumps from being exposed to the cold. I still can't find my voice.

He grabs my waist, pressing me against his erection, rubbing against my wet and soapy skin.

"You have to give me an answer." He flicks my nipple again before caressing it between his thumb and forefinger, increasing the pleasure that courses through my body and settles in my stomach.

"It's been a long time, hasn't it?" he asks, grabbing me by my ass and lifting me up.

I wrap my legs around his waist.

"You're only ever speechless when it's been longer than a month since you've come." He kisses my neck, and my eyes close on their own accord. Stephan always knows how to get me worked up. He fuels a fire in my stomach that he knows can only be satisfied by him.

"But it is decided, Luna."

"What!" I shout, a bit too loud, and so quickly that Stephan throws his head back in laughter.

He eases me back into the lukewarm water.

"We will sort you out later, but if we start this now, we will be late."

I splash the water like a child. Shocked at my behavior, I cover my face, but I still hear Stephan's laugh as he leaves the room.

Family Occasions

Stephan places a hand on my thigh, drawing my attention from the trees on either side of us. I turn to look at him.

"Still upset about the whole bathroom tease?" He is trying desperately not to smile, but one glance at my face, and his façade crumbles.

"A tease it was indeed, just make sure you make good on your promise."

"I'll have you screaming my name to the heavens."

Though Stephan is just being himself, those few words have the swirls coming back in full effect, and I'm forced to cross my legs.

He slows the car, making sure not to miss the inconspicuous turn on the left covered by greenery

He stops the car in front of a metal cattle gate before getting out and pushing the gate open.

His phone buzzes and I pick it up, sliding it across, and holding the phone to my ear.

"Hi Theresa, Stephan is just moving the gate."

"Was he late picking you up again?"

I laugh as Stephan's mother speaks on the other end.

"Of course, he was, despite him getting a hotel next door." I hear the loud tut and sigh on the other end.

"But he made me breakfast, so I guess he's off the hook."

"You're far too lenient on him, dear. I would've given Lloyd an earful if he did that," she says.

Stephan shuts the driver's door as I speak. "I'm roping him in with my charm, and that's when the earful will begin. Either way, your son is a lucky man. We will see you guys shortly."

He eyes me, mouthing the words "Mom or Dad?" I show him the caller ID, and Stephan represses the urge to roll his eyes. I put the phone back to my ear.

"See you in a bit, Luna," Theresa says.

"Lucky man, eh? "

I raise a brow at him.

"Don't you think so?"

He slows the car, pulling up outside the house alongside an army of other vehicles.

"I'll show you my appreciation tonight." He kisses me quickly.

A loud thud comes from outside, and there stand Charley and Kaleb with beers in their hands, arms wrapped over each other's shoulders.

"What took you so fucking long, *Slaouse*?" Charley shouts, and Stephan groans, opening the door, half stepping out of the car.

"How old are you, Charley? *Slaouse*, really, man? You haven't called me that since I was 13."

Charley shrugs, taking a long gulp of his beer before speaking.

"It is reserved for the days you are particularly late."

The door opens, and Kaleb stands on the other side. He gives me a broad smile, typical of the boys of the family.

"Oh Kale, the beard is coming through," I say, beckoning him forward so I can run my hand over the stubble.

"You think so? The guys think it still looks weak," Kaleb says, rubbing his chin to reassure himself.

"I say it's the jealousy talking."

The comment makes the young man chuckle slightly.

"How late was he today?" Kaleb asks, as he stretches out his hand to help me out of the car.

"Well..." I start, catching Stephan's attention as he tries to get out of a headlock. "He wasn't late."

Kaleb cheers, punching the air as Charley lets go of Stephan. Charley fishes in his pocket, pulls out a hundred-dollar bill, and slaps it into Kaleb's hand.

"But..." I begin. The boys freeze mid-transaction. "He did rush to get there on time, so he had a shower after we got back."

Charley's grip turns to iron as Kaleb tries to pull the note from his tight grasp.

"Hey, I won, Charley."

"No, the bet was Stephan here wouldn't be late," Charley clarifies.

"And he wasn't," Kaleb points out.

"That's because he cheated. If he had a shower, he would've been late, right, Luna?"

The boys turn to me: the deciding factor on who would win a hundred dollars. Stephan stands by my side looking down at me.

"Well, I gue-"

"Luna." Theresa's feathery voice cuts through the boys well before I see her emerge from the house. She separates Charley and Kaleb, the hundred-dollar bill ripping in half.

Theresa pulls me into a hug, which I return, and then holds me out by my shoulders.

"We've been waiting for you guys. How was the flight?"

I sigh, running a hand over my forehead.

"I still don't like planes."

Theresa gives Stephan a stern look before her warming brown eyes come back to me.

"I told him to drive."

Stephan gives his mother a hug, kissing the top of her greying brunette hair.

"And I told you that I couldn't." He lets go of her, heading to the car, his brothers hot on his tail to help with the bags.

"Come in, Luna. I finally got the kitchen island done."

"Lloyd finally got round to it?" I ask, excitement dripping from each word. She nods, hooking her arm around mine and leading me into the green and white house.

Stephan's family lives in a community in a teardrop formation. There are seven houses including his family's, whose house is at the top. They keep to themselves, almost isolated from the world. Nearly all the children are homeschooled. Besides Stephan, who moved to Seattle, they scarcely ever venture out for too long.

Tonight is their quarterly community feast. Everyone comes to Theresa's home to eat and spend time with one another. It is almost like a public holiday.

As the door opens, we are surrounded by people chatting and laughing. The general atmosphere of festivities and family unity is overwhelming, and I feel my smile falter just a little.

Theresa is smart to keep the ground floor open plan, merging together the kitchen, the living room, and the dining area into one large room with three large deer antler chandeliers hanging above us.

With about 20 people milling around across the living room, the outside deck and garden, it is as cozy as ever. I'm rubbing shoulders and catching up with people I haven't seen in months.

We navigate through the crowd to where the kitchen is. There stands Theresa's newest prized possession: an intricate oak island with white marble on top. I crouch down, inspecting the complicated design etched into the wood.

The design follows the trees we pass to get here, and the path that leads to the community. It reminds me of something Michelangelo would create, like a wood carving of the Sistine Chapel ceiling artwork: many stories weaving together.

I stand up and face Theresa, who is anxiously waiting for my response.

"It's beautiful, Theresa. Lloyd did really well."

"I did, didn't I?"

I turn around to the husky voice. Lloyd stands wiping one hand on his apron, a spatula in the other. Lloyd is a big man, both wide and tall, and whenever we hug, I get the faintest hint of cinnamon underneath all the oak and timber he plays around with.

"You guys are having a BBQ in December?" I hug Lloyd. His large hands wrap around my body and squeeze me slightly.

"Of course, we are. How else do you expect me to feed this lot if not with burgers, chicken and hot dogs?"

I look around; he does have a point.

Lloyd leans down to whisper in my ear, "was my son late again?"

"Dad, stop trying to get Luna to tell on Stephan." Marie squeezes past a few people and pulls me into a long hug, rocking us from side to side. I step back, taking in her stomach.

"Marie, you've grown." I can't contain my excitement as she blushes, tucking a brunette strand behind her ear as she rubs her stomach.

"I could just about get into this dress. When will this pregnancy be over?" She fakes a sigh as she places the back of her hand on her head.

"You should savor it; no work, just rest," Stephan says, emerging from the crowd, his brothers by his side. Charley cradles Marie from behind while Lloyd pulls his son into a hearty hug.

"Come outside, you guys, you must be hungry," Lloyd says, ushering us all out to the garden through the deck on the right.

Stephan takes my hand, and I am grateful. No doubt I'd get lost among the people.

The only illumination we have is the lights of the surrounding houses. The sun has taken its leave, replaced by the full moon.

We all stand huddled around the grill as Lloyd works away, flipping the burgers and basting the chicken and steak in marinade.

"Marie," I begin. The brunette turns to me. "When? When I was here last, you barely had a bump. Now..." I motion to her large stomach.

"For you, it seems like it's happened overnight, but she was always growing just a little more obvious." Marie giggles as I gawk at her.

"It's a girl?"

Charley wraps his arm around his wife as he speaks. "Did Stephan not tell you?"

I turn to Stephan, who is about to gulp his beer, and I nudge him in his ribs gently, causing him to choke slightly.

"No, he did not."

We all look to Stephan, waiting for an explanation.

"I forgot, OK."

We all groan, and Stephan gives me an apologetic look. I give him a small smile, telling him I forgive him.

Kaleb hands us a plate of food, the unofficial chef's assistant. Stephan and I follow behind Charley and Marie. We take a seat at the wooden garden table and chairs. There are only three chairs, so I settle on Stephan's lap, not that he minds much.

"What you guys been up to?" Charley asks.

"Work," we say in unison. We both stare at each other before laughing.

"You guys are far too compatible, " Marie points out, and I stroke Stephan with the back of my hand.

"It's probably why we've been together for so long," Stephan mentions, and I nod in agreement.

"I agree. We kind of just seem to fit. Our schedules work well with us."

"You say that now, but what happens when you get married and have kids?" Charley asks. Stephan avoids the question by taking a drink of his beer.

"We've talked about it. But Verna has to give us her blessing, right?" I turn to look at Stephan; he nods, still avoiding the question.

Marie puts her hand on mine from across the table.

"Don't worry, she will approve you guys. It's been three years together and two years of suitability."

I sigh, hanging my head. Stephan pulls me to his chest. It is a touchy subject, the suitability ritual.

"Luna does an amazing job. I know we are coming to an end; you won't have to do it for too long now."

I smile, but it doesn't reach my eyes. Stephan brings me close, kissing the top of my head and whispering words of encouragement as his brother and wife watch.

"Stephan."

We all turn to the old woman as she shuffles towards us, her hands clasped over her yellow blouse.

"Abuela."

I get off Stephan's lap so he can hug his grandmother. He has to crouch down to properly cradle the old woman. As she finishes pinching his cheeks, she turns to me, her arms open wide.

"Verna," I say, hugging her, breathing in the flowery scent.

"You know you can call me Abuela as well."

I let go of the hug.

"I know. I want to be officially part of the family before I do."

Verna hugs me again, taking a look at the second eldest grandson.

"I always said I liked this one."

Stephan side hugs me, kissing the top of my head.

"You and everyone else, it would seem."

Verna peeks around us to Charley and Marie, who are still seated.

"Marie, the kids are in bed, but they insisted that Luna tuck them in. Is that, OK?"

Marie looks to Stephan and me as she speaks. "Is it OK?"

I wave my hand nonchalantly.

"Of course. I haven't seen the guys in so long."

Marie nods in approval and leans back in the chair. I hand Stephan my half-eaten plate and head back into the house.

The guests have begun to thin out, just a few seniors talking in the corners of the room. I take the staircase by the garden door and head upstairs to the bedrooms.

As always, Claire and Austin are in the first one. I open the door slowly, the constellation night light causing stars to dance across the wall.

Claire is the first to see me, and she jumps out of bed. She hugs me at the waist before Austin comes and joins her.

"I thought we'd be asleep by the time you arrived, Luna," Claire whispers.

I usher them back into bed and take a seat on the floor between the two.

"Abuela told me you wanted me to tuck you in."

Claire nods quickly, sweeping her golden-brown hair out of her face.

"Claire wanted you to tell her the story."

I look to Austin, who has the covers covering most of his face. Only the family green eyes peek out.

"Liar. You want Luna to tell the story as much as I do," Claire points out.

"Did not," Austin retorts.

"Did too."

"Did not."

I raise my hands, shushing the pair.

"It doesn't matter who wanted the story the most. I'll still tell you the story. But you need to be quiet, deal? "

"Deal," they both say. I sigh happily, clasping my hands together.

"Right, do you want the scientific version or the far more interesting version?"

"Come on, Luna, when have we ever wanted the scientific version?"

I laugh at Austin's comment and shrug.

"It doesn't hurt to ask." I clear my throat before I begin.

"I was born on a full moon, but there's nothing special about that as there's a full moon every month. However, what made my birth special was what happened. My parents were star enthusiasts. I'm sure if you asked them any question on stars, they would have an answer. They never missed a chance to see the stars. For a long time, they decided that my name would be Lyra after the constellation.

"As they were watching the stars shine, my mother's waters broke, and they were on a camping trip that day. Like I said, big enthusiasts for stars, so even a baby on the way wouldn't stop them examining the sky. There was no way my father could get her down the hill, let alone to the hospital. They always wanted a home birth, and this was the closest they could get to it. My mother really wanted to give birth under the stars so that they'd be the first thing I'd see."

The door creaks open, and I turn around, seeing Stephan leaning on the door frame. I blow him a kiss, which he catches before I return to my story.

"The birth, from what my parents told me, was fairly easy, aside from the screams of labor, of course. The best part came when I arrived; they said I didn't scream or cry, but simply stared up at the sky just as they intended. They said that, as I stared at the moon, a small chunk of my front hair turned white, replacing the black color. My mother said it was the moon that did so, and it was only right they named me after it."

"Is that how you got your name?"

I nod at Claire.

"That's right: Luna, Cassiopeia, Lyra, Stanley." I stand up and tuck the sheets around Austin and Claire's.

"Is that why Abuela has let you into the pack, because you were touched by the moon?"

I rub the back of my neck as I think of a suitable response.

"I think so. Your Abuela doesn't do anything without the moon's approval. I wouldn't say she let me in, but the moon did."

"Then if the moon allowed you into the pack, why have you and Uncle Stephan been participating in the chase even after two years? Why aren't you married yet? Christian said his brother only had to do it for a month before he got married, and Mom and Dad only had three runs before they got married."

I look to Stephan, as Austin has asked some tough questions. Stephan steps in when he notices my unease.

"It's difficult, Austin. Werewolves and humans rarely interact so intimately. Luna is right for our family. She's right for the pack, but because she's not like us, she has to prove herself more than female werewolves."

"Well, what if the moon decides that she isn't, what then?"

I place a hand on Austin's shoulder. He is clearly distressed and knows far more than we all care to admit. It won't be long before he undergoes his first moon.

"I don't think the moon would let this go on without a good result. Don't worry, Austin, I'll be part of the family when the time is right." I stand up, and Stephan takes my hand, squeezing it slightly.

It seems like everyone is asking the same question. Why am I not part of the family yet?

"What's the scientific reason?" Austin asks suddenly. I smile slightly at his thoughts, directing him somewhere more pleasant.

"That I have poliosis, causing that part of my hair to be white."

Austin rolls over as he speaks, "yeah, the other version is far more interesting."

I laugh lightly, stroking his head.

"I think so too, Austin. See you guys in the morning." I take Stephan's hand, leading us out of the room.

Moonlight Escape

The house is quiet, with only a few murmurs from the family as we walk down the hallway to our room. The creaks of the wooden floor echo across the empty space.

I sit down in a clear huff on the bed.

"You're stressed, aren't you?" He shuts the door, leaning on the wood.

"Yes, I'm just worried this won't go anywhere, and that the moon won't approve of us."

He walks over and pulls me up into a hug. Despite him doing the best he can to comfort me, the problems in our lives still linger with me.

In werewolf culture, family is everything. A female is made to leave her blood family when she finds her mate; it shows her loyalty and that she'll know no one else but her husband's family. Even with a mate, they shift every full moon until their firstborn has gone through their first transformation.

It is imperative to find your mate, because the older you get, the more dangerous it is on your body every full moon. I have heard stories of wolves dying after a moon simply because their bodies could no longer handle it.

Ideally, by the age of 30, you should have had your first child. Parents send their children away to travel in the hopes that they will find their soulmate, that their sons will return with a Luna, and the girls, they hope, will not return at all.

But I am human, and in the archaic times, I wouldn't bring anything to the pack. If the pack was under attack, I couldn't fight. I can't heal as quickly, I'm not particularly fast, and any children I have could be just human, thereby decreasing the strength of the pack. Logistically, it's not practical having a human as a mate.

"Austin is right," I finally say, and Stephan looks down at me. "What happens if I'm not approved? What usually happens?"

Stephan holds me at arm's length as he says, "I don't know, Luna, a mate is a mate, and usually, they are werewolves. Why do you think we are still participating in the chase? As archaic as it is, you have to prove yourself as a suitable woman to mother my children, and you also have to bring something to the pack that'll increase our strength."

I want to cry. The chase is a horrendous a ritual that two potential mates have to go through during a full moon. The male chases the female in their wolf forms. It is so each family can assess the two parts. Is the male strong enough to produce equally strong children? Could the female take over as leader should her husband die?

At times, the chase is brutal – the couple fights, testing their strength and skill. Making sure that they know how to protect the children if need be. If they aren't true soulmates, either could easily die. It is a massive risk on both the families' part, but the chance of success is worth it.

Stephan sits down, bringing me onto his lap so I am straddling him. "Oh, Luna, don't cry."

A tear drops onto my lap, and I wipe it away.

Stephan holds my hand, running a thumb over my open palm.

"You know it's just Abuela who's very traditional, and she loves you too much to not have you as part of the family. The whole family loves you."

"What about Marie's family?" Though Marie is no longer part of her birth family since she married Charley, she still told me how strict they were, how hard they were on the pair during their own chase ceremony. Immediately after they said, "I do," her birth family caught the first flight back to Athens and never spoke to her again.

Usually, today's technology keeps people in contact even if they aren't supposed to be, like Stephan's family. Theresa knows what her sisters are up to, but never speaks to them; she just browses Instagram and Facebook, making sure they are still alive.

"You know how they are. They don't even know about Austin. You have nothing to worry about." Stephan kisses my wet cheeks, stroking my face. His lips gently find mine, his hands cupping my cheeks, deepening the kiss.

His hand trails down my top, removing my cardigan while I unbutton his.

I pull my lips from his just to remove my shirt, and he takes the opportunity to pick me up and lay me on the bed. He throws off my shoes and pulls down my jeans as he kneels in front of me. My body shivers as I watch Stephan remove his shirt, dropping it to the side as he crawls over my body to hover above me.

He leans down to whisper in my ear, "let me distract you." He kisses my ear as his hand trails down my body, snaking under my pants. He rolls his thumb over my clit. It has been too long since my body shook with pleasure, and as Stephan kisses my neck t, I let out a small whimper.

My eyes close as his kisses begin their descent. As his kisses find their way to my navel, my breath quickens, my thighs instinctively squeeze together, making Stephan laugh: a low rumble vibrating against my leg.

"You'd think you were a virgin, Luna." He kisses my inner thigh. "Relax."

I feel his hot breath against me, revealing the dampness of my desire. His fingers hook around my underwear, and he slides them off, exposing me to his warm breath.

Stephan kisses my folds, a shudder going straight to my head. His tongue swipes across the slick opening, and a moan escapes my mouth. His tongue goes in again, sliding inside, curving and forcing my body to arch, and a loud gasp escapes me. His hand goes to my breast and pulls it out of its confines.

His tongue goes in again as he pinches my nipple before soothing it between his thumb and finger. His tongue licks gently against my clit, making my body shudder with pleasure.

"Don't make me come from this, Stephan," I breathe out, his tongue going for another dip. He gives my clit one last kiss before moving away, my body missing his warm air.

I sit up slightly, watching as he removes his trousers, pulling down his boxers, revealing the thick and throbbing penis.

I pull him down for a kiss, my mouth open and my tongue wanting to wrestle with his. He matches my intention and opens his mouth, sliding himself inside, both of us moaning with pleasure. He places my legs over his shoulder, deepening the slow, pleasurable thrusts. I manage to open my eyes and notice the blue that has begun to grow in his irises.

He grabs my exposed breast, pinching the nipple, knowing full well that is the one thing I crave. I place my hands flat against the headboard, using it as momentum to push myself against him. Stephan hangs his head back, his hands sliding down to my hips, bringing me down hard with every thrust.

"St-Stephan... " Moaning his name out loud causes him to smirk. He knows what I want, knows what I crave. He pulls my legs off his shoulders, wraps them around his waist, and his mouth goes straight to my erect nipple.

He sucks on it, his other hand pulling the lonely right breast out of the bra and caressing it before pinching the nipple while he soothes the other.

My back arches, forcing more into his mouth as my hands tug his hair.

"I'm so...so close. "

His mouth detaches from my nipple, moving to my ear. "Will you come for me, Luna?" His hot breath fans my ear as he thrusts deep inside me.

I can't help but whimper, my hips pushing with his thrusts.

"Will you say my name as your body shudders, riding that orgasm that's been denied to you?" He sucks on my nipple once more before going back to my ear. "When's the last time you've come?"

The knots in my stomach begin bunching up, close to unfurling. Stephan ups his speed, holding my hips in place, so that I feel him slide in and out as he sucks on my nipple.

"Stephan...St-Stephan..." My calls spur him on as my voice grows louder, repeating his name over and over again. I hold on tight around his neck, the knots reaching their limit.

Stephan's breaths become ragged as he plummets into me.

"Stephan...Stephan..."

"Fuck, Luna. Fuck." Stephan growls. His hands on my waist become painfully tight. We both breathe out each other's name as our orgasms meld into one.

The Chase

I eye Stephan, who is lying on the bed watching me intently as I pull my hair into a ponytail.

"Yes, Stephan."

He slides off the bed. The only thing containing him is a pair of black boxers.

"Even though I know the repercussions of tonight, it's still a huge turn-on watching you get dressed." He leans his head on my shoulder, staring at me through the mirror.

I pull at the nude-colored shorts. From afar, I look practically naked. It is the closest I can be to a werewolf equivalent, minus the fur.

There is a knock at the door, and Stephan gives me a lingering kiss on my temple. He cuddles me one last time before letting go and allowing me to open the door.

Verna stands in front of me, her gloved hands cupping a ball of wolfsbane. I take it from her, holding it by the small, roped link at the top.

"Nervous, Luna?" She places a hand on my lower back and guides me down the stairs.

"Always, you'd think I didn't know what I was doing."

We head out of the house through the front door and stand in the dark.

Without the illumination from the porch light and other lights from the neighboring houses, there is nothing but complete darkness. I am completely and utterly out of my element.

Verna takes my hand so I can look at her.

"Don't forget, Luna, not until the first scratch; otherwise, you'll just upset him," she reminds me, and I nod.

When it was decided that Stephan and I would participate in the chase, I was fortunate enough to be given a few handicaps. I have a longer head start, and I also have wolfsbane to increase the overall effect. Without it, I would be caught in less than a minute, and that wouldn't bode well in terms of our suitability.

I take a deep breath, my nerves starting to build. Verna gives me a small squeeze before heading back in the house. I know I can't stand there and watch her retreating figure. I grip the wolfsbane in my hands and jog into the dark, dense forest.

I leap over a fallen tree, making sure to land with my knees bent. *The last thing I need is a sprained ankle.*

Several howls echo through the forest, and my heart sinks to the bottom of my stomach.

The howling first, then the thumping of feet – I shake my head. I can't get distracted, especially here of all places. I continue running, careful not to catch myself on hanging branches.

Growls erupt around me, and my body shivers. It is dark, below freezing, and I have to balance being fast but alert. I can't see well, and that is a considerable disadvantage.

Several twigs snap behind me, and I know what will happen. I pluck the turquoise stone from my bracelet and crush the gem, sprinkling the dust over my head for protection.

Oh God, here it comes!

A stabbing pressure hits my back, causing me to fall forward. I manage to roll over, picking myself up quickly, but I am caught, and another stab of tension bursts across my lower back. I spin around, throwing the wolfsbane in a guessed direction, my eyes still dizzy. A puff of dust explodes, and I cover my mouth with the crook of my arm.

The dust settles, coating the giant wolf in a greenish-yellow color. Its eyes shoot open, the blue irises bloodshot from the pain. Teeth bared, it lunges recklessly at me, and I dart to the right. Another swipe of its claws grazes my forearm, knocking me into a tree as he also goes flying into another.

I hold my arm to my chest, running off. Without the turquoise crystal, I probably would've been paralyzed with the shock of being slashed several times. Another howl echoes through the dense forest, and I switch directions. Heading with no clear destination, the sounds of hard breaths can be heard. I'm not sure if they belong to the wolf or me.

The wolf's substantial body drops on top of me, causing me to land with a hard, painful thump on the ground. I scream, my back arching as twigs dig into the exposed flesh. The gem only nullifies the pain, splitting the connection from the brain to rest of the body. But sometimes pain transcends mere connections.

Through cloudy eyes covered in tears, I stare at the wolf. It looks up at the sky, howling one last time. I roll over onto my side. The effects of the crystal reach its capacity and the real force of pain seeps in.

The wolf curls up next to me, licking the wound on my arm. I wince, crying as blood escapes from my body, pooling onto the forest floor and coating the muddy surface. If the injuries don't kill me, infection surely will.

My body moves again against my will and my eyes nearly roll back into oblivion. I choke slightly on the bile that is filling my throat. I can't move, and when I do, I am electrocuted with pain and fire.

"I'm sorry, I'm sorry," Stephan whispers as he picks me up. I can't see; my eyes are open, but they are covered with blood and tears.

The paws of two giant wolves approach us and my eyes struggle to match their gaze. Standing just a few feet away, their colors are masked by the dark atmosphere. Verna emerges from between them, a small candlelit lamp illuminating the space immediately around her.

"Abuela, " Stephan says quietly. Verna looks at her grandson and shakes her head. As the last bit of protection magic evaporates, so does my consciousness.

The wolves take to the moon, howling in pain.

Scarred Wounds

I step out onto the plane's stairs, the winter air slapping my face. I pull my scarf tighter around my neck, pick up the small suitcase, and carry it down to the car parked in front. I take the keys from the chauffeur, pop open the trunk, and throw my suitcase in.

My phone buzzes with a call from an unknown number, and I frown.

"What!" It is mid-afternoon, and I am tired from spending two weeks with Freya, fixing problems with our shipping containers and other paperwork. *Apparently, having the Aldrek name is more of a disadvantage than advantage these days.*

"Sir," the voice on the other line begins, "there's been a problem."

I listen carefully as the person on the other end explains. My hands tighten around the phone, and my teeth clench together to the point of breaking.

Once the conversation finishes, I slam the trunk shut, the force causing the car to shake. I get into the car, driving straight to Mae's safe location.

I fling open the plastic door to the supposed yoga studio. It is vacant at the front, but I hear murmurs and cries from down the hall. I walk quickly to the solitary white door, and the screams increase.

The smell of blood fills my nose.

Mae. She is bleeding. A part of me salivates as I imagine her blood crashing to the floor, splattering across the white floor. But that feeling is replaced with searing hot rage.

She's bleeding, and it's not because of me.

I pull open the door, ripping it off its hinges, and throw it behind me. Several doctors rush in front of me, their aprons covered in blood. I head towards the small cries and whimpers. The painful sounds only intensify my anger, acting as my driving force.

Mae's hair is the first thing I see, but when the doctors disperse, I see her lying on her side. Deep scratches stretch across her back, and when the doctor peels another cloth from her wound, her back arches in pain, her whole-body shuddering.

"What the FUCK is going on?" My voice echoes through the room, and everyone stops to look at me.

"Dominic, should you be here?"

I turn around to look at Magenta, who emerges from a corner. The tips of her fingers are coated with blood, and from where I stand, it seems she has already touched Mae.

"What do you mean should I be here? Why is she hurt?"

Magenta looks to Mae, who is still crying on the metal table, before her gaze comes back to me. What angers me the most is how none of this seems to faze her and how unsympathetic she appears.

"Occupational hazard. This isn't the first time Mae has participated in a chase ritual."

"A what..." I look towards Mae, making sense of the scratches on her back. *Her loyal client is a werewolf, and if that isn't bad enough, she allowed herself to partake in a suitability ritual.*

"It's part of her job."

Those simple words send me over the edge. I bound for Magenta.

It's part of her job' my fucking ass.

A small doctor blocks my path, and I can't control my hands as they tear through the doctor's neck.

You made her bleed.

I gouge and tear, blood splattering against my face.

You made her hurt.

Blood drips down my forearms, ruining my clothes and the floor.

And you made her cry.

I chuck the poorly decapitated doctor's head aside, licking the back of my hand as I taste the salty blood of what I now know is a siren.

I will kill you for this.

Magenta doesn't seem fazed as I squeeze her neck and, without a second thought, bite down on her, pulling and tearing at whatever artery and vein I can get my teeth on.

I step back, wiping my mouth with the back of my sleeve as Magenta continues to remain unfazed. She swipes at her neck. The blood stains her hands as though half her neck isn't hanging out.

Magenta's amethyst eyes catch mine as she smirks. My vision becomes blurry. The image of Magenta splits into two, then four, then eight. She is surrounding me as she folds her arms. I stumble back, slipping on the pool of blood from the dead doctor.

I roll over onto my hands and knees, coughing violently as black, ink-like liquid spews out of my mouth, sizzling as it makes contact with the floor.

As the – what I believe – last bit of ink leaves me, I suddenly feel very cold. I collapse onto my side, shuddering as Magenta's heels enter my view before I black out.

Taking Work Home with You

I groan loudly. Before I can even open my eyes, I notice my head is heavy, and my throat is on fire. I rub it gently. It isn't something that can be satisfied with water.

This feels like a hangover. *I only get hangovers if the person I drank from was intoxicated. Mae d-* I sit up, immediately looking around the foreign room.

"Jesus, Dominic, don't move so suddenly."

I turn to Mae, who is sitting, feet perched on the chair, her knees close to her chest. I move to get up, but something snags onto my arm. I look down at the piece of yellow fabric wrapped around my forearm, holding down a needle.

My eyes follow the plastic tube before it rests in Mae's arm. She is staring at me, a pencil tucked behind her ear; her hands rest on her lap.

"What happened?"

Mae stands up, slides her own needle out of her arm, and lays it on the chair, tucking what I now realize is a sketchbook under her arm.

"You collapsed at the studio. I couldn't take you to the doctors, and I don't really remember how to get to your house, so

I had to take you back to my place. You've been asleep for two days, in and out of a fever. It's good to see you've pulled through." Mae attempts a smile before speaking. "Have a shower. It's just gone six pm. Sybil sent a driver with some clothes and stuff." Mae points and my eyes follow to the black leather duffle.

"I'll be downstairs making dinner."

I watch Mae head down the stairs beside her chair. She glances over her shoulder and notices I am still watching her. She smiles slightly at me, before continuing.

Mae's room isn't what I expected of her. It is noticeably light: shades of white, beige and cream are everywhere from the sheets to the floor and furniture. I reach over to the duffle bag, pulling it up on the bed before unzipping it.

I can only imagine what Sybil thought when Mae requested my clothes and things, whether she was skeptical or how Mae even went about asking for them. *What could she have said? What did Sybil say?*

Somehow, I manage to pull myself off the bed. Glancing around her room, on the bedside table is a picture. I instantly notice Mae and her mother, and a man and a small boy accompany them. *Her mom remarried, had a son.* Mae looks the most out of place, as though she'd been photoshopped into the picture.

She is standing off to the left slightly, almost out of focus and not all there. Despite her smile, I see in her eyes the emptiness. *Is it sadness? Regret? Both?* I shake my head. *Who am I to pry into her family life?*

I grab the duffle bag, carrying it into the bathroom. I pull off my clothes. Standing in the small bathroom, I can tell that I haven't showered. My clothes seem to stick and cling in every area that produces sweat, and when my shirt comes off, you'd think I had just come back from a full-body workout at the gym. I can't even imagine what my breath smells like.

I turn on the water, making sure it is just below scalding. Being dirty is not my thing, and it is certainly not something I am often. Having the hot water hit my back is pleasurable and, as I scrub myself vigorously with soap, I feel layers of grime fall off me and swirl down into the drain.

By the time I leave the bathroom, I've showered, dressed and brushed my teeth. I feel relaxed, considering I am in a stranger's house. I hear Mae humming with a song from the kitchen directly underneath the bedroom.

I didn't take Mae as a loft kind of girl, but not to say it isn't nice. It's just that her bed is like a balcony overlooking the living and dining room.

There isn't a divide, and if she had guests over, they'd see everything. There is no privacy. I can't imagine Mae bringing a client home. *If I remember correctly, no client is even supposed to know their employee's date of birth or even their last name for that matter. I doubt they'd know where they lived.*

I head down the stairs and see Mae. Her back is to me while her music plays, and she talks on the phone.

"No Lara, Magenta said it was fine to bring him home." She is stirring something in a pot.

Her little island has food ends scattered across it and a blender with a red liquid at the bottom.

I stalk forward as Mae continues to reassure this Lara person.

"What...take him home, which might I add I don't actually know where his home is... I've only ever been conscious twice when I've come and gone from that house..."

I step behind her, watching as she stirs a large pot of what looks like soup.

"Tha-" Mae screams, turning around.

I look down at the knife pressed to my throat. Her hand is still shaking as she tries to calm herself.

"The sneaking, Dominic. God, I forgot you were here." Mae turns around, pressing her earphone.

"Lara...No, I'm fine... Honestly...I'll call you or see you soon, whichever comes first...yes, I'll be," she eyes me slightly, "vigilant... Love you too, bye." She pulls her earphones out, discarding them on top of her fridge.

I watch as she drops the knife into the sink and stares at me.

"How are you feeling?" Mae is dressed in a tight, fluffy pair of caramel leggings, figure-hugging to be exact. She doesn't have a top on, just a black sports bra, and I'm not surprised. The heat encased in this small loft is impressive. I feel sweaty already.

I turn her around, staring at her back.

Nothing.

The deep gashes, the peeled skin, and crusting blood isn't there. In fact, it is more like it never happened. No scarring, not even a small indent to suggest something happened.

"Your back," I whisper, almost scared that I could jinx it and the magic would lift. Mae turns around, almost embarrassed by the whole thing.

"It's fine." She steps back as though she could still feel the pain that had left her crying on a metal slab only a few days ago.

"How...I saw the..." I can't even bring myself to mention the sight. The thought and image of it make my stomach roll.

"Magenta. The doctors did the surgery, and Magenta polished up the scarring. Come." Mae takes my hand, running it over her side. It feels exactly as it did when I had left her: smooth and soft. My body releases a held breath as I close my eyes.

"Mae," I open my eyes to stare at her. I place a hand on her shoulder, my tongue running over my teeth as I think carefully on my next words, letting my silver eyes caress her brown ones.

"What is Magenta?" I remember the burning in my throat as I regurgitated her blood, how Magenta didn't even squirm after I practically tore her neck out.

Mae stares at me, her eyes still captured in mine. My words slithering around her head, sticking to the section where she would be compelled.

My head suddenly whips to the side, my cheek burning as Mae grips her sore hand.

I hold my cheek, more shocked that she hasn't been compelled and less on the fact that she has slapped me.

"Don't," she points a stern finger at me. "Do that again. You don't think Magenta made sure that I wouldn't succumb to things like that?"

Fuck. I hadn't thought of that. The witch is a lot craftier than I gave her credit for.

"I'm sorry." My shoulders slump as I look to the floor. "I know she's your employer and... well, that event in the yoga studio baffles me. You've got to appreciate that this doesn't happen at all. I don't have trouble feeding, and I certainly don't sleep for two days in and out of a fever," I explain. Mae listens to my apology as she tidies her small kitchen.

"Understand, Dominic. I don't bring clients home. What happened in the studio was stressful as it is without you being there, but I'm used to it. What happened to you because of it was another added stress. You're better now, and quite frankly, that's all that matters."

"Magenta hasn't called off the arrangement."

Mae shakes her head, chucking her blender into the sink.

"No, she understood that the situation was very distressing for you."

I'm surprised I haven't received a two-year suspension and maybe even a legal case in the mail in the next few weeks.

I watch her run some water over her cookware before turning to me to speak, "If my other client is going to be a problem, then we should call it quits."

I rub my chin, scratching the short hair.

"Your client is a werewolf, and if that wasn't bad as it is, you're partaking in their weird mating ritual. Does Magenta even allow things to go that far? What happens if you guys pass? Where in the pricing is marriage?"

She places her things in the dishwasher next to the fridge, contemplating her answer. After the last utensil goes in and Mae starts the cycle, she can finally address me properly.

"Magenta will sort it out, Dominic. Will it be a problem?" Her stare is cold, and her eyes are desperately trying to look through me instead of at me, but I can tell she doesn't have the answers.

There is a chance that Magenta will keep profiting off her arrangement with this werewolf right up until her deathbed.

"No. It won't be," I reply curtly.

Playing House

"Shouldn't this have already been done?" I ask, pulling another bauble out of the plastic container and handing it to Mae. She looks down at me as she positions the golden ornament on the tree.

"I've been busy. With you."

I hand her another, a silver one to match the other Christmas-colored balls and bells.

I have decided to stay at Mae's house. Not only has Sybil brought me enough clothes, but I don't want to have to meet her gaze and the words to follow.

After Mae places the last decoration on the 6-foot tree, she hops off one of the chairs and puts it back at the dining table. I gaze up at her handiwork. She has been very adamant that I only hand the ornaments, never place them, as she has already picked out the design.

It is close to geometrical – the baubles are placed in a spiral formation of gold, silver and burgundy, and the same colors are never adjacent. The transparent bells are placed seemingly sporadically between the spirals, but I am sure Mae has done it with purpose and precision.

The star at the top is not your typical metal star and is certainly not a fairy. Instead, it is plastic with small LED lights inside. The whole tree is without wires, no fairy lights, and certainly no tinsel, which Mae found a horrendous notion when I suggested it to her.

"The best part is when you turn off the lights," Mae says quietly. She hurries off to the switches. The curtains have already been drawn, the blackout blinds shading the whole place from any outside light, so when Mae switches off her mood lights, the entire room almost succumbs to darkness.

I feel Mae's presence as she comes to stand beside me, marveling at her work. There is a clear reason why she insisted on precision. The ornaments are covered in glow-in-the-dark paint, but these are not the neon colors that I am used to when Lincoln holds a blackout event in the club.

The baubles shine burgundy, silver and gold, nearly illuminating the tree but instead just seem suspended in the air. The transparent bells look like frozen snow.

"Pretty, right?" she whispers. Her arms are around mine as we stare at her achievement.

"It is indeed."

Mae takes my hand, leading me away from the picturesque tree and to her room. She turns on the small side lamp, the soft orange glow not able to detract from her glow-in-the-dark tree.

I stand by the foot of the bed as she removes her clothes. Oddly, there is no rush of blood to my lower half, I don't look at her body hungrily, and there isn't a sudden urge to bite down on her neck.

Perhaps the fever was a lot worse than Mae said.

Instead, I just watch her glide over to her drawers and pull out a grey crop top. Mae slips into bed before her gaze fixes onto mine.

"You're not coming in?"

I am taken aback. I haven't slept with Mae. I've forgotten that this is what people do after sex. I've been used to sending her on her way. Not that we need to have sex now; I just can't imagine any other situation where we'd be lying in bed together.

"In the days that you were asleep, I wasn't on the sofa. We've already shared a bed."

For some reason, that relaxes me – it makes sense, not only to make sure I didn't deteriorate in the night but because it is her place. Mae pats the space next to her before lying down on her back.

I pull off my clothes far too slowly for my liking, hanging them on the chair she had been sitting on earlier. In just my boxers and a shirt, I slip into the bed beside her. It is large enough for both of us, but I still find her body heat caressing my own.

"What happened after Glasgow?" I ask, trying to distract myself. I turn my head to face Mae. She is staring at the ceiling, almost frozen except for the beat of her heart and the rise of her chest.

"Nothing good," she replies.

My keys fumbled in my frozen hands as I struggled to pull out the correct one. They dropped onto the floor, the sound of metal hitting rock making my heart jump, and I groaned, kneeling down to pick

them up. *A searing pain ran through my arm as the grooves of the key slid across the slash in my hand.*

I slotted the key, my eyes burning as my vision doubled. It was four in the morning, and I didn't want any unnecessary noise that would wake up my mother. I closed the door, quietly sliding the lock across.

I kicked off my shoes, hung my woolly coat on the coat rack, and dropped my bag by the radiator before dragging myself up to my room.

As I hit the top of the stairs, I glanced to the left. The light underneath Mum's room was off. I opened my door and turned on the small switch near the floor, illuminating my room with the fairy lights that hung around the perimeter.

I crashed onto the bed, instantly regretting that decision as a pain shot through my stomach, almost making me want to vomit. I didn't want to change. Right in this moment, I wanted to cease to exist.

Bringing my knees to my chest ached, causing the bruising on my thighs to burn and throb. My throat was incredibly dry; all the screaming I had done had left my voice so cracked and raspy that it even hurt to breathe. Or that could've been the fact that I was sure at one point a knee had pushed down onto my lungs.

I pulled the covers over my mangled frame, taking in a large gulp of air that made my chest ache and my head spin. But somehow, I managed to fall asleep, or perhaps I lost consciousness from internal bleeding.

I played with a loose bit of fabric of my sleeve, pulling the red thread, watching it come away from the knitting before letting it fall on the floor.

Surprisingly, I had avoided my mum; being a bartender meant that I had become a night owl. Sleeping throughout the day and working at night, meaning that I didn't see much of the sun, and most people in general, but working as a bartender certainly supported the household.

The door opened slowly, and a brown-haired woman stepped through. She had her hands around two Styrofoam cups, steam rising from them.

"I wasn't sure how you took it, so I brought some packs with me." She laid one cup in front of me before placing hers down on the other side. Before she sat down, she fished out the said sugar packets and placed them beside me.

"They said you wanted to speak to someone," she said, taking a seat opposite me. I stared at the swirling brown liquid, watching the caramel outer ring begin to decrease as small bubbles popped.

My middle finger instinctively rubbed the bandage over my palm. I took another long breath, my lungs instantly seizing up before I was able to exhale.

"I want to report a murder."

Christmas Festivities

I sit opposite Dominic as I bite into my toast. His eyes are glued to his phone as he types away furiously. *Being practically dead for five days must've sent the companies into freefall.*

"Not exactly, Mae." Dominic glances up at me, his usual charm back again as he picks my thoughts.

"But there are things that do require my attention." He places his phone facedown before resting his elbows on the table. "We should go out tonight."

I eye him as I take another bite before saying, "really. I didn't take you as a celebrator."

"I'm not, but I do need to get out of your place. Get some breeze on my face. And my car has been sitting outside a yoga building for five days now, and I know that it's probably been towed."

"I think you're fine. It's a private property car park for customers, and well, you're an extension of me, so you should be fine."

"Nonetheless. We've both been inside for too long, and I wasn't exactly asking you, Mae."

I smile, shaking my head as my grin grows.

"I guess Dominic Aldrek is back. You were a lot quieter when you were recovering."

Dominic stands up, his plate in hand.

"I wasn't me, Mae. I will text you the address and the time I want you there." Dominic doesn't even allow me to reply and heads to the kitchen, places his plate on the side, and heads toward his shoes.

I stand up and lean against the wall as he heads down the stairs.

He picks up the duffle bag, slinging it over his shoulder.

"I will see you tonight, Mae."

I nod at Dominic as he opens the door. I wait until he rounds the stone steps before shutting the door behind him.

It is good he is gone. A part of me was considering calling my mum from the bathroom so she wouldn't overhear anything and begin asking complicated questions.

I head up the stairs, pull my laptop from the drawer, and lift the top. Immediately, I start the FaceTime call.

I wait patiently as the ringing continues. It has been nearly ten months since I've seen everyone. Moving to the states was always going to be difficult, but missing birthdays and holidays makes it even harder.

Max's face pops up; he is talking to Mum before he gives me his attention.

"Daniele." He waves his hand, frantically beckoning my mother towards him.

"Mae's on the phone. Hi, Mae." He waves at the screen, and I wave back, my face in a smile.

I lose Max's face suddenly; it being replaced with a smaller version of him. I hear Max's annoyance as Kenzo takes the iPad off him.

"Hi, Maisie," he screams. He presses his lips to the camera, and I do the same, making loud kissing sounds before removing our faces from it.

"Hi, Kenny Benny. How's my favorite monster?" I ask.

"As monstrous as ever," Mum replies in the distance. Kenzo pouts slightly, but my face on the screen makes the pout disappear quickly.

"I'm fine. Hey. Hey, look what Santa got me." Kenzo turns the tablet around to the mountain of wrapped boxes, all various sizes, stacked under the Christmas tree. He turns the tablet back around so he can see my expression. I place a hand over my mouth, my eyes wide.

"Wooh, you must've been perfect throughout the year, Kenny."

Kenzo nods wildly, his black hair falling over his eyes. "I've been the goodest. When are you coming over?"

My lips move to the side as I think up a good answer. Saying not until this time next year will be heart-breaking to them all, but then it is the truth.

Before I have a chance to reply, the tablet is taken from Kenzo's grasp, much to his annoyance, and my mum comes into view. She is still looking down at Kenzo, who is sitting on the floor as she speaks, "don't ask your sister such difficult questions, Kenny." My mum turns her gaze to me.

"When are you coming home, Mae?" Her eyes look sad. This is not the first time I have stayed home for Christmas, typically because of work. *No rest for the wicked.*

"I don't know. I've been working on a big project since October the 31st. If I want to make the deadline, I can't take time off."

My mother sighs, the camera lowering slightly.

"But I will come down for my birthday, I promise," I say quickly, hoping not to ruin the Christmas mood emanating from my family. "I've got to go, Mum, I have dinner with a client later, and need to get dressed," I bite the inside of my cheek as I tell my mum a half-truth, which she luckily buys.

I watch as she moves the iPad so that I can see her, Max and Kenzo smiling and waving.

"Love you, Mae," they all say.

"Love you too, guys." I kiss the camera before ending the call.

I flop back onto the bed, groaning. It is easier to do my job now that I live several hundred miles from home, but I still have to juggle the lies and half-truths, and to say it isn't exhausting would be another lie.

I lay my fifth option of clothing on the bed. I glance at my watch. I have another two hours before I am definitely going to be late, and I still need to shower, do my make-up and hair.

My phone buzzes. I pick up, seeing the incoming FaceTime call from Stephan.

I pluck a gem from the bracelet and sprinkle it on my hair before sliding the unlock bar across. Immediately, I am greeted by cheers and all-around happiness. Stephan is chatting to someone, unaware that I have answered the call.

"It's great to see you guys celebrating," I shout, catching his attention. His face lights up when he sees me, taking himself to a more secluded area so we can chat.

"Merry Christmas, Luna," he says.

"Merry Christmas, I see everyone is in the festive mood."

"Yup, it's their favorite holiday. Mom has even got the matching sweaters out." He tilts the camera down so I can see the red Christmas sweater. It has stitching of Christmas lights across his chest and Christmas trees at the bottom.

"Well look at that, you'd make Saint Nick so proud."

Stephan laughs and takes a gulp of his beer. Theresa's hair appears at the bottom of the screen, and soon enough, the phone is in her hands.

"Let me talk to my daughter-in-law," she orders Stephan unnecessarily, as she has already taken command of the phone.

Her attention turns to me as she speaks, "Merry Christmas, Luna, it's a shame you aren't spending it with us."

I pout before sighing.

"I know, I have a meeting with a client, then I'm flying out to Moscow for a premiere of the new year's fashion line, and you know, Theresa, I'm not a big public holiday celebrator, not after..." My voice trails off.

"I know, dear, not after your parents died. It's such a shame they were both only children." Theresa tuts, shaking her head as though she is the reason for my fictional parents' death.

"Don't worry, Theresa, I'm sure they are more than pleased for me for getting you guys as my new family."

"Right you are, Luna, right you are."

Stephan comes into focus, rolling his eyes at his mother.

"Can I speak to my girlfriend now?"

Theresa blows me a kiss before handing the phone back to her son and heading back to the festivities.

"Moscow. Is that where you're heading?" He cocks his brow as he asks his question.

The one thing that I love about Stephan is that he is none the wiser about our arrangement. Thinking he'd been conned by Magenta's promises and ended up finding his dream girl all on his own. He doesn't know who I am when I head home; he is so wrapped up in the person I have made for him that to think I am anyone else is preposterous. Magenta even went as far as to have the money taken out discreetly, so that if anyone, including himself, saw any transactions, it'd be under something as mundane as a purchase or a renewal of a subscription. He and Luna have been dating for three years, and he doesn't even know my name.

"Yes," I reply, "you know, Zaytsev, the name you refuse to pronounce no matter how many times I try and get you to say it."

Stephan laughs, nodding.

"Yeah, I remember, it's that time already? You said in the new year you'd be heading up there."

"No, I said it's for the new year line. Anyway, I have to go and oversee the finishing touches, maybe make some changes." I roll my eyes at the thought. "He's so particular about the smallest details."

"That man stresses you out, doesn't he?"

"He really does, babe."

"I can see you're busy getting packed and everything. Let me know when you touch down, and Merry Christmas. I love you."

"I love you, too." I blow him a kiss, which he catches, holding it to his chest as I end the call.

I pick up a dress off the pile of clothes and bring it into the bathroom as I go to get showered.

Merry Christmas

The door swings open, and I take the gloved hand of the chauffeur as I step out of the car. I hold the golden clutch tightly in my palm, instantly regretting braving the December air with nothing but a dress on.

My heels click on the cold pavement as I hurry to the entrance of the restaurant.

It isn't busy, but then again, it is Christmas Day, so I am surprised it is even open. The front is made out of glass, aside from the wooden sign that says *Qusa* hanging at the front. An orange glow emits from inside. I push the glass door open and step in.

The room has been completely cleared, the tables and chairs swept to either side, and that confirms my suspicions. *This place isn't open.*

"It's open for us, Mae." I turn as Dominic speaks, stepping out from a door. He fixes his cufflinks as he approaches me.

"Why am I surprised that you've rented out this place?" I smile at Dominic as he stands looking down at me, the dim light bouncing off his bright silver eyes.

"I didn't rent it out, Mae, I own this restaurant," he replies.

I cover my mouth in fake shock.

"I wouldn't have ever guessed." I take a step back to get a good look at him.

"You look very nice."

Dressed in a white tailored shirt, Dominic has discarded his suit jacket, revealing the burgundy suspenders.

His suspenders match my dress, a fitted, midi, off-the-shoulder dress with a sweetheart neckline. Complementing the outfit, I had straightened my hair and wore black open toe heels.

"And you look beautiful." He offers me his arm, which I take, and leads me to the solitary table in the center of the room.

As I sit down, soft jazz dances through the room.

"How are you feeling?" I ask, as the waiter lays the starter in front of us: a small bowl of soup with a single coriander leaf in the middle.

"Better." Dominic takes a small sip of the soup before he speaks, "I don't think I ever said it, but thank you for looking after me."

"Well, if you die before the year ends, FolkWore is contractually inclined to refund you." Dominic smiles as he stares, amused by my response.

"But I'd also hate to see you come to such a terrible demise," I finish, bringing the soup to my lips.

"And so, the truth reveals itself."

I raise a brow at him before speaking.

"What truth?"

"The arrangement benefits you and me," he concluded.

"Financially, yes."

"Sexually, emotionally, maybe even mentally."

I dab my lips gently before laying the napkin down.

"I don't mix work with pleasure, Dominic," I say, leaning back in my chair. "It creates problems which I would rather not have."

"I can see your every thought, Mae. I know this situation benefits you."

My eyes narrow ever so slightly and I don't notice that our plates have been taken away. "And pray tell, what do my thoughts tell you?" I ask, holding the glass of white wine to my lips before taking a sip.

"That's it's been a long time since you've been you?"

I set the glass down hastily, the liquid sloshes slightly, and a drop falls onto the white tablecloth.

Dominic takes it as a sign that he's hit something and continues, "that for however long you've done this line of work, no one has asked for you. That if you're not careful, you'll forget who you are, and your deepest fear is what shell of a person you'll be revealed to be when you retire. *If* you manage to get that far."

I place my hands on my lap. Dominic is completely correct; the moment the words leave his lips, my brain shuts down and I want to hunch over and throw up, chuck up all the memories and fears.

I stare at him, forcing those silver eyes to pierce into my mind and pick up the tumbleweeds that are floating around.

"Is that why you bought me for a year? Show me a life where I'm with someone who knows me and loves me?" I reply almost robotically.

"No, I want someone to have my child," Dominic says simply.

A laugh seeps out my mouth before I have a chance to stop it. Dominic's eyes narrow before they soften, and he smiles, his dimples showcasing themselves. I haven't seen him smile like that since we first met.

"That is quite funny, Dominic, but I think you might have struck out with me."

"Why's that?"

"I chose not to have children."

"Chose how? Surgery? Implant?" I see curiosity dancing across Dominic's eyes as he questions me.

"No nothing like that, nothing so invasive. After I passed my training, I was granted a wish."

"Magenta?"

"Magenta. Anything I wanted. Most chose materialistic things, but I was looking at the bigger picture."

"And what was that?"

"That I was in a job where I had to pretend to love people that I don't actually love. My main concern was that all that faking would make it difficult for me to find the real thing. So, I asked Magenta to stop me from getting pregnant unless it was with someone I loved."

"That's a dangerous game, Mae. What if you got pregnant by someone truly horrendous? What if Magenta removes her wish to manipulate you? What if you change your mind?"

"Those are a lot of questions, but it's been doing me well these last few years, so..." I shrug. "Besides, I'm with you for a year. You concerned that I might get pregnant now?"

"No, like you said, you separate work from pleasure. Despite me being both, I'm sure you can manage."

I lean forward onto my elbows as I speak, "So, tell me then, the real reason you bought me for a year."

It is Dominic's time to lean back into his chair. He sits up quickly as the main course is brought to our table: fish on a bed of kale and broccoli. I take a forkful, watching Dominic and waiting for his reply.

"As you know, my companies have come across various problems. Someone is messing with my money."

I watch as Dominic takes a sip of his wine, sighing heavily.

"I'm losing control, and I don't do well when I lose control. So, I need an escape." His eyes capture mine, and his face seems to soften, as though just gazing at me gives him that calm, he needs.

"You're that escape."

"But why me? You could've easily had your pick of any employee. It's a lot of money on a gamble."

"And that is exactly why you. I didn't want to have to think about it. My whole life is surrounded by smart choices and calculated risks. I had the money, so I did it."

I watch as Dominic bends down to retrieve something off the floor. It is a perfectly wrapped box covered in silver paper, decorated with white snowflakes, all with a golden bow on top.

"Merry Christmas, Mae," he says softly, handing the present over to me.

My mouth begins to ache as my smile grows wider.

"You really didn't have to." I try my best to contain my excitement, peeling the paper back delicately and with sophistication. As I tear the first piece off, my eyebrows knit together in confusion. The more I rip, the slightly less confused I get.

"Headphones?" I look at Dominic, then back at the box. In the back of my mind, I thought it would be jewelry, or something...shiny.

"So, I don't disturb you vinyasa again," he replies. My smile returns. This is by far the best present I have received. Jewelry is easy to get someone, but he has actually paid attention to me and bought me something I can use.

I place the box down and lean over the table, placing my lips against his now slightly flushed cheek.

"Thank you, Dominic," I whisper against his skin. I sit down, smiling at Dominic as he returns my smile with his own.

Family reunion

"Way to start the new year," I say, glancing up at the retreating sun falling behind Dominic's house. I hold my bag in my hands, my feet wiggling from inside my heels. The stomach flutters have returned

Having those small two weeks at my house threw me off my game. Sleeping in my own bed, being around my space, and then suddenly having to reintegrate back into someone else's home again is a lot harder than I imagined.

I sigh, slowly heading to the front steps of the house. I open the door and step inside. There is a small temptation to call out for Sybil, like a husband returning from work, but I suppress it.

"And who might you be?"

I turn to the purring voice, facing the lady who has emerged from the library, a martini glass in one hand and a fan in another.

"I am Mae," I reply politely. The lady takes a deep breath in, her eyes shut before opening slowly the dark grey stares at me intently.

"Dominic never said that he had hired a new maid." She tucks a small strand of chocolate brown hair behind her ear as she saunters closer.

"I'm not his maid," I manage to say, somehow my words struggling to leave my lips.

The woman twirls her diamond necklace around her finger, her gaze glazing me over but simultaneously never leaving my own eyes.

"Then who are you, my dear?"

I don't notice her hand caressing my arm softly, moving up and down in small strokes. My body warms from the inside, and there is a strong desire to tell her all my darkest secrets. Confess every desire I ever had and ever will have all at the same time, but just as the warmth reaches its peak, and my tongue rolls in my mouth to tell her everything she needs, the feeling flatlines. Falls off a steep cliff and leaves me extremely cold.

I step back, much to the woman's shock, and grip the handles of my bag tighter.

Did she just try and compel me? Female vampires have a stronger compulsion than their male counterparts, though it works best on the opposite sex. Still, I don't appreciate the invasion.

"I think that'll come better from Dominic," I reply, keeping an arm's length from the woman as I circle around her, heading to the stairs, not even giving her a glance back.

"Mother."

I look to the top of the stairs. A shocked expression is etched onto Dominic's face. I turn back to the woman, who continues to casually fan herself. *Mother?*

"Well, hello, eldest, you did say we'd meet up in the new year," his mother replies, taking a small sip from her glass. Dominic walks down to stand by my side, a possessive arm wrapping itself around my waist.

"I did, but I didn't expect you to come on the first day of the new year. Who let you in?"

"Sybil, of course. Your father and I arrived a few hours ago, and Freya not long after that."

"The whole family is here..."

"We are, and we are about to have dinner. Why don't you and your..." She lets the end of the sentence hang in the air briefly before Dominic speaks.

"My girlfriend. We will be down shortly." Dominic stares at his mother, waiting for her to leave, but instead, she opens her arms.

"A hug for your mother before I go."

I watch as Dominic sighs and pads down the stairs. He pulls his mother into what appears to be a loving embrace, and I take it as my chance to escape.

I stare at the small bedroom, extremely deflated. I already have my reservations on settling back into Dominic's house, but to suddenly be surrounded by more Aldreks is suffocating.

I drop my bag on the floor, pull my hair out from my hair tie, and fluff it slightly.

"I'm sorry."

I turn around to face Dominic, who is pressed against the door.

"You don't need to apologize for your family," I mention, taking a seat on the bed.

"I just don't want you to feel like you've been blindsided. I am as shocked as you are."

"Don't worry. It's not the first time I've had to do a 'meet the family' situation."

Dominic holds out his hand before he speaks. "If you wouldn't mind having dinner with my family."

I take his hand as he opens the door, both of us following the smell of cooked food.

The idea is to appear united as Dominic and I bound down the stairs. It is in this scenario that I wish there were a door, a small separation before we reach his family, but the archway provides no such thing.

There sits his family: his mother and three others.

"Well." The old man stands up, having taken the head of the table.

"How are you, son?" Dominic's father walks towards us, his smile wide as his curled moustache wriggles.

Dominic allows his father to embrace him, his father's cold silver eyes staring intently at me, never once leaving my gaze as they end the hug.

"Mae," Dominic begins, "this is my father, Callahan. You've met my mother, Ada." He places a hand on the shoulder of the female who is sitting to the left of him. She looks up from her phone, brushing some of her honey blond hair out of her face.

"This is my sister, Freya, and her husband, Christopher."

Christopher leans forward, pushing his black-rimmed glasses further up his nose as he gives me a small nod.

"Where's Elsie?"

"She's asleep back at the house. I asked Constance to watch over her while we eat."

Dominic turns to me.

"Elsie is Freya and Christopher's daughter."

"Everyone, this is Mae." Dominic wraps an arm around my waist, leading me to the table so we sit opposite Christopher and Freya.

Sybil walks in with plates of food laid across her arm and serves us all. I sit there, eating my food quietly, trying to disappear into the furniture.

"Right." Dominic's words cut through the silence. "Why are you in my house?"

Callahan drops the napkin onto his empty plate before resting his elbows on the table.

I can see where Dominic got his stern look from. Both of them have decided to let their hair grow. While Dominic's hair reaches his jaw, Callahan's is swaying gently against his shoulders, the salt and pepper color making his tanned skin seem even more striking, with silver eyes that can kill if need be. Unlike Dominic, Callahan has grown out his facial hair, matching the silvery look of his head.

"Should we perhaps discuss this once your lady friend has gone to bed?" His eyes quickly shift to me before returning to Dominic.

"That's not necessary. Mae is aware of everything. She knows I'm a vampire, and she knows that you all are, too. She can sit in on this discussion."

"Be that as it may," Ada begins, pushing her plate aside and bringing her wine glass closer, "She's not family."

Dominic narrows his eyes at his mother, but Freya steps in, subduing the tension.

"Dominic wants Mae to stay, so she will stay. We are going off track here. Dominic, everything is falling apart."

"Your sister is right. The shipping and airline companies that Freya and Christopher manage are being hit by governmental policies. We had that stupid drug incident; your mother has told me that property development is hitting a wall."

"I know this, Father, I'm dealing with it."

"That's not the point. All our companies are being disrupted. This isn't just some coincidence; someone is deliberately messing with my money," Callahan shouts.

"And who could that possibly be?" Dominic asks smugly, "I mean, we are the only people that look after vampires. Without us, they'd have no place to feed, no place to live, and no way to travel. No one would dare ruin that balance."

"Well, the Nazari family weren't shy of our destruction," Callahan points out.

Dominic sits back, sighing.

"I dealt with the Nazari family. They look after the East; we look after the West. That's always been the treaty."

I look between Callahan and Dominic before clearing my throat. All eyes find me, and I can feel the burns from them all.

"It was nice meeting you all." I push my chair back as I speak, rising to my feet. "I'm going to bed." I run a hand over Dominic's shoulder, and he kisses my hand.

"It was lovely meeting you, Mae, I just hope the next time will be in better circumstances," Freya says, giving me a small smile. I leave the dining room, heading for the staircase.

There is a knock at the front door. Usually, I would leave this to Sybil, but seeing as I am less than an arm's length away, I go to the door myself.

I open the door, and there stands a man. He has his back to me.

"And you are?" I ask, getting the man's attention, forcing him to turn around and address me.

The pair of grey eyes are the first thing I notice, well, I always did with Lincoln. Despite how cold they appear, there is a warmth and a sense of humility to them whenever he is on his hands and knees.

The moment Lincoln catches sight of me, he immediately falls onto his knees, kissing the toe of my heels. He caresses the shoe, rubbing my lower leg as he does. I pull my foot away, making him gasp.

"Have I not earned that?"

"You know damn well you haven't," I hiss. I shake my head, forgetting who I am. "Get up, Lincoln."

He rushes to his feet, his head bowed. I pull him in, shut the door, and continue to pull him into the library, closing the door behind us.

"Seraphine wh-what," he stammers.

"Shut up, it's Mae," I correct. Lincoln spins me around, running his hands up under my dress and over my back.

"Your...your wings." His smooth, warm hands remove themselves, and I turn around, fixing my clothes.

It takes a lot for me not to push him away, to tell him to remember his place in the arrangement we have, but that is Lincoln and Seraphine. Right now, I am Mae. But that doesn't mean that when Seraphine next sees him, she won't give him hell. Faery hell to be exact.

This situation could not be any more awkward. I've heard stories of clients knowing one another, but they usually ended up in a foursome.

This is not so steamy.

Lincoln and Dominic have very different requirements of me, and both equally share the same entitled trait that seems to have been engrained since conception with those two.

Lincoln is up for anything and doesn't want me to know more than his first name – not that our situation calls for Seraphine to remember his name. She prefers to call him "pet".

Dominic is very particular in what he wants and articulates it very well. Naturally, I want to know more about him. I don't particularly like mysteries.

"I'm not a faery currently, Lincoln. I'm just me," I huff.

Lincoln grabs my wrist, bringing me close, so I have to tilt my head slightly to look him in the eye.

"Does Dominic...know?" Lincoln whispers.

"About Lara? No, I don't think that should come from me."

"My family already knows about my sexuality. I doubt they'd care if I fuck a trans woman or not. I don't need them knowing that I like to fuck elves."

I yank my wrist from his grasp as the library door swings open. Lincoln instinctively takes a protective stance in front of me.

Dominic walks through, his eyes narrow, as I'm sure he knew who was behind the door well before he opened it.

With the two standing in front of me, I notice the faint similarities: while Dominic looks more like his father, Lincoln and Freya have a closer resemblance to their mother – a darker shade of honey blond.

How did I miss this?

"Lincoln, what are you doing with Mae?"

I move around Lincoln, walking away quickly. As I pass Dominic, he moves to grab my wrist, but I maneuver out of his reach and out the door.

I don't dare to look back as the two pairs of silver eyes watch my retreating figure.

Green-Eyed Monster

Dominic's family has left sometime during my shower, discussing not-so-sporadic problems across their empire. As I come out of the bathroom, my hair wrapped in a towel and another covering my body, the bedroom door opens. I stare at Dominic, who seems to be seething with anger.

With only the bed between us, I see how his eyes have gotten darker around the rims.

"You're my brother's Dom?" He shuts the door behind him.

I fold my arms as I match his stance.

"Lincoln tell you this?"

"Has he fucked you, Mae?"

"That's against compa-" I shriek loudly as Dominic slams both his hands against the wall on either side of my head, closing the distance between us in less than a second.

"Don't," he whispers through gritted teeth. "I spoke to Lincoln. Now I'm asking you."

"No, that's not the arrangement we have," I blurt out.

"Then what is it?"

"He just prefers to watch," I say, finally looking into his silvery eyes.

"Watch what?"

Must I spell it out to you?

Dominic growls, moving closer to me so I can feel his warm breath and thumping heart against my body.

"Lara and I have sex. He likes that Lara is a trans woman. It fulfills his attraction to both men and women. Or it could be because she's an elf." *Shit.*

My confession seems to appease him, and his high shoulders drop to their usual place.

"My brother likes elves? Has he fucked one?"

"I wouldn't know."

Dominic takes a step back, finally allowing me to breathe instead of suffocating on his second-hand air.

"I know my brother isn't picky, but an elf?"

"Many people have that fantasy, Dominic. There's no need to add your little tidbit to it. Your brother likes being submissive, and that's exactly the fantasy that Seraphine provides him."

Dominic grabs me by the waist before I can move away, pulling me against him.

"You may be his Dom, but you're my sub. Understood?" He rips my towel off, discarding it to a corner of the room, showcasing his dominance.

I somehow manage to pry his fingers off my waist. The towel on my head becomes loose and drops to the floor. I have one hand on my chest and another covering my lower half.

"I preferred it when you were ill. This lust-driven arrangement is very unbecoming. Surprisingly, Dominic, there's more to me than a vagina, if you hadn't noticed."

I jump back suddenly as Dominic approaches me. His face has softened, and his strides aren't so aggressive, but my body is on high alert.

Noticing my discomfort, Dominic doesn't approach me further. My eyes watch him like a hawk for any sudden movements.

"I'm sorry," he says. Those two words cause my shoulders to drop from beside my ears. He lifts his hands slowly, gesturing to me for him to come closer.

I nod.

"I said you were my escape, Mae." He tucks a strand of damp hair behind my ear, snaking his hands around my waist, caressing the dips in my hips.

"I don't like the thought of you being anyone else. I know this is your job, but it still hurts."

I let out a heavy sigh before I speak, "the arrangement that we have is exclusive. For the most part, that has been maintained. I wouldn't tarnish that for a quickie in your library." Somehow, I find the courage to look at Dominic, who already has his eyes cast on me.

Something is stirring inside me, whether that be the fact that Dominic, though jealous, shows he cares for me further than our contract, or perhaps it is that his emotions have entirely led this conversation instead of it being behind the composed and calculated responses that he always seems to give me.

He hooks his hands up under my ass, lifting me up to wrap my legs around his waist. As our noses brush against each other, Dominic leans in and kisses me, his mouth already open and his tongue pressing against my bottom lip.

Naturally, my mouth opens, my tongue caressing his as Dominic lays me on the bed. The kiss deepens as we both take a small inhale. Dominic removes his top, our lips immediately melding together the first chance they get.

Beyond the sound of our kiss, Dominic has managed to discard his trousers. Placed between my legs, Dominic moves his mouth, trailing kisses down my face to my neck. As his soft lips press against my neck, I stiffen. Dominic pulls away.

"Does it scare you?" he asks.

I open my eyes, realizing they are closed.

"Not as much as it did before," I whisper, immediately regretting my confession.

"I would never hurt you, Mae," Dominic replies gently. He trails his thumb over the puncture wounds, staring at them intently before his gaze finds mine.

"Trust me."

He leans in, and it takes every ounce of willpower for me not to tense; however, my heart has betrayed me and is firing quicker than it should. Dominic presses his lips again against the scars. Never once do I feel the sharp pain of his fangs penetrating my skin; instead, he continues to kiss the wounds, waiting for my heart to return to an average speed.

He's telling me to trust him. To trust that he'd never hurt me.

As the kisses soften my nerves, they begin to feel pleasurable, every contact sending small sparks across my body. Sensing my calm, Dominic leans towards my ear.

"Open up to me, Mae."

The way my name rolls off his tongue causes a sigh to leave my mouth. My body relaxes into the silk sheets, and my eyes slowly close, my mind removing the restrictions it has surrounding it.

My darkest fears and deepest desires roll out, filling Dominic's mind like a shaken bottle of cola exploding when the lid is opened.

Dominic breathes out slowly, his hands holding my waist as he slides his erection into me, the squelch of my own juices coating him as he pushes, every inch deep and angled.

I whimper as he touches my g-spot, noticing that he has hit the mother lode, Dominic prods the spot again with more conviction than before.

I can feel his smile against my skin as he continues to kiss me, his strokes slow and meaningful. I open my eyes.

"Look at me," I say quietly. Dominic lifts his head and, as our eyes meet, he hits my spot with more force, causing me to arch my back.

I manage to keep my eyes open as his strokes gain speed. Dominic's lips are parted, and his hands are balled into fists on either side of my head, but he maintains his gaze.

As he hits my spot again, I pull him to me, pressing my lips against him as I let out a moan, which Dominic matches.

I gently bite onto his lip, pulling it just enough to cause him to growl and for his strokes to increase. I release his lips only to suck on them. I notice the taste: a silver coat on the tip of my tongue.

Dominic pulls away briefly, swiping his finger across his lip to see a small smear of blood. He looks at it confused for a moment before he looks at me, his eyes dripping with lust and a smile spreading across his face.

I can't help but bite my lip at the sight, a part of me wanting him to punish me at this moment and send me spiraling into an orgasm.

Hearing my thoughts, Dominic takes hold of my neck as he slams himself into me. I breathe out loudly as he tightens his sexual grip around my neck.

His strokes turn from fast to slow and powerful. Each hit is like a quake that knocks me closer to the edge. My eyes try their best to remain open, each thrust rocking me to my core, and the thought of tumbling over the edge has me arching my back.

As I feel the last of my sanity shatter, my eyes open, and I hold his wrists, staring deep into those silver eyes. As the final piece falls, my nails dig into his wrist, the pleasure of the orgasm causing a scream to erupt deep within me, one that has been bubbling away.

I feel Dominic shudder slightly above me, his hold on my neck gone as his own orgasm leaves him breathless.

He rolls over onto the bed, immediately pulling me close so that he can rest his chin on my head. Both of us still soaked in sweat and cum, Dominic pulls the sheet over us as he holds me in his arms.

Functional But Impaired

Rebekah stands outside the wooden door, rotating a cup of coffee in her hands as she contemplates whether to knock, or to wait until someone takes note of her presence and opens the door for her. A part of her still shivers at the possibility of security charging down the hall, shouting at her not to take another step as they realize she has infiltrated the most important place in Seattle.

"Miss Calamba?"

Rebekah turns to the voice.

The slender woman bounds down the hallway, the authority only Naomi could carry. The Asian woman raises her hand, which Naomi gives a firm shake before dropping.

"You're here early. I'm Naomi Drynt." Naomi escorts her inside and opens the door to a small conference room that is bare of any windows or natural light. The room is a beige square of overflowing boxes and paper. Rebekah stares, horrified at the amount of paper that surrounds her, which she is very sure isn't in any efficient order.

Conrad's head snaps up when he hears the door open. He gives Rebekah a dry smile and offers a small nod to Naomi.

"Calamba, I expected you a bit earlier," Conrad says, maneuvering his way around the stacks of papers to approach the women.

"The FBI doesn't just let anyone in," Rebekah replies, stepping into the room and placing her things on a seat that isn't occupied by cardboard and paper. Naomi, refusing to step foot into the stacked chaos, holds the handle to the door instead.

"Conrad will get you up to speed, Miss Calamba. It was nice meeting you, and welcome to the team." With that, Naomi shuts the door, heading somewhere less claustrophobic.

Rebekah looks at the lid of one of the boxes, where *Aldrek Pharmaceuticals* is written in permanent ink.

"We're back on the Aldreks?"

"Not really. I doubt we will find anything useful in these boxes that we wouldn't have found when the task force was created. No, we are working on Mae and FolkWore." Conrad heads to a corner in the room, where stacks of boxes seem to be separate from the rest of the mess.

Rebekah opens the first box, containing pay slips and taxes, an IRS favorite thing to peruse through.

Mae is everything you'd expect of an average citizen, originally born in Seattle, but later moved to England after the death of her father. She has a BA in Fashion Design from a university in Glasgow. Then, she moved to the States, where she was employed by FW.

Rebekah pulls out the death certificate of an Elijah B. Geoffries. He died when she was three, resulting in her mother's move back to the UK. *Mae's got two passports. She is a citizen of both the US and the UK.* Rebekah tuts loudly before turning to Conrad.

"If this transaction is between Aldrek and FW, there's no way we can pressure her to speak. We can't force deportation on her," Rebekah comments.

"I know, and although we have an extradition treaty with the UK, I doubt they'd send their own person over, considering she's more British than American." Conrad huffs from his corner of the room, the wind lifting a few pages near Rebekah.

"We just need to keep looking." As Rebekah is about to put all Mae-related documents aside, she sees a trial and sentence document from the Crown Court.

"Conrad, I have something very interesting in my hands."

As she says this, two large hands reach over and take the sheet from her. Rebekah looks up as Conrad scans the document, a smile taking over his face as he reads it.

"This is a criminal case. It says here that there were two cases parallel to each other. Miss Geoffries was both the victim and the defendant."

"What? How is that possible, you can't be both?" Rebekah argues.

"Well, it happened in this case. She was a victim of sexual assault but was also accused of manslaughter."

"She killed her attacker?" Rebekah asked the obvious question, already knowing the answer.

"It appears so. I'm going to call Scotland police; they should be able to direct us to the officers in charge." Conrad leaves the room, letting Rebekah ponder.

She doesn't know Mae personally, but she has to wonder as to how the girl ended up in this situation. Best case scenario, Mae is everything her employer says she is, ignorant of this whole situation the issues around Aldrek the multiple lawsuits between people and FolkWore. If that isn't the case, then she's going to be in a world of misfortune. Conrad comes back with a post-it note attached to his chest.

"What time is it?" Conrad asks.

"10:27."

Conrad tuts, sitting down in a chair and grabbing the corded phone from the table.

"It's nearly seven in the evening over there. Let's hope this Detective Norton is a hard worker." Conrad presses a few buttons, the sound filling the room. There is a drawn-out silence before it begins to ring.

"Hello. Glasgow police station, how can I help?"

"Hi, this is Agent Grier from the FBI Seattle branch. I'd like to speak to one of your detectives, is Mr. Norton there? Do you need my badge number?"

"If you wouldn't mind."

"1811C1201198G."

The line momentarily goes silent, and the pair think that the lady has hung up right before the line comes back to life with loud coughing and spluttering.

"Detective Norton speaking, what yer want, Agent Grier?"

"I wanted to know about a case you worked on in 2012, the case of Mae Geoffries."

There's a loud, annoyed sigh on the other end. "Ey, of course you're calling about that one. What do you want to know?"

"Everything. What really happened?"

Norton sighs again before speaking. "We weren't made aware of the crime 'til the next morning when Miss Geoffries handed herself over to a local police station in Inverness. It was then we received a call from a jogger who had found the body. I would like to say that it was as simple as tying ya shoes, but when Miss Geoffries said that she was attacked and had no intention of killing the man, I cannae remember the last good rest I had after that."

"What was the story?" Rebekah asks.

"Who is that lass? I thought I was speaking to an Agent Grier?"

"That's my partner, she works for the IRS. Please, Mr. Norton, could you give us the witness's statement?"

A chair screeches from the other end of the line, accompanied by stomping feet. Conrad leans into his chair, waiting for the man to return.

"Still there?" Norton asks.

"Still here, detective," Rebekah replies.

"Mae had finished her shift from a nightclub in Glasgow and was on her way home. Four other guys were on the train and noticed her. From the train's CCTV, we saw the group of men repeatedly try to get her attention, and on one occasion, the deceased attempted to sit next to her and strike up conversation. We had witnesses from the carriage and the Inverness station report that the men were clearly drunk, and that Miss Geoffries was uncomfortable. The CCTV showed all parties getting off and heading out the station. There is one camera on the road by the station. Everything else is based off all parties' testimonies."

"What was Miss Geoffries' testimony?" Conrad asks.

"If I remember correctly, there's an alleyway that cuts behind the station, which Miss Geoffries used to shorten her walk home.

The men followed and continued their advances. When she continued to ignore them, the deceased made physical contact by trapping her against the wall. Miss Geoffries fought back, and that's when the other participants restrained and held her to the ground. Forensics showed that Mae had a bruise around her neck where the deceased had put his knee. There were also more on her abdomen and upper thighs where the group struggled to get her pants off. Miss Geoffries explained that in her panic to get the man off her, she had grabbed a broken bottle, which had cut her hands before using it to stab her attacker in the neck. The others confirmed that once the deceased was stabbed, Miss Geoffries used the momentary shock to escape. They also left the deceased and ran back to their respective homes.

"I told my superiors that I didn't want a circus show of the whole thing. BBC News would be all over the story, and that would bring unnecessary attention to the town. Luckily, a psychiatrist agreed that it would not benefit Mae and her family to be scrutinized by the press, so even though the lass was 18, the judge made a special ruling that her privacy would be treated as though she was underage, even though she went on trial as an adult. The accused and the deceased did not receive the same courtesy.

"Mae was acquitted for the manslaughter charge. Not only was she defending herself, but the jury found that, because she turned herself in immediately, she had no intention of killing the man that night."

"Any mention of a company named FolkWore?" Conrad asks.

There's a pause on the line.

"Ey, there was. They paid her legal fees."

"That's it?"

"Yes, that's it. Anything else?"

The pair can tell that Norton is tired, and irritated, and that his question is rhetorical.

"No, thank you, Detective Norton."

"No problem. That Mae girl was a good kid when I met her, clearly shaken up, but ready for a life sentence if it was handed to her. Whatever she's gotten into, I don't believe it's on her. Have a good night, Agent Grier, and to you too, IRS lass." With that, the phone call ends, and Conrad leans back in his chair.

"Do you believe what he said about Mae being a good kid, and that she just might be the middleman?" Conrad asks, looking to Rebekah. Rebekah thought from both an IRS and a person's perspective.

"I think we'll have to speak to her ourselves, but unfortunately, she's gone into hiding."

How to Bribe the Devil

Mae looks at me as she processes the question again. It is supposed to be a simple question, but Mae has taken it very personally.

"Why?" she asks.

"I want to set a meeting with Magenta. Is it that big of a problem?" I fold my arms, matching her stance by the entrance of her door.

"No, just suspicious."

"To apologize for last month. You never went into detail of what happened after I..." I let the sentence hang in the air, hoping not to finish it.

"I'll call, and if she's free, we can go today. Is that OK?" Mae heads into her room, leaving the door open as she pulls out her work phone from her bag.

"Yes, that'd be OK. Will you have to drive again... again to..." I scratch my head. Suddenly, my memory of when Mae drove is hazy, as though it is covered with a dirty film. She is typing away as I try my best to finish the sentence.

"No client should know the whereabouts of the branches," Mae says, her eyes still glued to her screen. I look up at her. I give it a second for it all to make sense. *I see. Enchantments.*

"Magenta is there, so should I go and get a car for us?" She chucks the phone onto the bed.

"Once you're dressed, sure."

I watch Mae hurry to the walk-in closet, deciding to pair her simple long-sleeved turtleneck dress with a camel-colored trench coat. She picks up her bag, slinging it over her shoulder, and approaches the door.

"Ready to go?" she asks me gently.

"Let's go see Magenta."

I know the place is shrouded in magic and enchantments, but my curiosity of who – more specifically what – Magenta is, only grows. I know of witches or those with an affinity of magic: moon witches, solitary witches, secular witches, cosmic witches. However, Magenta seems to be some, and none, all at the same time.

The crystals that Mae carries on her wrist are bits of her magic picked off and used to magnify the properties of her gems. I have never heard of such a skill, but Magenta seems to have it all.

"Are you coming in, Dominic?"

I notice that I am staring at the *FolkWore* sign, standing outside the store, the new year breeze creating goosebumps across Mae's legs as she waits on me, the door held open. I walk in, and there is a semblance of déjà vu as I enter. I know I have been here, but trying to recall the memory seems fuzzy.

"Mae, back so soon." *That voice...the faery...Clinton.*

"Hi Klaus, you're here again. Don't you have a job?" Mae asks as she places her elbows on the glass table. The male faery stands behind it, tracing small circles on her hands.

"No, it's been quiet for me. I'm half pleased and half bored."

Mae kisses the faery's cheek before nuzzling into it.

"It is your holiday, spend it like Gretchin and sleep."

The new year brings slumber for most Fae who participate, spending the first month rejuvenating and taking time for self-love and preservation, reconnecting with the person who matters the most: the self. I have been told that doing so means better interpersonal experiences in the future.

"Ah, not in this line of work."

Mae rolls her eyes at her friend and takes my hand, heading towards the emerald curtains.

We walk through the hallway, illuminated by small tea lights casting an eerie glow around us. Mae pushes through the other end.

The female faery is nowhere to be seen, so Mae takes me upstairs. The metal clangs as we walk up the stairs to the wooden door.

Before Mae has a chance to knock, the door creaks in.

Just like the first time, there sits Magenta, as radiant as ever. Her hair is clipped to the side, falling into the crevice of her exposed cleavage.

She clasps her hands together, leaning on her knuckles as she watches us enter, her amethyst eyes never once leaving mine.

Mae has to practically drag me in. There is yearning, as well as caution, surrounding her.

"Mr. Aldrek, I heard you wanted to speak to me." Magenta smiles, her pearly whites catching the artificial light. I take a seat in one of the plush chairs. The frilled fabric tickles my neck.

"I hear you have some new members," Mae says, easing the tension that swirls in the room. "Could I go see them?"

Magenta allows her eyes to leave mine and looks to Mae. She smiles.

"Yes, of course. They are with Martel practicing."

"Martel." I notice a spike in her heart rate and peer up at Mae, who is surprisingly grinning. "I'll be there then when you are done." She turns away, leaving us quicker than I imagined possible.

Magenta returns her gaze to me, studying me like a corpse ready to be dissected. I am sure she knows what I am here for. I just don't know how to go about it.

"I came to apologize for last month. Even more so for the poor girl I killed, and, well, you as well." My eyes manage to glance at her neck. It doesn't even have a trace of scarring, not even an indent.

Magenta waves it off, smiling.

"A superficial wound at best, Mr. Aldrek. I understand that the situation must've been very distressing. Seeing Mae like that and finding out her other client is a werewolf. I understand the tension between your kind."

I wouldn't say there is tension; there's just not enough humans for both of us. We need food, they need...well, something.

Werewolves are strange creatures. To think they live their whole lives relying on the orbital position of the moon is hard to believe. Their deity controls whom they fall in love with, have children with – any deviation is a certain painful death.

It seems like a curse they can't escape but make damn certain that every other person suffers because of it. Despite their traditions of the family unit, they are fundamentally prejudiced - if you aren't werewolf, you are second class in most cases.

"I still thought a face-to-face apology would be most suited, and perhaps a gesture of goodwill. A donation of some sorts."

"Are you trying to bribe me, Mr. Aldrek? You must've known that your contract with us is still being maintained. You don't have to worry about any suspensions."

"I understand, and I am grateful. Unfortunately, besides money, there's nothing I can think of to offer you as goodwill."

Magenta pushes out of her chair as she speaks, "Your money has already gotten me into trouble, Mr. Aldrek."

"A Detective Grier has come to see you?" I ask. Magenta rounds the table, showcasing her pink blouse and jeans.

"Followed by his very charming IRS partner." She opens the door, and I stand up. I start walking out and down the stairs.

"That is why we have procedures in place, Mr. Aldrek. Your recklessness will be our undoing if we are not careful."

"Then what can I do to help?"

"Stay away from here if you can. I understand you are trying to make amends for December, but your goodwill might do more harm than good."

I don't want to be indebted to Magenta or feel as though I owe her. Lincoln's words float around my head. *"Magenta is an opportunist if I've ever seen one."*

"Surely this goodwill could be processed through your usual channels?" I ask as we reach the bottom of the stairs.

Magenta seems to be mumbling to herself, leading me down a small corridor to our right. She sighs laboriously.

"Fine, if you insist. We hold an annual event here in Seattle, see it sort of as a staff party and an initiation event for the new ones. If you insist on financial goodwill, you can pay towards that. I'll send you the invoice for the event, which can be paid after your contract with Mae has ended. This will include the death fee."

My ears perk at the death fee.

"Death fee. I thought that was just for escorts?"

Magenta laughs, deep in her belly and patronizing.

"What made you think that she wasn't?" She spins around to address me, "My employees do more than just have sex with people. They need a profession to fall back on, they need to do other things, Mr. Aldrek. First and foremost, I run a costume store. One that is international. I may be the owner, but I need a workforce, I need designers, I need accountants, I need customer assistants, I need an HR department, I need techies that can make the escort business run, and I need doctors who don't ask questions. Why outsource when you can fund and train your own employees? And what I can't fulfill with employees, I get from clients. I do not employ one-trick ponies; I'm not their pimp."

Magenta seems to be brimming with pride. Her business for supernatural beings almost rivals mine dedicated to vampires. She has seen a market and catered to it: one that is three-dimensional and fully self-sufficient.

In any other circumstances, Magenta would be a worthy ally and business partner. Together, we'd monopolize the market and, with her international connections, could begin to control the world.

"So, if you aren't their pimp, what are you?"

"A smart businesswoman." Magenta pauses outside a door. "You have spent an awful lot of money on Mae." Without giving me time to respond, she slides open a door, revealing a dance studio.

Floor-to-ceiling mirrors to the right make the four white-washed walls seem larger than they are.

Mae stands in front of a group of people. They all look human enough, no outstanding features. However, the smells that lift to the ceiling suggest otherwise. A few greens indicate a nature beast; it's hard to distinguish which creature, whether it be an elf, Fae, or pixie, as they smell very similar. A dark blue for a djinn, and silvers for a siren.

There is a rumble in my stomach as I remember the taste.

Mae, like many humans, has a somewhat translucent, smoke-like substance, so hard to see until you're close, and by then, your teeth have found their target. There is the faintest shade of red around the edges. *Her time spent around me is rubbing off.*

Martel, however, is something different entirely. A thick, dark fog emanates from him like a warning not to engage.

I have always been fascinated by demons and their sub-categories, more so the lust demons. Hollywood depicts them and most demons as red, fiery beasts with tails and horns that end in a point, and for that, a lust demon can move around freely, not having to worry about crosses and rosary beads. You wouldn't think that a succubus' or incubus' skin resembles a shattered mirror with sharp, jagged edges – that, I hear, is surprisingly smooth.

I also hear that when you stare into their cloudy eyes, your deepest desire paints itself onto them: a complete reflection of your darkest and most lustful fantasy. That a lust demon finds no satisfaction from the sexual act itself, but the lust and desire that emanates from their prey is an intoxicating aphrodisiac that fuels them right before giving in. Some would even go as far to say that it is the evil acts that their victims do in a bid to gain their own desires. *After all, a demon thrives on evil and sin.*

Martel has a pair of shades on, odd for the indoors, but I overlook it. He pulls at the waistband of his sweatpants as he speaks, "In a few months, y'all will be attending the annual staff party. It's your chance to score some clients and build a portfolio. You'd be surprised by how many clients thrive on inexperience. You'll be expected to learn the dance routine for our showcase performance, aside from your usual dance practice."

The group mutters to each other. A sense of uncertainty clouds above them.

"Don't allow Martel to worry you," Mae says, her voice both calm and reassuring. "The first party is daunting, but you're there to enjoy yourself, meet some of the other guys, make money and build a portfolio. The clients will not be sampling any goods at the party, so your main objective is to be aesthetically pleasing, sell yourself for a good year ahead."

"Martel," Magenta whispers, "he's our Seattle branch dance teacher, teaches the new ones to be flexible and rhythmic. Mae is his partner when a client asks for couples."

Anyone beside Mae would instantly become as radiant as she is. There is a light in her that refuses to be extinguished, one of the things I li-

"We should get going, Magenta," I say quickly.

Magenta nods before clearing her throat, catching the groups' attention.

Mae looks to me, nodding slightly before giving Martel a side hug, who in turn kisses the top of her head.

Mae waves at the group before skipping over to us.

"Everything sorted?" she asks.

"Almost," Magenta begins, "I think it's wise if Mae makes the outfits for your event, Mr. Aldrek. I have no doubt that the FBI and IRS will continue to keep tabs on you well after the contract has ended. At least this way, we have physical evidence to uphold our claims."

"FBI, IRS. This is the first I've heard of this," Mae says, her voice a little higher than usual.

"No need to worry, dear, Mr. Aldrek and I have kept it contained, but this would help the situation greatly. At least if they catch up to you, Mae you won't be blindsided."

"That is fair. I'll start preparing when we get home." Mae looks to me for confirmation.

"Yes, I think that is wise."

Magenta hums a response, and we take that as our opportunity to leave.

An Opportunity Arises

"**M**ae..." *My eyes focused onto the creased dark brows in front of me.*

"Huh," I replied, as Leo sighed heavily.

"In light of what's happened, I want you to take the rest of the month off, maybe even 'til the trial ends. Full pay, of course." Leo twirled the pen between his fingers before tapping the tip onto the paper. It was my contract, he perhaps read over it before deciding whether they could afford to pay me during everything.

"Why?" I whispered. Half to myself and half to whoever bothered to listen. Social distancing was the last thing I needed.

"I live ten minutes away. I moved so that I wouldn't have tha-... this problem again."

This was a half-truth. I moved because I couldn't bear being near that alleyway again, let alone have to travel through it. I moved because I wanted to distance myself from it, albeit in doing so, I distanced myself from my mum. Though I earned just about enough to pay for a caregiver, it was still very much just her at home.

My mother thankfully didn't argue with me. I wasn't sure whether it was because she could see how broken I looked or that she'd been persuading me for the last few months that I needed to start thinking about my life and not worry about hers. Having her own caregiver meant that some of the burden would be lifted.

Leo pushed his hands towards me with all the intention of being comforting but retracted them in the last moment, afraid that it'd be too soon for me to be touched by the opposite gender. "

I know, but head office believes you need time to heal away from any triggering places, and this is one of them."

"I like being here." I felt like I was whining. Somehow, I had convinced myself in two seconds that I was being childish, that if I had been more vigilant and careful, I wouldn't be in this mess.

"You were attacked, Mae." The words stung, and I could feel a warm sensation in my throat. Bile? Blood? The feeling of a knee being pressed down on my neck.

"Two weeks ago. You need time to...process."

This meeting was not debatable; Leo was merely informing me of a decision that had happened several days ago. He just gave me the courtesy of doing it face-to-face rather than in a poorly written text.

"Sure." I stood up, holding my things in my arms. I knew I should've been more concerned when I came in this evening. The hush in the staff room, the dense cloud that seemed to drench the entire place.

I opened the door out of his office.

"When this is all done, Mae, we can get back to normal."

What is normal, if not a false sense of hope?

The door creaked open, and I snuggled further under the covers, trying to appear asleep. It was four in the morning, and the sun was beginning to rise, marking the start of summer. I had been staring at the growing lines of light for the last ten hours, seeing the transition between night and day through the layers of a fluffy duvet.

"Work was shit if it's any consolation. No big spenders today."

I remained silent, trying to uphold the assumption I was asleep. A body slumped against me before limbs started to wrap around me.

"There was nothing in the dishwasher. You either tidied up after yourself, or you haven't eaten." Dark blue hair brushed against my forehead as Adele placed her head on top of mine.

"Talk to me please, Mae, even if it's to say that I'm being annoying."

I rolled over, pushing the covers down as I spoke, "Of course, this had to happen to me. I should've just moved here from the start to avoid the whole commuting. I mean what the actual fuck was I thinking, I mean money alone, nearly half my wages were on traveling."

"Living in the center of Scotland is bloody expensive, babe," Adele replied.

"You do it just fine," I countered, and that was true. A two-bedroom apartment in Glasgow was pricey, and Adele had a luxury apartment: two bedrooms, one ensuite, a balcony, parking. She was living the dream.

"And you do it on a part-time wage. My mum couldn't help me the way your parents do. You know our situation."

Adele pulled away from me. I looked to her to find her biting the inside of her cheek.

"My parents don't help, Mae, they have their own bills to pay. I work two jobs."

"I thought you were studying?"

"That too."

"I know student grants don't pay enough."

"They don't, true, but my other job does. It's fun, and I enjoy it. If you are so concerned about money and the trial coming up, then I can ask my manager if we have any openings. Maybe you need a change of scenery, to start again somewhere fresh once everything is all done."

I thought about it for a while. Adele, noticing she had made an impression, got up off the bed.

"I'll set up the meeting. You can decline if you want when you get there, but at least you have the opportunity to do what you want," Adele said.

I fell back onto the bed, and Adele took a seat next to me.

"What happened to you was inexcusable, and how you reacted was just. I know you're worried, with the trial, your mum, and everything. I don't get it, but I get it. You got me, you know that, right?"

I opened my eyes, sighing heavily. Adele was my closest friend since I moved to Scotland. Meeting her at the bar was the only reason that I decided to continue working there. Her energy transpired through her bright blue hair, a contrast to her pale skin and smoky orange eyeshadow.

I should've listened to her when she said I could move in with her the first time.

"You're right. I need to take control of this situation. There's a good chance I won't find any employment after this. If you could set up an interview, at least I can get ahead of it."

"Anything for you, babe." Adele slid off the bed, pulling her phone out of her back pocket. "Now, the real important question." I sit up. "Pizza or Chinese?"

Tailored to Your Needs

"**H**ow many properties do you own?" I ask, as my shoes hit the concrete stairs.

"Just two. This one is mainly for when I'm designing clothes. My other place is my home. You'll notice I too have a bag."

"Yes, I noticed." I swing her duffle, touching her calf. Mae laughs, glancing over her shoulder.

"Don't be so childish." She smiles at me. "We are here." Mae kneels on the floor, feeling around the iron door for something. She slides a part of the metal aside, reaches her hand in, and pulls out a silver key.

"You don't keep the keys on you?" I can't help my shocked tone. Mae, however, does not seem bothered at all and dusts her knees as she slots it into the lock.

"No, I'd most definitely lose it that way. Besides, I have cameras." She points in several different directions before continuing, "so no one has successfully broken in." She pushes open the door, not explaining her choice of words.

I can only assume that while nobody has successfully broken in, they do try.

"Hopefully, if Klaus did his job, someone should've come over, dusted, and filled the fridge." Mae pushes the door further to let me in.

This place is way better than her other loft. It is a sanctuary.

The kitchen is directly to my right. It consists of a high table, a few bar stools, and a bowl glistening with fruit. To my left is a small two-seater sofa. There is no TV, just a fireplace and two tall bookcases, one filled with book while the others decorated with small ornaments. The stairs are behind the sofa and lead up towards what seems to be some sort of greenhouse. There are only three windows in this room: two at the back wall nearest the kitchen, while the other is a skylight directly above the glass room. I can make out mannequins in a corner. *That's her designing room.*

"Do you want to continue staring, or should I show you around?"

I laugh, taking my eyes off the glass room, and turn to Mae, who is standing near the windows.

I carry our stuff, heading towards her and past the stairs. It is there I notice her bedroom.

It is simple: a king size bed covered in muted pinks and off-white. With the exposed brickwork, the room is elegant yet straightforward. Mae doesn't have a bedside lamp like her other place but instead a tall floor lamp in a corner.

The entire loft has wooden laminate flooring, topped with a fluffy coffee-brown color rug.

Mae takes the bags out of my hands and chucks them on the bed.

"The bathroom is through there." She points to an open archway to our left. "Feel free to shower whenever." Mae checks her watch, biting her lip. "However, I have to do your suit and design some outfits for the event before the weekend is up." Mae kicks off her shoes and pulls off her dress. She takes out a pair of socks from behind her pillow on the bed and slips them on.

"Take off your shoes, relax. We will be here for a while."

"You work like this?" I ask.

She peers down at her underwear – a matching set of lavender. "Usually, I wear nothing. This is a compromise. I need you to stay focused. I can't have you attacking me every time I bend over."

"Who said I won't do that regardless?" I reply, causing Mae to roll her eyes, a hint of a smile playing on her lips.

"Come on, Dominic." Mae leaves me to the room. I shrug off my jacket and take off my shoes. As I leave the room, the floor feels cold. However, I feel the vibrations of the indoor heating kicking in.

I head up the stairs to the glass room. It has just gone past midday, and the light streams in through the room. *No wonder she wants me to hurry up; she's working against the sun. Once it sets, she's done, and that'll be in a few hours.*

I walk through the exposed entrance. Mae is already flustered. She has tied her hair up using an array of fabrics to keep every strand out of her face. She is mumbling to herself, looking over a small booklet of diagrams.

"Please stand in front of the mirror." She wiggles her finger at the full-height, curved mirror near the center of the room. There is a small, raised platform, and I move to stand on it. Before both feet rest on the platform, Mae is behind me, tape measure in hand. She strokes my back before sliding the tape measure across one shoulder to the other.

"Talk to me, Mae. You seem stressed, tell me what you are doing."

"20 inches, shoulder-to-shoulder."

I hear a screech as Mae drags a small stool around to the front, between me and the mirror. She stands up now, several inches taller than before, crouching slightly. She places the tape measure somewhat under my Adam's apple and wraps it around.

"14.5 inches, you have a small neck."

"And your breasts are uncomfortably close to me. I have this unnerving urge to attack you." I smirk at Mae, who in turn raises a brow before going to measure my chest.

Her overall measuring is rather efficient. It doesn't take longer than ten minutes before she moves the stool to her desk, one overlooking the rest of the loft.

Mae pats the stool next to her, signaling for me to sit. I sit down and gaze at her roughly drawn figure with my measurements in the appropriate places.

"A suit is a suit. The creative comes for the different designs. I'm think single breasted, notched lapel When's the event?"

"Late next year, I'll need to talk to my father. The colder seasons though for sure."

"Then a three-piece suit would be the best direction. It has the additional layer from the vest, and I think it's more formal than a standard two-piece. Modern design as well will look good on you. Any particular material? I was thinking velvet providing it doesn't rain. I think it'll look quite nice."

"Isn't that very high school prom?" I ask. Mae bites the end of her pen, thinking.

"Yeah, you're right. However, wool will be far too warm when you get inside and...well...I fucking hate corduroy."

"Why?"

"Because she's a bitch to sew, which is ironic because I think we will have to go with tweed. I say black, you can't go wrong with that. Now the inner lining, I was thinking that's when we could add some color." Mae gets up from her stool, hurrying to a floor-to-ceiling shelf with rolls of fabric.

They aren't large rolls but tiny sample sizes. About a hundred, all separated by color then organized by shade: dark to light.

"I was thinking an emerald color, but it stands out so much I don't think I could make the vest emerald in good conscience. So, I might just do the inner lining, a small pocket square and tie to go. What do you think?"

My lips slide to the side before I say, "I think it sounds tiring."

Mae huffs, which makes me smile. What I am looking at is Miss Mae Geoffries the designer, a very good one at that. She seems to know what she wants and what she is doing, and her passion and excitement make her even more alluring. I don't want to slow her process down with my own inexperience.

"Time, Dominic?"

I glance at my watch. "Just gone past one."

Mae zips past me, running down the stairs. I hear shuffling in the bedroom before she is back up the stairs. Her dress is on, and she is wearing pink sandals.

She pulls one of the green tubes down before pulling out a pair of scissors from thin air and cutting the fabric haphazardly.

"I'll be back in twenty minutes." She zips out again before coming back in suddenly. "You don't have any money, do you...

actually, never mind." And like that, she is gone, a small breeze left in her wake, and the slam of the door.

I'm not exactly sure what happened, but it makes me smile. *She's oddly chaotic. It's cute.*

The sun is warm in here. With the glass everywhere, it could almost be a greenhouse. I pull off my sweater and chuck it into a corner of the room. *I think I will take her up on that offer of a shower.*

My hand slides over to her sketchbook. I flip the pages near the end of the book. They are decorated with similar drawings, pieces of fabric cut off and stuck. Incomplete sentences orbit each drawing, and then there is a photo of the completed piece, taken in this room with Mae standing smiling next to it.

Each page is a different version of Mae. Sometimes, her hair is shorter, other times, it is straight, and in all of them, the woman is stark naked, proud as a newborn baby without a care in the world, in the most revealing of poses. As I peruse her work, I notice that Mae seems younger and has finally put on her clothes.

As I near the end – or rather the beginning – the background changes from this loft to another significantly smaller room.

I continue flicking through. The background changes again, and there I notice the first piece.

A woman is being held up by two men. Her wedding dress flows down her body and pools on the floor in white elegance. The woman has her back to the camera, but her salt-and-pepper curls are no different from the photo I had seen in the newspaper. Mr.s. Geoffries on her wedding day. Mae is in a pale purple flowy dress, and she has her thumbs up to the camera. *Her first piece was for her mother.*

I stroke my hand over the page, noticing patches of rougher paper, small little blotches near the bottom of the page. *She cried? When she made it? Or when she stapled the picture in? Both?*

The door slams and I scramble to put the book back where I found it. Mae is as quick as ever, aside from the crashes and bangs followed by a string of curses. It isn't long before she is running up the stairs.

I swivel on my chair as Mae huffs, holding her chest.

"You OK?" she asks as she chucks me the plastic bag. I catch it and drop it on the table.

"I should be asking you that. Did you run to raise awareness or something?"

"No, there's a fabric store one block down, and the woman comes from Spain and still siestas."

"Siestas?"

"For a guy who travels a lot, I'm surprised you don't know. She closes shop between two and five PM. I mean, by 5:30, she'll open for about an hour, but I'm racing against the sun. Anyway, I got the fabric. We can go there tomorrow to pick up the buttons and zippers."

Mae seems to glide over, unloading the folding streams of fabric: one black, the other emerald. She was right to only do the lining green, because I couldn't in good conscience wear that color as a vest. Subtlety is my thing.

She lays the black fabric out before heading to a filing cabinet next to her bookshelf of fabrics. She takes out a few sheets of thinly crumpled paper and smooths them out on top of the material.

"These are the pattern pieces. I'll have to cut them out, taking into account your measurements, and then I can sew. Do you know when the sun is setting?"

I pull out my phone, ignoring the hoard of emails, and open the weather app.

"3:30. It's not a lot of t-"

"Shush, I can do at least half today."

I purse my lips, a smile growing. I can only imagine this is how I am at work, highly motivated and scarcely deterred.

Mae pulls out a little chalk piece from a small flowerpot on the table and begins tracing.

Curry and Conversation

"**D**ominic..." I hear a rumble of Mae's stomach before she can finish her sentence. I check my watch; it is 3:34, and the red and orange of the setting sun are casting a hurtful hue around Mae, who is working tirelessly at her sewing machine.

While the sun still shines, she has managed to lay one side of the jacket against my frame to see whether the color is right – not that she has much of a choice if it isn't.

"Do you know how to cook?" she asks, the whirring of a needle piercing fabric slightly drowning her voice.

"I do. Hungry?"

Mae nods. "There's food in the fridge, with a recipe card somewhere on the counter." Mae looks up, her eyes big and dilated. "Would you mind?" She seems almost tearful at the potential rejection. I can see she is trying to work out whether she actually needs food if I decline her proposal, or whether she could just eat at midnight.

"Not at all." I get up off my stool, pick my sweater up off the floor, and leave Mae to her sewing.

Klaus has done a good job. The fridge is stocked with food, enough for the two days we'll be here. I close the door and see the recipe cards on the counter.

Prawns and broccoli stir fry, or lamb and lentil curry? Well, they'll both get eaten. It's just a case of when. I slide the recipe card for the stir fry aside. Mae seems very hungry, and I don't want to waste time deveining prawns.

I go in search of the ingredients, then get a frying pan and pot *Add lamb, onion, and garlic, and fry.* I pour a bit of oil in the pan and set the heat on low, then dice the lamb, onion and garlic, placing them in a small plastic bowl. I empty it into the pan, grab a wooden spoon, and coat the food in oil.

Add the curry paste to the lamb, then the tomatoes and lentils with water and salt.

I give the pan one last stir and watch the sauce bubble and pop.

"Smells nice."

I turn around to find Mae in an oversized shirt. The greenhouse is as dark as ever. With the sun retired for the day, so has Mae.

"Are you finished, then?" I pour in the tin of tomatoes, stirring the contents as I wait for her answer.

"After dinner. My stomach is getting agitated." Mae takes a seat on one of the stools, resting her head on her hand. "What's on the menu?"

I pick up the recipe card and flick it towards her.

"Lamb and lentil curry. I don't know why Klaus struggles with a simple pasta dish."

"You should see the food for tomorrow. I hope you like labor."

"I've got seamstress cramp," Mae whines as I place the lid on the pot.

"Would you like a massage also, Miss Geoffries?"

Mae holds her chin in deep thought. "I think that would be asking too much of you." "Dinner's ready," I say, turning off the heat.

"Salad?" she asks.

I open the fridge and check her salad drawer to find a fully prepared bag of mixed-leaves salad, emptying into the bowl.

Mae sits down, licking her lips, and I take a seat next to her. She puts her hands together.

"'Ai.' She reaches for the food.

"What was that?" I ask.

She frowns before saying, "What was what?"

"The hand thing, the word that came out of your mouth."

Her eyebrows dip before she makes an *o* with her lips.

"It's this thing my stepfather does. It means eat. Sorry, being here, I slip into old habits."

I purse my lips before bringing my hands together.

"'Ai.' I glance at Mae, who is smiling and nodding.

"Well pronounced," she says.

We dish out our food, digging in as though neither of us has eaten in days. "This event, aside from hearing about it yesterday, I don't really know much else. It'll help me if I understand who I'm catering for."

I lay my fork down before taking a gulp of water to wash down the food. "It's hard to explain without telling you everything about... well, everything I do and how it benefits people."

"If it's not too much trouble," Mae replies.

"There are four main sectors which Aldrek has an interest in: nightlife, travel, property, and medicine. Each industry is specifically designed to cater to vampires. My father started with just medicine; mostly blood. Best way to get it, store it, and distribute it. However, it's hard to explain why a company only focuses on that field, so that eventually became a small branch in the medicine sector.

"We couldn't just focus on ourselves if we wanted to hang around humans, so we opened the industry to anything medical-related: vaccines, hospital improvements, medical equipment, sponsoring hospital universities, and some international aid.

Once a year, we have a charity ball. Last year, we did an auction, and the money went to children in Brazil. This year, we want guests to buy some clothes and other one-of-a-kind items. Aside from you, we have Jeff Koons making a few paintings, Aston Martin has agreed with us to make a replica of the car they'll be preparing for the new James Bond film; and Tiffany's has given us roam of the staff and store in Seattle with a spending spree of $100,000," I explain.

"Well, paired against all those other gifts, mine don't seem nearly as fancy."

"Those are the big three. We'll have smaller gifts fluttering around. Your outfits will be the only thing of clothing available."

"Big expectations, Dominic."

"I'm sure you'll exceed them."

Mae smiles. However, there is a weighted look in her eyes from what I just told her.

"So, the other sectors of your empire?"

"Yes, as my siblings and I got older, the primary responsibilities were handed to me. By that time, my father had expanded the business into property. While it's great to be able to supply vampires with blood, it's also good if they have somewhere to live, a place where we don't have to worry about wandering humans and nosey realtors.

"We started off small, an apartment complex here and there. Then, as we got more money from the medical sector, we invested it into property going from apartments to small, gated communities to now, where we rival Beverly Hills. Ten houses to a community, and on average, four communities to a state. We have a share in most major water, gas and electric, and internet companies. We try to keep as many problems in-house as possible.

"My mother and father moved to Bali, revealing another potential market: travel. A travel company with our own fleet of planes for families and couples who don't want the stress of long-haul flights being surrounded by humans or other supernatural creatures. Especially with hungry and young children on board. Opening vampires to a private airline meant that we opened conversations with other countries, which naturally expanded our property and medicine sectors. Freya manages that sector. She's a stay-at-home mom, so traveling with Elsie to different countries works well for them both."

"And Christopher?" she asks.

"He's a pilot, so they are all on the move together most times."

"That's cute, but surely you must have the odd human who travels with you. I mean, how do you make something exclusive but open to the public at the same time?" Mae asks.

"We do. They get bumped to premium X. Kept away from the other passengers."

"That's very generous of you."

"Privacy is very expensive, Mae," I mention casually.

"So, nightlife?"

"Nightlife is fairly new and actually the only sector that isn't exclusive to vampires. It's just a venture that we thought would look good on the overall company. Lincoln handles the main club here in Seattle, and then we are shadow partners for a few restaurants in Seattle. I didn't want to focus too much on nightlife, so those restaurants are run by our partners. We have a 40% share in the businesses, so I don't really see a need to be breathing down their necks unless I have to."

"And that family you mentioned at dinner?"

"The Nazari family? They handle the Eastern side of the world. I keep out of their business; they keep out of mine. We had a falling out in 2011 as my father stepped back from company duties, but I was able to smooth it out with them. Keep the peace, and ultimately keep the money flowing."

"What is your net worth, Dominic? You must be on Forbes' list by now?"

"Me personally, 1.7 billion. However, Aldrek is 30 billion as of last March."

"How long has the company been around?"

"Well, my father likes to say we've been in the business for as long as time." I roll my eyes, which earns me a smile from Mae.

"However, we started up officially 1973. My father took a step back in 2010, then in 2012, I became his successor. April 15th, the day I turned 21."

Mae jumps off her chair and loads the dishwashers with our plates.

"That was quite the bedtime story, Dominic. You always hear how self-centered some creatures can be, human and supernatural alike. Though it was purely for a business venture, it's nice to think you haven't forgotten about us."

"Need help?" I ask.

"You could put the rest of the food in a few containers. Bonnie will want to try some."

"Bonnie?" I do as I am told, emptying the food into some containers I find in a cupboard.

"The woman who owns the fabric shop. Seeing as I didn't pay her and I asked if she could open tomorrow for me, I'll need something besides you to make it worthwhile."

"Besides me?"

"Well, when I said I was making a suit, Bonnie insisted on details. Though she's legally blind without her glasses, she's uncomfortably perceptive. She worked out that it was someone close, certainly not a friend, but not quite a husband."

"What did you tell her?"

"That it was for my boyfriend, and then I ran out of the shop." Mae's hip bumps the dishwasher, closing it shut before turning it on.

I wipe down the surfaces, and Mae ties the bin bag and leaves it by the door.

"We are at titles then, are we?" We are both heading to the bedroom, and Mae swivels on her feet to face me as she walks backwards, much like she did the first time we met.

"I am merely following your lead. I think you'll remember you placed the title of girlfriend on my head."

I switch off the lights to the kitchen. The whole room suddenly succumbs to darkness before Mae switches on the lamp in the corner.

"It's an easier explanation than the girl I bought to drink her blood and fuck."

"Whatever sounds better to your ears, Dominic Aldrek."

"You're blowing this way out of proportion, Mae." I grab my bag, holding it over my shoulder. "I'm going to take a shower."

"Do you need me to wait outside the door in my fuck-me shoes?" Her voice tingles the tips of my ears as though she is whispering it, and her alluring jasmine scent wafts up my nose. I grin and turn to see Mae has discarded her clothes and is standing with hands on her hips.

I lick my lips as my eyes trail over her skin, flecks of light making it glimmer in some places. The hourglass frame that dips and rounds in all the right places, the perfect shape for my hands.

"As my *girlfriend*, you can do whatever you want."

I walk into the bathroom and turn on the shower. I feel relaxed, aside from talking about the company. I haven't once reached for my phone. A part of me wants to see what has gone on in my absence, just to make sure everything is fine, but I disregard the thought.

I switch off the water and wrap a towel around myself before heading out of the steamy room.

There, snuggled under the covers, is Mae. I get dressed for bed – a pair of boxers – and slip in next to her.

"Goodnight, *boyfriend*," Mae whispers before rolling over to the other side.

I lie back onto the pillows sighing heavily, a huge smile on my face.

Perception is Key

"**Y**ou piece of shit."

I laugh into the pillow before throwing the sheets off my body and grabbing my trousers.

I head out of the bedroom, stretching. I see Mae above me sitting at her sewing machine trying to tackle the bastard tweed fabric.

"How long have you been up?" I ask as I ascend the stairs.

There is a large bowl on her drawing table, next to a cup of coffee.

"Since the crack of dawn. However, I've only been tackling this little bastard for...time?"

I pull out my phone from my pocket. The black screen stares at me.

"Battery's dead, sorry." I put it back in my pocket, writing a mental note to charge it at some point.

"Well, I'm going to say 16 'you piece of shits' ago."

I sit down, taking a piece of fruit out of her bowl.

"And how much have you completed?"

Mae takes a pencil from behind her ear and chucks it to her left, hitting a partially dressed mannequin.

"I've done the jacket, but you'll need to put it on so I can see if it needs adjustments and whatnot. Argh, you piece of shit." She rolls her eyes.

"17."

Trying to be as helpful as I can, I lift the jacket off the mannequin and carry it to the platform. I pull it on. Mae is still missing the buttons, but the overall fit is damn near perfect.

The fabric is soft like wool, but I don't feel weighed down by the tweed. It has an emerald silk lining with an inside pocket.

I pull the two ends together as though there is a button to see whether the front is the right shape and fit.

"Well..." Mae is biting her bottom lip as she peers around me to see my reflection in the mirror.

"I think after this, you'll have to become my tailor."

She smiles, taking a quick tour of the suit, flattening it against my body.

"I haven't made a suit in ... well, actually not since uni."

"So only a few months ago." I smile.

"I wish. I'm 26 years old this year, so four years ago. But I'm surprised I still got it." Mae helps me out of the suit jacket and puts it back on the mannequin before getting the fabric that is sitting beside the sewing machine and placing it against my waist. "Seems like I got the length right. Hopefully by lunch, I'll be able to get the trousers on you, and then I should be done by dinner." Mae grabs her phone. "It's just gone nine. I don't want to annoy Bonnie by showing up late on a Sunday. You free to come with me now?"

"As your sweetener?"

"Well, of course. Bonnie doesn't just open the shop for anyone."

"I guess I can lend a hand."

Mae grins and skips ahead of me downstairs to put some clothes on.

I sit on one of the chairs as I wait for Mae to get dressed, twirling my phone on the marble tabletop.

"Ready."

I glance up and see her dressed in a mid-length khaki sweater with a puffy turtleneck and flared sleeves. She has a plaid green hair band holding her hair back. At the bottoms of her long legs are ankle-length Chelsea boots. *She looks absolutely stunning.* I feel underdressed in nothing but some sweatpants and a sweatshirt.

"Dominic?" Mae's head is tilted as she watches me gawk at her.

I jump to my feet. "Ready."

Mae follows behind me as we leave her place. She pulls the iron door shut, locks it, and places the key back in her inconspicuous slot in the door.

She takes my hand, and our fingers interlink. She rubs her finger in between my knuckles as we step out into the cold February air.

Bonnie's shop is nothing exciting. Sandwiched between a small Starbucks and a laundromat, the italic, white cursive writing fits across the top. There are bars across the window, and the lights aren't on.

"Are you sure it's open?" I ask.

"It's open for us. Sound familiar?" Mae wiggles her eyebrows as I roll my eyes. She rings the doorbell, and a piercing *buzz* vibrates through the small shop.

Mae rocks on her heels as we wait. A light switches on and a small, hunched woman emerges from somewhere in the back. Her little hands clasp together as she shuffles towards us. She seems tired, but as she lifts her head and sees us on the other side of the glass, her movements are bit more purposeful.

Bonnie is mumbling something as she unlocks the door, opening it up to us.

"Hola, Mae."

"Hola, Bonnie."

"And who..." she lowers her thick spectacles to get a look at me. "Is this?"

"Dominic, the man I told you about."

"Oh, the boyfriend." She pulls open the door to let us in. Mae takes my hand and leads the way, allowing Bonnie to close the door behind and shuffle forward.

"You left quite quickly, *Mija*. I did not know it was for a *lechón*."

I don't know much of other languages aside from the basic greetings, but I have heard *vampire* enough through various languages to pick up the familiar tone of disdain. I narrow my eyes at the elderly woman. She has an earthy brown surrounding her, one I have not seen before.

"Ah, Mama." Mae has adopted a Spanish accent as she speaks, "so perceptive, Dominic is not like most vampires." She turns to me and smiles. "He's kind. Bonnie here is a ball-dòrain."

I raise a brow at the word.

"Don't confuse him with technical language."

I step back as Bonnie moves towards me.

"I'm a mole. We are rare and few."

"Why did you move to Seattle?" I ask gently, worried that if I speak any louder, her race may go extinct.

"It's cold and dark." Bonnie claps her hands. "Now, *Mija*, I'd like to go back to bed. What do you need?"

"Buttons and zippers."

"Come, come then."

Mae drops my hand and hurries behind the shuffling woman. I decide it is the wisest decision to sit on the small chair by the counter while the women work, placing the plastic bag filled with last night's dinner on the table.

I hear their low voices from the other side of the room somewhere near the cufflinks and zippers.

Who would've thought I'd spend my February at someone else's house? I rack my brain for why I insisted on accompanying Mae to her house.

Besides the measurements and the fitting, which could all be done in one night, there is no need for me to be here, and yet I'm here in downtown Seattle letting a ball-dòrain supply my suit.

I am so used to high-quality and expensive suits, yet Mae's suit will be the best suit I've owned. I trail my finger over the dust coating the table and rub it between my fingers.

"*Mija*, you brought me food?"

I turn as Mae and Bonnie emerge from the rows of fabric. Mae has a small brown bag filled with her treasures.

"I did not cook, but yes. We brought you food."

Bonnie rounds the counter, opens the bag, and smiles at us. She reaches over and grabs my cheeks, pinching them delicately. "What a kind little boy you are."

I rub my cheeks, feeling warmth grow on the tips of my ears. "Mae said you don't usually open on a Sunday."

"Well, Mae is the owner of the shop. I just run maintenance and look after the occasional customer. She's kind enough to let me live downstairs."

I turn to Mae, who is trying her best to not feel embarrassed.

"I think it's a fair trade, Bonnie." Mae fishes in her small bag, pulls out a few notes, and hands them to Bonnie.

"And, on the rare occasions she does pay, she pays way too much." Bonnie takes the three 100 dollar bills and opens the cash register.

"It's a balance, is it not, Bonnie?" Mae goes around the counter and hugs the small woman, nestling her hair into Bonnie's greying waves.

Bonnie smiles, holding Mae's arm before turning around and holding Mae's face between her hands and kissing each cheek.

"Take care, *Mija.*"

"You too, Mama." The two let go, and Mae comes to my side, holding my hand and leading us out the door.

"You take care of my *mija.*"

I glance over my shoulder to Bonnie, who has a stern but soft gaze on me. "I wouldn't have it any other way, Bonnie."

With the door to the fabric store shut, I take the bag off Mae and carry it in one hand while the other holds hers, my finger running over the back of her hand.

"I didn't know you own the store," I say as we head up the street.

"Bonnie is just exaggerating. She's the only fabric store for miles. I just have a share in her business to make sure it stays open. I encourage the other designers to buy from her when we can, and luckily, I get a discount from the suppliers we use at work."

Stepping back into the loft is a welcoming sight; winters are always cold in Seattle, and this one seems like an unusually cold one.

Mae is quick to undress, heading straight to her sewing room, making the most of the sun for the next few hours.

think I will make some breakfast.

Making is a bit of an overstatement as I pull the bread out of the bread bin and place two slices in the toaster.

I lean down as I survey her coffee machine. It is the same brand as the one at home. I attempt to make a white americano.

The toast jumps from the toaster, and I place it on my plate. I take the toast and cup of steaming coffee upstairs, completely forgetting my phone on the kitchen island.

Mae is sitting at the table, one foot on the stool as she sews a button onto the front of the jacket.

"What did you think of Bonnie?" Mae asks, her eyes glued to the movement of the needle.

"She kind of reminds me of Sybil."

"Really?" The shock and skepticism are evident in both Mae's voice and face as she looks at me.

"Yes, Sybil isn't nearly as steely as you think. She just needs to warm up to you."

"I've been in your house for four months, and I am convinced that all of them are avoiding me. I mean, she doesn't even give me chores anymore. I end up doing everything myself."

"Well, Sybil isn't exactly pleased you are there. She's also close to retiring. I eased up her responsibilities aside from the kitchen duties; it's just us in the house."

"Like we live together? Like that house is ours?"

"I guess in a way, yes." I take a sip of my coffee and bite into my toast. Mae opens the jacket, fluffing it out before holding it up.

"What's left to do?" I ask.

"One half of the leg, the vest, and then the pocket square."

"No tie?"

Mae makes a face. "No, I think black will be fine, and I'm sure you are already in an abundance of black ties." She plucks a slice of apple and sandwiches it between her lips before taking a bite.

"May I ask you something, Dominic?"

I swallow a lump of food before saying, "sure."

"Am I your first girlfriend?"

I cough slightly on the coffee before setting it down. "Why would you assume that?"

Mae casually shrugs. "Call it occupational insight. After a few years, you can tell who's new and who isn't."

"Well, then you would be wrong. I've had women whom I kept a somewhat exclusive relationship with, but it didn't last more than a few weeks."

"Why is that?"

"Aside from the fact I have to restrain myself from biting their necks every time we have sex, they are often looking for something more serious, and I don't want to think about more serious things."

"I'm sure your female equivalent would at least solve one of those problems."

"A female vampire, yes, sex would no longer be an internal battle, but that only makes children a higher risk." I run a finger over the rim of the cup.

I keep away from female vampires. Not only do I have to worry about the reason they are with me but also the implications of every time we have sex.

"Having sex with a human, there is less of a risk of conceiving."

"Well, that's not true." Mae replies, and I arch my brow at her.

"Please educate the vampire on vampires." I laugh.

"Well, to conceive, a vampire would require the female to ingest the males' blood before or during the act of sex while he ingests hers. We already know that a vampire's blood remains in a human a lot longer than a human's remains in a vampire. Take us, for example. I could easily just bite you during a heated moment, and well, we know your fetish already."

"Yes, we are a pretty good example, but what person bites another person? I can tell you that no woman has bitten me during a 'heated moment.'"

"I did," Mae's sultry voice tickles my ears.

"Because you're a little minx who pushes boundaries."

Mae laughs at my quick-fire response. She stands up and drapes the jacket back over the mannequin before sitting down and bringing the bowl towards her.

"If I never pushed the boundaries, you would eventually grow bored of me," Mae retorts.

We bask in the morning light as we eat breakfast. Occasionally, I nab a piece of unguarded fruit from Mae's bowl as she unsuccessfully attempts to sneak a sip of my coffee, as hers is now "terribly cold."

I don't think I will ever get bored of you.

The Highs and Lows

"**H**e fucking did what?" I shout. Lara lifts her head from between my legs, pulling off her mask and revealing her swollen bottom lip.

"Jesus, Mae. Must you be so loud?" She pulls out the small, soft swab from my cervix and slips it into a sealable plastic vial.

"Well, sorry, Lara. People tend to get riled up when they find out some prick used their best friend to come out, and, if that wasn't fucking sketchy as it is, when it inevitably backfired, turned on them. He used you like a safety blanket, Lara. It was a win-win situation for him. If his colleagues support him, great. If they don't, well, he can take it out on you and play the whole 'I didn't know she was a dude, I feel so cheated' card."

The elf drops the vial in a small plastic bag before pulling off her gloves and taking a seat in front of me.

Today is my bi-monthly checkup. Luckily for me, it is being performed by Lara, the branch's chief doctor. However, unluckily for her, it is the day after a brutal attack from a still-closeted little shit.

"Don't you think I realized that, Mae?" She drops onto the stool, rotating it slowly. I take my legs down and pull up my underwear before sitting in the chair next to her.

"Your vagina looks good, healthy."

"Don't change the subject, Lara."

Lara looks at me, her golden-rimmed eyes sparkling like jewels in the night.

"Magenta had me report him to the police. She said she had her reservations to begin with when he approached her but thought a small office party wouldn't go so terribly wrong."

"He deserves to go to jail for what he did. I mean, he's a fucking descendant of a minotaur, of course he has a temper on him. It was a hate crime, Lara. Plain and simple." I sigh. "Is that why she hasn't patched you up?" I stroke the lump above her eyebrow, the raised skin making my eyes water.

"Yeah, if this goes to court, which it probably will, I need to keep the evidence." Lara pulls out a blood pressure gauge and lays it on the table.

I lay my arm on the table as she wraps the strap over my arm.

"Now can you relax for me so I can get a proper reading?"

I inhale dramatically before exhaling. The strap tightens as it takes a reading.

"68 bpm, good. You took a urine sample before you came in."

I tap the small little pot on the table labeled with my name and date of birth.

"Now, I must ask. Is he hurting you?"

"Will you be telling Magenta?"

"You know the rules, *Maebell*."

"No, he is not, *Larissa*."

Lara pulls the strap off my arm and puts it back into the drawer. "Now, for your favorite bit."

I roll up my sleeve, exposing the veiny skin. Lara gets up from her stool and heads to go get a blood test kit.

"What did the police say?"

She takes out a plastic vial and a small needle wrapped in plastic.

"They say there's a good chance of conviction. He's been on their radar before, but the other cases were circumstantial. Hopefully, with my evidence, more victims will step forward." She presses the needle to my arm, and the blood begins to pour a steady stream into the vial.

As I watch the blood fill the vial, a slight roll of my stomach has me turning away. Before I know it, the needle is out and replaced with cotton wool and tape.

"I'll text you if I find anything concerning, which I doubt I will."

I roll down my sleeve and grab my jacket from the back of the chair. "Does that mean you're on holiday?"

Lara only handles the most severe cases.

"Yeah, until the trial is over, I'm on doctor duty."

I stand up, wrap my arms around Lara's head softly, and press her to my chest. I stroke the back of her hair, which has been braided, running my finger down the parting. Lara sighs, wrapping her arms around my waist.

"You're going to be OK." I pull away enough for the elf to look at me. "OK?"

She has begun crying, her tears staining her rosy cheeks and my dress.

"Oh, baby girl." I pull her in for another hug, caressing her head as she sobs, hushing her cries and stroking her hair.

"Have you told Lincoln?" I whisper. Lara shakes her head between my breasts.

"He'll have a fit, most likely go to you for more information." That is very true. While Lincoln lusts over Seraphine, he is in love with Lara.

However, the two find it very difficult to not be swayed by other people, and therefore don't pursue their feelings for one another outside their arrangement.

Lara pulls away, plucks a tissue out of the box, and dabs her eyes before blowing her nose.

"I've been waiting 24 hours for you to show up so I could have a good cry."

"I would've come sooner if you had told me."

Lara waves off my argument.

"Work comes first."

I roll my eyes before pulling her in for another hug, smothering the top of her head with kisses. "You will keep me up to date," I say, straightening out my dress.

"Yes, of course. Now off you go. I'm sure Mr. Bitey is getting agitated waiting for you." I give Lara one last kiss on the temple before throwing on my jacket and picking up my bag.

"See you soon, love you."

"Love you too, Mae."

I didn't want to leave. If I could, I would've run Lara a warm bath and showed her the affection the woman deserves.

A whole chunk of me felt guilty walking out of the yoga studio into the cold air, seeing Dominic sitting on the hood of his sleek black BMW, one leg casually draped over the other with his arms folded.

"Everything in good shape?"

"I've been told I have a healthy vagina."

Dominic smirks slightly.

"I could've told you that."

I can't help but smile at him as I open the car door and slip into the passenger seat.

"I have a request," I ask suddenly. Dominic turns his head to me to give me his full attention. "I'd like to see my family back in Scotland. I know it's not exactly work-related b-"

"That's fine with me. You can use one of my airlines. I think there's one scheduled for Gatwick tomorrow morning. Do you want me to drop you at your place to pack?"

"Uh..." I stare at Dominic. Not that I expected some drawn-out conversation where I gave him multiple psychological reasons why I need to see them, but I didn't expect this. *That was easy.*

"Yes, that'd be great."

The Nikos

The burgundy door is propped open slightly. A birthday sash has been draped over the frame; the number 20 written over to say 58. I shake my head, laughing. *No doubt Max bought the sash trying to make Mum feel younger than she is.*

I hear the thumping of bass travel through the door, catching the muffled words of music.

"Carry on standing outside. The party will be over before you step in."

I sigh, my lips curling into a smile as I spin around.

The Samoan man chuckles, tilting his head to me before opening his arms. I skip into Max's arms and wrap mine tightly around his back.

"She never remembers to get ice." I laugh, pulling away and attempting to take a bag off Max, who dodges me and tilts his head to the door.

"Your mother never gets ice; she enjoys sending me out."

I pick up my small suitcase and let Max lead the way into the house.

"We didn't expect you to come. I thought you said you'd be here in May for your birthday?"

"Yes," I place my suitcase by the door. "But you know Mum, and Kenny has his dance recital, doesn't he?"

Max heads past the living room to the sliding door at the back, and I am right on his tail.

"You guys still practicing?"

"Every Saturday morning. I promised I would join him this time."

"Your mother got that boy to tap before he could walk."

"And would she have it any other way?" I ask. Max slides the door open, and the actual volume of the music hits my ears, stretching them as wide as my smile.

Jesus, the Niko-Geoffries, are so loud.

The long garden is filled with various members of both families, a few cousins I haven't seen since Kenzo's second birthday, and some I haven't seen since Mum's wedding.

"Look who I found," Max announces, and all heads turn to me. The loudest of them all is a small brown boy, darting between family members.

"Maisey!" he screams. I scoop him up, twirling him around in my arms before planting the fattest kiss I can muster on his tiny lips.

"How are you, Kenny?"

Kenzo wraps his arms around my neck, squeezing me so tight that I am barely able to breathe. I cough loudly, bending my knees slightly like I am about to collapse.

"Must...breathe...Kenzo." I squeeze him back, nibbling into his neck, making him kick his legs in laughter.

"My daughter has returned."

With Kenzo still in my arms, I turn to the familiar voice. Mum is heading out of the kitchen, a stack of plates on her lap.

I put Kenzo down, much to his reluctance, and hug the 58-year-old. Her jasmine scent wafts up my nose, and I sigh contently. I kiss her cheek, trying not to get tearful.

I probably didn't address the accident the way she did. I still struggle seeing her in the chair. *Could it be because I'm never here, or am I just avoiding the pain that comes with change?*

Mum, however, adapted – as to be expected with someone so amazing. In her adjustment, she found Max, an honorably discharged army chef, and the two couldn't have been better matched.

I always believed my father was her perfect match. Max reckoned that remnants of departed souls implant themselves on people who will make a difference to those they leave behind. He's convinced that a part of my father emanates from him and that, in a different life, Kenzo and I are the children that he never had.

"Mae," my mother whispers, "I'm OK, baby. It's good you were able to come."

I pull away, still crouched to her level, and she tucks a strand behind my headband.

"Happy birthday, Mum."

She strokes the side of my face, wiping the traitorous tear that has escaped. I stand up, grabbing the plastic plates off her lap before she can protest.

"As the birthday girl, relax, Mum."

She rolls her eyes, taking herself to sit in the shade.

"Is that my *nieta* over there?"

"*Abuelo.*" I watch the tall man weave through the crowd with arms wider than the oars of a boat. The sprinkle of moles across his face rise as he smiles, his hazel eyes getting lost in his cheeks.

"You're looking more and more like your mother," he says as he hugs me. "How long has it been?"

"Far too long. Is *Abuela* here?"

I feel his head move up and down.

"Cooking, something that probably could be left for another time. She's worse than your mother. The next time she sits will be when she dies."

I make a face, trying to stifle my amusement at his dark humor.

"Then I'm heading to the kitchen." I let him go, straightening out his striped collared shirt before handing him the plates to set the table.

Abuela, as always, is dancing around the white-tiled kitchen, stirring pots and sprinkling seasoning here and there.

"You are micromanaging again?" My voice makes the olive-skinned woman laugh.

"You know I like using your mum's kitchen when there are family events." She turns from the stove to address me.

I hope that at the age of 86 I will have the same youthfulness: that surge of energy that seems to hit anything in proximity. Her hair is still thick and voluptuous by her collar bone, grey with strands of black. Puerto Rican blood that my grandfather, a single father with a newborn, fell in love with instantly. Abuela Joan took my mother, and she became her own.

My mum looks great for 58, and Abuela Joan looks ethereal at 86. She kisses both of my cheeks before returning to her work.

"You don't call enough, Mae," she says unprompted.

I lean on the countertop, plucking olives from a small bowl.

"Time zones are tricky to manage. I try my best, *Abuela*." As I reach for another olive, a ladle comes down, hitting the back of my hand. I hold my hand to my chest, rubbing it.

"Your mother worries for you, in America on your own. Never telling her what you get up to."

I sigh loudly, pushing up off the table.

"*Abuela*, I'm a designer. You know this. Luckily, a high-end one. America is where it's at. It's bigger, and so is the market. I tell Mum this every time. The UK is still my home, and I come back whenever I can."

Abuela Joan has been watching me, studying my choice of words as they came out of my lips. She purses her own, watching me a bit longer until she is satisfied, and turns back to the stove.

"Go take the food out before you eat it all."

I smile. I have passed her test. I take the bowl of olives in one hand and salad in the other. Just before I leave, I plant a kiss on her cheek.

"Of course, *Abuela*."

We all sit at the three tables in the garden under the shade of several large umbrellas. Mum is at the head of the table closest to the house.

Abuelo rises from his seat on the other end of table number one; he angles himself so he can be seen by everyone.

"Dear God," he begins. Everyone dips their heads, some holding hands, others with clasped hands in front of them. "We thank you for blessing Daniele with another year. We know she has been through tough times, but we know you only give us as much as we can bear. I thank you for the food we are about to receive, the hands that made the food, and the people who have come to enjoy it. Let the people say."

"Amen," we reply in unison.

I mouth the words 'ai' to Max, who in turn does it back to me. With our plates out and everyone hungry, we dig in. "Kenny," I say, grabbing the little boy's attention. He has one hand wrapped around a spoonful of rice and another hand around a drumstick.

Nonetheless, the little boy can speak, "Yeth." A few grains of rice slip out of his mouth.

"Dance recital tomorrow. Excited?"

Kenzo opens his mouth to speak, but with a mouth full of chicken and rice, he closes it, settling on just nodding frantically.

"Are you talking about the dance recital tomorrow, Mae?" Mum asks. "Do you plan to join as well?"

"Finally, yes. I just hope my partner is as good as his."

Kenzo is part of a contemporary party that my mum consults for. Once a year, they have a family performance. I skip it most years, and Kenzo has to settle for an extremely rigid and stiff Max, but tomorrow, I will dance with him for the first time, with a partner who should be able to lift me elegantly.

I just wonder if I can still hold my form.

It is like I have never left: the laughter, the jokes of past Christmases and family gatherings are everything to make my heart warm. I've forgotten how much I miss them, how much I miss the family unit, that love and emotion that sweeps the floor and everyone around. Most importantly, I've forgotten how much I miss being me, around people who know me. Know Mae.

I sigh contently as I lean back into the white plastic chair. The sun has begun its descent, and with the orange and red hues playing across the garden, a low glow emits from the kitchen.

"Happy birthday, to you," Abuela Joan begins. I turn slightly to the cake that is being brought out into the garden and join everyone in singing.

Mum tries her best not to look embarrassed with all this attention orbiting around her. She smiles sheepishly as Max stands behind her, rubbing her shoulders.

I place the cake in front of her. The number *20* with two small fires emanating from it only makes my mum smile wider. Max kisses the top of her head and she, in turn, kisses his hand.

With the song coming to an end, Mum clears her throat. "Thank you all for coming. I told Max I wanted something quiet this year. 58 is not such a big deal."

"Well, for your 60th, we're renting a hotel," Max counters. We all laugh, but the man is most likely serious. He'll work out something, with his charm and unwavering love for my mother.

"I wouldn't want to spend this birthday with anyone else," she finishes. We all raise our glasses.

"To Mum," I shout.

"To Daniele," everyone replies before clinking glasses and cheering as she blows the candles out.

Cautionary Precautions

"I thought we'd given up on pursuing Aldrek," Rebekah hisses as she slows towards the guard booth at the entrance of *Dove Valley*, a gated community which Aldrek has built just outside main Seattle.

"I had, then we got a ping off Miss Geoffries. Turns out she's gone to England using no other than," Conrad points sternly at the silver gates, "this man's airline. So much for 'they liaison on her behalf' bullshit. That's why we are here."

Rebekah sighs heavily. The car coming to a halt, she rolls down the window as the guard on the other side rises from his chair.

"Who have you come to see?" he practically growls, holding the edge of his booth with two tight fists.

"Mr. Aldrek," Rebekah replies kindly, noticing the immediate strain and tension in the air. Conrad doesn't give the man a chance for a rebuttal and flashes his badge, Rebekah quick to follow suit.

"Open the gate."

His eagle-like eyes narrow and he draws the window booth shut, the force causing it to rattle slightly.

Conrad slides back into his chair as the man talks on the phone inside the booth.

"We can't get what we want with aggression," Rebekah says.

The window slides back open, and the guard eyes the pair. He presses a button, and the gates begin to rumble.

"Last house."

Rebekah smiles meekly at the man, telepathically apologizing to him for Conrad's behavior, then follows the road. Passing detached three-story, red-bricked homes, small front lawns, a car every now and again on the driveway, some with sprinklers on and others with children perched on the grass.

"This place seems nice. I wonder how much they go for?" Rebekah voices absentmindedly.

"Don't worry yourself about that. You see any middle-class people here?" Conrad replies in a snarky manner.

Rebekah gives him a sideways glance. Something is pestering the FBI agent. He'd seemed fine when he called her to meet him by the coffee shop, they now frequently go to and still fine when he'd told her he wanted her to drive somewhere. However, as they turned off the freeway, his mood dropped, and his aura soured.

I thought he wanted to come here?

"Of course, he has the biggest house," Conrad mumbles, and Rebekah focuses her attention on the large house at the end of the road.

She stops the car, putting it into park before engaging the handbrake.

"What the hell is wrong with you today?" She turns to Conrad, who has already begun unbuckling his seatbelt.

"And don't tell me nothing; you are snappy this morning."

"Sorry," Conrad breathes out, "I feel like we missed an opportunity when Mae flew to England. I mean, I just about convinced Naomi to put a small hit on her name, but if they had just put her on a no flights list like I asked, we could've used that card to get her to talk. They don't think she'll try to run, neither do I to be honest, but I'm getting squeezed by every senior who has a stake in this investigation. They need some results. Otherwise, I'm going to be the scapegoat for explaining away the waste of FBI resources and staff."

Rebekah puts a caring hand on his shoulder, the best she can offer.

"We are going to get answers, but right now, let's try and be approachable. Dominic might slip up if he doesn't see us as any more of a threat than we already are." Rebekah opens her door, Conrad in tow as the pair walk up to the double mahogany doors.

Conrad presses the doorbell. The tone disperses inside the house, only to be replaced with the steps of approaching feet.

The door swings open, and there stands Sybil. She looks extremely deflated as she meets the pair, several hundred years older than she is.

"How may I help you?" she asks politely, her hands held together in front of her.

"We are looking for Mr. Aldrek," Rebekah replies.

"Unfortunately, Mr. Aldrek is not here. He's away tending to business. I'll happily take a message and tell him you dropped by."

"Thank you, could you tell him that Agents Rebekah and Conrad stopped by hoping to talk? He has my business card," Conrad adds.

Sybil nods, her hands holding the edge of the door as it moves a little bit more closed.

"Will do, thank you for stopping by."

Rebekah turns on her heels, heading for the car, while Conrad lingers a little more, staring into the house a bit more than necessary. He clears his throat before smiling slightly and taking his leave as well.

Rebekah sits in the car, playing around with the navigation so that they can get back home. The passenger side door slams shut, and Conrad slumps into the seat.

"Sorry, that was a huge waste," he admits, defeated.

"Not at all. Yes, another dead end, but that just increases the chances of stumbling onto the ends that aren't dead."

"I just want to know where the fuck those two are."

An Uninvited Invitation

I *should not be here.*

I move the bouquet of flowers from one hand to another. I have convinced myself that flowers will be enough of a gift to hand to Mae before she asks what the hell I am doing at her house. *Not her house, her mother's house. Her family home, which she wanted to visit. Alone. This is low even for me.*

Borderline obsessive is what it is. No, actually this is just obsessive.

"Can I help you with anything?" A tall man is standing by the open burgundy door, his hands deep in his pockets.

"You've been standing outside my house for the past twenty minutes." It is here I am grateful for the fact that we are in Scotland, and he most likely doesn't have a firearm on him.

I rub the back of my neck, suddenly blank for any reasonable excuses.

"I'm here for Mae." *Well, that just sounds possessive.* "I'm her boyfriend, she said she would be here." *And now you're lying.*

He stands there, glazing me over, unimpressed and not swayed with my reason. I place the flowers under my arm as I reach for my pocket.

"I have a picture of us." That part is correct.

As is traditional for Mae when she completes an outfit, she'd taken a photo of it on me for her notebook and another for me, which she insisted I have.

"*Come on Dominic, I'll put a timer on. Smile for me please,*" *Mae said, angling my phone so it could capture us and the mannequin in between.*

"*Wasn't the first photo enough?*" *I asked, leaning an arm on the shoulder of the doll.*

"*I hardly ever get to take these photos with clients.*"

"*Fine,*" *I mumble.*

Mae pressed a button, skipped next to me, and did a thumbs up. A light flashed several times, momentarily blinding us before it stopped. Mae went to the phone and turned it over before frowning. "*Damn, I cut us off at the bottom, lets-*"

I snatched the phone out of her grasp, lifting it high above her where I could still see, but she was unable to reach.

"*It'll do, it got our faces in it.*" *That was true, though the photo stopped just shy of our waists, leaving out our legs.* "*And besides, you have the other photo.*"

I show the man the evidence, and he takes my phone to survey it closer. I am lucky it isn't precisely to Mae's tradition.

"She made you a suit?" He hands the phone back to me. "My name's Max. I'm sure you know that already, being Mae's boyfriend and all."

The "and all" couldn't have been anymore dismissive, but I smile the best I can with my hand outstretched.

"Dominic, nice to meet you."

Max shakes my hand hard and firm before dropping it and shutting the door behind himself.

"I guess you brought the flowers for her performance this afternoon?"

I stare down at the bouquet of white and pink flowers, most of which I don't know the name of.

«*I'm surprised she'd tell him of Kenny's performance*»

I clear my throat as his thought drifts through my head.

"She's performing as well? I thought it was just Kenny?" I try to come off knowledgeable, as though Mae and I had discussed this like a proper couple.

"Kenzo will be dancing as well, it's a family thing. They dance together. Have you seen Mae dance?"

That is a good question. Aside from our first night together, which I would call more gyrating of the hips, I haven't seen her dance.

"No, though I can imagine she's as good as her mother when she was Mae's age."

Max narrows his eyes slightly at the mention of his wife. Maybe I crossed a line. *Mae's mother is in a wheelchair. Is that a touchy subject?*

"Well, Daniele consults now." He checks his watch quicker than the average person would. "Show starts in about 20 mins. Did you drive?"

I turn slightly to point at the four-year-old silver Mercedes across the road that I had rented when I arrived to be as inconspicuous as possible.

Again, playing into the possessive trope, Dominic. I frown at my inner thoughts.

"Great, follow behind?" Max doesn't give me much time to reply and heads to the black ford next to me. I take myself to my own car, start it up, and wait for the man who will no doubt leave me to the winding streets of Inverness the first chance he gets.

I step out of the car and slam the door shut behind me as Max steps out of his own next door.

The dance studio, or at least where the performance is to happen, is in a drama hall, an extension to a high school.

The double doors are open, and Max leads the way inside.

Chairs have been set up in several rows with a walkway in between them, and the rest of the space is filled with mingling family members.

The pressure of what I have done weighs on the back of my neck. *You honestly could not have maimed yourself anymore. What excuse can I make up to leave? Could I compel Max to make him forget?*

I stare at the man ahead of me talking to someone, faint creases in his light brown skin. There is no smell emitting from him that suggests he is anything but human. In fact, glancing around, I notice no colors. The whole room is human.

"Mae is in the back getting ready," Max is standing next to me, a drink in either hand.

"Squash?" He hands me the orange liquid, and I smile, taking it from him.

"What can I expect this afternoon?"

"She didn't give you a schedule?" Max sighs, placing the cup on a nearby table before pulling out a folded piece of paper from his back pocket and handing it to me.

1. Sarah & David
   Time Apart
2. Kristin & Layla
   A Summer Breeze
3. Margret & James
   A Midnight Song

I trail my eyes down the list of unimportant people until I find her name.

6. Kenzo & Lillian with Mae & Charlie
   Dancing on my Mind

I hand the paper back to Max, who folds it away.

"It thought it was Kenzo and Mae?"

"It is, Kenzo has a dance partner for his piece, so Lilian's brother is paired with Mae. He performs professionally. She's in good hands."

"Could you call me when Mae is up?" I ask.

"Not trying to watch the other performances, I get that."

"But you're going to have to." A velvety voice breaks between us and I turn, my gaze lowering to Mae's mother.

Despite her sporting a grey buzz cut, she reminds me of Mae in every possible way: the broad smile that makes her cheeks rise and begin to cover her brown eyes, the jasmine scent that wafts around her. Hers feels tamer, with a hint of honey to it, while Mae has a hint of chocolate. Either way, the smell is intoxicating and enriching every inch of my body.

"Mr.s. Niko," I smile politely. "My name is Dominic." I hold out my hand to her.

"Daniele is fine. I haven't heard of you before, Dominic." Daniele takes my hand, shaking it firmly. "Who is my daughter to you?" There is a bite to her words, another reminder of Mae's own voice.

"Boyfriend, would you believe, Daniele?" Max says. Daniele raises her brows, making an *o* with her mouth.

"Well, that would be a first. Where has she been hiding you?"

"In America."

I notice that voice and gulp loudly, looking past Daniele to Mae, her arms folded, a smile that is wavering with every passing moment.

Dancing on My Mind

Daniele glances over her shoulder to her daughter before turning slightly.

"Is that what you've been doing in America, having a boyfriend?"

Mae gives me a quick glance, her eyes extremely cold.

«*What the actual fuck, Dominic?*» I fight the urge to wince as Mae practically screams at me through her thoughts.

"Mother, I was going to tell you about Dominic, but yesterday was your birthday. I didn't want to take the light from you." Mae smiles, gliding towards us.

Dressed from head to toe in all black, her hair has been tied up in a bun, and she looks everything like a ballerina.

She kisses me gently on the cheek. Her lips are a bit more pursed than usual, and she exhales as she does.

«*We need to talk about this.*» Her thoughts are softer this time; the shock has died down.

"Well, the man traveled all this way for your performance. Let's get him a good seat before the show starts."

"You save him a seat. He will meet you later."

Daniele heads towards the front, as do all the other people in the room. Max gives us a lingering glance before he trails after his wife to the front.

Mae grabs my hand, dragging me out of the hall and into the corridor, taking me further into the school. We don't stop until we are hidden between two flights of stairs.

"Explain." Mae folds her arms, unimpressed.

"I d-"

"If you wanted to come, you should've asked. I wouldn't have been able to say no. Yes, it would mean I'd have to lie, but I'm somewhat OK with that with warning. I don't appreciate being blindsided and taken by surprise, Dominic. You don't even know me outside of... " she waves her hands frantically. "This. What if I have a husband, or a wife, or any partner, and you claim to be my boyfriend. How do you think I could explain that?"

"Do you?" I hadn't considered that. I thought escorts kept themselves free, so they didn't have to worry about those things: no one to be mindful or considerate of.

"Thankfully, I do not. However, you have to remember that this ends in eight months." Surprisingly that stings, like a shot of heartburn I'm not prepared for.

"Now I'm going to have to give a reason for us breaking up. Now I have to lie to my family."

"I'm sorry. I had every intention of letting you go visit your family. I just found myself here; it was a pull. You felt vulnerable and nervous about something, around six pm, and it concerned me, so I got the next flight here." I watch as a flurry of emotions run through Mae: concern, shock, fear, and the slightest bit of reassurance.

It has been a while since I have built up such a connection with another person. They call it tagging. When a vampire feeds enough times on the same person without killing them, that person is tagged as theirs. They emit a scent which can be recognized by others as taken and, in the rare cases that other vampires try to attack their prey as a sign of defiance or challenge, the owner senses it. No matter how far they are, they know. In rare cases, they get glimpses of their prey's last moments. Though I had tagged Mae in the first month of our arrangement, the cleanse she went through with Magenta caused the connection to break down slightly, almost muted it. However, it was still there. As long as she spent time around me and I fed off her, that link would remain, and it has been a while since she's cleansed, so the connection has only grown stronger.

"I went back to the bar I worked at. It was a lot more triggering than I care to admit." Mae's face is lowered slightly, and her gaze is pointed to the floor.

I hold her chin, lifting it up to look at me. A small well has developed in her eyes, and I stroke her cheek with my thumb.

"Are you OK?" My voice is barely over a whisper. The well of brimming tears increases, and a small tear drips from the corner.

"Maisey. Who is this man?" A tiny voice breaks the moment we are sharing, and Mae quickly wipes her face, revealing a wide smile as we both turn to the owner.

"Kenzo, this is Dominic."

I look down the stairs at the small boy dressed in all black as well; both he and Mae have the same nude ballet shoes on their feet. His hair has been brushed back into a low-hanging ponytail.

"Hi Kenzo, I was just talking to your sister here."

Kenzo has the same unimpressed look as his father. He turns to Mae, and his smile widens.

"Is he your friend?"

"My bestest friend." Mae giggles. "Now I'm sure you're here to tell me it's nearly our turn."

Kenzo nods. "Penelope has just finished. Charlie was looking for you."

"Thank you, Kenny. You and Lillian finish your stretches, and I'll be there to join you, OK?"

"Bye, Nick," Kenzo says quickly before running off down the corridor.

"Mae..." I begin.

She gives me a look, one that isn't stern but almost scared of heading down that path.

"If you've really tagged me, you'll know that I am fine. My parents have left a seat for you. Enjoy the show."

I have tagged her, and Mae is not OK. However, now isn't the time for this conversation.

"I'll be rooting for you."

She lets out a breath like a laugh and heads down the stairs after Kenzo. I sigh and walk back to the hall, holding the limp flowers in my hand.

The room is darker, the curtains drawn, and only a few lights display the stage. Max and Daniele are in the first row. A seat has been left for me on the edge, and I sit down.

The pair look at me, and I smile slightly, turning my head to focus on the performance.

The piano kicks in, and the spotlight falls onto Kenzo and his partner Lillian sitting while they play with toys. They are happy. They pick up the toys, twirling and running around each other. Lillian leans on Kenzo as she extends her leg, his hands holding her hands out.

They both stop and look at each other before running in different directions off the stage.

Mae and Charlie emerge: a representation of the older versions of the two children. They stumble into each other, the force pushing Mae slightly, and Charlie catches her. They stare at each other as the realization of old friends emerges.

Mae smiles at Charlie as he pulls her close, twirling her before catching her in his other arm as Mae lifts her leg. Charlie holds her up, picking her up as she spins.

Kenzo and Lillian appear as Charlie puts Mae down. The two pairs mirror each other: a balance of the young versions of themselves being reacquainted in their older years.

Charlie and Kenzo lift their partners as Lilian and Mae hang their heads back. The girls are twirled, both in complete synchronicity, leaping and jumping together as a unit.

As the song concludes, the two pairs hold hands as their legs stretch high. While Kenzo and Lilian go back to the floor to play with the toys, Charlie bends down to one knee, holding his hands as though he is proposing.

Mae nods, and Charlie picks her up, spinning around before bringing her down slowly, her hand never leaving his face, a smile as wide as anything.

The audience applauds, and I find myself on my feet clapping with the rest of them.

Luna and her Wolf

"We can't get married," Stephan says, setting his coffee cup down on the table.

I lean into the chair, holding the chai latte close to my nose as I peer out the window. April had begun, and with it, warmer weather: fewer clothes and more time spent outdoors. *I'm going to have to change this to an iced chai.*

"Luna," Stephan begins. I finally turn my attention to him. "Did you hear me?"

I sigh, slowly setting my own cup down on the table.

"Yes, I know. These chases will end up killing me. Magenta can only fix the scars so many times. She says I'm at my limit of magic consumption. Three more heals, that's all she can do."

Magenta has become Luna's witch best friend, a fill in her story to explain why she never has any scarring. A mysterious witch who shares a flat with her, a witch who has set a restriction on this arrangement. *Magenta really did think of everything.*

"We can't simply break up. I wish you were my mate; I really do, but-" Stephan clasps his hands together and holds them across the table. They are shaking. *He is scared.*

"I know, but we knew what we'd be getting into when we thought we'd give it a chance." If I was Stephan's mate, the moment I told him my full name, his wolf would've told him, his heart would've told him.

"I have an idea. It would require a lot from you, Luna." Stephan lifts his head to gaze at me. The moment our eyes connect, he returns them to his drink.

"We should run away."

I let go of his hand and put mine on my lap. What he is proposing is insane, to completely abandon his family for a human. Worse yet, a human that isn't his mate. Stephan would turn his back on his tradition, his morals, and when he found his mate, he'd have to kill me to rejoin his family, and he would because that's what his mate would ask of him.

"Stephan...you're giving me a death wish," I whisper. His love for me will ultimately kill us both. My stomach churns at the density of our relationship.

"Not if I never leave the house, if I only see you. I can't possibly find my mate if I'm a hermit." Stephan dryly chuckles at the last bit.

"You understand the physical and mental repercussions of that, right? That's solitary confinement. I don't want to be some sort of warden over you."

"It's voluntary confinement."

"And kids, are we just abandoning that idea as well? You realize that if we have kids, not only would they be destined to never find their other half out of the goddesses' spite for true love, but it would mean you'd all die. You'd all die by 40; constant changing at the full moon would break you in half over time." I settle into my seat, noticing how I hold the arms of the chair, and the occasional glances from other people.

This is their coffee shop: a small, tucked away place. The exposed light bulb buzzes along with the lo-fi hip hop playing in the background. This is where they first met, where Luna was born. Call me sentimental, but I have grown connected to her. At first, I wanted to challenge myself and be someone slightly different than Mae. However, over the years, we melded into the same person: light and dark shades but still the same color.

"I know, Luna. I'm willing to have all the babies in the world with you. I'm willing to have none at all and die early. I don't want to be with anyone else. Trust me to know that I couldn't love anyone more than you."

I bite my lip, hoping the damn thing will start bleeding and realign this pain I'm feeling in my chest.

"Don't answer now. But at least think about it."

I stand up, and so does Stephan. I fall into his arms, taking in his cologne, holding his body close to mine as I feel the rhythm of his heart. Stephan holds me tightly in his arms, stroking the bottom of my hair, his chin resting on the lie that is the white chunk of hair.

"I'll think about it, Stephan. I love you." *But I worry what it might make us do.*

"I love you too, Luna. Would you like me to walk you to the station?"

"I have a meeting upstate. I'm going to get a cab." I look up at Stephan, peering into those sad, green orbs and pull him into a kiss, a deep one, one that expresses more than the words we've said.

Luna and Stephan love each other, and they are both ready to risk it all.

I stand somewhere up the road from the coffee shop, waiting for the car to arrive when my phone rings. I pluck it from my bag. *Dominic.* I slide the button along.

"Miss me already, birthday boy?" I smile into the phone as he chuckles on the other end, the black car pulling up to the curb.

Skeletons in the Closet

"**M**orning, Calamba."

Rebekah looks up from her small fort of boxes as Conrad walks in carrying two large cups of coffee.

"You texted black americano, right?"

"Yes, don't tell me you got me a white americano?"

"No, I just got a strange look when I ordered it. You know it has six shots of coffee."

Rebekah takes the cup, ignoring the skull and bones drawing on the side of the cup just under her order.

She takes a sip of the just-below-scalding liquid and purses her lips, feeling the lava incinerate her insides before she speaks.

"I've organized the boxes: Dominic over there," she says, pointing to the corner furthest from the door. "Mae there." Gesturing to her right. "And FolkWore here." She taps the small stack of boxes surrounding her.

Conrad gazes at the ten separate boxes of documents: every skeleton is in front of them.

"Is this all, pay slips and tax refunds?" Conrad asks, pulling a chair from the corner and lifting one of the lids. He chucks it aside, much to Rebekah's dismay.

"You'd think that. If you were a lawyer for this business, what do you think their cases would be on?"

Conrad shrugs, taking a gulp of his chocolaty coffee.

"I guess licensing, drawing up supplier contracts. Maybe the occasional franchising scuff."

"Would it surprise you that most of their cases are criminal, and they are always the prosecutor?"

"Then I call bullshit," Conrad replies.

Rebekah tilts her head, pulls out a random file from the open box, and hands it to him.

Conrad takes it from her and flips it open. Here is just one of those cases: a court document where FolkWore is prosecuting a person for harassment of one of their staff. "Harassment. Did this person not get their slutty elf outfit on time or something?"

"It's unclear, but it's not the only one. Half these boxes have similar cases spreading over the last 35 years."

"35 years? That Magenta lady couldn't be more than 35."

"Well, it's a family-owned business. It's just been passed down from one woman to another. That doesn't explain the fact that these guys have way too many criminal cases under their belt. What the hell do they supply?"

The Next Chapter

Babies.

Designed to control the subject's desire to protect them, from their round heads to the creases in their arms and thighs, and this baby makes me broody.

Tia could not have been any cuter. The tuft of hair on the top of her head, her button nose that seems to float on her face, and small dimples in her cheeks that deepen the wider her smile becomes. Most importantly, the bubble of saliva she creates every time she is taking in the world, and that is often.

"Can I take her home?" I lift the small human, rubbing my nose into her stomach, making her gurgle, prompting her to grab a fistful of my hair. I sit her on my lap, sliding some strands out from between her fingers.

"You know how to change a leaky diaper?" Marie asks, folding another sleep suit and placing it in the basket.

"Can't I just hose her down?"

Marie looks at me, shocked, before a wide grin spreads across her face.

"You can't hose down a three-month-old baby, Luna."

"No, you can't." Stephan's arm wraps around my neck, stroking the top of Tia's golden hair.

"A compromise would be giving her a bath or get better diapers." He pinches her nose, making the little girl go cross-eyed before she smiles, her pink gums on full display.

"I've always wanted to bathe with my baby when I have one. I think it's great bonding."

Stephan jumps over the couch, landing next to us, forcing the weight to shift.

"We can all have a bath together," he whispers, kissing my temple. "Sorry we couldn't be here when you gave birth, Marie."

"Honestly, you wouldn't have seen much. I was holed up in the basement for a month and a half. Only Verna and Charley were allowed to see me."

Allowed is one way of describing it. When a female werewolf gives birth, the next moon forces her to take her wolf form for the first month or so of her child's birth, to protect the child from other predators and those who wish her harm. I'd heard stories of mothers attacking their own children during this time, seeing them as a threat. It is mother instincts on steroids.

"Do you remember much of it?" I ask, genuinely fascinated by the ingrained habits of werewolves.

"Not really. I remember the labor, meeting Tia...but the next full moon was the next evening, so it was hazy from then on out. I just remember waking up in bed and Charley holding her."

"I guess that's one upside of having you, Luna, no worry about a territorial wolf stuck in the basement." His finger trails up my arm.

"No, instead an exhausted mama who wonders when her body will tighten back up again."

Stephan chuckles, draping an arm over me as I snuggle close, bouncing Tia on my knee.

"If I know you, it'll snap right back." Stephan rubs his hand along my shoulder.

"You guys look like a family," Marie says. She has finished her folding and is just watching us. "Have some babies. I want Tia to have someone to play with."

"Take it up with the goddess." I laugh.

I cradle Tia as she begins clenching and unclenching her fists, a sign she is getting tired. I use the tip of my finger to stroke from her forehead down to the tip of her nose, the motion causing her eyelids to shut.

"You can't tell me that she isn't a natural," Stephan whispers. I catch him staring at us, his green eyes sparkling with wanting. I somehow manage to shuffle off the sofa and place Tia in her basket, draping her blanket over.

"Luna, want to help me put this stuff away?" Marie asks. I ruffle Stephan's hair, who in turn pinches my butt and picks up the basket from the other sofa.

"I guess I'll just watch the kid?" Stephan whispers.

"Please do. Get some practice in while they're not yours," I reply, following Marie up the stairs.

Charley and Marie's room is right next door to Austin and Claire's room. I haven't seen it before, but I am sure the sidecar crib has been refurbished since the arrival of Tia.

Stephan's family lives for heirlooms, and this is one of them. Carved from the trees in the forest, the smell of pine and oak is embedded in the grain of the wood. Lloyd's father shared his passion for wood carving with his son. On the bottom are the names of all the children that have slept in this crib from Lloyd all the way down to Tia.

It is protection: a connection between their ancestors and them. Tia will be cradled by her great grandfather every time she sleeps; he and his wolf will watch over her. I graze my finger over the newly carved name.

"Your family is so sentimental," I say quietly, running my hand over the top bar of the cot.

"Werewolves are sentimental creatures; we treasure family and memories. They tie us together and with the goddess. Our wolves keep that information to pass on when we die. When they reincarnate, a bit of us lives on."

"You're immortalized."

"Maybe, however, our memories travel across more quickly than we do."

Movies suggest that when a werewolf dies, so does their wolf, but that is false. Every werewolf will once again reincarnate into the body of another person and become their wolf. Every wolf has been human, and every werewolf will one day be someone's inner wolf. It is a cycle that connects everyone together, simultaneously allowing them to live and create their own memories.

"I can only imagine what it's like to have a thousand different memories inside you. What is it like, Marie? When you shift." I sit on the bed, handing the brunette a small pair of socks for her to put away.

"It's like falling into a beanbag." Marie laughs, pushing some hair out of her face as she tucks the socks away. "Probably not the most glorious comparison. Anyway, you've fallen into the bag, and it's deeper than you thought, but it doesn't worry you. Instead, you let the bag slide over you like a warm blanket, and there's a calm that envelops your mind. It's almost euphoric. Sometimes, when I concentrate, I can hear the odd word or catch a fleeting emotion or feeling in my body, but the beanbag is so cozy, and it's hard not to just fall asleep."

"When you put it like that, it sounds almost intoxicating," I mention.

"Yes, however, when it's time to get out, it's painful and tiring. The beanbag seems warmer, cozier, and every time you leave, your body aches. You're that much more tired than you were the last time you got out."

I hand Marie another item of clothing, allowing her insight to settle into my mind. Luna wants kids, she wants a big family to compensate for the lack of one she has now. No grandparents, both parents dead, and no aunts and uncles to call. She wants to never return to an empty room, never to be surrounded by silence. She's spent enough time in silence for a lifetime.

I, on the other hand, am surprisingly just as lonely as she is. However, while it is forced upon Luna, I have willingly accepted the silence and the empty room. It suits me. *It's a choice, every day it is a choice for me like it's always been.*

But how long before there is no more choice left to make, and the silence of the empty rooms kill me?

The Road to Hell

Folk Wore?

    I pulled down the sleeve of my blazer, one I hadn't worn since sixth form, as I stared at the sign.

"Funny right?" I turned to Adele, who was biting the corner of her nail.

"It's certainly different," I replied.

A quaint little store that was nestled in the back roads of Oxford Circus. Adele and I had booked a hotel before traveling back to Scotland tomorrow. What kind of job I'd be receiving was beyond me.

"What is it that you do, Adele?"

"Currently just studying, Mae. I'm on probation at the moment until I finish uni, but once that's done, I've got a job here as an HR assistant. Payroll and stuff like that. I come here maybe once a month to shadow the current manager so I can hit the ground running."

Adele pushed the door in and walked inside. I followed. There were racks of clothes lined up across the floor.

Sequins, jewels and gems decorated the costumes. Some even had a pair of wings attached to the back. I handled the fabric delicately in my fingers. The thin, papery substance was thinner than chiffon, but there was a heaviness to it.

"Mae."

I lifted my head up toward Adele, who was deep into the shop. She gestured me to come on, and I picked up my fallen bag, hurrying after her.

"Mae, this is my manager, Natalie."

Natalie stood tall next to Adele. Her short blond pixie cut waved about her chin, brushing against her caramel skin. Her dark blue eyes pierced mine, scrutinizing me before she smiled, and held her hand out.

"Hi, you must be Mae." Her voice was like silk: soft and weightless.

"Adele says you're looking for a job?"

"Yes, of a kind. Sort of. It's a bit complicated."

Natalie chuckled. She held my shoulders, smiling.

"You're nervous, I can tell. Relax, take a few breaths. In."

I did as I was told, rising on my toes with an inhale.

"And out."

I exhaled, sinking into the carpet slightly. It did make me feel better.

"Now, usually I'd be conducting interviews, but you're in luck. The owner is in."

Adele gasped, and my once-calm demeanor shook and fell off the edge of the earth.

"Magenta is in?" she squealed.

"Yes, she'll be conducting your interview. If you could head through those curtains, up the stairs, and the door on the far end."

I looked to Adele, though I knew she wouldn't be able to come in with me. I became extremely nervous. I held the straps of my bag, and breathed out, before smiling at the pair.

"Sure, thank you, see you in a bit, Del?"

"See you in a bit, Mae."

I followed Natalie's instruction, heading up the narrow stairwell to the polished wood-floored corridor. All the doors on either side looked the same to me. However, the one at the end of the hallway seemed to shine, the light hitting the doorknob like I was opening the pearly gates.

I knocked, rocking on my heels. The door swung open, and the dazzling scent of hazel filled my nose while fiery orange hair encircled me. I tilted my head slightly to a pair of dark brown eyes.

"Mae Geoffries, I was just about to get you. Come in." Magenta stepped back, fixing her rose gold Panama hat. I caught sight of her rings: at least two on each finger. Adorned with various gems and stones, they sparkled and gleamed in the light.

"Thank you for this opportunity."

Magenta rounded her desk and sat down on one of the chairs while I sat on the other side, sinking slightly in the furred fabric. I pulled out my CV and placed it on the table.

"So, tell me a bit about yourself, Mae?"

I cleared my throat, sitting up slightly.

"Well...um...ah, I live in Inverness currently after moving from East London with my mum. Finished sixth form with an A level in design, art, business, and psychology. To be honest, I only chose the last two subjects on a whim. My main focus was on design, and I thought art would go quite well with it. Got an A for design, a B in art, business and psychology I'm convinced I just about made that C grade." I laughed slightly, noticing the hard gaze Magenta had on me. I cleared my throat again.

"Currently working at a bar in central Scotland called the Bridgely. It's like the only good bar near the university, so we get all the uni students, but then at the same time during the holidays, it's really quiet: a few stag and hen dos every now and again, but nothing much."

"And why are you looking to work here?" Magenta asked.

Ah, what a question. Well, to be honest, I've been put on involuntary holiday for an upcoming trial which could result in me going to jail for a long time.

I clear my throat.

"Just a change of scenery really, something a bit more mature, I guess. I don't want to be 36 and still pouring tequila down some young adult's throat."

"So, it's not because of your potential life sentence?"

My body seized, and the room began to spin like I was on a helter-skelter that got faster with each turn. I squeaked, the only sound coming out of my mouth.

"It was very easy to put what you said together. I like to keep track of what's happening around my employees, and your issue made the news, albeit they excluded the fine details. They did, however, mention the bar. I put two and two together. So, Mae, why are you looking to work here?" There was a tone of light warning. Magenta wanted the truth, but I believed she would not judge me for it.

I cleared my throat.

"Uh...so I was maybe minutes from being gang raped. The only reason it didn't happen was that I killed someone. Now, because of the laws, there's a good chance I'll be sent away, for a long time. My mother is in a wheelchair from an accident that could not have been any unluckier, and we've moved hundreds of miles from her closest

relatives. Could you imagine her having to move back to her parents so they can look after her? My grandfather is 72 years old. And... and..." I started to laugh, holding the side of my head.

"The funniest thing is, when this is all done, if I get acquitted, I will have to find a new job. I need to find a new job, but this thing is following me like a dead body." I huffed loudly, wiping the sides of my eyes, trying to not let more tears fall down my face.

A box of tissues slid my way, and I looked up to Magenta sitting on the desk next to me. I took the tissue from her, dabbing my eyes and wiping my nose.

"Has Adele told you what we do here?"

I shook my head.

"We are a luxury costume store; we provide tailored costumes for clients. However, we do more than that. Tell me, Mae, what do you know of the supernatural?"

I frowned slightly.

"I've seen Twilight, a few TV shows."

"And what if I told you they are real, and very much among us?"

"Then I'd say this must be a Wattpad story."

Magenta laughed and stroked my head.

"I'd like to offer you the job."

My eyes widen. After everything I'd just said, I'd been offered the job.

Wait, what is the job?

"Now you won't be able to work immediately; I expect all my employees to be graduates. You say that your main passion is design. Have you considered taking that further?"

"I..." This was insane. "I have, but with everything, I just haven't been able to."

"Don't worry about your trial, Mae. As of now, you are an unofficial employee of FolkWore. One thing I ask of you is, in these next months, to think about what you want to do. We can meet again after the trial. That sound OK?"

"Yes, Magenta, that sounds excellent." I stood up and shook her hand, stuffing the tissue into my back pocket. I shut the door behind me. And for the longest while, I felt optimistic.

Swimming in Our Feelings

"**I**t's time you tried Voyager. It's hands down my favorite place to trade and buy cryptocurrency. It's 100% free co-"

I take out my earbuds and bring the treadmill down to a light jog.

I wipe my face, leaning my arms on either side as the belt slows to a walk. Sunlight streams into the room. Even with the windows open and the AC on, sweat rolls down my neck.

My eyes catch her figure immediately. Mae is swaying to the music coming out of the headphones I gave her for Christmas, twirling and rolling her wrists.

She drops her towel at the edge of the pool, revealing an orange and black tie-dye bikini. A woman in a bikini is no different than one in underwear, yet somehow Mae looks more alluring.

Could it be the tight fabric disappearing in between the round-ness of both of her cheeks? Or that she'll be dripping wet when she gets out? Either way, I have the urge to finish my workout with a swim in a pool I haven't used in years.

This woman never ceases to turn me on.

I head to my room, change my gym wear to swimming shorts, and pull a towel from the bathroom, hurrying to the garden.

By the time I make it to the pool, Mae is swimming back and forth. I kneel as she reaches the far end. She rolls over in the water, kicking off the wall to propel herself forward.

Mae slows down, emerging from the water. Her hair lies flat against her face.

"You also swim?" I ask, dipping my feet into the cold water.

"It's a good skill. Besides, it makes the body work harder." She lays her arms on the edge of the pool, looking up at me, her chocolate brown eyes peering through the streaks of her hair.

"Do you swim?"

"Not enough to really own a pool." I laugh, discarding my towel and slipping in beside her. Mae bobs up and down in the water, causing little ripples to stretch away from her.

"Do you trust me?" she asks suddenly, gliding towards me, her body practically cutting the water in half.

"Yes."

"Lie down and float."

I didn't expect this to take that turn, but I turn around, lowering myself further into the water. I feel Mae's small hands cup around my head as I lift my heels, taking in the clear blue sky as tiny clouds float by.

"What's th-"

"Shush."

I see that Mae has closed her eyes, leading me around the pool. I allow my body to relax in the water, and her hands.

"Have you ever been in an isolation tank?" Her voice is soft.

"No."

"It's the same temperature as the human body, and you feel as though you're floating. No idea when the water ends, and your body begins. That kind of connection and infinity gives you time to think."

It's silent. With my eyes still closed and the feeling of weightlessness, I speak.

"When Lincoln told me about FolkWore and how much fun it brought him, I was skeptical. I didn't quite understand how paying someone would ever make you feel more than just lied to. However, having you here, I wish I never signed up in the first place."

"Why is that?" Mae asks.

I sigh, the realization weighing me down into the water.

"Because I would have rather met you outside of this."

"And who says you still can't," Mae whispers. I feel her hands travel from my head down to my sides, before her hair brushes against my forearm.

I open my eyes. She is floating by my side. She turns to me, smiling as she interlocks her fingers with mine.

We both turn to the sky, watching the clouds roll above us slowly, floating in a pool of water, and our feelings.

Hell's Doorstep

"*Congratulations on being acquitted, not that you needed it.*"
Natalie pulled away from the hug, stroking my arm.

"*Thank you, I'm just glad it's over with. Though reporters are still hanging around the bar, looking to catch sight of me.*"

"*Well, you won't ever have to go there again. You work here now.*"

This month could not have gone better. Receiving my contract with FolkWore and handing in my resignation felt like I was truly moving past it all. Mum was happier. She and Marlene – her caregiver – had noticed a positive change in me.

"*You applied for the designer position, which is great. I'm always looking for fresh ideas. Luckily for you, I am the manager for this shop, so you'll shadow me when you come here. Have you found what uni you'll attend?*"

"*Yes, I explained my situation to the university, and I'll be enrolling in late September.*"

"*Excellent. Well, seeing as you'll mainly be in Scotland, you can send in any designs you have via email, or we can FaceTime if that's easier. You'll also need to come to the shop once a fortnight for company training.*"

"*Company training?*"

Natalie took me through the back of the shop. We headed up the stairs, and she immediately opened the door to her left. She stepped aside so I could see inside.

Four other people were sitting down in a row in front of a projector. Most were talking while one was in a corner scrolling through their phone.

"To learn about supernatural creatures," Natalie finally replied. I frowned, turning towards the woman.

"I thought that was a joke, a curveball question in the interview."

Natalie laughed and closed the door while the eight pairs of eyes watched on. Natalie opened another opposite, ushering me into the empty fabric room.

"What exactly did Adele and Magenta tell you?"

"Not much. I didn't want to get my hopes up with the trial, so I didn't really ask too much."

Natalie mumbled a few profanities before leaning against one of the shelves.

"On the outside, we are a luxury costume store. Sometimes, we dabble in streetwear, and designers do projects with other companies on occasion. However, behind the scenes, we offer a more intimate service, a fantasy that's quite bespoke."

The words settled in my brain for a while before the gears began to turn.

"This...this place is an escort business?"

"Particularly tailored to werewolves, vampires, fae and the like." Her sentence seemed to fly over my head. I was still spinning from realizing that I had just been employed to be an escort.

"I-I have to have sex with people?" I whispered. My stomach turned as imaginary hands caressed my body, making me squirm.

"In time, yes."

What should've been a great opportunity suddenly turned very sour.

"Then I can't work here. I'm sorry, but this won't work." I smiled weakly at Natalie, who had a piercing gaze on me as I headed for the door.

"Then we'd have to ask for the expense of your legal fees returned to us."

I spun around, gob smacked.

"What?" I was stunned, they were sinking that low.

"We hired that lawyer and paid those fees for an employee of the company as we would do any employee. As you are handing in your resignation without a month's notice, we will need that money returned."

"Then here is my one month's notice," I replied. I guess in some sense, I was lucky to be in Scotland. I could just avoid their calls and start searching for a new job.

"One month's notice is for employees who have completed their six-month probation after they become a full employee. As you will spend the next couple of years studying, you are not regarded as a full employee until after your studies have finished."

"So, you're saying that I can't leave for the next several years?"

Natalie nodded. A flicker of emotion went through her eyes.

"You must see that this company is flawed, right? You can't honestly expect to manipulate me into having sex."

"I have not done anything, Mae. You're free to leave. We just expect our money back."

"And you know damn well I can't afford that." I felt a rise of heat from my chest. What I thought was a beacon of hope, had now become a cloud, raining shards of glass.

"*Then am I really forcing you? If you are worried about the escort business, I can assure you that you will not be having sex with clients until after you've completed your studies, supernatural and otherwise, and that won't happen for a long time.*"

I don't know how she managed to spin this situation into a positive, but I relaxed slightly, the knowledge that I wouldn't be having sex with strangers until five years from now somehow comforting. At least by then, if I left, I could've saved some money to pay the legal fees back.

"*Your safety is our utmost priority. You may attend a few parties, be a bit of arm candy but nothing more, and at all events you will be with an experienced member, never on your own. Clients are contracted to treat our employees with respect and kindness. No one would tarnish that. You'll be safe with us.*"

Of course, no one would hurt me with the devil in my corner.

Fatherly Advice

Another jacket flies out of the closet, landing on the growing pile on the chair.

"Mae, if you continue throwing things, we won't be doing this again."

One more piece of clothing darts through the air, and I stand up. I walk to the room to find her bent over, surveying my shoes.

"Have you found something yet?" I ask, watching her look behind her, hair falling in front of her face.

"Patience is a virtue," Mae says, standing straight and turning to face me, clothes draped over her shoulder and a pair of brogues are in her hand.

"Besides, I only see you in the evening. I'd like to contribute to your morning."

"It'll be evening by the time I leave the house."

Mae rolls her eyes and pushes me out of the room and onto the bed. I watch her lay my clothes out.

"I want you to complement what I am wearing."

"You're wearing all black, my dear, that won't be very difficult."

A thigh-length pencil skirt with the smallest slit on both sides, and a thin-strapped silk top that ripples in the center: I don't see how they pair with a white tailored shirt, grey trousers and black brogues."

"The grey matches my underwear." She lifts her skirt, showing me a peek of the grey lacy fabric. "So you are, but no one will know." She smirks, taking the pile she created, and going back into the walk-in wardrobe, allowing me time to finally get dressed.

The phone rings halfway through lacing up my shoes. *Mr. Aldrek* displays on the screen, and I slide the button across.

"Father? Everything OK?" He tends to keep to himself, playing golf with friends, or going to visit Freya. Mom usually calls on his behalf.

"I'm outside." With that sentence, he hangs up.

Callahan Aldrek is very to-the-point. So, when I hear the door opening, I grab my coat, phone and keys, and leave the room.

He is standing, as dominant as ever, by the large table near the front door, hands behind his back, dressed in a tailored three-piece grey suit. I probably look even more like his son in my own grey suit trousers.

Father brushes his long hair behind his ear before stroking his full beard.

"Good morning, Son." His voice is baritone, and rumbles with every word.

"Good morning, Father, nice to see you again." I'm halfway down the stairs when my door closes. I watch as Father's eyes dart slightly to my left, and his jaw tightens.

"Mr. Aldrek." Mae's voice is sweeter than usual. I glance quickly over my shoulder to find her standing by my door, her hand still on the handle.

"I was just tidying up Dominic's clothes. He allowed me to dress him today."

I feel a rising heat tickle the tips of my ears as I turn to look at my father's reaction.

"Then you must be psychic. Dominic knows I like a united front when we head into the office together." He grins at her revealing perfect teeth

"Psychic powers would work well in my line, so maybe I am. You look very handsome today." Mae brushes past me, heading down the stairs as she speaks to my father.

"Did Bernard do your suit?"

Callahan looks down, mildly shocked, before nodding to Mae.

"You know of Bernard's tailors?"

"Oh, yes." Mae takes his arm, lifting it up to inspect the cufflinks. "He has a thing for Greek cufflinks. Did you know he designs them himself? Has his own metal man to make them for him somewhere in Athens." Mae gently removes her hold on my father's arm, yet her control over his attention prevails.

I shift uncomfortably as Mae and my father exchange more compliments. This woman has got my father smiling in record time and joking like lifelong buddies.

"As much as I love chatting with you, Mr. Aldrek, I-"

"Callahan, please, Mae."

"Callahan, I'm sure you didn't just come to talk about suits."

He smiles at her, clasping his hands together to finally address the actual person he came to see.

"Yes, I came to help finalize this year's charity. I want to see which cause we are focusing on this year, and how the companies are going; seeing the owner always boosts productivity. Mae, you should join us. I could use your womanly touch with some of the elements."

Mae sighs, smiling slightly.

"Unfortunately, I can't. I have a meeting with my boss, but I'm sure Dominic will do a fantastic job."

"If his decisions are anything like his woman, we will do fantastically, right son?" They turn to me.

"You're in good hands, Father."

Callahan nods, heading out the door to wait for me in the car. I look to Mae, taking her hand and pulling her towards me.

"How did you manage to do that?" I whisper, our faces a few inches apart.

"Your father isn't nearly as stoic as he makes himself to be. You both are very similar, and I know *you* all too well."

"Is there anyone who doesn't immediately fall in love with you?"

"None to date." Mae holds my face in her hands, bringing my lips to hers. A slow and gentle kiss causes my hands to wrap around her waist, stroking her back as the kiss deepens.

Mae pulls away, and my eyes flutter open.

"Have a good day at work, Mr. Aldrek. I'm taking one of the cars."

I smile at her, letting her body go.

"Don't destroy it, Miss Geoffries, or you'll be in trouble."

"Is that a threat or a promise?"

"If you're not careful, it'll be both."

Mae giggles, and I give her one last smile before heading out the door. Father sits in the driver's seat of his Porsche, tapping the wheel as he stares through the passenger window. I hitch my trousers up as I climb in.

The car pulls out, heading out of the community.

About halfway into the journey, as the tall buildings begin to eclipse us, Callahan clears his throat.

"I like Mae," he begins simply. "She seems suitable."

"Suitable for what?" I have an inclination of where he is taking this conversation. *Children.*

"She would bear great children."

"I couldn't ask that from her, father. She's human. It's not even as simple as that if she isn't. I could really hurt her."

I could end up killing her. To be specific, the child could. Bearing a vampire is no small feat, even for a female vampire. Those nine months are agony. The excessive and almost addictive feeding habits are just one of the things females have to consider. With Mae, if she didn't consume blood, the baby would consume hers, leech its own human mother, unaware of the damage it would ultimately do to itself.

"We've only been seeing each other for six months. It might not even last," I add.

And we only have six months left.

The impending sound of sand hitting the bottom of a timer echoes in my head, and I sink slightly in my chair.

"You have my blessing," he replies, pulling under the tall building of the company, refusing to engage on the matter, as we have arrived at a place of business.

Callahan Aldrek likes surprising people. He prefers to see people's true nature regularly to remind himself who to keep close and who to distance from, so entering the building with no warning is like dropping a shark into a fishing pond. Blood and panic.

I haven't bothered to text anyone. I have faith that my workforce will be presentable when my father arrives, a reflection of my leadership through their conduct.

As the elevator doors slide open, nobody on the floor even takes notice. They all continue with their work as we saunter through, heading straight for my office at the end of the hallway. I shut the door behind us as Father takes the seat behind the desk.

"Tell me about the cause we'll be focusing on," he says, running his hands over my desk.

Probably to check for dust.

"My PA has drawn up a few. May I?" I motion to the phone on his right. Callahan pushes back in the chair, giving me space to reach for the phone. I dial Delilah's room phone. The simple flash and caller ID will have her turning up at my door.

I put the phone down, waiting for the knock, which occurs within a minute.

"Come in," we say in unison. Delilah steps in, folder in hand as she smiles at the both of us.

"Good morning, Mr. Aldrek, and Mr. Aldrek Sr."

"Delilah, my father would like to see the potential charities we will be fundraising for this year."

"Also, the guest list and potential venues. I want the event to be near the end of the year, one of the colder months. I'm tired of the hot weather," Father says.

Delilah nods and lays a few files down on the desk, each a different color with a small title on the tab.

"Last year, our charity focused on international awareness: lack of water in Kenya, improving medical services in Brazil, child brides in Southeast Asia. I thought this year could be more in-house. With the mishap of the Citalopram recently, I thought we could focus our efforts on the youth: homelessness, poverty, lack of opportunities, mental health. They are the future and will one day be the contributors to the country's economy.

"I like that. Long-term, we need those people on our side."

Delilah pulls out the purple folder and lays it on the top of the pile. "I have a few venues here. In terms of staff, I recommend we strive for the younger crowd: the same type of children we hope to raise awareness for, with the incentive that they would get standard pay of other employed staff members, providing that they train, and pass drug and criminal vetting. Perhaps keep them on for future events; at least then, we don't look like we are doing it as a publicity stunt. All I need to know is the date."

"October," Father answers quickly, "perhaps near the end of the month."

"The 31st would be good, a theme of mystery and anonymity. We could supply masks to guests and staff, and have a silent auction. A classy black-tie event," Delilah suggests.

"Halloween? Isn't that a bit high school?" I point out, trying to appear casual, and merely floating opinions.

"Yes," Father begins, "if we were to have everyone dress up and decorate the venue with cobwebs and tombstones, but like Delilah said, black tie. Masks are the extent of the Halloween theme."

"We could still do that mid-October," I counter.

Father turns to me in the chair before speaking.

"Give us a moment."

Delilah takes the folders off the desk and leaves the room.

"Why are you arguing with me?" he asks.

"I just think that we shouldn't use Halloween as a crutch for our charity." This is true in a sense. I just don't want the last 24 hours with Mae to be spent working. I don't know what I want to do on my last day with her, but certainly not this. He stands up from the chair, straightening his suit jacket.

I had outgrown him by the time I was 21. However, when his eyes fix on me, every inch of his presence screams to be respected.

"The event will be held on the 31st of October. Now, if you continue being counterproductive, or playing devil's advocate, I'm sure there are other things that need your attention."

I keep my mouth shut. What can I possibly say other than the truth? *I can't exactly tell him that I have six months left on my contract with her, which expires on the 1st of November.* The sound of the sand becomes even louder as a grain hits the bottom.

Father moves to open the door, revealing Delilah, who is studying her folders.

"Now Delilah, let's work out the finer details."

A Midnight Realization

I toss and turn under the sheet, before throwing it off entirely with a loud huff. The clock glows a dim 12:06, and I groan, swinging my legs to land on the carpet.

Maybe she's awake as well.

I grab shirt and trousers, and head to Mae's room.

Maybe she'd be up for another round? Good sex always makes me tired afterwards, and since Mae is around more times than not, I usually sleep like a baby. Not to say last night wasn't great, but there is a weight on my chest that makes it damn near impossible to sleep.

I open her door slowly. Her bed is bare, and there is no light coming from the bathroom.

Where is she? Midnight snack?

I head down the stairs, but there is silence in the kitchen. The weighted feeling gets heavier, enough to force me to grab the side of the table.

This is her pain. Mae is experiencing a negative emotion, and my cursed vampirism is enhancing it tenfold.

With my vision slightly blurry, I rely on my sense of smell to guide me. The scent of jasmine wafts through the wall closest to the garden.

I hurry out the room, bumping into walls and furniture. As I make my way to the front door, another wave of emotion washes over me, and I nearly smack into the door. I pull it open, wobbling my way to the garden, her smell getting stronger along with the crushing weight of her emotions.

Mae is sitting with her back to me on one of the deck chairs overlooking the covered pool, her laptop resting on her lap. As I progress closer, I see it is a video call, and my ears pick up her singing.

"Happy Birthday dear Mae and Kenny, happy birthday to us." Mae blows at the screen as the candles on the cake dance before being snuffed out. Mae claps, laughing as more emotions invade my body.

"Happy birthday, Kenny Benny."

"Happy Birthday, Mae Mae."

"I need to go. It's midnight where I am, and the birthday girl can't be tired. I love you guys."

"Love you too," they all shout, Mae blows them a kiss before disconnecting the call and shutting the laptop. She sighs, bringing her knees to her chest as she wipes her eyes quickly as though she didn't even want the tears settling on her face.

I can't breathe.

It's sadness she's feeling.

And not a sadness that you get occasionally. This is deep-rooted, and festering inside her, and on rare occasions, the small container she has for it cracks, and some of it seeps out.

Mae gets up from her seat, and I'm grateful that she heads to the garage as opposed to using the front door. I don't think she'd want me to see her like this.

If she wanted me to know, she would've said it was her birthday. As she shuts the door to the house, my legs buckle, and I'm finally able to collapse under the weight of her emotions.

The Designer Named Mae

"*Stay away from here if you can.*"
If it's work-related, does that still count? I hold the door open for Mae as she steps in, pulling me behind her. As we draw closer to the cashier the faery is not there but someone else.

Her hair is as curly as Mae's and lies on the glass counter as she looks down at something. With the padding of our footsteps, she looks up.

Her eyes are a milky white with no irises before they change to a recognizable brown – speckles of gold if the light catches them right.

A version of Mae stares back at me from across the counter yet the Mae next to me is holding my hand. The copycat across the desk moves to one side, her hand sliding across the glass. She cocks her head as she blinks slowly, her eyelashes long and delicately framing her eyes. She smiles, her cheeks rising slightly.

She is crossing the threshold, her hips swaying gently. I inhale sharply, expecting the whiff of jasmine.

I begin coughing as an overbearing smell fills my nose.

The Mae I know is gentler, her scent more caressing. This person is overwhelming, and slightly painful.

I take a step back, and the imposter frowns. A crack forms just above her eyebrow, stretching towards her forehead. Her face begins to crack further, pieces of it falling off, revealing the reflective material underneath.

It is horrifying but fascinating to see the shell of Mae being chipped away and dissolving to dust.

Two soft hands are placed on my face, directing my eyes somewhere else. A pair of warm brown eyes with flecks of gold if the light catches them right, and the gentle warmth of her jasmine scent and trail of chocolate to follow.

This is my Mae.

"Jesus, Fauna, put on your glasses," Mae says, her voice stern and hard. I want to look at the imposter again to see what she is doing, but Mae has a firm hold on my face, and her eyes have completely absorbed mine.

There is some fumbling behind us before a slender hand rest on Mae's shoulder. Mae turns around, and my eyes can take in my surroundings again.

Fauna is rubbing the side of her head.

"Sorry babe," she whispers. She raises her head to me, her blue eyes like the sky just before a hailstorm. In her human form, the succubus is nothing like Mae; she is shorter and most definitely appears no older than 20.

Mae pulls the girl into a hug, stroking her burgundy curls.

"This one," Mae jabs her thumb at me, "is off-limits."

Fauna and I both raise a brow at Mae.

Fauna goes back to her space behind the counter, closing the book that she had been reading. "The girls have been working tirelessly to make your designs a reality."

"And I couldn't do it without you lovely ladies. When you're free, come to the back and help with some of the fittings. Your slender body will work well in some of the gowns, providing you wear your glasses."

Fauna rolls her eyes before saying, "if no one comes in, I will."

Mae takes my hand, pulling back the emerald curtain to the bustle of five other worker bees and their queen. It doesn't even faze me to find no long corridor but instead four workbenches in the center of the room, each with a line of mannequins in different stages of design, some with almost completed looks, others still have the basic shape of the outfit. With the curtain drawn, Magenta lifts her head up from her work and smiles, standing up from her stool and shifting everyone's attention to us.

"Mae, you made it."

Mae lets go of my hand and goes in for a hug with Magenta. I admire the change. When Mae comes here as an escort, there is a clear hierarchy, but as a designer, even though Magenta is her manager, they are just like work friends.

"Thank you again for spearheading the designs," Mae says as they finally detach. "I'm sorry I couldn't give you more than a brief outline."

"Brief outline." Magenta laughs and looks at me over Mae's shoulder, rolling her eyes. "This one practically sent me a thesis, from the suppliers she wanted to the type of stitching."

Mae bows sheepishly before dropping her bag beside one of the tables.

"Gracie, show Mae the completed items to get her final approval."

The tall Amazonian like woman stepped forward her skin a rich brown that seemed almost reflective and her sapphire eyes are piercing, expected of a djinn.

Who is Magenta's source?

Her hair is in the traditional buzz cut of her kind, while her pierced ears are decorated with pieces of gold and silver.

"I don't believe your boyfriend has ever seen a djinn before." Gracie's voice drags me out of my staring, and I smile awkwardly.

"Sorry, she just caught me off guard."

Gracie nods, seeming to forgive my blatant staring, and takes Mae by the elbow, leading her further into the room to the back.

The other workers continue, no longer interested in my presence. Magenta pulls two chairs from the corner.

"You change the back of the shop regularly," I say as I sit down.

Magenta laughs lightly.

"Change, I guess it's something like that. I like to think of it like revolving rooms, and I always display the one I want people to enter."

Mae and Gracie return, chatting quietly, discussing color schemes and fabric textures. I tilt my head slightly to watch as Mae directs some of the others.

"She's a good employee," Magenta says suddenly, her amethyst eyes directed at Mae.

"As an escort or as a designer?" I ask, a bit more bitterly than I care to admit.

"Does it really matter?" she says, turning to me, her features soft and endearing.

"I see her as a daughter. She reminds me of me in my prime. There is a passion and light to her that's just-"

"Intoxicating," I finish. "Makes one hate this service of yours."

"Why's that?" she asks. I frown deeply as Mae smiles and laughs with her colleagues.

"Because she can't date clients." I feel something slide into my hand and look down. It is an invoice for $200,000. *I guess this is how much her goodwill will cost.*

"Then perhaps you should stop being one," Magenta says softly.

Superstition and Shared Showers

A large hand glides over my body to lay across me, heavy and full of warmth. My eyes open lazily, and I roll over, my nose bumping against Dominic's ear. The sun is sneaking through gaps in the blinds and resting on his head like an imaginary halo.

I trail my finger from the top of his head down to his nape, causing the man to stir awake, his eyes slightly opening, the silver shimmering as his pupil's contract.

"Surveying the goods, are we?" he mumbles into the pillow before rolling onto his back.

"Seeing what all the fuss is about," I whisper, causing Dominic to smile. He props himself up on his elbow, leaning in close as my hands cup his face. I place a soft kiss on his lips.

"Good morning," I whisper.

"Good morning. Breakfast?" he asks.

"It must be my birthday or something."

"Well, it will be at one point, but seeing as the staff have the day off, if you don't make breakfast, I'll have to."

I nod. "Breakfast would be great."

Dominic pecks my lips before sliding out of bed and heading out of the room.

I lean back into the bed before rolling out and doing my morning stretches.

This thing between Dominic and me has developed. Since New Year's Eve, the lust and animal urges have subsided, and something else is pushing through. More times than not, we sleep in the same room, either mine or his, and most nights we have sex, he doesn't even feed off me.

To be fair, he's an adult vampire. He probably only needs a cupful a month to keep going.

I hold the banister as I descend the stairs, hearing the sizzling of oil from the kitchen. I get a whiff of bacon well before I see it frying in a pan while Dominic pours batter into a waffle iron.

"Well, you have been busy, Mr. Aldrek. Is this how you treat all your females?"

Dominic turns around, smirking.

"Only my favorite one."

I take a seat on one of the stools, running my feet along the cold metal as I fill two glasses with juice.

"Any plans today?" he asks me, and the question takes me aback.

"Uh...no I guess, I mean, what are my options? What are you doing today?" I reply with my own array of questions.

Dominic laughs, turning off the cooker and placing two glistening pairs of bacon strips on plates. I watch him scrape the waffles from the machine and lay them next to the bacon before placing the plates in front of me and rounding the island to sit.

"It's the weekend. I refuse to answer any business-related queries, and the girls are out for the day. We are both completely untethered."

I cut into the soft waffle as I think about what to do with my weekend.

"Well, it's June, and my Christmas tree is still up. It's getting to the point where if I leave it any longer, it might as well stay up for next Christmas."

"You know, it's bad luck to leave your Christmas tree up after a certain time," Dominic comments, taking a gulp of his juice.

"Then I am in for the worst luck of my life."

We both laugh.

I fold the last artificial branch and lay it on top of the others.

"Finished on your side?" I ask, glancing behind me as Dominic places the star in the plastic box.

"Yup, done to your very particular instructions," he says, smiling at me.

I close the lid of the tree box and push it into the storage cupboard by the front door. Dominic hands me the box of decorations, and I place it on top before shutting the door with a heavy sigh.

"You look like Max when you sigh. I didn't notice it before, but meeting them last month, you all have similar features."

I smile slightly at the thought.

"You think so?"

"Yeah, I know we pretty much headed back after the dance recital, but in the time between the recital finishing and you getting ready to leave at their house, I noticed. Especially Kenzo, he looks just like his father, frown and all."

I laugh, pushing up off the door.

"Kenny is adopted. Mum and Max wanted another child. A few years after they married and just before I moved to the states, the agency found Kenny. We are not sure what his heritage is, but we think his father was from the Polynesian islands. Max is from Samoa, and he says Kenzo looks a lot like him when he was young, and his mother thinks so, too." I open the front, door holding out my hand for him.

"Ready to go home?"

Dominic takes it, and I walk out of the apartment with him, closing the door and heading to the car park.

We both get into the car and sit in the dimly lit interior. I feel Dominic's hand slide over mine, squeezing it slightly.

"You've gone awfully quiet, Mae," he says. He rubs my knuckles, waiting for a response.

"It's nothing." I turn to Dominic, putting on my best smile. He observes me before turning his head to the window, pulling out of the car park and heading home.

When we arrive home, the first thing I want is a shower. Without giving much time for Dominic to talk to me, I race up the stairs to my room, stripping myself bare before I even reach the shower cubicle. I turn the heat up high and the steam covers the entire room.

My eyes are closed as I allow the water to fall on my face. Even with the noise of the water, I hear the opening of the door and the soft thuds of Dominic's feet on the carpet.

"You can join me. Neither of us has had a shower today." I keep my face to the showerhead, picking up the delicate sounds of Dominic undressing.

His hands run down my shoulders, and I lean my head onto his chest.

"It was your birthday last month." My heart stops momentarily. "I felt your sadness, Mae."

My hands clench together, and I hold them to my chest. Curse the tag he has on me. It was one thing to have him picking up my thoughts, but to feel what I was feeling was so ... so ... *reassuring?*

Was this all I needed, for someone to peak into my mind and decipher the feelings I couldn't do so myself? Could only someone like Dominic be able to overcome this mountain sized wall I've spent years building?

"You miss them, don't you?" he whispers. Dominic begins rubbing my shoulders, easing the built-up tension inside.

"I...I just...it's hard...uh..." I rub my face, annoyed at the mess of my response. Dominic moves my hand from my face. He turns me around, and I open my eyes to look at him. His silver eyes are soft, reminding me of a dense cloud.

"You're away from your family, and you're missing out." He runs his thumb down my cheek, and I sigh. My eyes fall closed at his touch.

"I understand. You haven't properly addressed any of it, have you?"

As he removes his hand from my face, I open my eyes slowly to find him pulling his band from his hair. His hands go for my hair, holding it delicately, pulling the band over it, only to have it snap and bounce off the glass.

Dominic frowns, and the reaction causes a laugh to come out. He looks down at the band before laughing along with me, pulling me into a hug as both our hair gets wet by the shower.

"You make it a lot easier to communicate how I feel without having to say the words," I say against his chest.

"Sometimes it's not so bad being intimate with a vampire. I see your needs, and I hear them, too."

"Are you showing me what I could have?" I look up as Dominic looks down at me, referencing the conversation we had on Christmas Day.

"And what do you think?" he asks.

I think I like it.

Dominic smiles. His hands play with my hips as he leans down, kissing me. I place my hands around his neck, pulling him closer, my tongue pressing against his lips, forcing them open and stroking his tongue.

Dominic pulls away and turns me around, kissing my neck. I moan as he nibbles the spot, his hands gliding up my torso and cupping both breasts, massaging them as he rubs his growing erection against me.

I place my hands on the glass, pushing myself out, encouraging him to go further. Instead, one of his hands slides down my exposed body, rubbing a finger gently over my sensitive clit. The sparks that fly around my body at the sensual touch force me to push myself out further.

"This isn't about me, it's about you," Dominic whispers. As he pushes two fingers inside of me, I'm surprised I don't orgasm immediately.

With one hand sliding in and out of me with unprecedented ease and another teasing my erect nipples, I am mewling with pleasure.

As my walls tighten around his fingers, Dominic removes them painstakingly slowly, grinding my approaching orgasm to a halt. I whimper at the loss of his touch. My hands ball into fists as Dominic holds my waist, pushing his erection into me.

I push against his rhythm. The crescendo of wet skin hitting against wet skin makes the shower steamier.

"Fuck, Mae," Dominic says. The glass vibrates as he slams a hand onto it, his other hand gripping my waist as we both pound into each other, steaMr.olling to that orgasm. I push him deeper, and he curses louder. He holds my hand that is pressed against the glass, causing my walls to tighten and my toes to curl.

My knees buckle, but Dominic manages to keep me held up as I reach euphoria. Dominic hugs me close as he reaches his own finishing line, kissing the underline of my jaw.

Sexual Betting

I play with the hem of my skirt as Lara rummages around my nether regions with a cotton swab.

"I'm guessing I still have a healthy vagina," I say. Lara pushes away on her chair, pulling her mask down, her face like the picturesque beauty it always should have been.

"It is. No wonder Mr. Bitey enjoys you so much." She winks at me and pulls off her gloves.

"How did the court hearing go?" I swing my legs off the side, pulling on my knickers.

"He got three years for my attack, and other victims came forward, so he might get more, and he's been blacklisted."

I hop off the chair and pull my best friend into a huge hug.

"That's good news, right? He can't hurt you or anyone else." I take my seat by her desk, exposing my arm.

"It is, but you know there's always that fear when you get those clients that just won't let things be."

I understand her entirely. It is the whole reason Magenta has clients name their chosen employee. Aside from medical issues, clients aren't even allowed to know our surnames or date of birth.

"I hope he tries, just to see Magenta's wrath first-hand." I laugh, and so does Lara; it is good to see her smiling. Last time I saw her, her eyes were dimmed, and she had shrunk into herself.

There is a knock at the door before it opens. Gretchin steps in, carrying a notebook in her arms, her hair a paling purple.

"What are you expecting us to buy now?" I ask, causing the faery to pull her hair in front of her eyes. One of these days gretchin will dye her hair and completely throw us off with what emotion she's having.

"Staff party is tomorrow, bets on who makes the most on their portfolio," she says, taking a seat on the bed opposite.

"It's a scam, that stupid game. The demons are at an unfair advantage. Fauna, Martel and Lilith are lust demons, this job was made for them, even Gweneth has an unfair advantage. One small tune and she's got a whole five-mile radius on their knees," Lara protests.

Gretchin scoffs loudly.

"Says the elf. With your brief foresight when aroused," Gretchin counters, "you're practically gold dust. Any stockbroker would die to have you."

Lara visibly shivers. There was a time when elves were enslaved, used as horny crystal balls for other creatures, humans included. They were such docile creatures, focused on knowledge that things such as violence and war were beneath them. Simple in one truth to learn all that there was to learn. Then Seraphine liberated them. Sex shouldn't be caged and monitored. That's when pixies were born, and finally, the fae and elf separation, forbidding them to interbreed.

"That's rich, Gretchin. Everyone wants aerial sex. No one wants a human they can get off the street. Feigned innocence is the only thing I've got going for me." I pout, my eyes going that little bit bigger for the girls.

"Well prove them wrong, Mae. How much are you betting?" Gretchin purrs, her hair deepening into a violet.

"Minimum cash in?" I don't like to spend recklessly. Not that I can't, but I worry about what I will do when this all ends. *How long can I survive on this nest egg I am building?*

"$20,000, about a month's pay if you're booked enough," Gretchin replies.

I shrug casually as Gretchin lays the pen and paper on my lap for me to sign away a month's work.

"I'll sign mine after I've done my checkups. I'll come find you, Gretchin."

The faery nods, leaves the room, and shuts the door behind herself.

"Did Magenta say anything about my blood?" I ask, watching Lara play with the sealing bag.

"No, you know how she is when it comes with foresight. She won't even tell me."

Magenta is something of a unicorn. She is a witch, yes, but her powers extend further than the levels of a nature witch or even a lunar witch. Hers have developed, evolved into something beyond our imagination, and foresight through blood is just one skill she uses. Simply touching someone's blood gives her insight from a month up to a year for that person.

"But don't worry, Mae. Magenta won't let harm come to her employees."

Guest #3092

I tap my fingers on the steering wheel, waiting for the line in front of the large mansion to move, checking my watch. It has just gone past ten.

Is this what a $200,000 party gets me? A queue?

The FolkWhore invitation lies on the passenger side. The gold font sits delicately on the black card, shimmering under the moonlight, next to the equally shimmering black mask that had been sent with it.

Privacy costs money.

A FolkWore event requires what seems to be the biggest house in the state. Located near the edge of Seattle, the house is as big as a school, and with good reason, too. Every single important figure seems to be here, or at least that's what Lincoln had told me when I called yesterday.

"Think of it as a runway show, but with an auction element to it."

I frowned, twirling the corner of the letter on the desk. I could hear Mae tidying her room before her car arrived.

"I don't like the idea of people seeing me there, not with the FBI and IRS perched underneath me."

"That's the beauty of it, dear brother, no one will know. Did you get the mask?"

I opened the black velvet box to reveal the black mask. I ran my thumb over the velvety material. "What does it do? I mean, I'm not in a superhero movie. Covering my eyes won't change my identity."

Lincoln laughed on the other end.

"Well, the mask distorts your projection to others. You'll see when you get there. Go enjoy yourself. See how much your girl is worth."

"You not coming? You don't want to see how Lara will fare?" There was some silence on the other end. Lincoln and I hadn't talked about the new year's fiasco. We simply pretended that we hadn't both been intimate with Mae at one point, nor that my brother liked a bit more than the LGBTQ+ community.

"No, I'll end up spending too much money on her to make sure no one else gets her."

"Oh," was all I could say. **At least he's honest.** The door to Mae's bedroom closed.

"I'll need to go, Link."

"Let me know how much she gets you to spend."

I hung up the phone, dropping the invitation on the table and heading out of the room.

The mask feels warm against my skin as I fix the satin ties to the back of my head.

I step out of the car and hand the keys to the valet. The flight of stone steps in front of me has been draped with carpet. The doors are open, and the lights, chatter, and soft music are evident before I reach the top.

A gloved hand stretches in front of me, preventing me from progressing into the main hall. I turn to the owner.

The Oni mask is painted in black and gold, which seems to be the running color scheme of the event. The teeth and horns are gold, the eyes are completely empty. I crane my neck slightly to get an inclination of his scent, but nothing.

It's certainly not human. This is what Lincoln meant by distorting projection.

"*Nǐ hǎo.*"

My eyes travel from the seven-foot Oni-masked thing to the chipper Chinese boy next to it. He pulls out a tablet from a small box on a side table and hands it to me.

"Here you will find our available employees tonight." He presses the home button, and the screen lights up; rows of numbers and pictures are visible.

"There is a filter tab if you have a certain type you'd like, and a search bar if you know their number. Tap on the employee number, and you'll find where they are based on site." The boy presses a random employee: a brown-haired woman who seems to hail from the eastern side of the world. Just underneath her number is the word 'Kerchee'— a fae type creature who lives under the sand dunes in Egypt. Rare, and extremely hostile to non-natives.

The employee index minimizes, revealing the layout of the area, a green dot flashing at the back of the house.

"You'll also see the three highest bids." He points to the top right corner, a box of ever-changing figures next to guest numbers, the highest being $13,000. At the bottom is the text tab with the guest number #3092, my number.

"How will I know who's up for sale?" I ask.

"If they aren't wearing a mask, then they are up for bidding. Enjoy your evening. There's a bar in each sector, and food will be making its way around the floor."

I take the tablet under my arm, walking into the bustling guests, not a scent in sight.

I just hope my projection is the same.

Streams of black masks weave in between one another, some attached to suits, others to dresses. I feel Magenta's gaze long before I see her perched at the top of the stairs on the far end, leaning on the railing as she watches her money accumulate below.

I came here for Mae, and I'm not about to trail through "black, female, human" filter results to find her.

I keep to the edge of the room, heading to the stairs, not even giving the other guests a glance. Magenta doesn't even look my way as I approach her, her amethyst eyes still surveying the fruits of her labor.

"Excellent turnout," I say, folding my arms and resting them on the railing.

"There always is. People travel from far and wide to get priority. Our personal financial year begins in July; employees are open for new contracts."

"Where is she?" I ask simply, bored of upholding the false interest I have for Magenta. My money has been spent; she is making all the profit.

"Employee number 4902."

I type in the number in the search tab, and there is Mae's picture, the words "human" underneath. I press her image, and the green light flashes in the left wing of the map. My eyes subconsciously travel to the top right-hand corner, my teeth rubbing against each other. Compared to the Kerchee woman, Mae's highest bid is at $30,000, and the event only began 45 minutes ago.

To be expected. She knows how to gain a man's favor.

"If it's any consolation, bidding starts at $10,000."

"Thank you, have a good evening, Magenta."

"Let the girl work, Mr. Aldrek. She's not yours tonight."

I *tsk* loudly, taking my leave and following the direction to where she is.

Drinks flowing a mile a minute, escorts open for buying, I'd be more surprised if they didn't have gambling. The map leads me to the casino section. Three rows of six roulette tables stretch down the room, and from the pulsing green light, Mae is at table number four.

At the entrance, another employee stands with their own personal Oni-masked giant beside them. *Bodyguards to protect the merchandise.* The blonde stands by an identical black box on a tall side table. She is waiting for me to be close enough to speak.

"Welcome. Complimentary chips, sir?" She pulls out a small, sealed, clear box and hands it to me. "If you'd like more chips, our dealers have a chip and PIN machine on hand. We only accept debit tonight. Enjoy your evening."

Mae is dressed in a white tailored shirt with a short red tie. Her hair has been slicked into a high ponytail, her curls resting near her ears. She is catering to three guests; two of them taking their leave while the one still sitting down is talking to her.

I take a seat to Mae's left, two stools down from the floundering, stubby man. It is hard to see much of him after that; his face is fuzzy.

"So, I said no, I won't spend money on a new boob job, and that is how marriage three ended."

Mae laughs, giving the man her full attention. I open the transparent container with three rows of different colored chips. I pull out a red one, $1,000 marked on its face.

I watch Mae turn her attention to the spinning wheel and ball. It bounces between numbers before landing on a red three. She takes the chips that the other guest has put on black 29. He is down to about six chips and shows no signs of stopping.

"Welcome to the table, sir," she says, smiling. "Gentlemen, place your bets." Mae turns her smile to the other guest, who is all too happy to receive her attention. I place the chip on one of the numbers. I'm not too bothered where it goes; it is complimentary.

"Blow on this, would ya, doll?" The other guest holds out his hands: three chips of varying color and value. Mae giggles and leans over the table, pursing her lips and blowing onto the man's hands. The guest places all three chips on a single number.

Mae spins the wheel before turning the ball in the opposite direction. It bounces before landing.

"Black eight, congrats, sir. Your reward is $49,750." Mae smiles, pushing a small stack of chips towards me. The guest two stools down curses loudly, hitting his palm down on the side.

Mae goes to grab the chips the man has lost, and her hand is caught inches from them. She looks at the guest, who has a hold on her, and my eyes narrow.

"Unfortunately, sir, you have lost these chips. Please unhand me so we can begin the next round."

"You unlucky little bitch," he spits, his grip on her wrist tightening. My stool screeches as I stand up, ready to tackle this guy to the floor, yet Mae's personal Oni mask is quicker.

A bigger, thicker hand seizes the guest's wrist, forcing him to swivel in his chair to face him. The beast removes his mask slowly. The lights begin to flicker, causing guests to gaze up at the ceiling in awe.

Tension corrodes the air, and a sense of fear creeps up my spine. Even at my distance, I want to be further away. I can only imagine what the guest in front of me is feeling. His hold on Mae is weakening as it shakes violently. What he is witnessing is the real face of the demon: the embodiment of damnation and evil.

The demon has only moved the mask an inch downwards, but it is enough to get the point across. Mae's hand is free, and she has taken the chips away.

The beast goes back to its position beside Mae. She turns to the Oni mask, smiling as her tongue makes movements inaudible to everyone. Her pupils dilate until the black covers the entire eye. It looks like little more than a quick flash, but I notice it.

She's speaking the language of Hell.

I shiver. That sort of realization makes my stomach roll. Most human words are branches of supernatural origin, mutations of kinds; but Hell is a different level: to hear it is instant insanity, and to speak is immediate damnation to the soul.

How? Why? Mae isn't as human as I thought.

"Gentlemen, if you make your way to the garden, the show will begin. Feel free to cash in your chips with our employees near the entrance." She smiles at both me and the other guest. His hand has begun to turn to stone. A part of me laughs at the fight or stone mentality of gargoyles.

Employee #4902

I head to the garden with the wave of guests. We all sit a couple of feet from the stone steps, in front of a platform.

"Welcome to our annual show and catalogue," Magenta begins, taking her stance at the top of the stone steps, microphone in hand. "I hope our employees live up to your satisfaction. Now let's begin the show."

The lights dip, only casting their beams on the path down the stairs and onto the runway. The first of the employees begin to stream through as the music starts.

"Our nature born," Magenta announces.

Fae, elves, pixies, kerchee, and water sprites walk out. Their employee numbers have been painted on various exposed parts of their bodies, glistening a pulsating deep green. Their wings flutter as they hover above the ground.

"Or perhaps you desire something with a bit more darkness."

The next section is creatures of the night: female werewolves, their numbers a luminous blue. Vampires, their numbers blood-red and dripping. Sirens, their mouths taped shut with their numbers written across the tape. djinns, and a range of incubi, succubi and Lerans.

Lerans, a descendant of the infamous phoenix, have skin that is black and crumbly, much like ash, but underneath, they're dipped in gold and can emit the sun's heat. Parts of their skin were in the shape of their numbers. They glimmer under the spotlights.

The sky is lit up with scents from across the world, like paint to a canvas.

"Maybe you prefer innocence." Magenta's words seem to whisper in my ear as though she is talking directly to me. I look to the stairs as a line of men and women dressed in white descend.

Humans.

There are about ten of them trailing through, their clothes untouched by everything around them, pristine white. Mae is at the back wearing a white dress that sways at the knees, almost like a wedding dress.

Somehow managing to divert my eyes, I check her bidding. She has soared to just under $100,000. My fingers itch, hovering above the bidding tab. I could easily win. If I add one more zero to that top bid, I can have her.

But I don't want to buy her. I don't want to be a client anymore.

I look up to Mae, who is reaching the end of the platform near where I'm sitting. Our eyes connect briefly.

«Hey.»

With that, she turns on her heels and follows the trail up the stairs and into the building.

She saw me out of a crowd of hundreds; she knew I'd be listening to her.

With the lineup of employees coming to an end, the guests head back to do some more shopping. I, however, hang around the outdoor pool, sipping on passing trays of alcohol as I wait for the party to end.

"Mr. Aldrek?"

I lift my head from the whiskey in my hand to none other than Fauna. She has her glasses on, keeping her body in its human form.

An elegant jumpsuit coated in rose gold brings out the warmth in her light brown skin tone.

"Hello, Fauna."

"The event is coming to a close, would you like to come get Mae?"

I stand up from my seat as Fauna leads the way.

Instead of heading through the main event, we round the back of the house. I remember Mae mentioning that guests wouldn't be sampling the goods, so it makes sense why Fauna is taking me to Mae discreetly.

She opens a side door, revealing the bustling of a kitchen: cooks still preparing entrees and waiters refilling their trays before heading back out. We walk past the people at work to the back, another door that seems to lead to the employees' section.

A house this big, of course it has live-in staff.

"I've only come across one other person who resisted their lust," Fauna says as we walk through a narrow corridor.

She is referring to our first encounter, how her projection of Mae cracked and chipped away.

As we come to a single door at the end of the hallway, Fauna knocks on it gently.

"I just hope it's requited, Mr. Aldrek." She smiles at me slightly before walking away.

The door swings open, revealing a tall, brown-skinned man. He isn't wearing any shirt, using his muscles to somewhat intimidate me. The burning *H* has been stamped just under his left collarbone. He has a pair of similarly styled glasses, like Fauna.

Ah, an incubus. This must be Martel.

I see why he and Mae are often paired together; they look good. His strong, chiseled features display a contrasting difference to Mae's softer ones. His narrow eyes are like coal, showing dominance and temptation.

"You're here for Mae?" Martel looks over his shoulder. "Lara, he's here."

That name, the elf, the one who plays with Lincoln. What does this infamous Lara look like?

Martel heads back to whatever he is doing, and Lara replaces him. Her brown hair has been tied up. A single purple braid wraps around her neck loosely. She is dressed in a loose-fitting top, glitter sprinkled on her body and some equally loose-fitting silk trousers.

"She's sleeping. We asked one of the boys to bring your car around the back to be discreet. Come in." Lara opens the door wider, stepping aside to let me in.

I don't know what I expected of an escort business. I half-imagined all the employees to have one massive orgy, rolling around in the money they've earned. Nonetheless, I'm still pleasantly surprised.

The room is dimly lit, candles casing the perimeter, and the ceiling lights turned down low. It is about one in the morning, and most of the employees are asleep, all posted in different corners of the room. Some lie on folded out sofas, others in sleeping bags, and a few in hammocks attached to the ceiling. Those who aren't sleeping are quietly indulging themselves in conversation or watching the large TV at the back.

If you didn't know, you'd think you walked into a company retreat. Lara leads me to a small sofa setup, a three-seater facing a two-seater. One is unoccupied while the other has Mae sleeping under a blanket.

Lara crouches down to Mae's level, stroking her face, causing the woman to stir.

"Mae, sweetie, Mr. Bitey has come to take you home."

Mae smiles. She places a hand on Lara's face.

"I'll meet you out back, OK?" she mumbles, her words slurring.

"Five minutes. Otherwise, Nicole will drag you out," Lara says against Mae's skin, who in turn softly pushes her friend away, letting her hand lie limp on the floor.

Lara stands up, ushering me to follow her while Mae gets dressed.

We walk to the end of the room to another door, this one leading immediately to the pitch-black outdoors. It is still warm for a June morning, and I step out with Lara, heading down the stone path where the lights of the party illuminate above.

"I didn't know you and Lincoln were brothers," Lara confesses suddenly, stuffing her hands into her pockets, rocking on the balls of her feet as we stand next to a small back gate.

"Who my brother involves himself with is none of my business," I reply, eyeing Lara from the corner.

She isn't my brother's stereotypical type – men and woman alike. Elves are intellectual creatures; they are aroused by the mind and less by the body. Lincoln likes seeing naked people with little to no talking before, during and certainly after.

"I love your brother, and I think he loves me. He wanted to tell you but knows how you are with the whole service."

My jaw tenses slightly, not at what Lara said, but at the fact that Lincoln is seeking my approval.

He shouldn't care what I think.

"Next time you see my brother, tell him not to worry about my or anyone else's opinion. His relationship with you is not a team-building exercise. You are the only two involved, and therefore, the only two people who matter."

I turn to Lara and give her a smile. Her eyes widen before she gives me one of her own, the tips of her ears going a shade of pink.

The car headlights catch my attention as the valet spins the car around. A man steps out, a different one than the person I handed the keys to and pushes open a small entrance by the gate.

"Your car, sir." He hands me the keys, his djinn blue eyes sparkling in the night before nodding at Lara and making his way to the staff entrance.

My gaze follows his path, catching Mae coming towards us. She is dressed in the same outfit she wore when I spent Christmas at her house: cream-colored fluffy leggings and a matching crop top. She has her hair tied up with the help of a scarf, her curls falling on her face.

"Hey," she says, holding her bag in front of her. I take it before taking her hand.

"Hey," I say back. I look to Lara, who seems to be waiting for a good point to leave.

"It was lovely meeting you, Lara."

"And you, Mr. Aldrek." She looks to her friend. "See you soon, babe, love you."

"See you soon, Lara, love you too."

Lara takes her leave, heading back in. We watch the door close before we head to the car. I open the door for Mae and place her bag on her lap. Once she's seated, I head to the driver's side.

I pull off the mask and drop it onto the back seat. Mae yawns, covering her mouth.

"Tired?" I ask, eyeing her.

"Extremely."

"Get some rest, because once we get home, I'm sampling your goods."

Mae laughs as I smile, the sound of her voice tickling my ears and my heart.

Blacklisted

Rebekah and Conrad struggled to make any headway. After deciding that FolkWore had far too many court cases to not be suspicious, they decided that the only way to know would be to talk to the defendants themselves. However, that proved difficult with everyone being "far too busy to answer some questions," and those were the ones in jail.

SeaTac is like any other prison in America: tall and grey. Rebekah parks the car, grabs her bag from the passenger side, and slings it over her shoulder. She cradles her piping hot coffee, the sweltering sun keeping it warm for her.

"Miss Calamba, early as usual."

Rebekah slams the door shut and locks the small car before she answers Conrad.

"It's our first breakthrough in months. My bosses are starting to breathe down my neck. I have to give them something by the end of July."

Conrad pulls his shades off his face and tucks them into the front of his shirt.

"Well let's be efficient then, partner. People are expecting results." He leads the way to the entrance, neglecting to say his job is also on the line.

He opens the door for his partner, and they stride into the squeaky hallway, heading to the booth on their left.

A tired-looking man stares at them, chewing something obnoxiously as he waits for them to introduce themselves.

"Detective Grier and Agent Calamba. We have a meeting with a Francis Gogola. He's a recent inmate."

"ID?"

The agents pull out their identifications and slide them under the transparent plastic wall separating them from the guard. He takes the cards, inspecting them before handing them back along with a clipboard.

"Sign in, please," he replies slowly.

Conrad takes the form and signs his name before handing it to Rebekah.

It isn't long before the door opens, and a slim woman walks in. She isn't dressed like the other guards – no black trousers and blue buttoned shirt. Instead, she has a knee-length black pencil skirt and matching jacket, the central button fastened over her blood-red shirt. She fixes her round spectacles as she smiles at the agents.

"Hi, I'm Warden Bennett. We spoke on the phone."

"We did, thank you for allowing us to see Mr. Gogola," Rebekah says.

"Anything to help, detectives." She opens the door, holding it for Rebekah and Conrad.

"Unfortunately, since arriving, Mr. Gogola has been very difficult. Fights with both inmates and staff alike have resulted in him being isolated until he learns to behave."

"So, I guess he has quite the temper." Conrad shoots a worried look at Rebekah.

He is a big man and can hold his own, but his five-foot-five partner can snap if the right pressure is applied to her.

Rebekah looks to Conrad; she has read through Mr. Gogola's file. She knows what to expect.

Sent to prison after being convicted of assault against one of the FW employees, the jury was convinced it was a hate crime, and that Mr. Gogola targeted the victim for being a trans woman. However, after statements from other women, and men as well, Mr. Gogola was sent away very quickly, for more than one charge.

Conrad and Rebekah take a seat on one of the metal benches in the visitor's room, waiting for Mr. Gogola to arrive.

"Let me do the talking, Rebekah," Conrad says, catching her by surprise. He's never referred to her on a first-name basis. She drops her bag on the floor, taking out her small A5 notebook and pen.

There is a loud buzz from the other side of the room, and the door swings inwards. A man dressed in an orange jumpsuit shuffle in, his hands held together by cuffs as he is accompanied by two guards on either side, a firm hold on his arms.

Francis Gogola is not what someone charged with several counts of GBH, rape, and a pending sexual harassment case would look like, and that is probably why he got away with so many crimes. With curls of caramel breezing against his forehead and eyes like the fields of Athens, he is Greek, that much is for sure. His hard jaw and angular features could have been sculptured from stone.

A healing bruise on his cheek and a split lip ruin his good looks, and his eyes are full of rage and violence.

Francis is quiet, waiting for the guards to take up a post on the back wall before he huffs, steam seeming to escape out his nose.

"What can I do for you?" He has his eyes on Rebekah, smiling, his teeth as straight and perfect as his features. Conrad clears his throat, trying to disrupt the uncomfortable gaze Gogola has on his partner.

"We wanted to ask you more about the case that got you incarcerated."

Francis' features harden as he narrows his eyes at Conrad.

"You mean that little shemale?"

Rebekah visibly flinches at the harshness of his words, and the clear transphobia.

Francis picks up on her flinch and smirks.

"I took what I thought was a her to an office party, something fun and light-hearted. He didn't mention that he had his own tool between his legs." Francis growls at the recount. "Embarrassing really, for him, mostly. Imagine trying to have a good time, and you get a feel of that in your hands." Francis spits on the floor in disgust.

While Rebekah feels repulsed by the man, Conrad appears neutral. Seeing his supposed indifference, Francis seems to have no sense of boundaries.

"And what do I get? Fucking blacklisted." His hands clench in their confines as his face reddens, blowing more air out of his nose.

"Blacklisted, from a costume store?" Rebekah frowns as she speaks. It seems odd to be so riled up over a costume store. Francis laughs.

"Do you think I give a shit about some fabric, you mindless cunt? I got blacklisted from their service." He rises. The air billowing out of his nose has taken on some translucency.

"What service?" Rebekah asks, seeing the man is about to say something.

"That stupid bitch Magenta and her rules. You pay good money, and there are still boundaries. You pay for something; you should get it. I should be able to do what I want." Francis slams his hands down again, the table shaking. "I should get my money's worth. Is that not customer satisfaction?"

Conrad stands up, fixing his jacket as he speaks, "I can see you're getting upset, we need a credible source. One that could go up in front of a jury. I think we should return when Mr. Gogola is calmer." Conrad nods to the guards, who begin to approach Francis.

This only enrages the man, causing his face to flare up.

"Don't fucking patronize me, you fucking mutt. I'm in here for ten years, you piece of shit. His little statement got more people talking."

Conrad has already begun to walk away from the crazed Francis, forcing the man to turn his anger on Rebekah.

"Do you know how much money is gone because of that Jezebelle?" Francis has rounded the table, enough to stop Rebekah from leaving.

The guards take point on each side, trying to drag him away.

"More money than you will see in your fucking lifetime, and she just took it, no refund nothing, blacklisted and at a huge deficit." Francis unclenches his hand, revealing a scrunched piece of paper, and chucks it at Rebekah.

Rebekah instinctively catches it.

"Have a goddamn look, give yourself some fucking clue at this cash loss." Francis struggles against his guards. Having said all that he needed to say, he headbutts one of them square in the nose, causing the guard to topple back onto the table.

With only one guard and many more rushing to their colleague's aid, Francis continues to headbutt the incapacitated guard in the chest. Rebekah stands terrified, clutching the ball of paper in her hand.

A rough hold grabs her arm, pulling her away and out the door as guards tackle Francis, who is growling like an animal, to the ground.

Rebekah fumbles in her bag as they stand outside of the prison. She has her head so far into the bag that she reminds Conrad of an ostrich.

"Rebekah?"

She is trembling as she lifts her gaze to Conrad. She clears her throat, exhaling loudly to calm her body and her mind.

"First interview with a prisoner, and an extremely violent one at that," she says.

"You've only received basic training, not quite ready for the field in that way. I'm sorry I brought you in there." He lays a kind hand on her shoulder, and that seems to ease her stress a little bit.

"Would you like a lift home?" Rebekah asks.

"I think you should go home, have a bath and relax for the rest of the day. I'm going to head back to the office and see if we can speak to someone else who had a court case with FolkWore. Someone with a bit more zen."

Rebekah laughs slightly before huffing. Seeing his partner ease up warms Conrad. He pats her shoulder before jumping into an ordered car.

Rebekah watches her partner being whisked away. She unfurls the crumpled paper, seeing the first line of information.

FD: 2,400

Needs Must

When Conrad suggested that Rebekah should have a bath and relax the rest of the day, he should've specified that he wanted her to do it immediately.

Rebekah stands back, studying her investigation board. After having a thorough look at the sheet of paper Francis Gogola had given her, she has found that there are two sets of acronyms and numbers on either side. The front seems to be typed on one side. On the other side, the words seem to have been burnt into the paper.

Rebekah has photocopied the paper. During her *relaxing*, she's stuck post-it notes and written on the copy. She chews her pen, staring at the acronyms.

"It doesn't make sense," she whispers to herself, "why would Francis have such a breakdown of pricing for costumes? FD... FD...formal dress?" She shakes her head.

"Full design? No, that wouldn't make sense." She taps the pen on her lip.

"Fairy...doctor...two thousand four hundred dollars for a dress, it's very specific. Could they charge by the hour?" She laughs at herself, pacing as the pen goes from tapping to back to chewing. "24 for an hour" *I wonder how much they'd make in a d-*

Rebekah's eyes widen as she holds the lid in between her lips.

"It's not 24 for an hour but 24 for a whole day. FD, full-day, 24 hours, $100 an hour." She writes *full day* next to *FD*, which helps make sense with the following acronym: *HD 1,200.*

She drops into her armchair, crossing one leg with another.

"It seems weird to charge by the hour, especially as that means all purchases would work in the company's favor. They could easily take several weeks to create outfits and reap the most return." She rifles through some of her papers that have been stacked neatly next to her. Though Rebekah is becoming frazzled by this situation, her workspace remains as neat as ever.

"Aldrek spent $881,000. If I use FD as a figure, that means." Her fingers twitch as she works it out. "That works to about 367 days, but that is more than a year." She looks at the other acronyms that don't seem to coincide with time.

"Perhaps he has additional things alongside that." The words of Francis Gogola ring through her ears.

"*Do you think I give a shit about some fabric, you mindless cunt?*"

So, we can rule out costume making as the "service."

"Not many professions charge by the hour." *What about drugs?* "You sell an amount, you wouldn't charge by the hour, but it's certainly something illegal." *Guns?* "I guess it could be if they're renting, but why would Aldrek rent guns for a year, you'd rent then use it then hand it back right. . ."

Rebekah is clearly spit-balling to herself as she taps her foot. *What does Mr. Aldrek have in common with Francis Gogola?*

"They both have a lot of money."

Francis mentioned boundaries and rules. Magenta having rules to be specific.

"He also mentioned that he should've been able to do whatever he wants." *If he's referring to the reason, he's in jail, and the reason he is in prison is for GBH on an FW employee, would that mean tha-*

And like that, it all clicks. The last piece of the puzzle snaps into place. The large sum of money between Aldrek and Mae Geoffries, the fact that she would be away during that time, the terrible stitching she noticed, the multiple court cases where FolkWore was the prosecutor, and finally, why Francis Gogola was blacklisted.

"I need to call Conrad."

Conrad heads up the porch of Rebekah's house. It is rather large for just her – an extended bungalow with a driveway on the side.

She had been somewhat cryptic with her message, but sounded the most frantic he'd ever heard her, so instead of heading home, which was a few minutes from the office, he instead traveled to the outskirts of central Seattle.

He rings the doorbell and hears the running steps. The door blows open, and Rebekah wheezes as she steps aside, allowing him in. He kicks off his shoes and hangs his jacket on a peg.

"I'm glad you made it so quickly." Rebekah leads the way towards the living room, zigzagging between boxes.

"You moving in or moving out?" Conrad laughs, following her movements to not topple four-tiered boxes. Going past the kitchen, Conrad sees her handiwork.

"I didn't want you to be blindsided by the meeting tomorrow."

The FBI agent's eyes widen at the sight before quickly narrowing at the price list tacked to the wall.

"Meeting?" he says curiously.

"Yes, I organized a meeting with Naomi and Michael tomorrow afternoon showing them our findings."

"And what findings, Calamba?"

"FolkWore. I've worked it out. They do costumes. That much is true, however, it is also a front for soliciting escorts. I'm not sure where the costume employees stop and the escorts begin, but if Mae Geoffries can be both, there's nothing to suggest that they both don't coincide." Rebekah jogs to her board.

"FD, 2,400 dollars, it's to do with time. $100 per hour. However, I don't know what this other sheet means."

Rebekah is so busy in her explanation that she does not see the dark grey cloud looming over her partner's head. It is only when she turns to Conrad to make sure that he is still following that she notices it.

"I know that it's a bit crazy stumbling onto a prostitution ring. I mean, if Aldrek is involved, who is to say that other big figures don't pay for it?"

"I know about FolkWore," he says, "I've known for a while."

Rebekah frowns. How could her partner know when she didn't know?

"Then..." she shakes her head. "Why didn't you tell me sooner?" She looks to Conrad, who has a sullen look on his face.

"It's a bit more complicated, you ca-"

"It's not complicated at all, Conrad. You'd think that you'd lap up any opportunity to put Dominic behind bars."

"For anything but this. FolkWore has a lot of influence. Aldrek is just the tip of it all. Magenta's reach is more than just people."

"Has she got grips on government?" Rebekah asks.

"Not exactly."

"Resources?"

"No."

"Then what?"

Conrad sighs heavily, his face becoming very tired and drained, mustering up the courage to shatter Rebekah's stratosphere.

"Vampires, werewolves, fae, elves, supernatural creatures, Calamba. An escort business specifically for those kinds of people."

Rebekah scoffs, and that is understandable.

Conrad takes a pen from off the table, heading to her board.

"This other sheet, the writing is different, right? That's magic. Magenta, she's a witch. This side is for supernatural beings, tailored to the needs of each creature. Did you notice how much Francis breathed through his nose, and how his face was going red?"

"I-I guess ..."

"It's because he's a minotaur. They resort to violence very quickly." Conrad shakes his head, going off track. He circles one of the pricings, *M 13,000*.

"This is minor, minor injuries. That is small cuts and bruises, nothing that won't take a few days to heal. S is for serious, and C is for critical."

"You mean to tell me that employees can suffer critical wounds, and clients won't be reprimanded as long as they pay?"

Rebekah whispers. She disregards the whole supernatural revelation and instead focuses on the extortion of it all. "Then even more reason that Magenta needs to be stopped. Do you not see a problem with what she's created?"

"I do, Calamba, but she is a lesser evil. Imagine if Francis did what he did to a random person, or at a party. It seems backwards, but Magenta keeps those kinds of guys in check, and without her, literal Hell will break loose."

"Conrad, what are you suggesting? What do you expect me – us – to tell our superiors tomorrow? Gee, sorry guys, no breakthrough. It looks like it was just a harmless transaction. By doing nothing, we are enabling this behavior."

"Rebekah, I don't know how high up Magenta's powers go. She could have anyone on her service. They'll do anything to protect what she offers."

"I think it's time for you to leave, Conrad."

"What? Rebekah, you can't just-"

"Go. I have a lot of thinking to do."

Conrad opens his mouth to speak but closes it even quicker. He nods, leaving Rebekah to the largest conspiracy in Seattle.

Rebekah Calamba

Torn on how she should approach her newfound information, somehow Rebekah falls asleep. Her laptop remains slightly open in her living room with an unsent email depicting everything, albeit omitting the supernatural elements, but surely enough to start a full investigation into every party involved.

Rebekah has always been a light sleeper, so when her unconscious mind picks up sound in her lounge, she stirs awake. Only allowing her eyes to open, she listens for more noise. It is quiet and, as her lids begin to fall, another soft pad of her carpet. She sits up, slowly pushing up on her arms, and stares at the door to her bedroom.

Perhaps it's Nicholas?

She shakes her head. Nicholas isn't the type of man to show up without a call or text. She turns her head to the clock on her side table. *1:23*. Nicholas also wouldn't arrive at this unreasonable hour.

She slips out from her bed, trying to make no noise whatsoever. She hopes whoever is in her house assumes she is asleep and will burgle her house in peace without anything becoming violent.

All she needs to do is get into the ensuite and out the window. She crawls around her bed, keeping her body low in case she has to roll under it and hide. The soft steps outside her room are sporadic and are neither getting closer or further from her, making Rebekah nervous.

What if Conrad told someone? The thought makes her uneasy. She doesn't really know Conrad well enough to judge his character but wants to think that he wouldn't sell her out, considering they've been working together for more than half a year.

He did know about everything. Maybe he was playing me from the start? Perhaps supernatural beings are real. Rebekah shivers. The thought of a creature skulking outside her room scares her. As she crawls further to her bathroom, all she can imagine are red piercing eyes and a detachable jaw tearing her apart.

She kneels by the bathroom door and pushes it an inch, testing the waters. Another inch, no noise, then another, enough to squeeze her petite body through.

Once in the bathroom, she rises to her feet, pulling the latch to her window open. This is where being small has its advantages. If Rebekah can just stand on the toilet and push the top of the window out, she can wiggle through. She moves the window until she hears a loud, obvious *thunk*. She pushes again, expecting more to give way, and another *thunk*.

With only the light of the moon to guide her, she feels around the window, and her hand brushes against the plastic childproof lock stopping the window from opening further. She crouches down slightly, reaching her arm under the window for the latch on the outside.

Her fingers fumble around with the latch, unscrewing the resistance bar so the window can open wider, and the window begins to loosen.

A tight hand wraps around her shirt pulling Rebekah away from the window, her arm slicing across the metal underlining, and she tumbles into her bedroom. She is slightly dizzy but steadies herself, nonetheless.

Forgetting her bloodied arm, she picks herself up as the attacker stalks forward, completely shrouded in darkness. She can't make out even one distinct feature. Still, it doesn't matter because they've thrown her close to the bedroom door, and this is Rebekah's house.

Rebekah runs down the hall. She rounds her small kitchen island and heads for the back door.

The assailant predicts her moves, sliding on the table to send a kick straight into her shoulder, popping it out of its socket. Rebekah smacks into the stove edge, causing a pipe at the back to snap, and gas hisses out.

Rebekah hits the floor, but again, jumps to her feet. The back of her pajamas is grabbed, yanking her down causing her to hit the tile floor again, cracking it.

Her vision is spinning, the assailant picks her up by her clothes, placing a hand over her mouth, only now noticing she is whimpering. They begin to drag her back into the bedroom.

In a last attempt to flee, Rebekah summons all her strength to her mouth and bites the assailant's hand, drawing blood.

She feels as though she is underwater but hears the muffled shout of her assailant as they drop her on the floor. She lands on her knees. She gets back up, but her clothes get caught again.

They spin Rebekah around and deliver a punch straight into the side of her mouth.

Rebekah feels her teeth break free as her head whips to the side. She hits the floor, her back colliding with the cold tiles. Her assailant kneels over her, wrapping their hands around her neck, squeezing.

Rebekah's eyes widen as her legs kick wildly, her arms trying to hit at their hold on her neck. She feels them pushing their weight onto her throat, feeling the cracking and punctures of her larynx being crushed.

Her face contorts in fear. Her heart hammers away, trying to keep her alive.

Rebekah chokes on her last bit of air and sees a whisper of her soul begin to leave, ballooning out her mouth and into the sky.

Blood trails on the floor. The assailant lays Rebekah's lifeless body onto the bed.

The shadowy person watches her before going to close her dull brown eyes. They tuck her back into bed. The carbon monoxide is visible to them, and they are thankful that the effects take longer.

Leaving Rebekah in the room, they head to the kitchen. They open the cupboards, take out some alcohol and grab a small flannel from the drawer. Opening the back door, they exit quietly but not before they take the laptop and tuck it under their arm.

Now at a somewhat reasonable distance, the assailant lights a match and sets it to the doused flannel. Watching the orange flame grow and eat away at the fabric, they chuck the Molotov through the open bathroom window.

The explosion could not have been any more immediate; it rocks the floor they are standing on, alerting every single person.

With the covering of the night, the assailant heads into the dark as Rebekah's house stands ablaze.

When Two Alpha Males Meet

"**H**ave dinner without me. Work went on longer than expected. My life does not begin and end with you, Mae."

She laughs on the other end of the line.

"I suppose not. However, it works out well that you'll be home late. I have something for you," she says, and I hear the sound of tissue paper being pulled back.

"Oh." I smirk. "What have you done?"

"Get home, and you'll see, Mr. Aldrek." With those lasting words, she hangs up before I can reply. *What a minx.* I chuckle to myself, hitting the gas a bit more as the car speeds out of the city.

I drive up the long road to the house, noticing that Sybil and the girls' houses are lit. They are done for the day, and Mae is at home cooking something up.

My phone beeps as I near the front door, and I glance at the text message.

Come through the front door ;) - Mae

I smile, cutting the engine and getting out of the car. The door opens, Mae's enriching scent cradling my nose and leading me forward. It is more potent than usual, and I lick my lips.

I push the door, loosening my tie.

"Mae?" I call.

«*I'll be down shortly.*» Even in her thoughts, Mae's voice is light and tempting.

"Dominic."

I swivel round to the strange voice, narrowing my eyes at the intruder.

"D-detective Grier..." My words slow to a stop as I look at the detective. His hair is disheveled, sweat settles on his forehead, and his smart attire has been swapped for sweats and a jacket.

"Get out of my house," I say quickly, realizing that in about thirty seconds, Mae will show up.

"We need to talk."

I only now notice that he has stopped the door from closing, and instead, pushes further into the house.

"Then you can schedule an appointment at a decent hour. This is trespassing," I say, my voice getting louder.

"S-she was about to ruin everything. Dominic. Sh-she found it."

My eyebrows dip as Grier mutters in front of me, his hands shaking as he speaks.

"Detective Grier." My voice is soft, hoping to catch the man's eyes and guide his thoughts to leave.

"You look tired, distressed even, let me call you a car to take you home."

"Sh-she worked it out." *Who is this she?* "Goddamn," Grier growls, his green eyes beginning to melt to blue.

"You idiot!" he shouts, "why did you have to do it?"

I'm taken aback by his sudden outburst, unsure if he is talking to himself or me.

"I had to do it! I had to do it for us. She was about to make an enemy of Magenta."

All thoughts of tonight fly out the window when Magenta leaves his lips.

"What are you talking about, Grier?"

"Rebekah, she found out what Magenta does. I tried to talk her down. She was about to blow a lid off the whole operation, bring literal hellfire down on us. All because you had to buy a whore for a year!"

My teeth grind against each other. *How dare he try to blame me for this?*

"If you knew, then you should've handled it from the start," I argue, my own temper beginning to match his. "You should've had better control over your investigation."

"And let you walk free. Again!" Grier shouts. "At some point, you need to come face-to-face with your consequences, Dominic, stealing from Seattle to feed your own personal gain. At least you used to keep it somewhat hidden, but this? You couldn't just fuck a random chick in the bar? You had to go see Magenta? You had to solicit a fucking prostitute?"

"Dominic?"

Her sweet, delicate voice is like a knife through the rising tension. I spin around and see Mae standing at the top of the stairs, her hands crossed over her surprise: a blood-red underwear set.

"Mae," I whisper. Her eyes are wide as they stare beyond me.

"Luna?"

"Stephan."

Conflict of Interest

Conrad checked his watch again before cross-referencing it against the large wall clock on the other end of the room. They both read 1:38.

She's now an hour and a half late. Should I just go? He stirred the cooling coffee, eyeing the untouched croissant. *Maybe if I had brought my laptop, it would at least look like I came here for something other than a coffee date.*

A date was a bit of a stretch, as he didn't know who he was meeting, nor did he know what she looked like. There was a good chance that Magenta had swindled several thousand dollars off him, preying on his desperation, and Conrad was pretty desperate.

As a werewolf several hours from his pack, he couldn't have made himself any more vulnerable. His parents were already disappointed that his idea of strengthening the pack would come from him working with the FBI. Conrad frowned as he remembered the long fights between his parents as he made preparations to go to the academy. If it wasn't for his gender, they might have completely abandoned him.

But Conrad was glad he stuck by it. In this world, you needed more than brute strength, and he hated how archaic the Grier pack was: secluding themselves away in the middle of Colorado. So many other families had evolved, expanding their reach and their influence, and he had to be the first one to show his family change.

But now he was paying the price for being the first man to lead the way. It had been four years since setting his roots in Seattle, and he hadn't found her, he hadn't found his Luna, and if he wasn't careful, he would die a very early death.

That was where FolkWore came in. His parents were worried for their second son. Had the goddess forsaken him for forsaking his morals? So, he needed a girlfriend, just to show that he was trying. She'd be human, of course, to avoid suspicion. He couldn't possibly have a female wolf; his pack would be able to sense their lack of connection.

And the two would date maybe for a few months, let their "love" guide him to his real mate, and then all would be good in Conrad's world.

He checked his watch: 1:40. Perhaps he had gotten the time wrong, or even the location. The coffee shop was somewhat hidden from the world, tucked away in a side street. Conrad had since drowned out the lo-fi, it became background music to his thinking.

He sighed, taking a large gulp of his coffee and placing the croissant into a paper bag. Next time he'd take the girl's phone number so they could at least communicate. But he had a flight to catch. It was a risk starting this two days before he was due to see his parents, but he wanted to return with the news of a potential relationship.

"Don't leave so quickly." Her voice was soft, causing Conrad to look up to meet her brown eyes. She had her hair tied up, a center fringe resting on her forehead, a chunk of it ice white. Interesting.

She took a seat, crossing her legs, revealing her shimmering brown skin that complimented the caramel skirt and the burgundy heeled boots.

"May I?" she asked, though it was pointless. She had already sat down and had set her coffee on the table.

"Sure, I was just leaving," Conrad replied, pulling his jacket off the back of the chair.

"Stood up?"

Conrad looked to her, watching her take a sip of her drink, staining the rim with her brown lipstick.

"I've been here a bit longer than you. You were checking your watch but never made a call or text, so I figured blind date that never showed up."

He laughed, laying his jacket on his lap before he spoke, "that obvious, huh?"

"Don't worry, I was the only one watching you. To everyone else, I'm sure you looked cool and collected."

"Well, that's a relief. At least I have a bodyguard looking out for me, but I'm a big boy." Conrad smirked. "I can handle myself."

"Well then, see me as your guardian angel." She smiled. Her eyes seemed to sparkle with the entering light.

"May I ask: if you've been watching me, why wait until I'm about to leave?" he asked.

The female pouted, stroking her chin, her grey nails running along her skin.

"To make sure there was no competition." She smiled, the twinkle in her eye looked more mischievous now.

"Oh," was all Conrad managed to say. Had he lucked out? Had one door closed and another opened? Was this the goddess' way of telling him she had not forgotten him?

"But this is only the first date, so it's early days," she said, taking another sip while her mouth curled into a smile.

"Oh, so this is a date?" He smiled at her, leaning back in his chair.

"You were waiting for a date, a blind one at that. I have merely filled in the position. So yes, it's a date."

Conrad couldn't help but feel the goosebumps growing across his arms. She was captivating, and quick, and every word had a hint of sexual tension he was sure was conscious. Her voice sounded innocent and light, but something told him she was a temptress behind closed doors.

His phone chimed, and he looked down. A jasmine scent wafted through his nose, and something blocked the light to the table. He looked up, his face a few inches from hers, and noticed her eyes were on his phone.

"Checking to see if the competition is back on?" he whispered, causing smiles to spread across both their faces.

"You know me too well. However, it would seem you'll miss your flight if we continue chatting." She stood up, grabbing her leather jacket off the chair and picking her bag off the floor.

"Should we get going?"

Conrad looked surprised. Was she suggesting she'd come with him? Was it too early? Yes, it was too soon, but Conrad had not been in many relationships.

In his silence, the woman was watching him before she stifled a small giggle.

"I've been here far longer than I care to admit. I have things to do, but I wanted to talk to you before I left. Perhaps I can get your number, so we can chat further?"

Conrad sighed, causing the woman to giggle again. He grabbed his food and his jacket, letting her lead the way out of the coffee shop.

They both stood outside as she pulled out her phone.

"May I have your number?" she asked. Conrad recited his number to her.

"And what should I call you?"

"You can put Conrad S. Grier on there."

The woman wiggled her nose as she thought about his response. "That seems awfully formal. What does the S stand for?"

"Stephan," Conrad replied. Conrad was his birth name, but Stephan was the name his mother in her wolf form called him.

"I think I like Stephan better. If you don't mind."

Werewolves had two names: one for humans, and one for the wolf that would one day reside in them. Conrad had always preferred Stephan, just like the woman had said it did feel formal while Stephan felt approachable much more like him.

"Sure."

She smiled at him, pressing the call button, and his phone began to vibrate. Satisfied that he had her number, she ended the call.

"And what should I call you?" His heart began to flutter, and his wolf began to stir. She showed so much promise. He felt relaxed and excited. All his senses were heightened.

"Luna, Luna Stanley."

There was no embrace, and Conrad felt somewhat cold, but he didn't allow that to show on his face. He wanted a quick relationship with something to show his parents, and this could be it.

"That's a lovely name," he said and typed it in. "Well, I need to catch my flight. Maybe we can meet up for a second date?"

Luna smiled and lifted her hand for him to shake, which he did.

"That would be fun, Stephan."

And even though she was not his mate, his heart still fluttered at the sound of his name on her lips.

To Be or Not to Be?

I run the cold rag over the small bite marks on his hand, wishing the ground would open and swallow me whole.

What can I even say? This is way more intense than the brother situation. Not only am I dating both, but Stephan is investigating Dominic, and it's to do with me.

"Luna?"

I look up to Stephan, who is studying me intently, his green eyes filled with sadness. He reaches out, running his thumb over my hair. My missing white streak.

God how I wish I could die in this moment.

"You should've told me," he whispers, his hand caressing my own, warming me to my core.

"You know I couldn't. Magenta said it was all under control, and that was three months ago."

"Was he the client you had to see in December, and when we met for coffee?"

I nod, unable to let the truth slip between my lips.

"Was any of it real?"

I choke. How can I answer such a question truthfully? It has been so long that I have forgotten where the truth ends, and the lies begin.

"Were you ever a random girl in the coffee shop?"

"Sometimes, the best lie stems from an element of truth." Stephan's eyes well up slightly. "Your job makes it difficult for the company to proceed in their normal way, so we had to be smarter with our approach."

That is true. Working with the FBI means that Stephan is subjected to random security checks that range from internet history, phone calls and expenses to ensure he isn't a security threat.

"I didn't want it to get this far." He sighs, pulling his bandaged hand away and holding it on his lap. "You were supposed to be this girl that would show my family that I hadn't completely abandoned my morals. You weren't supposed to stick around, much less be a candidate for marriage. But I fell in love with you, and so did they."

I can't breathe under the weight of everything. Stephan loves Luna, and for some reason, I feel that they both deserve it. *Or maybe I'm just projecting.* However, there is a gnawing feeling in my chest, a pang of jealousy towards my alter ego, towards Luna, but it quickly subsides as Stephan lifts himself from the toilet seat.

"Do you want me to come next month?" I mumble, scared of his response.

"We have a plan, Luna, and I love you too much to end it here. I just killed someone for you. I'm not letting this go."

I keep my head bowed. Two arms wrap around my body, and it takes everything in my power not to sob into his chest. Stephan kisses the top of my head, and I feel tears soak my hair. He lets go of the embrace first, getting up off the floor and heading out of my room.

I sit there half-dazed as I hear some light chatter before the door closes and footsteps ascend the stairs. I don't want Dominic to see me like this. It is far too conflicting, and quite frankly, embarrassing.

I run to the bedroom door, closing it shut before his face comes into view, locking it to convey a message. Dominic probably knows my feelings well before I shut the door, probably feels it slapping against his body like an untamed wave.

«Just...just let me.»

"I understand," he says from behind the wood. It takes a few seconds before he walks away from the door, and I crumple to the floor in a mess.

Lying To the Moon

I hold Tia on my hip as I fill my glass with a spoonful of punch. I pinch one of the orange slices and hand it to her, which she gratefully takes and sucks on before her eyes squeeze shut.

"What is Auntie Luna doing to you?" Charley says, entering the house through the side.

"You make me sound like a criminal, Charley." I hand Tia to her father, putting the thin towel on his shoulder before his top gets dirty with orange-flavored drool.

"Are you excited about tonight's run?" Charley leans on the countertop as I lean on the kitchen island.

"If Verna believes it's the one, I'm nervous, to say the least." I take a sip of the beverage as I hear laughter from outside.

Today isn't like December. It is just the Griers this evening: an intimate gathering for the family to celebrate.

"More importantly," I begin, catching Charley's attention, which is on Tia, trying to share the orange slice between them. "Are you guys excited for Austin? The firstborn going under his first moon, no more shifting for you guys."

Charley's face sinks slightly. You'd think not being at risk of dying is a godsend. Now that Austin is going through his first moon where he'll meet his wolf, Charley and Marie will no longer shift at every moon.

"It's weird. I never really liked changing, but knowing there's a chance I'll only shift in a flight or fight situation feels kind of ... vanilla."

I laugh loudly, not expecting that response.

Charley holds out his hands, his mouth stretched wide with a smile.

"Don't get me wrong, I'm no sadist. It's just that ... it feels weird to watch my life from the backseat. I can still hear Caleb, and he can hear me, but he's told me he's done these hundreds of times and was once in my position."

"And what's his advice for you?"

Caleb is Charley's wolf, a man – from what I've been told – born somewhere around 1600BC, though his name has changed over the years. Things such as names and dates are hazy over reincarnations. Memories seem to cling on longer.

"He says not to worry, and this is just another step on the goddess' chosen path." Charley shrugs before nuzzling his daughter's neck, making her giggle.

"Luna, may I ask you something?" Charley's voice turns serious, and my heart seizes.

"Sure," I whisper.

"Is everything alright with my brother? You seem like your usual self, but Stephan..." He angles his head toward Stephan, who is standing on the balcony under the light of the moon, while the rest of the family is in the garden by the fire.

I sigh, knowing the real reason for his pain. *He is heartbroken. I've broken his heart.*

"His partner was in an accident, died in a house fire. That's what he told me. He said he's dealing with it, but I'm not too sure." *Close to the truth.*

Charley nods slowly before glancing at his brother, who seems to blend further into the shadows.

"I'm going to get this little one to say goodnight so Marie can put her to bed. If anyone can make him feel better, it's you, Luna."

I wave to Tia as the two exit. *I don't think I can, Charley.*

Since my arrival in Colorado, Stephan and I have been on and off. There are times when we fall into our old ways, and then he looks at me, and his eyes well up, and he distances himself. I understand why, though it still hurts to see him run away.

"Hey," I say, standing beside him.

"Hey," he whispers, his eyes fixed on the tree line.

"Your brother is worried about you."

"What did you tell him?"

"I told him your partner died."

"I guess that's part of it."

Pain stabs me in the chest, a feeling of guilt and misery oozing through me. I hold the railing, so I don't fall.

"Please try to act normal," I plead, though it is wrong of me. "Your family will begin to worry."

A painful silence follows my words, cold and lifeless. It wraps its talons around my neck and squeezes tight.

"I don't think you should've come L-Luna." The pause on my name makes the pain worse. *He is struggling to see her, see Luna for anything more than a facade.*

A whistle echoes across the space, and we both turn to face the owner. Kaleb waves at us, beckoning us to come over.

"Food is ready. Let's go!" he shouts, heading to the laid table and all the family waiting.

"After this, I will be gone. I promise." I stroke his arm, my fingers tiptoeing towards his, testing the water.

Stephan snatches my hand, causing me to look up. He is crying. I hold his face, wiping the tears.

"My love for you is real, Stephan. Three, almost four years together. I couldn't fake it all, even if I tried."

His tears subside and a tiny sparkle finds its way to his eyes. He sniffles, lifting his head to see the family chatting amongst themselves.

"Tell them I've gone to the bathroom. I'll join you in a second, OK?"

"OK."

"I love you, Luna."

I bring his face down for a kiss, my action speaking a thousand words that my voice can't say.

I watch Stephan head back in the house while I retreat to the waiting Griers.

"Stephan has just gone to the bathroom, but you guys can start."

No one needs to be told twice as they all pile on the food, Charley and Kaleb especially.

With Stephan back beside me and everyone with a plateful of food, Lloyd stands up. He straightens out his collared shirt before clearing his voice.

"Tonight is going to be a special night. Austin, alongside some of the other children of the pack, will be going through their first moon. This is the first step for you to one day take over the pack as alpha when your father retires."

"No time soon," Charley interjects, ruffling Austin's hair. Austin pushes his hand away and fixes it back down.

"Not only will you be taking your first step, but your parents will be taking a step of their own. They will no longer be shifting under the moon, and that is the sign that they will soon be taking over as the alphas of the pack while your mother and I go into retirement." Lloyd is smiling, but under the rims of his eyes, tears begin to form.

Theresa, on the other hand, has a napkin permanently to her eyes, dabbing as her husband speaks.

"And like the four phases of a werewolf, we start at the beginning, where love first blossoms and builds the foundation. My mother believes tonight is the night for our long-awaited couple, and all I can say is: two down, one to go."

I laugh with the rest of the family as Lloyd picks up his glass and raises it in a toast.

"To family, to the pack," he shouts.

"To the pack," we all reply, and dig into the food.

Lying To Me

I pull off my jumper, drape it on the bed, and roll my neck. I sigh deeply, feeling the tension in my shoulders weighing me down.

Stephan seems better after our brief encounter on the balcony, and Charley notices it as well.

I wonder what would happen if he told them. Would he be banished? Would I be killed? The thought terrifies me. Werewolves are traditional, and my presence here is like spitting at the goddess.

I don't even hear the door, and soon enough, two warm hands run around my waist before cupping my breasts.

"Are you sure?" I whisper. Stephan lets out a breath, tickling my ears and warming my neck.

"Having sex with you connects us." He kisses my neck, and a warmth spreads through my chest. "Besides, this might be our last time."

The last part is still bathed in sadness, but there is a hint of acceptance. He is beginning to understand.

My body relaxes for the first time in the last three days, and I lean a weary head on his chest. Stephan brings his hand down my body, sliding it between my skin and my skirt. He hooks a finger over my underwear and tugs it down.

The fabric drops to the floor, and I step out. My body tingles as he runs his hands over my back, bending me over to lie on the bed, lifting my skirt to get a good look.

I look as far as I can over my shoulder, and my eyes meet his, the green iris melting to blue as he growls.

Stephan unzips his trousers, moving them just enough to pull himself out and letting it hang on top almost threateningly. My toes curl at the anticipation of feeling him push and stretch me.

He holds his throbbing penis in one hand while the other hooks itself around my waist, holding me steady. He doesn't push it in but instead brushes it against my opening, revealing my cum-dipped folds.

"Jesus, Luna. Wet already?" He brushes against my core for another confirmation, and I exhale into the sheets, trying to move my body so he'll slip inside.

I feel his body lean over mine.

"Not so fast," he whispers, his husky voice tempting me. "Patience is key." He kisses my ear. His hand has let go of his piece and is using my cum to massage my clit gently, coaxing the slow build of an orgasm to bubble inside.

"Please," I say, my voice broken.

Stephan unhooks my bra, and pinches my stiff nipple, fingertips still wet from cum. His hips are pressing against my ass.

Stephan knows more than anyone that, for me, the best orgasms come from penetration. What felt like acceptance earlier now seems a little bit more like revenge.

"Stephan...don't-" I moan loudly as he pinches my nipple. My legs are beginning to wobble. Anticipation is like nitrous to this increasing pressure.

"It'd drive you mad if we left it here. Not being able to feel us connected in the most intimate way." Stephan positions the head of his member, pushing it in enough to do more harm than good, his other hand on my waist, making sure that I can't move back to take his full size in, and the thought is killing me.

There is a knock at the door, and I stifle a scream into the pillow as Stephan slides himself in.

"Who is it?" he calls, holding himself still and me with him. Any second, I'm about to create a pool of euphoria on this carpeted floor.

"Bro, it's time, where's Luna?" Kaleb says from the other side of the door.

"She'll be coming in a second." He rocks his hips, burying himself deeper, applying pressure on my hips that is both dominating and arousing.

Oh, you bastard.

His cheeky comment turns me on further, reminding me of the early days of our relationship.

"See you downstairs."

It isn't until he hears the last of Kaleb's footsteps and the slam of the front door that Stephan lets me have it.

Skin hitting skin echoes through the room as he fucks me. The sensation of his balls hitting my clit is an added bonus of pleasure and has me face-deep in cotton with a fist full of bedsheets.

Hearing him curse and hiss as his orgasm approaches is enough to expedite my own. I raise my hips, getting the angle just right.

He pulls himself free, and I feel the ache begin to settle in. Rough sex is fun, but the aftermath is sour. I sink to the floor, taking a peek at Stephan. He has his back to me as he fixes his clothes.

"I-"

"You should get ready, Luna. They are waiting for you."

I close my mouth and head to my suitcase. I take out my usual brown attire for tonight. His posture is enough to convey his intended message, and I head into the bathroom to get changed.

Laying the clothes on the bathroom sink, I pull my arms around my chest, consoling myself. An empty feeling from our interaction settles heavy on my shoulders. I lost myself in the lust-driven moment, only now noticing the absence of the loving feeling that usually follows.

Dressing quietly on my own in the bathroom is akin to a bad one-night stand, or the end of a relationship. Something about it feels humiliating and depressive.

I come out of the room to find the bedroom deserted, and sigh. Usually, Stephan would give me some words of encouragement, but today would not be one of those days.

I head out of the house, finding the path lit with tea lights. Verna stands at the top with Stephan and Kaleb. The others have gone to support Austin for his transition, as would most of the other parents and grandparents.

I keep my eyes on Verna, who takes my hand and squeezes it.

"You ready, Luna?"

I exhale loudly.

"Yes."

"There will be no handicaps to test the strength and dexterity of your relationship."

I nod, feeling slightly dizzy from the sound of blood rushing past my ears.

"May the goddess be with you."

An upcoming wind extinguishes the tea lights, leaving the light of the moon as the only illumination.

May the goddess be with me indeed.

I'm surprised that I have made it much deeper into the forest in the first twenty seconds. The air seems crisper tonight, and the light of the moon appears brighter, making it easier to see fallen trees and exposed roots.

I skid to a halt. catching my breath. *If I want to last longer, I need to pace myself.*

Stephan can catch me if it is a case of distance. I must be strategic. I pick up some mud from the ground and rub it against my exposed skin, a little bit smearing my hair.

This would've been a lot easier if it had ra-

"Oh, thank god we fou-"

I look up from my task, seeing a pair of flashlights and the two hikers that hold them. We both stare at each other. One has a map in their hands, and it doesn't take much to realize they are lost.

It probably doesn't help that the first person they meet is covering herself in mud like a wildebeest. My body trembles as small vibrations course through me.

They are dead, regardless of if I help them, so I run, heading in the direction they'd just come from in the hopes of masking my scent.

I'm sorry.

I cover my ears as I hear their screams. It isn't Stephan's fault. Anyone can be attacked during the ritual. Anyone who involves themselves purposefully, or otherwise, appears as a threat, and competitor.

A blur catches my eye, and I switch direction, not fully paying attention to my surroundings and stepping onto a steep slope. I scream as I fall forwards. My hands sprawl out as I tumble down the hill.

Scrapes and cuts tear my skin, shredding my clothes, my body bruised and bleeding.

Somehow, I manage to raise to my feet, slightly disoriented. My vision is cloudy, but I can still make out the large wolf at the top of the hill, its teeth bared, almost in a grin.

The knock of adrenaline is enough to push me into action, and we both begin to run: a cat and mouse chase in its purest form.

I pull the blueish gem from my wrist and crush it, raising my hand to sprinkle it over my head but I'm knocked against a nearby tree, the dust flittering to the ground and the air leaving my lungs.

The wolf stalks me from afar, enough distance to give me time to run. I get to my feet before crouching down on all fours, one leg further back than the other.

I growl in defiance, enough to have him charge towards me. I leap to one side, hearing the crack and splinter of the trunk of the tree breaking, and I run off.

I'm smarter than I-

His massive body drops onto me, forcing me to the ground. Stephan bites my shoulder to roll me over. The scream that echoes through the woods is piercing.

His snout blocking the light of the moon, he growls at me before howling at it. Saliva mixed with blood drips from his mouth and onto my chin. He has his paws on either side of my head, and I catch a whiff of blood.

I watch as his fur begins to molt, creating a warm covering over my body, his face shrinking and going into itself, back into his human features. His back legs lower, causing Stephan to lean over me on all fours in his human form.

His eyes have phased back to their summer green, no longer the ice blue his wolf has.

"Stephan...Luna?"

I turn to the side, seeing Verna holding a small gaslight.

My heart drums in my chest as I wait for her response.

Would I have to do this again?

"The wedding will be in December." Her smile stretches across her face, and I lay gob-smacked, not even noticing the tears that drip from my eyes.

They are not happy tears at all.

The Separation of Two Identities

Marie pulls another layer of bandage over my shoulder before using some medical tape to stick down the edge. I wince slightly, and a dull pain rolls over the joints.

"I forget how slow you heal," Marie says, rubbing the bandages softly with her hand.

"Unfortunately, we can't all be quick healers." I chuckle dryly, pulling my arm through the sleeve. "How was Austin's shift? I wish we'd been able to come."

"It was frightening. It's like giving birth all over again, yet it wasn't me doing the birthing. Charley and I were in tears through the whole thing. It was hard having to show who was in charge when it was time, especially as Austin is the same height as me."

Parents during their child's transition must show who is senior and they have to do so in their human form. A wolf must be respectful of the hierarchy in both human and wolf forms. Otherwise, the balance would be thrown off before it began.

If a parent cowered or showed any sort of inferiority, they'd be attacked as a bid to take their spot, and a child could be killed. There needs to be absolute loyalty and respect between wolves. Otherwise, all chaos would ensue.

"But you managed, right?"

"Of course. I'm his mother, and he and his wolf will remember that."

I giggle at Marie as she puffs out her chest.

"But enough about me. You're about to be my sister-in-law. A wedding in four months? I think I can do that, and no, Luna, you can't help."

"What? As a designer, it's in my nature t-"

"Uh, uh, uh." Marie wiggles her finger. "No, I already know what you like, so you needn't worry. Your sister's got you."

My throat seizes, and a pained smile cracks across my face.

I've always imagined getting married and having someone to gush about it with, but not like this. Not when the foundation of this marriage is fake.

There is a knock on the door, and Stephan pokes his head around, smiling at the two of us.

"It's time to go, Luna."

I check the clock on the far end of the room.

"A little early," I say, noticing that we'd be at the airport six hours earlier than usual.

"Not if we are driving. If it's OK, I want to spend more time with you."

"Twenty-hour drive is a long time to be cooped up in a car, Stephan," Marie points out.

"Not if it's with someone special." He smiles at Marie, his gaze turning to me.

He's right. This is our last encounter. I want it to last longer, too.

"But promise we stop at a motel. I'm not having you drive a thousand miles," I say.

"Don't worry, I've got us a hotel booked on the edge of Idaho. I'll get the bags into the car." He shuts the door, and I stand up.

I wrap my arms around Marie, and she does the same, rocking from side to side.

"Keep me updated, OK?" she says, and I nod. We let go, and I tiptoe to the cot by their bed, kissing my finger before putting it on the top of Tia's head.

"Say bye to the kids for me," I say. Austin has been asleep since he returned home, and Claire is playing with friends.

"Will do, Luna. Have a safe trip."

I head out of the room, down the stairs and out the door.

Lloyd and Theresa are by the front door watching Charley, Kaleb and Stephan pack the bags. The three hug.

"I guess I'll see you guys soon, probably next month to see how the wedding prep is going."

Theresa smiles, tears beginning to well in her eyes.

This must be a huge relief for her, forever worried that Stephan would never find his Luna. I hope he really does one day.

She pulls me into a hug and Lloyd wraps his arms around the both of us.

"Goodness, I am a mess of tears this weekend." She sighs.

I laugh. "Well, it's been a very emotional two days."

"Besides, it doesn't take much to bring you to tears, Theresa," Lloyd adds, getting a slight jab in the ribs.

We all detach before I'm scooped up by Charley, spinning me around, and making me lightheaded before placing me on the ground.

"See you soon, Luna. Finally, a baby sister," he says.

I laugh, holding my head.

"See you soon, Charley, and I'm not little."

I see Verna heading down the path, away from the other houses. She has her hands wrapped around a small spherical parcel. I walk towards her.

"I guess you're off, Luna."

"We are. Is this a present from Elanor?"

In werewolf culture, there is one witch: one female throughout each generation who shows an affinity for magic. She still has the attributes of other werewolves, aside from the shifting every full moon.

Elanor is the most senior witch, having succeeded the previous one for Verna's generation. I have never seen her before, as she hides away deep in the forest when she's training Beatrice, who will eventually become the witch for Charley's reign.

"It is. She let Beatrice make this one for you, so let me know how it turns out."

I unwrap the packaging to find a glass ball, filled halfway with pinkish dust.

The echinacea flower helps with healing. I'm very accustomed to it due to the rituals with Stephan.

"As always, my child, sprinkle some on your food and in your drink to help your body heal. You will be susceptible to infection."

I nod and hug the frail woman.

"Thank you, Verna, for believing in us."

"The moon never lies, and it can never be lied to."

I hum in response. Verna pulls away from the hug, kisses both sides of my cheeks and ushers me towards the car.

Stephan has an arm on the roof, watching me approach the car before sliding in and popping the door open on the other side. I wave again at the family before sliding into the passenger side.

Stephan pulls out of the community, heading towards the freeway that will take us home.

The sky transitions slowly from a bright blue to a burnt orange with brick-red hues. Even as it reaches eight p.m., the sun is still resisting nightfall.

Our journey has been quiet. At first the silence feels like a heavy ocean, but as we roll into the seventh hour, it dries up to a muddy puddle.

"Can I ask you something?"

I jump at Stephan's voice, almost forgetting who is driving.

His voice is low, and his words are slow, as though he's been mulling over this question for most of the journey.

"Sure..."

"Did you know I was investigating Dominic?"

I have been expecting this conversation, but hearing the words still catches me off guard.

"No, I was unaware up until February. I didn't even know there was an investigation. Magenta and Dominic said they had it all under control."

Stephan lets my explanation hang in the air as he turns off the freeway, driving into a small motel.

He parks the car and gets out, heading to the kiosk as I get out on the other side.

He and the customer assistant talk for a while before they hand Stephan what I suppose is the key. He points to one of the rooms closest to him. I shut the car door and walk towards him as he locks it remotely.

The door opens to a simple bedroom, a bathroom near the other end, a king-sized bed and a slim TV. I step in, kicking off my heels and letting my feet sink into the purple fibers of the carpet.

The door shuts behind me and Stephan brushes past, chucking his jacket onto the chair by the window.

"Do you remember what we discussed back in April?"

I do. I have been thinking about that meeting in the coffee shop since I saw Stephan standing at the foot of the stairs next to Dominic.

I nod.

"Yes, you wanted to run away."

"I thought my biggest problem was going to be having to accept that the universe didn't approve of us. A part of me still wishes that were the case. But..." Stephan sighs, stroking his arm with his hand.

"But hearing that we did it, that we will be married in December." He laughs. "It was the happiest thing to my ears, Luna."

"S-Stephan...you know we can't," I whisper. He is making this so difficult, so conflicting, and forcing a wedge between Luna and me.

"Who says we can't? Magenta never put a restriction on this relationship."

I feel a bubble in my chest, pockets of air pressing against my ribcage as Stephan is speaking.

"I don't know how you're not my mate, but there is something between us that has won the approval from the highest order."

It aches and strains against my skeleton, looking for a way out.

"You said you loved me, Luna. You said it was real."

And then my chest bursts.

"I'm not Luna!" I scream, "She was never real, it was all me! I put in the effort, and I don't even reap the benefits. I don't care if Magenta hasn't put a limit on this contract. I've put a limit. I refuse to allow her to take something I worked for. She is just a name, Stephan, a name to entice you. It was me who went backpacking with you for six months, it was me who calmed you down the night before we met your parents, it was me who was ripped to shreds under the moon, and it was me who was approved."

Three years of unconscious jealousy towards my own created identity spills over. I realize I hate Luna, hate her for having a better life than me, hate her for finding someone to love and someone to love her, hate her for being free while I'm caged in contract after contract of loveless sex and relationships.

"Luna is nothing but a chunk of white hair and a name," I whisper. My hands are shaking, and so are my knees as trails of tears drip down my face and onto the floor. "I want to go home."

I feel the branded *A* warm slightly before there is a knock at the door. I head to it and open the door to reveal Martel, drenched in sweat.

"Mae."

My name on his lips is like cold water that burns my skin. Everything I want, and not at all what I expected.

I turn to Stephan. Even in the distance, I see his eyes drowning in tears. I want him to hug me and reassure me, but he'd be reassuring Luna, not Mae.

I lower my head. I can't even say goodbye. I walk out of the motel room and shut the door behind me. Martel takes my hand, scooping me up in his arms.

"You OK?" he says quietly. I nestle into his chest, feeling empty and vacant.

Martel strokes my hair, holding me close as a gaping portal opens, and we step through.

Wounds and Pain

I sit in the kitchen, an elbow resting on the countertop, scrolling through the latest news while my free hand twirls the hour-gone-cold pasta.

My nose picks up her scent well before my ears hear her moving. It is strange. I expected Mae tomorrow afternoon, not today, somehow already in her room.

I stand up and speed walk out of the kitchen and up the stairs to the bedroom. As I reach the top of the stairs, Martel is exiting Mae's room.

Now, closer, her smell is masked, wrapped in the scent of him. Detective Grier. An earthy aroma with a hint of smokiness.

"What happened?" I ask.

"She called on me. She was in some motel in Idaho with a werewolf."

I growl, stepping forward as Martel raises a defensive hand to stop me.

"Easy there, big man. He didn't do anything to her at that moment, but she wasn't in a talkative mood when we left. I've already sent word to Magenta. Someone will come patch up her shoulder."

"I thought you said he didn't do anything!" My mouth curls into a snarl.

"At that moment. I don't know about before. It's a wolf bite gone a tiny bit septic. With the addition of shadow walking, it might have angered the wound more than it should have." Martel sighs, running his hand over his hair.

The guy is not dressed like someone who planned to leave the house this evening. His clothes are soaked with sweat stains, and behind the rims of his glasses, his eyes are bloodshot.

"Anyway..." Martel begins, noticing me looking him over. "I need to go. Magenta kind of interrupted my own work when Mae called." He smiles slightly, turning on his heels and disappearing into the shadows.

Not allowing a second to pass, I head through the door. items of clothing are left as breadcrumbs leading to the bathroom. Mae's hair drapes over the rim of the bath with her back to me.

As I approach, I see the deep bite marks in her shoulder, and a hiss pushes through my lips. She is covered in tiny scratches and growing bruises.

I pull off my clothes and lift Mae gently, stepping into the water and laying her body on top of mine. With her pressed against my chest; I feel the vibrations of her sobs coursing through me.

"I'm here, Mae," I whisper, stroking the top of her hair.

"Why does no one love me?" she croaks. A tightness invades my chest, and I wrap my arms around her, being gentle to her wounds.

"Mae, I-"

The door to the bedroom creaks open. I tilt my head to see Lara entering, dressed in purple scrubs. She sighs heavily.

"Jesus, Maebell."

Mae gets out of the tub quickly, running to Lara, who grabs the naked woman in her arms. I sit up and pull the plug. I grab two towels, wrapping one around my body.

Lara guides Mae to her bed, and I put a towel on her lap.

"Sit in the middle for me, babe."

Mae does as she is told, wrapping the towel loosely over her body as she sits cross-legged, facing me.

I kneel to her level, holding her hands as she tries to avoid eye contact.

I watch Lara pull out a needle and thread. She runs two fingers down the underside of her arm, revealing light grey runes that run past her wrist and through to her fingertips.

"Take a deep breath, Mae."

I feel Mae inhale sharply as Lara places her hand against the wound. Mae's skin hisses, and steam drifts to the ceiling. I expect to smell burnt flesh, but instead, I get a whiff of melting iron.

Mae's hands around my back aren't as tight as before, and she seems to slump into my body. I look at Lara worried, pushing Mae back and holding her in my hands. Her head is forward, strands of hair covering her face, and I notice one chunk at the front of her hair is ice white, setting more panic to bubble on my chest.

"She's unconscious."

"Crossing two sources of magic will do that to a human. Magenta won't mind on this one occasion. It does make the next part easier. Lay her on her side, please. You'll have to hold her up." Lara reaches over and unlatches the charm-filled bracelet.

"I'll return the bracelet in her next checkup. The last thing she needs to be doing is cleansing spells and illusions."

I do as I'm told, laying Mae gently on her right side, slipping into the bed next to her to support her body with my own.

Lara threads the string before climbing on the bed and stitching each incision in Mae's shoulder. I move her hair out of the way as Lara begins on the marks on her back.

When the stitching is done, she pulls out some grey fabric before pulling out a small syringe filled with an equally grey liquid. She squirts the liquid on each stitch before wrapping Mae's shoulder in the cloth and sealing it with some medical tape.

"Thank you, Lara," I say quietly.

"It's my job, Dominic. Make sure the dressings stay dry. They will harden over time, but don't worry. The fabric and string will decompose on their own."

I would've accompanied her out of the house, but my body refuses to move from Mae's side. All I can do is watch Lara lean in, kissing Mae on the top of her head before leaving the room.

I snuggle closer to Mae, wrapping an arm over her waist to make sure she won't roll over in the night. I breathe in the scent in her hair, picking up the light jasmine amidst the woodland and grass-like smells.

I kiss her neck, listening to her rhythmic breathing, and wish that I hadn't fallen in love with her.

Death of a Friend

"And though she is no longer with us, Rebekah Tanya Eurdaschia Calamba will always be with us in spirit."

Conrad keeps his head down and focuses on the freshly dug grave.

To most, he looks like he is just in mourning, but in truth the man refuses to watch her body be lowered into the ground and sealed away by the earth.

You did it for love. You did it for her.

"Mr. Grier?"

Conrad lifts his head, spinning around to come face to face with a man.

His eyes are red and swollen. He brushes his black hair away from his face.

"Nicholas Calamba." He stretches his hand towards the detective. "I'm Rebekah's husband."

Conrad shakes it with forced calm, but inside, he is in a frenzied state.

"I saw Rebekah just before it happened," he says in a low voice. "I didn't know her for very long, but she's not someone who allows you to forget about her."

Nicholas laughs lightly, sniffling from all his previous crying.

"Yes, indeed. For such a small stature, Rebekah makes an entrance."

"How are you, Mr. Calamba, if you don't mind me asking?" He remembers when his grandfather died, though that was from prostate cancer. Rebekah died from strangulation. Either way, he remembers the sadness that drenched his grandmother, how difficult it was for her to exist at one point. How difficult it was for his father as well.

"We are here," he says sadly Nicholas crouches down and picks up the small boy version of Rebekah.

The frenzied state in Conrad's chest goes nuclear.

"My son Robin and I moved to Canada. Rebekah was due to join us after her last investigation was over. But then this latest one came up and, well..." He sighs turning his head away from Robin, wiping his face with his sleeve.

Conrad stands awkwardly, guilt seeping out his pores. A warm hand lays on his shoulder and he turns to find Naomi. She ushers him aside.

Conrad nods before clearing his throat, getting Mr. Calamba's attention.

"I'm sorry for your loss, Mr. Calamba."

Nicholas nods, taking his son to mourn with the rest of the family.

Conrad walks towards Naomi, who stands underneath a tree, leaning on a closed umbrella, the point digging into the ground.

"I didn't think you'd worry yourself with funerals, Naomi," Conrad says, leaning on the other side of the tree, watching family and friends pack themselves into cars to head to the wake. He stares at the large, framed picture of Rebekah. She is in a wedding dress with a tiara perched on top of her head.

"I don't usually, but we have reason to believe this was murder."

The word *murder* rips through the last of Conrad's soul and he swallows heavily to force it back down.

"I thought it was a house fire?" Conrad is in shock. Could this be the moment armed men would jump out of the ground and arrest him, arrest him in front of the picture of Rebekah?

"Yes, but the autopsy proves otherwise: signs of fighting, and on top of that, Rebekah scheduled an emergency meeting for the next morning."

"Were there any cameras? Surely there's something to give us a good lead."

"She did. Rebecca was due to move to Canada. They had their contract and equipment transferred. Lucky for the perpetrator." Naomi huffs to herself. "Seems a bit convenient she'd die the day before the meeting. You saw her, didn't you? The night of?"

"Yes, I did." Conrad is surprised he can speak so clearly when his thoughts are ablaze. The irony of it all.

"She called me over; said she had a breakthrough. That she wanted to run some ideas by me."

"And what ideas were those?"

"We never got a chance to discuss them." He sighs, giving himself time to formulate an exceptional lie.

"We saw an inmate that day, and…I'm sorry, Naomi, the inmate was hostile, attacked the guard. Rebekah was practically shaking, so when I headed over, she broke down in tears. I comforted her for a while, hung around until she fell asleep. I left her a note saying I'd be back in the morning to run through the ideas." Conrad looks at Naomi, who has her eyes on the emptying funeral.

"I see," she says simply. She turns to him dramatically, her eyes piercing and forever scrutinizing.

"Do you think Dominic has anything to do with it? Or even FolkWore?"

Conrad's mouth moves to the side before he speaks, "There's a good chance. If Rebekah had a breakthrough that could lead to a conviction, they both had a reason to take her out."

Naomi drums her nails on the handle of the umbrella.

"You're right. The next few months are crucial. Forensics are combing through the house. It'll take some time, but we're hoping not all the evidence is ash."

"What about a task force? I would like to be on it. Though I didn't know Rebekah for very long, she was still my partner, and I feel responsible for her."

"And that's exactly why you can't be. You're too close, Conrad. A task force has already been put in place. We've agreed that a covert investigation is needed on Dominic Aldrek, FolkWore, and their connection to Rebekah's murder."

Naomi rests a hand on his shoulder.

"I want you to take some compassionate leave, Grier. We've got this. Rebekah's murderer will be held accountable."

Conrad gives his boss a dry smile, letting the woman take her leave and head to her car.

You did it for love, you did it for her.

Fanged Christmas

It has been two days since Mae has come home, and ever since then, she's progressively shrunk into herself.

Her jasmine scent feels muted. Her hair is flat. It could be because she won't be able to shower properly until her bandages dry and crumble away, or it could be because her last scheduled night with Grier couldn't have been any worse.

I don't want to push her. More specifically, I don't want to know. I fear what I would do to Grier or – even worse – Magenta.

I scratch at my throat as I feel a tingling from the last time, I let what happened to Mae drive my decisions.

Mae sighs quietly as she shuffles into my hold. I lift my arm. It is going on one a.m. I kiss the back of her head, crawling out of bed.

I open her drawer slowly, pull out the sky-blue incense stick, and place it in the jar with the others.

Surprisingly, Sybil gave this to me.

"To help with her sleeping."

I looked down at the light blue incense stick and rolled it between my finger and thumb.

"Mae needs a bit more than incense, Sybil."

Sybil tutted loudly at me.

"It's more than that. Calms the mind, and those that inhale it sleep better. Good sleep equates to faster healing."

I light the incense. A pink flame gnaws at the end before it extinguishes itself, the smoke snaking into the air. My eyes feel woozy as I inhale the sweet citrus scent. I shake my head from the daze, heading to the door before sneaking one last look at Mae.

I pick up the black leather duffle bag outside my room and head to the garage. I unlock one of the cars and pull out of the house.

I drum on the steering wheel as the lights from neighboring houses illuminate the streets: several cars parked on driveways and on the road, residents milling outside before heading in.

I slow the car to a stop, pushing my bag to the back seat before stepping out. I'm ashamed to admit that I might have given Sybil the better house.

While most houses are two-stories and semi-detached, Sybil's house always stands out. A cottage-like feel emits through the brickwork and the support beams. She's planted a tree right in the center of her lawn, its overcasting branches creating a tunnel to her doorstep.

I don't even have to knock. Sybil steps out holding two bags, which I quickly relieve her of.

"Happy *Bashta*, Sybil. You never mentioned that the incense was a Sosa stick," I say.

Bashta is a vampire celebration: the importance of blood and the longevity of vampires. It is almost like a vampire Christmas of sorts. Gifts are shared and dinner is eaten with family.

"I'm surprised you've even retained that information," Sybil quips, making me laugh lightly. "Happy *Bashta.*"

We get in the car, and I place her things next to my own bag before driving away.

"How is she, Dominic?"

I prefer when Sybil is informal with me. There was a time when she was the closest thing to a grandmother, so when my siblings and I "outgrew" the need for her services, I couldn't bear to leave her.

"She's healing...but something happened that night. She asked me why no one loved her." Repeating Mae's words feels like a rusty blade carving into my heart. I hold the steering wheel tightly, trying to keep my eyes focused on the road ahead.

"And you love her?" Sybil says.

"I do. I do love her." I can feel my heart bleeding along with my emotions. Saying those words feels soft on the tongue, light on my chest.

"I love everything about her: I love her drive when she works, I love how big her heart is for her family, I love that there's never a dull moment with her, I love her laugh, I love her smile, I love the way her eyes can hold so much innocence one moment, and then fire the next." Through my ramblings, I barely notice Sybil is chuckling quietly beside me.

"Oh, my dear, Nicky. Never in your life have I ever seen you so smitten. Here I thought I'd become a *müle* by the time you found someone worthy."

I can't help but grin at her cheeky comment.

A *müle* is what vampires evolve into when their life is drawing to a close: a skeletal type being that sleeps in the darkest of pits, their heart on the other side of the world, the closest thing we can get to natural death. Very few willingly become one; most prefer a brimstone torch to the heart so they can die permanently.

"Some faith in me would be nice, Sybil. Why is everyone convinced I will die alone?" I mumble.

"Well, it could be because you're so hard-headed and difficult to please. I believe you get both traits from your parents. I'm still somewhat skeptical of Miss Mae. However, I can't deny the positive effect she has on you."

I grin, my eyes fixed on the approaching inner-city lights. "And neither can I."

We pull the car up to the restaurant Mae and I had visited on Christmas Day. I see Freya and Lincoln chatting through the window.

As we enter, Freya goes in for a hug from Sybil.

"My, my, Freya, the shorter hair looks good on you. Where is my great-granddaughter?"

Freya moves to the side, allowing access to Elsie, who is perched on Christopher's lap. Her eyes are beginning to close, but when she catches a glimpse of Sybil she jumps straight out of her father's arms.

"Granny!"

I watch Sybil crouch down slightly and scoop the child up, planting a kiss on her cheek.

"Hello Freya," I say, dropping the bags by the door.

"Hello, Nick. No Mae?"

I shake my head. Apart from Sybil, I couldn't possibly tell the others what has happened. The judgment would be unbearable.

"No matter," she says, hooking my arm and leading me to the table to find Lincoln and my parents chatting. "You can give her our gifts when you go home."

"Mother, Father, Lincoln. Happy *Bashta*."

Lincoln raises his glass to me while Mother gets up off her seat, rounding the table to pull me into an embrace.

"Happy *Bashta*, Dominic." As we let go, my father gives my hand a firm shake before sitting down.

I take my seat next to Lincoln as Sybil ushers Elsie back to her seat between her parents.

With us all seated, my father stands, beginning his annual speech. "Happy *Bashta*, everyone. I'm glad we were all able to make it and spend time with each other. I know sometimes work and other business can get in the way, but there's nothing like family, and that should always be treasured. May our year be prosperous."

He lifts his glass, and we all do the same in a toast before taking a sip.

My father sits down as the first starter arrives.

I lean on the wall as Elsie rips through her presents, scattering wrapping paper across the room while Christopher desperately tries to pick it up.

"Lara spoke to me," Lincoln whispers, taking a sip of his rum.

"And your response?" I say, my eyes fixed on my niece, giving Lincoln the discretion, I know he appreciates.

"Thanks for not making it awkward," he replies.

"It's the least I can do, Lincoln. I wouldn't have met Mae otherwise."

Lincoln rests a hand on my shoulder. "I'm just glad you found someone to keep around."

I scoff playfully, ruffling his hair.

Freya, noticing our chat, walks over, squeezing herself between Lincoln and me.

"Go play with your niece. I need her tired before we head off."

Lincoln sighs, but I see the childish grin emerging. He hands Freya his drink before sneaking up behind Elsie, picking her up and chucking her into the air.

Her blue eyes are wide as she kicks and laughs, Lincoln swinging her around and Christopher pinching her calves.

"Freya, may I ask you something?" I say, eyeing Freya, who is sipping on Lincoln's drink.

"Let me guess: you want to know how I knew I wanted to be with Christopher forever?"

Always the perceptive one.

"Why do I even bother with intros? But yes," I laugh.

"I wish I could be of more help, but you just know. I tried to avoid it, Christopher being human and all, but I just gravitated to him, and when he was willing to change before we had Elsie, that was all the evidence I needed."

"You ever considered not changing him, keeping him human?" I don't want to even consider posing that question to Mae. I am content with the longevity of my life, but some people just aren't meant to live forever.

"We talked about it for a long time, and Chris knew the risks, but he loved me too much to grow old without me and couldn't even bear to think of Elsie getting old before us."

I sip my whisky, pondering Freya's words.

I wanted that. I wanted marriage, children, grandchildren, and I wanted that all with her.

With Mae.

Wishful Thinking

My body shakes, a groan seeping out. I roll over, landing on the velvet floor of the car as it slows to a stop.

"Good morning."

I look up at Dominic, who has a warm smile on his face. It causes a pain in my chest.

He's smiling at the person you're projecting, not at you.

I push myself to my knees, smiling at Dominic.

"Good morning. I was sure I fell asleep in bed."

"If we wanted to enjoy the whole day, we had to leave early," he replies.

"Oh, have you got something planned?"

Dominic winks at me before exiting the car. I sit up, allowing him to open the door for me. He stretches his hand out, which I take.

My bare feet touch the gravel and stones, but only momentarily, as Dominic scoops me up into his arms.

"I would say that I am perfectly capable of walking, but you forgot my shoes."

"I packed you a bag. You can shower on the boat."

The boat?

I turn and see we are on a private dock. At the end of the wooden walkway is a boat. Four staff members stand on the edge as we walk through.

"Mr. Aldrek, we embark in 15 minutes," a man says.

I have never been on a yacht before, but with three tiers, the boat seems to have enough space to live happily.

Dominic places me onto the wooden deck, takes my hand. He brushes my hair aside before he leads me up the stairs on the side, heading to the front of the ship. Through the windows, I make out a living room with a circular sofa facing a mounted flat screen and a bar at the back with its own island and stools.

Dominic leans on the railing overlooking the water. The sun is still making its journey up the sky, and a September breeze wraps around me, making me shiver.

I miss summer, when the mornings are just as warm as the evenings.

Dominic pulls me closer, and I wrap my arms around his waist. I lean my head on his chest as the boat's engine roars and hums to life, ripples spreading and pushing us forward.

"Today, there's no contract. Dress how you want. Do what you want. Today is for you to be you, Mae." His voice is soft, his words carried by the gentle wind.

"Then first order of business is a shower and some breakfast."

Dominic looks down at me. His face spreads in a smile.

"Let me show you your room." He takes hold of my hand and leads me up a flight of stairs.

The bedroom has floor-to-ceiling windows, a view of the ocean from every angle, and a king size bed. As Dominic shuts the door behind him, all the noise of the engine disappears.

"Soundproof," I say.

"So, no one can hear you scream my name," he whispers, kissing the side of my neck. His breath against my skin sends goosebumps across my thighs.

He wraps his arm around my waist, pulling me back against himself. A growing erection presses into my back.

"But," he says, pecking my cheek and letting go. I spin around and see him standing by the door.

"I have other things planned for us. I'll see you downstairs in the living room for some breakfast."

Dominic shuts the door, giving me one last look before heading down the stairs. I sigh heavily, heading to the bathroom.

I close the door and switch on the shower, and steam begins to cover the room.

I drop my clothes onto the floor, catching a glimpse of Stephan's bite marks on my shoulder, the skin swirling like an aerial shot of a tornado. Against the rest of my somewhat flawless skin, it is painfully obvious. It might as well have been pulsating blue.

I compulsively pull at the white streak in my hair, wishing it would fall out.

There's nothing I can do until I see Magenta.

I grimace, watching the mirror steam up and hide the finer details of my reflection.

The shower is scalding and, in the last few weeks, that's how I've liked it: painful and numbing all my other senses. I let the heat stab my skin like hot needles, hitting me from all directions.

It's not anyone's fault but my own.

I've done this to myself. Since the day I was attacked, it has been one lesser evil to the next.

I drop to my knees, pressing my head to the floor.

Nothing is going right for me; nothing ever goes right for me.

I want to cry right there, but I can't. As much as I hate it, I'm still working. October is only around the corner, and then the year will be over.

I sit up, exhaling, letting the water wash my invasive thoughts away.

When I walk downstairs, Dominic is sitting at the table sipping on some coffee as his eyes are on the TV, a football match going on. His plate is empty, crumbs on it suggesting he'd waited a while for me.

I slide open the door, catching his attention. His gaze lingers. A sparkle dances around his silver eyes.

They are warmer than when we first met.

They used to be quite piercing during the beginning, scrutinizing like he was dissecting me, but now they remind me of steam that rises, swirling and wrapping around the atmosphere, shades of silver that add depth and entice me to unfold the layers they create.

"Mae?"

I blink rapidly, noticing that I've been standing with my hand on the door far longer than I should have.

"Sorry, I took a while in the shower. I hope you didn't have to wait long," I say, hurrying to a seat next to him.

"Don't worry," he chuckles and rubs his thumb over my hand. "I had a guess at what you'd like."

A door by the bar opens and a waitress step through holding a plate. She lays it down before taking Dominic's empty one and leaving.

I look down at the English breakfast glistening with oil and seasoning. I arch a brow, looking at Dominic.

"And you still forgot the black pudding," I say, my lips breaking into a smile, causing him to laugh.

"If I remember correctly, you said you didn't want any."

"Ah, so you were listening?"

"I'm always listening, Mae."

Those words spark small embers of feeling inside me. I look to my food, my eyes watering. I take a forkful into my mouth, allowing the flavors to dance and spin around.

"What have you got planned for us?" I ask, sitting back into the wooden chair as Dominic clears his throat.

"Nothing that exciting: lunch, dinner, being all-round tourists. There's a quaint little secluded town up the river. We will be there in about five minutes."

"Quite frankly, that sounds wonderful," I say. I push my half-eaten breakfast aside, bringing the glass of freshly squashed orange juice closer.

"Good." Dominic's ears perk up slightly. "It would seem we are drawing closer to port. We may be out all day, so bring something to keep you warm."

I stand up and press my lips against his temple, causing the silver-eyed vampire to sigh contently.

"So that means you won't be cuddling me constantly?"

"Cuddling with you always ends up with your legs over my shoulders," he replies, causing a slight flutter in my stomach.

I kiss his head again before heading out of the room.

Dominic stands on the dock, his eyes on me as I step off the boat, flipping the black scarf around my neck.

Stretches of cobblestone and grey-bricked shops are lined up in front of us, like stepping into France. The smell of several bakeries dance in the air, and pigeons coo at our feet.

Dominic reaches towards me, and I hook my arm through his, leading the way into this town. The streets are quiet, just a few shops beginning to open. The atmosphere is both calm and serene and, for the longest while, my mind is quiet. Leaning on Dominic's arm while we walk is all I need right now.

"How did you find such a place?" I whisper.

"My mother is very particular with her wine. However, she didn't like outsourcing all the way to Italy and France, so she found a small wine vendor here. They have a field of grapes, and make their own brand of white and red."

The streets begin to thin. The shops and buildings become scarce, opening to a single stone fountain in front of a church. The fountain is carved from white stone and looks pristine.

I let go of Dominic's arm and walk towards the fountain, noticing the bronze plaque on the front: *Divine Requiem.*

The angel stands nearly seven feet high and thrusts a sword into the air. Water arcs out of the sword. The crook of the angel's arm shields their face. However, their wings are spread broad. Detailed feathers add to the realism.

I notice water trickling from their face as though they are crying, tears sliding down the statue into the base of the fountain.

I look down, noticing several colored coins seated at the bottom.

"Want to make a wish?" Dominic whispers. He has a coin between his fingers. I take it from his hand.

I close my eyes, taking a deep breath before exhaling and flipping the penny in.

"What did you wish for?" he asks.

"If I tell you, it won't come true."

Dominic shakes his head gently, a broad smile on his face. He leads us up a flight of stone steps, away from the church.

With the sun at its highest, the air begins to warm – not like August but enough to allow me to remove my scarf. With most of the town behind us, we walk along a roughly laid out stone path across a small field.

A cottage lies at the back of the field right next to a large barn, with a few smaller ones surrounding. Smoke puffs from the cottage chimney, signaling that someone is at home.

Dominic ushers me into the field. There in front of us is a picnic: a large blanket lying on the ground with a basket in the middle.

"Oh my, Dominic," I whisper. I kneel at one corner while he sits beside me, laying his arm across my back.

Surrounding grapevines hide us from the autumnal breeze and allowing the sun to warm our skin.

"And what do we have for lunch?"

"Something light," he says, opening the wicker picnic basket.

He pulls out a board, polished to expose the grain of the wood, then adds three different types of cheese: ones that crumble and ones that you can spread with a knife. A pair of crackers, and some meats and olives to finish it all off.

"I've seen a few cheeseboards in my life, but this one takes the crown," I say, making him chuckle as he brings out a pair of wine glasses and an unmarked green bottle.

"To an almost one year," I say, raising my glass.

This chardonnay is different. I want to say apple, but the flavor changes the further it goes down my throat. It is warm in the stomach, and a tingle rises from the tips of my toes.

"This is beautiful. I could tell your mum has rich tastes, but this. Wow."

"I'm glad that no big company has bought their recipe," Dominic replies, taking a sip of his own. I lay the glass down on the ground and peer at the sky.

"Do you ever just think about staying here?" I ask. "And not returning to Seattle?"

"And abandon my responsibilities?" he replies. I am sure I can sense some sort of readiness in his words, that all I need to do is say the word, and this would become our home.

"Or just a break from it all." I'm being lax with my words, but I'm mainly talking to myself – just quit FW and do something else. Rebuild.

"Everyone needs a break once in a while. It's natural to want to switch off from time to time. Just take me with you when you do."

I smile, a laugh trickling out from between my lips. I crawl over to him, laying my head on his lap as he takes another sip of his wine, his deep silver eyes inspecting me.

"What are you thinking, Mr. Aldrek?" I ask, noticing a slither of emotion graze over his face.

A warm breeze brushes past us before he replies, "Just noticing the fine details of you, Miss Geoffries, and how enthralled you make me."

I beckon his face closer with my finger, allowing our lips to brush against each other.

The sweet scent of the wine we share lingers between us until Dominic closes the gap.

The Last Hurrah

Dominic has both hands on my waist as I lead him back onto the boat. The evening paints the sky in deep hues of purples and settling blues. The autumnal air begins to nip at my exposed skin.

The boat is illuminated by small lights dotted around the deck.

I stretch my arms across the balcony, allowing the breeze to carry my hair slightly and lift my dress. The cool air is both numbing and calming. It is precisely what I need for my mind to be in the present.

"Enjoying the view?" he asks, leaning on the railing next to me.

"The ending of a day could not be more picturesque," I reply. My fingers tiptoe towards Dominic's hand and he grabs it, pulling me close to his body.

"Mae," he breathes out his words, the air nearly carrying them away before I can hear them. His soft tone is enough to cause me to look at him.

"Everything OK?" I ask, noticing the serious look he has on his.

"Everything is more than OK...being here with you, I wouldn't want to be anywhere else right now ... I- you're-" Dominic drops his hold on me, turning away as he reorganizes what he intends to share with me.

"Dominic," I say. I rub my hand on his shoulder. "Look at me...please."

He turns around, and I can see the conflict within his eyes. I stroke his face, smiling.

"You're worse with words than I am."

A small smile breaks through his serious face, making mine bigger.

"Make love to me," I say, my words carrying more meaning in the tone than the words themselves.

He knows what I mean; if he can't express what he feels through words, then express them through action. I lean in towards him, placing a soft kiss on his lips.

It is gentle, resembling a small breeze that grazes across your skin and makes you shiver.

As I pull away, I see Dominic's eyes are closed, his lips flushed slightly as he savors the feeling of my lips on his moments ago. His eyes open slowly, and he takes my hand, leading me into the bedroom.

The door closes, encasing us from the outside world. The only thing audible is the heavy breathing shared between us.

Dominic traces his hands up my arms, finding the zipper at the top of the dress.

My hands wander up his shirt, opening the buttons, exposing his chest.

I unhook his belt, open his trousers. As his clothes fall, so do mine, rippling to the floor by the door.

We both stand there, memorizing each other's bodies as though it is the last time.

My hands work their way to his face as his slide downwards, hooking around my ass and lifting me to eye level.

I feel like I'm seeing Dominic for the first time: thin strands of lighter blond that hide among the darker shades, the tiniest indication of freckles sprinkled across the bridge of his nose. His cheeks tinged pink.

I rest my head on his, eyes closed as I breathe a sigh of relief, holding myself around his neck and waist. I feel his head tilt, our lips brushing against each other, and I hold his face as I push mine against his.

Our mouths open simultaneously. I press my body close to his as Dominic walks us to the bed, our lips melding together as he lays me down.

With my eyes closed, my body is sensitive to his every touch. How his thumb trails over my waist, following the curve of my hips and thighs.

He runs his hands on the inside of my thighs, spreading my legs, both his thumbs running over my wet core.

Dominic pulls his lips from mine, forcing my eyes open. There is a lightness to his silver eyes as he stares at me. Our eyes captivated by each other, I feeling the emotions spread over our features as he slides himself inside.

He holds my hip as he strokes slowly, almost musically. Our hips rolling and lifting together, we hold the gaze.

I brush my hair aside, exposing my neck.

Do it.

If this is to be the last time, I want to be the last thing on his tongue.

Dominic approaches me slowly, his strokes still keeping their slow and angular movements. He kisses the scars, and his hands move from my hips and interlock our fingers together.

I feel the puncture of his teeth as my hands squeeze his. I feel his veins on the tops of his hands as he drinks from my neck.

It is different. There is no immediate fatigue, but a softness spreads across my body. I sink further into the bed.

I wrap my legs around his waist, arching my back slightly to force his penetration deeper. His eyes are lighter, more vibrant than before. He holds both my hands in one of his. His free hand goes back to my hip, holding me as his strokes become more aggressive.

Pulling his whole shaft out before plummeting back in makes my eyes water. The arousal that spreads from my core causes double vision.

My hands wiggle in his grasp as he fucks me. His hold loosens and he leans down, taking a breast in his mouth. The stimulation of both is arousing, and the tight knots that are grouping together grow close to unfurling.

The expansion of his own oncoming orgasm is another shot of pleasure as I'm stretched that little bit more. My head is spinning as Dominic sucks hungrily between both breasts.

Making noises I only now realize I have in me, my eyes shut firmly

The magnitude of my orgasm leaves me floating.

As I slip back into reality, my eyes manage to open. Noticing the sheen of sweat that coat both of us, I laugh.

"And this is why I work out," I say. Dominic lets a chuckle slip out. Laying down on top of me, he kisses my chin.

"Then I guess you're ready for round two?" Dominic smirks, rolling us over so I am on top of him.

I pull a hair band from my wrist and tie up my hair.

"Keep up, Mr. Aldrek."

"Always, Miss Geoffries."

Love and Business

I hate to admit it, but Delilah (like always) has done a fantastic job. She's rented out a museum, allowing investors and stakeholders to look at the auction items.

I scratch at my black mask. It is nothing like Magenta's, which is covered in rhinestones and velvet.

A tall woman walks over, holding her clutch tightly in front of her. Her brunette hair falling over her shoulder, exposing her olive skin. As she draws closer, I notice her brown eyes graced with long eyelashes fluttering at me behind her grey mask. A mask which matches her long evening dress.

"Miranda Ubenachi." I put my hands on either side of her arms, giving her a light kiss on each cheek.

"How are you this evening?" I ask, letting Miranda take a spot next to me, grabbing a passing champagne flute.

"Here to spend money. That's all that matters, isn't it, Mr. Aldrek."

I nod in agreement, watching the mingling of important people.

"It is, especially for a good cause. Work has steadily been progressing on the community. I hope to have the foundations laid by the end of the year."

"That is excellent news." She sips her drink. "I was concerned when I heard about the delays earlier this year."

"You know me, Miranda. I love a challenge. Yes, we had some hiccups; it seemed mainly a communication error between contractors, but we sorted that out."

"That is good." Miranda turns to me, leaning an elbow on the high, circular table. "We are hoping for another community development, in another state."

"That sounds like a good idea, Miranda-" My voice catches in my throat as Mae descends the stairs in a green dress. It hugs her figure in the best possible way, pooling on the floor slightly and catching everyone's eyes.

Held up by two thin straps, the front droops into the center, giving us a peek at her cleavage. Her hair is curled, and bounces past her shoulders. She has a hand on her mask, similar in style to my own.

Has she designed my suit to compliment her dress or vice versa? The emerald green, the exact shade she has used for my outfit.

I have forgotten all about Miranda and her proposal.

"If you could excuse me, Miranda." I signal to Delilah, who is talking to a few waiters, giving them instruction.

She hurries towards me, a single strand of hair blowing in the breeze as her silver gown trails behind her.

"Delilah, schedule a meeting with Miranda in the coming weeks." I gesture Delilah towards her and take my leave. I scan the room for Mae and catch sight of her dress outside on the balcony as she watches the city.

My mother is beside her, and the two seem to be chatting. I weave through the crowd towards them, trying to avoid getting into any conversations.

I haven't seen Mae at all today. Being busy with final touches and working on my speech, by the time I had gotten home, she had gone to get her dress.

As I escape the sea of people, my mother walks away, heading back into the party through another entrance. A cool breeze lifts Mae's hair and carries it in the wind; everyone is inside enjoying the appetizers and champagne, leaving us alone together.

I inhale quietly. *This is it. This is where I tell her I love her.*

I couldn't do it back on the boat, convincing myself that I didn't want to ruin our last moment if she didn't feel the same way, but then she kissed me, and we made love. I feel my heart swelling from the power she has over me.

"Mr. Aldrek, looking but not touching." She glances over her shoulder at me, her mask highlighting the darkness in her eyes. "We must really be at a business function."

I stride towards her and wrap my arms around her waist, laying a tender kiss on her temple.

"I don't care where we are. I'll touch my girlfriend whenever I want." I feel her hands rub against my own and notice how cold they are.

"What are you doing out here? You're freezing, Mae."

"Looking for an excuse for you to keep me warm," she whispers. I turn her around before I take off my mask and hers as well. I want to see her face and for her to see mine.

"Mae, when we first met, there was only lust between us. You certainly know how to keep a man intrigued. Then something happened. I stopped seeing you as an employee and then I called you my girlfriend, and the phrase seemed better suited. You aren't just someone to feed off of. Mae, I love you. I've tried to push the feeling away, but every time I see you, it comes back like a train. I love you and I want to be with you. One day, I even want to marry you, have a family with you, relinquish my immortality for you."

Mae stares at me wide-eyed. I'd hoped she already knew these feelings, but the last one caught her off-guard.

If done correctly, a vampire could give up their immortality. Burning their heart within an inch of death would allow them to heal, but that would be it. That amount of restoration would drain their immortality and, over time, their craving for blood would diminish, and so would their powers. I'd happily do that for her.

"Dominic ..." Her eyes are beginning to well as she speaks, "I-"

"Son, they are ready for your speech."

If it had been anyone else interrupting us, I would've told them to fuck off, but hearing my father's voice, I turn around while Mae looks back to the balcony.

"Yes, Father, I'll be there shortly." I'm sure he knows he's disturbed something important, but nothing is more important than tonight, and whatever he has disturbed can wait. He nods and heads back into the party.

I turn back to Mae and find her facing me.

"Go," she says. She pulls on my arm pecking me on the lips. I sigh. This is why I didn't want the event today. I'm being torn away from her at a crucial moment.

"Fine, but don't go anywhere, please." I overlook the way she avoids my eyes; I'm in too much of a hurry to get this speech over and done with and find an excuse to leave and go home.

The guests huddle to the front as my father speaks, explaining the long and recycled history of the company.

I make my way to the stand and wait to be introduced. My eyes fix on Mae, who stands by the balcony.

"But I could not have left the company in better hands. My son: Dominic Edward Atticus Aldrek. He's taken the company further in every possible way."

A round of applause echoes through the wall as I replace Callahan on the stage.

I take one quick glance to the balcony, relaxing as I see her still there.

"Thank you, Father. I appreciate your faith in me. Tonight, we wanted to focus our efforts on the problems within our state, more specifically securing our future." I look to the balcony quickly. *Good she's still there.* "The future is with the children of today who will become our doctors, our police, our entrepreneurs, our businesses. We must give them the best possible hope for the future we leave them." When I look again, she is gone.

I try not to panic as I scan the room, continuing my speech.

"That is why today's earnings will be dedicated to that future: improvements to district city schools, apprenticeships, internships, networking between the businesspeople of today and those of tomorrow. Now please, enjoy the food and the drink, spend some money, and have a good evening."

Everyone claps as I walk off the stage, allowing a few compliments to come my way. But my eyes are still searching for Mae.

A waiter approaches me. Instead of champagne on his tray, he has a sheet of paper. I take the folded sheet and look inside.

Sorry I couldn't stay longer. If you ever miss me, you know where to find me x — M

Outside of Work

My hands drum on the steering wheel as I watch the dial spin slowly. 12:58:39. One minute and 20 seconds, and our contract will end.

I can approach Mae outside the agreement and hope that my feelings will be requited. I press my head on the wheel, sighing heavily.

When I got home last night, her room was vacant, but not the vacant where you know someone has left. Her room was still decorated as though she would walk up the stairs at any moment, and that was a far worse feeling. I'm not ashamed to say that I slept in her room, but it felt larger and colder than any time before.

I catch sight of Mae pulling out of an underground garage in her own sleek black Audi. Her hair is tied, and both windows are wound down. I check my watch: 13:02. This is it. At this moment, I have gone from a guy who bought her, to a guy that has begun to follow her.

I'm not entirely sure that's an upgrade.

I hadn't thought past this moment. Initially, I hoped we could speak at her place, but now I'm one car behind, wondering at what point should I stop following her. What if she is heading to Magenta? That would go against the rules of the contract. *Even worse, what if she's going to meet another client?*

I gulp loudly. Can I bear to see her friendly with another person, reminding me of what she and I had started as? I pull open the contact book on the dashboard, praying that she still has the phone I gave her.

I see through her back window that she's pulling something out of her bag.

The car separating us honks at Mae – not because the light is green but simply because they have a horn to press.

With her eyes not on the road, Mae moves the car forward, trusting the prick who hasn't got his eyes on the road, either. She's still searching for the phone, her car rolling slowly forward.

Shit.

I open the door and step out before I'm choked by my seatbelt.

"Fuck!" I rip the material off the car.

It is quick but slow at the same time. The loud drone of the HGV van and the sound of tires screeching, trying to come to a stop. Metal crunching and cracking while her scream echoes through the street. The ground rocks and shakes as the back of the lorry rounds on itself from the sudden brakes, forcing the whole machine to tumble and roll, crushing Mae's car that has already crumpled in on itself.

I drop to my knees, the sound of sirens filling the November air.

Owned by the purple-eyed devil

I scream, throwing my hands up in the air.

"Mae, Mae, it's OK." Magenta holds my hands, which are both clammy and shaking.

I look around and find that we are in her office.

Oh, thank God.

I pull her hands over my face, stifling my sobs. In that moment, watching the grill of the van charge at me, I thought I was about to die.

I take a few calming breaths. *It's fine, you're OK, you're not dead.* I hold my arms, hugging myself.

"What happened?" I whisper. Magenta sits on the edge of the sofa.

"You nearly died, sweetie. Luckily, it works in our favor," she says cryptically.

"What do you mean 'in our favor'?"

"Luna is dead. The golem I used to replace you will prove that. Mr. Grier can save face without having to marry you." Magenta looks almost pleased with herself. *How long has she planned this? Why didn't she tell me?*

The fight in the motel hits my chest hard. Had I known there was something in place, our last moment wouldn't have been me screaming at him, leaving him alone in a motel in Idaho.

Before, I was shaking from almost dying, but now, I'm shaking because Luna died. How could I have been so blind? Why did I allow Luna's life to worry me? Of course, Magenta had a plan. She always did.

I hold my mouth, feeling the build-up of vomit bubble up my throat.

Magenta brings the bin already on hand to my lap, allowing me to chuck up all the contents of my stomach, she strokes the back of my head.

"You must calm yourself, Mae. It won't do you or the baby any good."

What?

I lift my head slowly, seeing Magenta's amethyst eyes glint at me. My mouth is open, and she closes it gently with the tips of her fingers.

"But my wish...not unless-"

"Yes, not unless you loved them."

"Them?"

Magenta sighs, brushing her hair aside.

"I am having trouble concluding who the father is and how far along. Mother nature has hidden that much. It's the price of your wish, my dear."

"Then abortion. I'm dead to one and my contract ended with the other."

"That I am afraid I can't do."

"Why the hell not? Lara could do it, magic or science. I can't have a child. I refuse to have a child."

The air around me grows tense. The sunlight in the room dims and thunder cracks around us. My knees buckle as a swarming heat encases my body, spreading from the "H" on my skin, making breathing painful.

Magenta bends down to my level, her eyes glowing a deep purple and a snarl across her lips.

"I will not relinquish my position of power because of you." She grabs me by the throat, a show of dominance without having to exert any force on me. The burning sensation is doing that already.

"You are my golden goose, Mae. The biological father is irrelevant. It's who you are to them, a multibillionaire and an FBI agent. Why would I allow you to remove the hold you have on them?"

Magenta drops her hold and I crumple to my knees, my heart pumping a mile a minute as I try to suppress the overwhelming anxiety attack that is trying to drown me.

I feel her cool hands on the nape of my neck, stroking the skin as the burning begins to cease.

"I think it's wise to see your parents, Mae. I know you've missed them. Who knows how long before you won't be able to fly anymore." Her cool touch makes me lightheaded. More importantly, it makes me extremely tired.

I don't want to close my eyes but can't fight the cinderblock lids falling shut. Magenta hums, stroking the back of my neck as I fall asleep.

Epilogue

It's funny how two people in different locations can experience the same emotions simultaneously.

Both men sit in their respective rooms. While Stephan has his eyes on the black funeral suit, Dominic has his hands around a bottle of whiskey, half of it already marinating in his stomach.

Both surrounded by a similar sense of loss. While Stephan's loss sets him free to find his true Luna, Dominic's sends him into a perpetual state of loneliness not even he can fathom.

Both surrounded by the dying light of the November sun.

A perfectly timed knock sends a shiver through both men, like a ghost running its hand down the napes of their necks.

Both feel compelled to see who it is. Both need to see who or what is behind that door, and sadly, both assume it will be her.

But it is not.

On the floor lies a letter no wider than their palms, held together by a purple wax seal. It is warm to the touch, as though the wax has only begun to cool.

Together, in complete synchronicity, each man pulls the seal away, revealing three things inside the letter.

The first: a picture of Mae. Both men assume this is an old photo as, of course, Mae is no longer of this world. However, the second item is both a punch to the gut and a bucket of salt to the eyes.

A sonogram, a sonogram clearly dated two days ago. You can't see much of the growing fetus except a small space of black against a sea of grey, but both men know what that means.

And finally, the third item. Here is where the true slice of pain escapes both men: a letter five words long and enough power to force both men to their knees with a deafening crunch.

Thanksgiving is all about family — M

TO BE CONTINUED

Acknowledgements

For the daughter who started it all, the man I manifested, K5Rakitan for stumbling across my book before she got banned from Wattpad and hooking me up with one of the best editors I could've asked for, and finally, to the small inner child who has vivid dreams that turn into stories. Thank you all.

About the Author

Born in Seattle, Ajrea Huar grew up in East London. She's a mother and real estate agent, when she isn't writing or watching an obscene amount of anime. Drawing inspiration from her wildest dreams, you can expect to find more books from Ajrea delving into different genres. One thing all her books have in common in the DreamShelf Universe is that they touch on thought-provoking themes and tend to have a more grounded ending despite the fantastic elements. Ultimately, Ajrea is simply a book girly who's been given a moment to share her work and give her readers a glimpse into her mind.